BLAKEWELL MAGES BOOK ONE

GHOST WHISPERS

BRITTANY ARDEN

Veritas University
Airport
NEW TOWN
McDara's apartment
Motel
The Obsidian Quill
OLD TOWN
Police Station
The Black House
BLAKEWELL

Contents

1

Chicago hummed with life, its twilight-drenched streets pulsing beneath the neon glow of flickering signs and the rhythmic lull of distant traffic. A saxophonist played in the corner, his notes weaving through the electric charge in the air, a sound both melancholy and defiant. I clutched the neatly wrapped package under my arm, the brown paper crinkling beneath my grip.

A birthday gift. The *perfect* gift for my dad. It wasn't much, but I knew he'd love it.

But I was late.

A surge of panic clawed through my chest as I checked my phone. Shit. My shift started fifteen minutes ago.

I ducked down an alley damp and slick with the city's grime, and slipped through the back entrance of the high-end French bistro where I worked. The greasy scent of seared duck and melted butter clung to the air. No smoke break stragglers today—small mercies. I wedged my fingers into the door's gap, courtesy of a loose concrete block, and yanked it open.

The stainless-steel chaos of the kitchen roared to life as I stepped inside. Clanging pots. Barked orders. The sharp hiss of something hitting scalding oil.

High-end restaurants were hell to work in, no doubt about it. The stress made it an industry with sky-high turnover, but I also knew it was the fastest way to climb to the top of the haute cuisine world—a dream I'd chased ever since I'd decided to attend culinary school. One day, I swore, I'd open my own restaurant, see its name glowing in lights, and watch the pride in my parents' eyes.

My locker clicked open, the hinges smooth from countless uses. I shoved my father's present inside, along with my cobalt suede jacket and feather-shaped purse—expensive indulgences for someone living paycheck to paycheck. But sometimes you just needed something pretty to remind you that life wasn't all survival and struggle.

The second I turned, I felt it.

A presence behind me, dripping in condescension.

"Sneaking in again?"

Terry.

She leaned against the break room doorframe, all cherry-red lips and sharp smirks, her buzzed hair slicked with confidence. She'd been gunning for me since day one, sharpening her knives on every misstep I made.

I gritted my teeth and yanked a crisp white chef's jacket from a hook. The matching hat settled over my black bob, a small act of defiance.

Unlike you, Terry, I actually follow the rules.

"Excuse me," I said, voice even as I pushed past her.

"What excuse will you tell Long this time?" she purred, feigning concern, her painted mouth curving with mockery. I'd almost compliment her on the color if she weren't so spiteful.

I held my breath and ducked past her. The constant confrontations during our shifts were enough, but I couldn't shake the fact that Terry had a point. Things happened around me—odd, sometimes deadly things that would make anyone wonder if I belonged in a mental institution. Even in a world where Magicals were known and lived, albeit strained, among humans, what I could do...made even the *other* creatures of the world wary.

Jack's frantic whisper cut through the din. "Sonia! Where have you been? Long is in a mood, and you're late—"

"Has he been back here yet?" I muttered, grabbing the night's meal specials—my usual station—and hurried through the busy kitchen to my stove. A pot of simmering soup awaited me. If Terry had been in charge of the special menu, there'd be no way this masterpiece would be on track.

I glanced over my shoulder and Jack was on my heels.

Jack grimaces. "Not yet. But he will be."

Great. Just my luck.

I moved through the kitchen on muscle memory alone, collecting the last ingredients for the soup, the sharp heat of the stove curling against my skin, the rhythmic chopping of knives grounding me in familiar routine. Cooking had always been my refuge—a place where chaos had rules, where fire and steel yielded to technique and patience.

"It should be almost ready," Jack said with a lopsided smile. "I've been trying to stir it regularly, but there hasn't been much time."

"Thanks, Jack," I replied, nearly melting with relief at his kindness. His cheeks bloomed a soft pink as he ducked back to his station.

Terry sneered. "Someone's trying hard for his own special menu." It was loud enough that even Chef Morgan shook her head. I lifted the lid of the soup pot, wishing I could crouch behind it—with my small stature it would be the perfect disguise. I took a deep breath, then another, forcing my spine to straighten despite the heat on my face and my eyes to fix on the bubbling soup. I had nothing to be embarrassed about, and I refused to cower because of Terry.

But just as I reached for a handful of spices, the air shifted.

A shiver skated down my spine.

The heat of the kitchen should have been suffocating, but suddenly, the left side of my body felt numb.

A hush settled over my mind, thick and cloying.

Not now.

I kept my eyes on the bubbling soup in front of me. Pretended the cold wasn't licking at my skin, weaving through the air like a noose tightening around my throat.

Then, the ice appeared.

Frost spidered along the far left side of the stove, creeping over the handle of the soup pot. From a void, spectral fingers reached out, stretching into my world. Delicate lace, attached to a billowing sleeve, draped over a hand as more of the ghost forced its way into the Living Lands, stubbornly clinging to life.

Jean.

The ghost was back.

I snapped my eyes shut as a cold breath puffed over my ear.

"Please."

The whisper slithered beneath my skin, coiling tight.

I didn't open my eyes. I didn't acknowledge him. I couldn't.

Not in the middle of service. Not with Manager Long ready to snap my neck over one cold dish.

"Please."

It's a plea, raw and jagged. Then—a sharp, wet sound.

My eyes popped open but I didn't have to look to know what came next.

The gunshot wound in his throat would gape open, black tar dripping from his spectral form. He would clutch at it, over and over, replaying his final moments. His hollow eyes would bore into me, begging.

I bit my tongue so hard I tasted blood.

Not now. Not today.

The pilot light flickered out.

The soup went cold.

Ice locked around my fingertips.

I jerked back as the frost receded, the ghost slipping back into the narrow walkway between stoves. Probably the exact spot that he had died in. My hands shook, but no burns marked my skin—just the phantom memory of death-ice.

I glanced around the kitchen but I knew no one would notice anything except a mild temperature change. They were all human. Their senses as absent as magic in their veins.

With a mix of desperation and resignation, I struggled to relight the pilot, forcing my eyes away from Jean as he replayed his final moments—an occurrence all too common with ghosts. I had researched him the first time he appeared. In the early 1900s, he owned this building, only to be killed by his younger brother for inheritance. His history wasn't particularly riveting, except that he insisted on reliving his last minutes over and over for me. I had even tried speaking to him—once.

After my first month here, I'd snuck back into the building with Phontine's help, to see if I could make Jean move on. Phontine calls ghost like him, that repeat their deaths and can't seem to interact in any other way, a Pest. Other's, however, that can fill a room with ice and look me directly in the eyes as they scream? She calls those TTG's. Toddler Tantrum Ghost. I just call them scary. Not that any master guide of classification existed.

It was nice, though, for her to try and organize the apparitions that plagued my life—if only to keep what's left of my sanity intact.

It had been my first major ghostly upheaval at sixteen that drove me to seek help from a Mage House. Since then, I'd groveled at the doors of Chicago's six Mage Houses, only to be turned down every time I explained what I was—a Mage who sees and speaks with ghosts yet couldn't muster enough magic to cast even the simplest of spells. So, with my loyal best friend—a Pixie—I had begun classifying ghosts based on how they interacted with me and the world, the Living Lands.

The apparition lingered, a translucent figure casting shifting shadows across the stainless-steel surfaces. A surge of frustration and helplessness swelled in me as I tried to focus on my tasks, yet his ethereal gaze haunted me. Eventually, the ghost dissipated, leaving me alone to face the aftermath. The soup began to warm again, the lingering frost melting away with him. If only I could have ten more minutes before a customer ordered it—

A pot clattered to the ground, and the kitchen froze—not just in temperature, but in time.

And then—

"Ladle."

Manager Long's voice snapped through the kitchen, sharp as a blade.

I jumped.

The soup. Shit.

I grabbed the ladle, lifted the lid—too cold.

Long didn't wait. He dipped the ladle into the pot, brought it to his lips—and stopped.

His face darkened.

A string of sharp Korean curses ripped from him. I blinked, recalling that on my first day he had tried to speak to me in his native tongue, only to learn that although my heritage is Korean, being adopted by an aging Caucasian couple who had never spoken the language rendered me a disappointment in his eyes. Every little, inexplicable mistake had only deepened that judgment.

"Why is this colder than a Chicago winter?"

I swallowed hard, throat tight. "The pilot light went out, I just—"

"How," he interrupted, his voice slow, deliberate, dangerous, "does a pilot light in a temperature-controlled kitchen extinguish long enough for the entire pot to freeze?"

I wondered if telling him that it was the dead landlord from the 1900s paying a spectral visit would change things, but while magic was very real and known of, humans did not like reminders. And being told that not only could Mages do magic that scared the ever-loving life from humans, but that a Mage, *me*, could talk to the dead…Yeah, that would go over great. Magicals might have existed because of the Woods that sprang up in 1872, but humans preferred to live as if fairytales were mere stories. Telling Long—or any human employer—that I was a Mage would shatter my dream of becoming a renowned chef even more than my personal plague of ghosts.

So, I did what I always did.

I said nothing.

"I have given you four months to prove that this—" he began, then stopped to draw a deep, disapproving breath. "This was a mistake. Please gather your things from the back and leave."

The words hit like a knife to the gut.

"Wait—" My voice cracked as I stepped forward. "I can fix it. I swear, I—"

"Your last paycheck will be deposited at the next pay period," he said, voice flat. "Don't make a scene, Sonia."

A scene.

My hands curled into fists. I was so tired of ghosts ruining my life.

I stormed toward the break room, ignoring the way Terry chuckled under her breath. My locker slammed shut as I shoved my things into my bag.

Out the back door. Into the night. The cool air did nothing to soothe the fury clawing at my chest.

My father's gift pressed against my side. A reminder of why I fought.

Why I couldn't keep losing.

The ghosts had won this round.

But they wouldn't take anything else from me.

Not again.

2

Disappointment had become a shadow in my bones—a quiet, relentless thing that curled around my ribs and whispered in my ear, *You should have seen this coming.* Four months. That's all I'd lasted. A new record.

I walked toward the bus stop, the weight of failure pressing into my shoulders, settling into my chest like lead. My fingers curled tighter around the strap of my bag, knuckles white, muscles aching. I didn't even care about the sharp Chicago wind needling through my thin jacket. I just wanted to go home.

Home, where the smell of garlic and fresh herbs would wrap around me the second I stepped inside. Where my mom's voice would drift through the kitchen as she hummed over a simmering pot, casual and warm, like she wasn't waiting for me to come home shattered—again.

Julie Byrd would take one look at me and know. She always did.

I exhaled sharply, rubbing at my face with one hand, willing the burning behind my eyes to stop.

It wasn't just losing the job. It was knowing my parents had never been angry about it. Concerned, sure. Disappointed, maybe. But I'd spent my entire life dragging ghosts into our house, into their lives, into their carefully built normalcy, and still they had never once made me feel like I didn't belong.

They should have.

Any sane person would have sent me back to foster care years ago. But somehow, *somehow*, my parents had looked at the haunted eight-year-old child they brought home and decided she was worth keeping.

They'd listened.

They'd believed me.

Even when the ghosts stole my peace. Even when they had cost me every damn job I tried to hold down.

The scent of snow-laced lavender tickled my nose, interrupting the downward spiral of my thoughts. I didn't have to look up to know who had arrived.

"Seriously?" I muttered under my breath.

Phontine fluttered beside me, her delicate, iridescent wings shimmering even in the dimming city lights. Smooth lavender skin speckled with periwinkle caught the last hints of the setting sun. She was barely taller than my forearm, but right now, her unimpressed stare carried all the weight of a full-grown human.

"You're not supposed to show up out in the open like that," I hissed.

She flicked a strand of my hair out of my face with a wing, entirely unfazed. "You're in a mood."

I shot her a glare. "And you're about to get swatted by some paranoid human with a broom."

Phontine had learned the hard way that not all humans handled Magicals well. Some saw a Pixie and assumed it meant tricks, theft, or worse. But I wasn't a Pixie. As for me—a Mage, though not entirely of the Wood—the origins of my kind were tangled. Our ancestry began with humans two decades after the Three Great Woods exploded onto the scene like a twisted April Fool's joke, each Wood with a hidden trail that led to a massive Heart Stone.

A human's touch transformed them, infusing them with magic, creating Mages. That magic trickled down through generations ensuring humans could become Mages one of two ways: Hereditarily or by going to one of three, perfectly circular Woods, walking down its singular path, and touching the Heart Stone. If it didn't kill you, then congratulations, you became a Mage in a world that hated magic.

Magic may have come from the Wood, but humanity had twisted it, wielded it, feared it. Now, it belonged to us, and yet we were still feared.

"Fine," Phontine sighed, rolling her eyes as her form faded into a translucent shimmer, visible only to me now. "Happy?"

A lie. I wasn't sure I'd felt happy in weeks.

The bus still wasn't in sight.

"Why aren't you at work?" she asked, her voice softer now.

I hesitated. She already knew. I could see it in the tilt of her head, the way her wings slowed their idle flutter.

"Jean did his choking bit again," I muttered, keeping my eyes on the road.

Phontine landed on my shoulder, patting it lightly, as if that could fix the fact that a ghost had cost me my job. Again.

"Well," she said, far too cheerfully, "it's not the end of the world."

I scoffed, my laugh flat and humorless. "No? Because it sure as hell feels like it."

"We live in Chicago." She spread her arms dramatically. "There are thousands of restaurants."

I turned my head just enough to glare at her. "It doesn't matter how many restaurants exist if my résumé makes me look like I can't last a year without getting fired."

She hesitated.

"Yeah," I muttered. "Exactly."

An older man walked up to the bus stop, pausing just long enough to stare at me, his brows furrowed.

I tapped my phone, pretending to adjust an earbud. "Talking to someone," I murmured.

He gave a stiff nod and took a few steps away.

Great. Now I was scaring the elderly. *Fantastic.*

Phontine, oblivious to my growing irritation, sighed dramatically. "Hopefully your mom's making kolduny tonight."

"What?"

"You always calm down when you've had a good helping of potato in your system," she mused.

I huffed. "I'm not hungry."

She shrugged as if that changed nothing. "Comfort food."

I pressed my lips together and stared hard at the pavement, willing the bus to just show up already.

"Geez, okay," she relented, curling closer against my neck in a quiet side hug. "Didn't realize losing this job hit you that hard."

I swallowed past the lump in my throat.

It wasn't just the job.

It was the feeling that I'd never escape this. That, no matter how hard I worked, ghosts would always be there, lurking in the corners, stealing everything I tried to build.

"I don't want you to joke about it like it's nothing," I murmured.

Her voice softened. "I know."

"Can humor get me a job where ghosts don't ruin my life?"

She hesitated just a little too long.

"Probably not."

A bright flash of headlights cut through the street, the growl of an engine pulling up to the curb.

"The bus is here," Phontine said, like that solved anything.

I sighed.

The wind slammed into me, sharp and unrelenting, slicing through the narrow Chicago street like it was trying to flay the city open. I turned away, shielding my face with my collar, while Phontine's tiny fingers dug into my hair to keep herself from being swept away.

Movement at the edge of my vision caught my attention. Across the street, in the mouth of a grimy alley beside an old deli, an elderly woman rummaged through a dumpster, her frizzy gray hair whipping in the wind.

My stomach twisted.

"Come on, doors are opening," Phontine murmured, tapping my temple lightly.

But I barely heard her.

I was standing here, drowning in the weight of my failures, agonizing over a dream that felt impossible—but I still had a home to return to. A warm kitchen. A mother who would hum as she cooked dinner. Parents who had chosen me, had loved me, had never once sent me away despite the ghosts that haunted me.

A home I had not earned.

I exhaled sharply and reached for my wallet. Just enough for the bus.

My fingers hesitated.

Without a word, I turned and marched straight into the deli.

Fifteen minutes later, I placed a neatly wrapped sandwich and a small bag of chips beside a battered shopping cart filled with someone's entire life.

The woman startled, her faded brown eyes darting from the food to me, wary and sharp. She didn't speak. Neither did I.

I let go of the bag.

For a moment, nothing but understanding passed between us. Then I turned and walked away.

Every step back toward the bus stop felt like a steady drumbeat of exhaustion and determination.

Losing one job wouldn't break me. Being fired a hundred times wouldn't stop me. This was my second life, and I would not waste it.

I had not been born Sonia Byrd. Before my adoption, I hadn't even had a last name. But at eight, I had been given one—with warm smiles and patient hands, by parents old enough to have been retired, but who had chosen me anyway.

I would make them proud. I would repay them.

One day.

Phontine huddled closer against my collar, her delicate legs curling beneath the fabric of my too-expensive, cobalt, suede jacket—one of the only indulgences I allowed myself.

The wind cut between the towering buildings, forcing me to brace against the chill.

Chicago. The only home I had ever known.

"Three more blocks," Phontine announced, her voice laced with the same exhaustion weighing on my limbs.

I nodded, barely paying attention as we crossed the invisible border between the cleaner, human-dominated streets and the weatherworn brownstones where Magicals lived.

Magicals weren't legally forced into the slums, but the division was clear. Humans got government assistance to stay in "reputable" neighborhoods. Magicals got the scraps.

Shifters. Goblins. Trolls. Fairies. And somewhere, scattered between them, Vampire and Mages like me.

Phontine was the only Pixie I had ever met.

Not for lack of trying.

I had asked her once—"Where are the others?"

She had smiled at me, too bright, too sharp, and changed the subject.

I didn't ask again.

The rusted copper gate of my brownstone screeched as I pushed it open. I barely noticed.

Copper and steel were favorites among Magicals, barriers against certain types of magic. It was a quiet declaration—*This place is ours. You are not welcome.*

It had been installed before we moved in.

The wind howled as the gate slammed shut behind me.

Phontine sighed, patting my shoulder. "Let's go."

I climbed the steps, pulled the key from my pocket, and slipped into the house.

Warmth. Butter frying in a pan. The scent of vanilla candles, and something clean and bright.

Home.

I exhaled slowly, pressing my palm against the door for just a moment, grounding myself in the familiarity of it.

Phontine shimmered into visibility, stretching her wings with a quiet hum.

"Sonia?"

My mom's voice, soft and trembling with weakness ever since her heart attack some years back, drifted from the kitchen.

"It's me," I called back, shoving my hands into my pockets, trying to shake off the weight pressing against my ribs.

The living room unfolded before me, a warm palette of beige walls, mocha-stained wood floors, and couches in a vibrant, deep pink that looked almost purple in the dim light.

I had picked them out. My first real decision in this house.

I stepped through the open archway into the kitchen, leaning against the counter as I took in the sight of my mother at the stove—long gray braid trailing down her back, thin pink lips pursed in concentration as she flipped a pancake.

She glanced up, eyes tracing over my face with that quiet, all-knowing look she always had.

"How was your day, sweetheart?"

I forced a shrug, tilting my head toward the stove. "Breakfast for dinner?"

She smiled. "Felt like a pancake night."

I swallowed hard. I didn't deserve her.

I slid onto a barstool, watching as she set a plate of fluffy, golden pancakes in front of me. Butter melted in rivulets, pooling at the edges, waiting for syrup.

She reached for the bottle on the counter but paused.

"You know," she said, tone light, "if you wanted to...try something else, you could."

I blinked. "Try something else?"

"The restaurant business is brutal," she continued, pouring the syrup in slow, even drizzles. "You're smart. Talented. There's nothing else that interests you?"

I picked up my fork, stabbing into the pancake but not eating. "If I want my own restaurant one day, I need the experience."

"Yes." She nodded, flipping another pancake onto a fresh plate. "But you have time."

I shook my head. "I'm twenty-four, Mom. Not exactly a spring chicken. Everyone I graduated with already has steady jobs, promotions, connections."

Her hands stilled on the spatula. "And you think they all have it figured out?"

I swallowed hard. "They're doing something. I'm just—" My voice cracked, and I clenched my jaw.

She set the spatula down, turned off the stove, and wiped her hands on a dish towel before stepping in front of me.

I didn't resist when she pulled me into a hug.

Her arms were soft but steady, her grip firm, the scent of jasmine and warm fabric softener wrapping around me like a memory of safety.

She kissed the top of my head, whispering, "Finding your place isn't about making decisions. It's about living enough to know which ones matter."

I squeezed my eyes shut, pressing my face into her shoulder. "And what if it takes too long?"

She pulled back just enough to cup my face, her fingers warm against my cold skin. "Then it takes a long time."

My breath hitched.

She smiled, brushing back a stray lock of my hair.

"If I had poured all my energy into my failures instead of my life, I never would have met you."

She reached for a glass of orange juice and slid it in front of me.

"And that would have been the biggest mistake of my life."

Tears burned behind my eyes, but this time, they weren't from failure.

I turned my face away, blinking hard. "I got Dad's gift today."

Her gaze softened. "Let me see."

I pulled the package from my bag and peeled back the paper just enough for her to see the gold-lettered spine of a vintage Frank Sinatra record.

She inhaled sharply. "Oh, sweetheart."

I shifted uncomfortably. "He's gonna love it, right?"

She smiled, brushing her thumb over the exposed edge of the cover. "He's going to love it."

For the first time since I left the restaurant, the weight on my chest eased.

At least I could get one thing right.

"How much was it?" Mom asked, her voice soft but knowing.

I tightened my grip around my glass, barely pausing before I waved a dismissive hand. "Don't worry about it, Mom—"

"Nonsense." She cut me off, her delicate fingers fluttering through the air in a familiar, no arguments gesture. The veins in her hands, deep blue and pronounced by time, traced delicate patterns against her skin like rivers of quiet strength. "Leave the receipt on the counter."

I swallowed a sigh. We both knew that if I didn't, she'd find a way to slip the money into my bag anyway—an old habit of hers, one she refused to break no matter how much I insisted I could handle things on my own.

Before I could argue, a deep, gravelly voice rumbled from the doorway.

"Receipt for what?"

My mom startled, whipping around so fast that the package nearly slipped from her grasp.

"Nothing, love." Her words came quick, light, and paired with a too sweet smile that would have fooled anyone but my father. Clutching the paper-wrapped record to her chest like it was the last secret in the world, she leaned up and pressed a kiss to his cheek. "I need to run something upstairs."

Dad hummed knowingly, but he let it go. He always let her win.

She disappeared down the hall before I could so much as blink, leaving me to face the warm, amused eyes of Martin Byrd.

My dad.

He turned to me with his usual easy smile, his arms opening without hesitation.

I didn't hesitate either.

I stepped into his hug, letting the steady weight of it press against my shoulders, grounding me in a way I hadn't realized I needed until this moment.

He smelled like coffee and old books, like the faint spice of his cologne and something unshakably familiar—home, safety, unwavering love.

When he pulled back, his eyes sparkled with something teasing. "Are you and your mother keeping secrets?"

"From you?" I scoffed, shoving my plate toward him with an exaggerated flourish. "Never."

His laughter—deep and rich—wrapped around me like another embrace.

And, true to form, he stole a sausage from my plate.

I rolled my eyes as he hummed in approval, chewing with deliberate enjoyment before pouring himself a glass of juice.

"Did you have a good day?" he asked, too casually.

My smile wavered, just a fraction.

The sharpness in his gaze told me he caught it instantly.

"That bad, huh?"

I hesitated, then shifted the conversation before the concern in his eyes could dig too deep.

"Dad," I started, voice light, feigning nonchalance as I twirled my fork in the remnants of syrup, "when did you know you wanted to be a professor?"

He didn't even hesitate.

"The moment I saw your mother working in the educator's administration office at our college."

I groaned. "Dad."

He grinned, utterly unrepentant. "Truly," he said, mischief flickering in his gaze despite the lines of age etched at the corners. "It was love at first sight for me. And there was no turning back."

I huffed, trying to keep my smile in check. "So, what? I should base my entire career path on a guy?"

His brow shot up. "Heavens, no." He chuckled, shaking his head. "There's no man good enough for you."

I let out a short laugh, but the ache in my chest was still there, lingering just beneath the warmth of the moment.

"This isn't really helpful," I muttered, even though I couldn't quite stop the smile playing at my lips.

"I'm just an old man, sweetheart." He leaned against the counter, swirling the juice in his glass. "Whoever said age gives you wisdom clearly wasn't talking about the ordinary folk."

I frowned. "You're not average, Dad. You're a tenured professor at a prestigious college, you've been published multiple times—"

He held up a hand, stopping me mid-sentence. His expression shifted—not the teasing warmth I was used to but something softer. Something steady.

"You know why?" he asked, and there was no humor in his voice this time. No teasing.

I shook my head.

His gaze held mine, his words measured, firm. "Because I loved what I was doing, and I wasn't going to stop until I reached my goals."

He tapped the counter once, the sound sharp against the quiet weight of his words.

"And because I had someone like your mom rooting for me every step of the way. Even when it was hard."

The knot in my chest pulled tight.

Of course, he'd say something so simple. So obvious. And yet, it unraveled something inside me.

I curled my fingers around my glass, exhaling a slow breath as my heartbeat evened out.

My dad never gave up.

And neither would I.

He watched me carefully, like he wanted to say something else, something heavier.

"Sweetheart, if—"

I cut him off before he could voice the worry in his eyes.

"So, what you're saying is that it *really* matters who I marry."

A short, booming laugh echoed between us as Dad shook his head, wiping a hand down his face.

"You'll be luckier than a king if you find someone half as good-hearted as your mother," he said with a grin.

"Well," came a soft, trembling voice from the hallway, "isn't that nice to hear."

I turned as Mom stepped back into the kitchen, the brown paper package no longer in sight.

She shook her head at Dad, exasperation warring with affection.

He winked at her.

I laughed, the sound surprising even me—light and unburdened, even if just for a moment.

The weight of the day wasn't gone.

But for the first time since I'd walked through that door, it didn't feel so heavy.

3

The sun chased us all day, streaming through the windows in warm golden streaks as Mom and I raced around the house, setting up streamers and filling bowls with caramel taffy—Dad's absolute favorite. The scent of sugar and warm laughter wove through the air, an invisible thread binding us in the quiet joy that came with celebrating someone you love.

Across the living room, the oversized *Happy Birthday, Martin* banner shimmered in neon blue, letters glistening with actual twinkling stardust. The fabric undulated in slow, mesmerizing waves as if caught in an unseen breeze.

Phontine's handiwork, of course. A pinch of Pixie dust, a whispered spell in a language older than the Living Lands itself, and suddenly a party banner had more life than most people I knew.

I grinned, the ache in my cheeks a reminder of how much I had smiled today. Birthdays in the Byrd family were sacred. Not just a day, but an event. A celebration stretched from sunrise to the last lingering embers of the night, wrapped in the warmth of phone calls from faraway relatives, the rich scent of butter and sugar wafting from the kitchen, and the pure, unfiltered love that had built this home.

I never knew you could love the day of your birth until I was a Byrd.

Before, birthdays had been blurry, distant things—sometimes acknowledged, sometimes forgotten, but never cherished. Then I was adopted, and suddenly I had aunts, uncles, and cousins who sent gifts, sang songs into static-filled phone calls, planned surprise visits just to see the look on Dad's face when they showed up on the doorstep.

And this year, we had pulled off something spectacular.

I snorted as I helped Phontine arrange plastic-wrapped candies—each treat nearly the size of her torso—on a purple glass plate. She huffed, rolling her shimmering periwinkle eyes before sticking out her tongue at me.

"Sweetheart," my mother's voice floated from the kitchen, soft but knowing. "Don't pester Phontine. She's doing a marvelous job."

Phontine straightened, preening at the compliment. "Thank you, Julie."

I crossed my arms, feigning innocence. "What? How did you know I did anything?"

My mom didn't even turn around. She simply tapped a wooden spoon against the rim of a mixing bowl, glancing toward the microwave's reflective surface, where her smile winked back at me like it held a secret.

For a few blissful hours, I let everything else fade—the weight of another lost job, the gnawing uncertainty of my future. None of it mattered today.

Birthdays were a pause in time. A moment where the world didn't demand answers.

By late afternoon, the kitchen table was buried under a spread of Dad's favorite dishes—rows of meat pies, golden and flaky; desserts stacked like edible architecture; and my own small contributions carefully arranged, even if pastries weren't my specialty.

And then—

A sharp rata-tat-tat sounded at the front door.

The air in the room shifted—not a big thing, not even something that anyone else would have noticed, but I noticed.

I always noticed.

My gaze flicked to Phontine.

She stilled, wings fluttering once before she met my eyes.

We didn't have to say anything.

We both knew that not everyone who stepped through that door would be as welcoming as my parents.

Julie turned, voice gentle but firm. "Phontine, my dear, it's time for you to become invisible."

Phontine nodded. No argument, no hesitation. She understood.

Her form shimmered, flickering out of sight, but not before I felt the faintest pressure on my shoulder—her version of a reassuring squeeze.

I exhaled slowly, rolling my shoulders as if that would rid me of the tension curling up my spine.

I never really understood how Pixies worked. How Phontine existed the way she did—flitting between the edges of the Living Lands like a ghost who had simply never died.

I only knew she was from one of the Three Woods, like all Magicals. That she had been with me since before I could form proper memories.

And that, without her, I would have lost my mind before I'd even turned four.

My first ghost sighting—at least, the first one I remembered—had been at three-and-a-half years old.

Terrifying.

Unreal.

All-consuming.

I had been too young to understand what I was seeing, but I felt it. The way the air warped. The way ice bloomed where warmth should have been. The way my chest locked up with a kind of fear that had nothing to do with the dark and everything to do with knowing, knowing that something was there when it shouldn't be.

If Phontine hadn't been there, whispering in my ear, keeping me anchored—

No.

I didn't want to think about what I would have become.

I glanced toward the door as the knock sounded again.

Tamping down the unease pressing against my ribs, I forced a smile and moved forward.

Today wasn't about ghosts.

Today was about celebrating life.

The door swung open, and Aunt Debbie filled the entire frame, her arms overflowing with neon-yellow wrapped presents. It was almost a shock to see her without her usual entourage of corgis. Though, after last year's disaster—where four of them had nearly shattered Mom's china cabinet—I figured she'd learned her lesson.

"Sonia, my girl!" Aunt Debbie boomed, launching herself at me in a bear hug that crushed the breath from my lungs.

I laughed, wrapping my arms around her sturdy frame, feeling the familiar warmth of one of the first people to ever make me feel like I truly became one of the Byrds. Every summer since I'd been adopted, Aunt Debbie had claimed me for two weeks—eras of wild bonding, endless ice cream, and an impulsive perm that still haunted me in family photos.

More guests trickled in—family members, Dad's friends, a few old neighbors—all carrying gifts that were piled like a mountain of celebration in the kitchen. The sight of it made me grin. These people might have been in their sixties, seventies, some pushing eighty, but birthdays still made them giddy like kids.

Mom bounced in place, clutching the carefully wrapped package I'd found just yesterday. "I think that's everyone," she said, her eyes gleaming with excitement. "Put yours by the coffee pot. We'll open it last."

I moved to set the gift down, watching as Phontine hovered over the jam tarts like a starved little gremlin, her longing gaze practically burning holes into the flaky crust. She dodged between presents, darting back toward the living room with a reluctant sigh.

Then—the moment arrived.

Julie clapped her hands, moving toward the door. "Alright, everyone! Get into hiding—Martin always gets home at five."

A scramble followed: Elders groaning as they crouched behind couches, uncles grumbling as they tried to squeeze into spaces between furniture and walls that were clearly not wide enough to conceal fully grown adults. A chair tipped over. Someone laughed under their breath. The last thing I saw before the room plunged into darkness was Aunt Debbie trying to wedge herself behind the TV stand.

Anticipation buzzed through the air, thick with the promise of celebration.

Five o'clock came and went.

A strange unease crept into my spine, but I ignored it. Dad was late sometimes. Maybe he stopped to pick up flowers for Mom like he always did on his birthday.

But then—five-fifteen.

The excitement dulled into a restless silence. People shifted. A whispered conversation started in the back of the room.

Five-thirty.

The unease that had been a whisper turned into a scream in my gut.

Then—the knock.

Sharp. Solid. Final.

Every head in the room snapped toward the door.

My breath stilled.

Why hadn't Dad used his key?

Aunt Debbie struggled to get up from behind the TV stand, grumbling under her breath. Mom hesitated, her fingers trembling as they reached for the handle.

I rose to my feet, my pulse hammering against my ribs.

The door cracked open.

Something was wrong.

Mom didn't move. Didn't speak. Just stood there, rigid, like someone had just drained all the air from her lungs.

Then—her fingers snapped over the light switch.

The room was flooded with searing light.

I blinked, blinded by the sudden brightness, my vision filling with white spots. But as the door creaked open the rest of the way, I saw him.

Not Dad.

A police officer.

His hat in hand. His face streaked with grime.

And the world tilted.

4

The house that had once hummed with warmth and laughter now felt like a grave. The air, thick with the scent of wilting lilies and burnt coffee, pressed against me, suffocating in its stillness. Grief clung to the walls, wrapped itself around the furniture, settled into the spaces between murmured condolences.

It had been two weeks since the police officer knocked on our door, and yet the pain felt as raw as the moment my mother's sobs had split the world in two.

I watched her move through the crowd, exchanging solemn smiles, accepting platters of food, murmuring her thanks like she wasn't barely holding herself together. Her mask of composure was flawless—so perfect that, if I didn't know her so well, I might have believed it.

But I did.

I knew that once the last guest trickled out, once the leftovers were wrapped and stored, once the final glass was rinsed and placed on the drying rack—that mask would shatter.

And then we would be alone.

Just the two of us. Half of our family gone forever.

I clenched my fists against the growing ache in my chest.

No.

Not forever.

I slipped past the quiet conversations, past the soft clinking of dishes, past the murmur of sympathy. In a shadowed corner, away from prying eyes, I caught Mom's hand and pulled her aside.

She let me, though the tension in her fingers betrayed her exhaustion.

"Mom." My voice was barely above a whisper; the weight of what I was about to say pressed down on me, squeezing the breath from my lungs.

She turned to me, her weary eyes meeting mine, and I nearly lost my resolve.

But I had to say it.

"I think I can reach him."

Her fingers tightened over mine.

"I think I can use my magic to see Dad," I pressed on, forcing the words out before fear could swallow them whole. "To talk to him—just once."

The thought had been a spark in my chest from the moment the officer uttered the words, *fatal accident*. That couldn't be the end. A hurried birthday kiss on the top of my head couldn't be our last moment.

If I had this power—if I had spent my entire life plagued by ghosts, haunted, hunted, torn apart by the dead—then surely, I could bend that curse to my will. Surely, it could give something back for once.

I waited for hope to flicker in my mother's expression.

Instead, fear darkened her gaze.

"Sonia." Her voice, always so soft, so careful, wavered under the weight of unspoken things. She cupped my face, her thumb brushing my cheek. The touch was warm, steady—but it was a warning. "Sweetheart, no."

I shook my head. "Mom, I—"

"No." This time firmer. The kind of no that wasn't up for debate. The kind of no that had nothing to do with logic and everything to do with terror.

But I wasn't backing down.

"I can do this," I insisted, my voice fierce, my hands shaking. "I know I can. We could see him again, we could—"

"You don't know that." She cut me off, the crack in her voice nearly breaking me. "Sonia, you don't know what will happen if you try. What if it doesn't work? What if it—" She stopped, pressing her lips together like she was trying to hold in something far worse than words. "What if it breaks you?"

My heart slammed against my ribs.

I swallowed, my throat burning. "It's already breaking me."

The room around us blurred, grief pressing in, the weight of it threatening to crush us both.

She could see it, I knew she could.

The desperation in my eyes.

The unbearable need to fix this.

To undo the cruelty of fate, even if just for one moment.

"I can handle it," I whispered, more to myself than to her.

Mom exhaled shakily, looking at me like I was still that little girl who clung to her after every nightmare.

But I wasn't a little girl anymore.

And I was done letting ghosts destroy my life.

I would not let this be the end.

We could have one more goodbye.

One more moment.

Even if I had to drag him back from the edge of the Deathscape myself.

A violent shudder ran through me at the thought. I had seen the Deathscape. Just a glimpse. A nightmare of shifting shadows; a wasteland where souls dissolved into nothing.

And yet, if I had to carve a path through that hell, I would.

I had to.

Mom's hands dropped from my face, but she still watched me.

And for a moment, just a moment, I saw it.

Hope.

The same wild, reckless hope that had kept me standing when my world crumbled.

But then—

She shook her head.

"I can't bear it, Sonia," she whispered, tears slipping down her cheeks. "I can't bear to lose you, too."

I froze.

The air in my lungs stilled.

I hadn't even considered—

She wasn't afraid of failure.

She was afraid of losing me.

The realization hit like a dagger between my ribs.

But I couldn't stop.

I wouldn't stop.

I had spent my entire life being haunted by things I could never control.

Now, for once, I was choosing to walk into the darkness.

For him.

For her.

For one last moment.

She wiped her eyes, forcing a wavering smile. "Sonia—"

"I'll find a way," I whispered, stepping back, my chest burning with resolve.

Her brows furrowed. "Sonia, please—"

But I turned away, the decision already made.

Mom might not be able to bear it.

But I could.

I had to.

I would.

Six months later.

There was a little shop on Clark Street where belief clung like incense—thick, heady, and stubbornly refusing to dissipate.

Valier's Mystic Shoppe.

The humans who came here? They wanted to believe. They held tumbled stones in their hands like lifelines, whispered affirmations over bundles of dried herbs, and bought hollow promises in satin-lined pouches. Charms that claimed to banish negativity, enhance intuition, attract love.

It was a nice idea.

But the truth? The truth was that none of it meant anything unless a Mage was the one who breathed real magic into the spell. And Valier? She would never risk that.

I exhaled slowly, my breath a thin wisp in the cold air as I watched the last customer drift out, their arms loaded with expensive placebo. A group of three women—laughing, chattering, believing.

A bitter pang settled in my chest.

They're lucky.

I pushed off from the lamp post and made my way toward the deep violet door where cheap gold paint peeled at the edges, betraying the shop's years of wear.

The bell chimed softly as I stepped inside, and the smell of dried sage and old wood enveloped me. The ceiling was draped in layers of faded purple and blue scarves, their fabric gently shifting as though touched by unseen hands. Satin-covered tables gleamed beneath flickering candlelight, each one cradling boxes of crystals, glass jars of moss and lavender, runes carved from river stones.

Aesthetically pleasing.

Useless.

I didn't linger.

I knew where the real magic was.

I strode past the counter with the ancient brass register, the scent of fortified tea and brandy already curling in the air.

"Valier?" My voice carried easily over the quiet hum of the shop. "It's Thursday—we had a meeting, remember?"

I slipped past the shelves of glittering charms and overpriced incense, my steps practiced, weaving through narrow back hallways stacked with old stock and forgotten spellbooks that never held any real power.

This place had been my first job.

Three summers of working the front counter, peddling hope to the hopeless, until Valier had found out about my magic.

After that? She had other plans.

She tried to use me—tried to make me see the spirits of our customers so I could share information I'd otherwise have to research. When I explained that it didn't work like that—that I could only see ghosts if they were already lingering or if I somehow called them from beyond—she'd promptly banned me from the séance room.

Except, of course, when she needed someone to clean it after hours.

I found other jobs.

But every winter break, every holiday, she'd let me crawl back for a few shifts, as long as I promised not to scowl at the customers or make snide comments about their life-altering purchases.

The beaded curtain rattled as I pushed into the back room, just as a familiar, smoke-rough voice called out—

"Yeah, yeah. Get over here, girl—it's almost time for supper."

I sighed, pivoting back toward the séance room.

The candles inside flickered like watchful eyes, their glow casting jagged shadows against the worn wooden table.

Valier was already there, lighting a candle, her flowing white dress ghosting over the floorboards like an apparition of a woman long since faded from her prime.

I hesitated for half a second—then, with a breath, I stepped inside.

"Thanks for letting me do this, Valier," I murmured, my voice barely above a breath.

The air was thick with the smell of candle wax, old books, and the faint bite of charred herbs. Shadows flickered along the velvet-draped walls, the dim glow catching on gold-tasseled cushions and the polished obsidian trinkets littering the shelves.

Valier, already sinking into her usual cushion, let out a slow exhale.

Her round frame settled, the little metal tassels on her seat jingling with the movement. Usually, her eyes—dark, magnified behind bright pink glasses—danced with mischief, her curling hair was a riot of gray streaked with orange and yellow and always wrapped in a scarf that screamed bold and unbothered.

But tonight?

Tonight, there was no cheer. No teasing. Just a deep frown cutting into her freckled face as she watched me.

"We'll try to contact your dad, Sonia," she said, voice smooth, lulling. "But you know I've never done this before."

She hesitated.

Then—

"And unless you've gotten better—"

"I can do it."

The words came out hard and sharp, a knife of pure resolve.

I had to.

For a fleeting moment, I almost believed myself.

Valier exhaled through her nose, then swept a hand over the table, clearing it. The hand-painted tarot cards, the crystal sphere filled with swirling smoke—all pushed aside like cheap illusions.

I watched, jaw tightening.

She was right to clear them away.

Real magic didn't belong with human tricks.

"Take my hands," she instructed, her worn palms resting open on the small, circular table.

I didn't hesitate.

I latched on, my fingers pressing against hers, chasing after that familiar, ghostly cold that always lingered in my bones.

"Close your eyes," she murmured. "Seek the tendril of your magic, deep within."

I obeyed, inhaling through my nose, diving inward.

At first, there was nothing. Just the usual void of black space, stretching endlessly behind my eyes. But then—a pull. A shift. A shiver deep in my ribs.

Like mist curling in an unseen breeze.

Like a door cracking open.

The fog stirred beneath my ribs, cold, twisting, something unseen moving within it.

There was a shape in there.

A presence.

My stomach knotted.

"Now," Valier's voice droned, a vibration against my skin, "call out to the spirit."

I swallowed hard.

"Dad."

His name tasted strange on my tongue, heavy, thick with grief. My fingers tightened around Valier's.

"Martin Byrd, please come to me."

The fog shuddered.

Something moved within it.

A ripple.

I held my breath—

And then—

Nothing.

The shape vanished, dissolving into mist.

A hollow ache cracked through my chest.

No.

No, no, no—

"Please," I choked out, desperation sharpening every syllable. "Spirit that is close to me, that is connected to me—come. Please, come and speak to me."

Something broke.

The air tensed, pulled—

And the world erupted.

A pressure shifted, a wrongness, like the universe inhaling sharply.

A glow blossomed in the center of the room, thick, otherworldly.

Then—

A scream.

Not Dad's.

Something else.

The specter burst through the fog, shimmering scales, long ribboning hair, her features sharp, otherworldly—wrong.

Not Dad.

Not human.

A mermaid.

A ghostly, furious mermaid, her eyes blazing with something far from peace.

She howled, a cry that splintered through the room, rattling the candles—

Then she collapsed.

Liquid erupted from her, thick and unnatural, spectral water oozing in slow-motion splatters, too heavy, too dense, sliding off the table in unnatural waves.

I didn't have time to scream.

The cold slapped across my face, dripping down my nose, pooling on my skin like frostbitten oil.

Valier ripped her hands away from mine with a sharp gasp, stumbling back.

The connection snapped.

The séance shattered.

I blinked wildly as spectral slime clung to my skin, a wet glob sliding from my cheek to the table with a sickening plop.

Valier was already moving, snatching off her glasses, her face twisted in pure rage.

"Don't—" she sputtered, then threw the ruined glasses down and stood so abruptly her cushion toppled over.

I barely registered her storming away before I was on my feet, scrambling after her.

"Why didn't it work?" I blurted, my voice raw. "I—I summoned a spirit. I did it. But why wasn't it Dad?"

Valier whirled on me, her eyes like embers, burning with a frustration that sliced straight through my ribs.

"Because, Sonia." Her voice snapped, sharp as a spell cutting through the air. "You asked for any spirit that was close to you."

A cold dread pooled in my stomach.

Valier stepped closer, her expression one of barely contained fury.

"You're a conduit, girl," she hissed. "A beacon for the dead. Do you know what you just did?"

I swallowed hard, the ghostly damp still clinging to my skin like a warning.

A door left wide open.

And something other than my father had stepped through.

"I—" I tried, but the words caught in my throat, strangled by the tight coil of failure lodged deep in my chest.

Valier didn't give me time to stumble through an excuse.

Her voice was low, strained, vibrating with something that felt dangerously close to fear. "Not all spirits are kind, Sonia. Some aren't lost souls at all. If you do not learn control before tapping into the spirit world again, you could be knocking on a door you'll regret opening."

A sharp, cracking sound tore through my ribs—grief splitting apart, giving way to something uglier, rawer.

I burst into tears.

Not the silent, dignified kind.

The shaking, gasping, collapsing kind—six months of failure trying to reach my dad spilled down my cheeks in hot, shameful streaks.

"I'm sorry," I sobbed, hands clenching into my sleeves like I could hold myself together if I just gripped hard enough. "I'll do it right next time—"

Valier sighed, defeated, and took my shoulders in her hands. Her touch was firm, grounding—but not reassuring.

"I cannot risk it. There will not be another time."

The words hit like a death sentence.

"What?" My fingers latched onto her arms, desperation digging in like claws. "No. No, I can do this. I just need to—"

A high, piercing ringing bored into my ears, drowning out my thoughts.

"The Mage Council forbids contact with the Deathscape," Valier stated flatly.

A sickening stillness filled the room.

"The Deathscape?" My voice barely escaped, a fragile whisper that carried the weight of impending horror.

Valier's face hardened, her grip tightening.

"Where do you think the spirit you just summoned came from?"

I shook my head furiously, panic clawing at my throat.

I didn't know.

I didn't know.

But I should have.

I should have known.

I should have guessed that the gaping maw of the Deathscape—the place where spirits went to be unmade, where the dead were meant to stay dead—was somehow involved.

The ringing in my ears grew louder, deafening.

I pressed my hands against the sides of my head, my whole body trembling under the weight of it all.

"No Mage House will take me on," I forced out, my voice shaking with fury, shame, despair. "They say I don't have active magic. I don't have anyone to teach me. I have no clue about anything!"

The silence that followed was worse than any reprimand.

I had learned over the past six months since the funeral that pity was the ugliest thing you could see on a person's face.

Valier pulled away gently, stepping toward the back of the room. She disappeared for a moment, then returned with two towels, handing one to me.

I clutched it limply to my chest.

"I'm sorry, Sonia." She worked the towel through her curls, still sticky with spectral goo. "But the penalty for meddling with the Deathscape is imprisonment."

A fresh bolt of fear surged through me, sharp and ice-cold.

"Then why did you let me try tonight?" My voice was barely a whisper.

Valier paused, her hands stilling in her hair.

A moment passed.

Then—

"Because I thought you might have gained some control since you were a teenager," she admitted, voice low, regretful. "But you haven't improved."

The words struck like a blade between my ribs.

She continued, quieter now. "And because I hoped you'd be able to see your father again. I thought this one breach of the Council's law would go unnoticed."

I choked on a breath.

"Let me try one more time," I begged, stepping forward. "Please, Valier—"

"Sonia—"

"Please."

I dropped to my knees.

I had nothing left to lose.

Valier closed her eyes, a tremor passing through her fingers before she set the towel down.

"I cannot risk it again," she murmured.

Then, softer—like a whispered confession—"But you...you can always try on your own."

I froze.

The words clanged through my mind, over and over, leaving only one undeniable truth.

I could try again.

Alone.

But what would that mean?

If I failed—if I summoned the wrong thing again—

Or worse.

If I got caught.

The Mage Council did not forgive.

Did not forget.

And I would not survive prison.

My throat closed, my stomach twisting into knotted steel, but I forced myself to lift my chin and stand.

I had no other choice.

"Could you—" My voice cracked. I swallowed hard, gripping the damp towel. "Could you teach me? About my magic?"

Valier's expression softened, but not in the way I wanted.

She looked at me like I was something broken.

"I do not have your gifting," she murmured. "I do not know of any Mage in Chicago that does. Sonia..."

Her voice trailed off, and I knew she wouldn't say anything else.

She didn't have to.

Her gentle hand found my arm, guiding me toward the front of the shop.

I didn't fight it.

There was nothing left to say.

The lights dimmed with a flick of her wrist. The door creaked open, spilling warm, orange streetlight into the shadowed room.

Valier patted my back once, softly, then pushed me forward, across the threshold.

Out.

5

I stumbled onto the sidewalk, still dripping in spectral goo, my mind a fractured storm of loss, fury, and resignation.

A quiet shimmer of air flickered beside me.

Then—

A familiar voice, high and exasperated.

"Eww! What happened to you?"

Phontine.

She fluttered midair, her tiny, iridescent wings humming with energy, her dress stitched from moss and woven starlight shifting in the cold wind.

She stopped just short of landing on my goo-covered shoulder, wrinkling her nose.

I didn't answer immediately.

I forced my feet forward, one step at a time, like if I stopped moving, I'd collapse.

"I summoned a ghost," I said flatly.

Phontine gasped, her wings twitching. "You did it!" She perched on my head, tiny knees digging into my scalp. "How was Martin? Can we summon him again? I want to say—"

"It was a mermaid," I cut her off, voice hollow. "Hence the goo."

She went silent.

I kept walking.

The city buzzed around me, bright lights and neon signs blurred by the fog rising from the pavement.

Phontine settled cross-legged on my head, deep in thought.

Then, after a long pause—

"You still don't know how to summon a specific spirit," she murmured, her voice softer now.

I didn't respond.

Because she was right.

Because Valier was right.

Because I didn't just need to learn control—

I needed a teacher.

A real one.

Someone who knew the Deathscape.

Someone who walked its edges.

Someone who understood what I was.

Phontine sighed, shifting her weight.

"All Mages have teachers, you know."

I knew.

I just didn't have one. And with no House that specialized in Mages who spoke to the dead...It meant I had nowhere left to turn.

Not to a Mage.

Not to Valier.

"There might be one or two Mages who could teach you about your magic," Phontine murmured, her voice barely a whisper against the cold night air.

The words slipped under my skin, needling their way into places I didn't want to examine.

"No." My answer was immediate, uncompromising.

Phontine huffed, stomping tiny feet of pain into my scalp as she jumped up. "But it makes sense, Sonia!"

I gritted my teeth as she hovered in front of me, wings beating furiously in agitation.

"Magic is hereditary. At least one of your birth parents must be a Mage, and they could share the same magic as you. There is no one better to teach you than them—"

"I want nothing to do with the people who gave me away." The words burned out of me like acid. "I have a dad, and I'll figure out how to contact him without their help."

I whipped my arm out, throwing the ruined towel onto the asphalt, my hands burying themselves in my jacket pockets as I marched headlong down the street.

A gust of wind lashed at my face, ripping through me like a blade, but I didn't slow.

Phontine, for once, fell silent.

Then, a sigh. A deep, resigned little puff of air.

"I'm here to help, Sonia," she said at last, voice floating somewhere behind me. "Even if you won't consider all your options."

I didn't look back.

The city hummed around me—the low murmur of cars rolling by, the occasional burst of laughter from late-night revelers, the neon glow of storefronts casting eerie, flickering reflections onto the slick pavement.

I barely registered any of it.

Phontine's words dug into my mind like hooks, each one tethered to something I refused to pull closer.

Magic was hereditary. Someone could teach me.

I shoved the thought deep down, locking it away in the same place where I kept the years I spent wondering why I wasn't good enough to keep.

By the time I reached my townhouse, its warm glow spilling onto the sidewalk, the sight felt strangely hollow.

A shudder wracked through me.

I tell myself it was just the cold.

Just the wind.

Not the gaping silence waiting inside.

Not the way my chest tightened at the thought of stepping into it alone.

I took a deep breath, pushed open the rusted iron gate, and slipped inside.

"Sonia?" Mom's voice floated from the staircase, thin, trembling more than usual.

"Yeah, Mom, it's me."

I rounded the corner just in time to see her struggling to drag a suitcase down the stairs.

My stomach dropped.

"Mom—what are you doing? Let me help!"

She exhaled sharply, pink-faced from exertion as she leaned against the banister.

I rushed forward, my hands closing around the heavy suitcase, carefully lowering it step by step.

"You can't exert yourself like that," I snapped, panic laced in every word. "You're a heart patient—"

"I know, honey."

The gentle reassurance did nothing to soothe the storm inside me.

She shouldn't be doing this. She shouldn't be pushing herself at all.

Not when her heart—fragile, damaged, stubbornly beating—had already betrayed her once.

The suitcase landed with a soft thud by the door.

I turned to face her, jaw tight.

She looked tired, but her smile was warm. Always warm.

I opened my mouth—to scold her, to beg her to take care of herself, to do anything but scare me like this—but she moved first.

She pulled me into a hug.

Her arms were soft, steady, familiar, and I let myself melt into her hold.

"I'm okay, sweetheart," she whispered.

I buried my face against her shoulder, the weight of the day pressing down on me all at once.

I didn't cry.

I wouldn't.

But my grip tightened, like if I held on hard enough, I could stop time from taking her away, too.

Mom pulled back first, smoothing wind-tangled strands of hair behind my ear.

Her brows furrowed slightly.

"Honey," she murmured, tilting my chin up, eyes scanning me like she could see every fracture beneath my skin, "why are you all wet?"

I blinked.

The spectral goo. It must have looked like rainwater to her, clinging to my clothes in faint, sickly blue patches.

I cleared my throat. "Got caught in the rain."

It was a weak lie.

But she didn't push it.

Instead, she gestured toward the suitcase.

"What's this for?" I asked.

Mom's smile faltered, her fingers twisting in the hem of her sweater.

"Aunt Debbie broke her foot."

The words slammed into me like a brick.

"What? When?"

"She'll make a full recovery," Mom rushed to reassure me, waving away my panic. "But she needs help with the dogs for a few weeks."

The Fine Breeds Show.

Of course.

Aunt Debbie treated her corgis like royalty. Otto—the current reigning champion—gets hand-cooked meals and his own dedicated velvet pillow throne.

Mom was the only person she trusted to take care of them.

And I got it, I did—

But a leaden weight settled in my chest.

Mom was leaving.

The house would be empty. For the first time since Dad died—

I'd be alone.

"If you want me to stay, I can call a sitter for her," Mom offered gently.

I shook my head, forcing a half smile.

"No, Mom, it's fine. No one has the money for that." I shrugged, trying to make it look like the idea of her leaving didn't tear something open inside me. "And it's just a few weeks, right?"

A cold tendril of dread wrapped around my ribs.

Mom watched me too closely, reading every flicker of hesitation.

She didn't believe me.

But she nodded anyway.

"Okay, sweetheart."

She dialed for a taxi.

I helped her into her coat, wrapping her scarf snugly around her before the October wind could steal her warmth.

The taxi honked from the curb.

She turned, cupping my face in her hands.

"If you need me, call," she said, voice soft, firm.

I nodded.

But my throat was too tight to speak.

Mom hugged me one last time, then stepped outside.

I watched the taxi pull away, headlights disappearing into the city haze—

And when I turned back toward the house, the warmth that once filled it was already gone.

The silence inside stretched too wide, too deep.

Phontine was nowhere to be found—off sulking, probably.

I made my way to my room, boots dragging against the floor, exhaustion settling in like a weighted shroud.

I didn't turn on the lights. I just sunk into my desk chair, head tipping back, eyes slipping shut.

Then—

A small sticky note, placed perfectly in the center of my laptop screen.

One word.

Blakewell.

And beneath it, written in neat, looping script—

I'm here for you, Sonia. Even if you won't consider all your options.

The words burned into me, an echo of Phontine's voice in the back of my mind.

Blakewell.

The one place I swore I would never go.

The place where my birth parents—the people who had left me—might still be.

The only place I might find answers.

I swallowed hard, staring at the name until the letters blurred together.

I didn't want to do this.

But I might not have a choice.

6

The air hummed with constant motion, the steady churn of rolling luggage, murmured voices, and intercom announcements weaving into a familiar airport symphony of chaos. As I stepped off the plane, the weight of the city pressed in around me, thick with the scent of jet fuel and fresh asphalt baking under the midday sun.

Blakewell.

The name sat heavy in my chest, as if saying it aloud might unravel something I wasn't ready to face.

Meanwhile, Phontine was a whirlwind of excitement, her tiny wings a blur as she zipped around me in erratic, dizzying loops.

"I can't believe you actually came here!" she crowed, gleaming like a shard of twilight against the glaring daylight.

I sidestepped her buzzing wings, my gaze locked on the endless parade of cars outside. Taxi. I needed a taxi.

Were they yellow here? In Chicago and New York they were. That would make sense, right?

And yet—

A shudder prickled down my spine.

Something felt off. Like stepping onto a bridge that didn't quite hold your weight.

"Sonia?"

A gentle tug at my messy bun pulled me back, Phontine hovering just inches from my face, her lavender glow flickering with concern.

I swatted at her halfheartedly and shook off the eerie sensation.

"What?"

"Taxi," she said simply, wings flicking as she gestured toward a burnt-orange car idling at the curb.

I frowned. That...wasn't the color I'd been expecting.

Still, I rolled my suitcase forward, worn boots rattling against the uneven pavement. The cabbie was a wall of muscle and stubborn creases, tucked beneath a faded black ball cap that had definitely seen better days. His wiry beard, permed into wild chaos, framed a scowl so deep it might have been permanent.

"Where ya goin'?" he grunted.

"Um, 108 Castle Bridge," I started, then glanced at Phontine for the rest of the address.

"New Town," she supplied promptly.

"New Town—"

"Blue Lane," she finished, landing delicately near the cabbie's window, though he wouldn't be able to see her. "The Blue Lane on Castle Bridge. Apparently, the neighborhood is sectioned by Mage House—"

The cabbie's gaze flicked toward me, his expression sharpening like a blade against a whetstone.

"New Town, Blue Lane," I repeated, trying for casual indifference.

He squinted, assessing me like I might spontaneously combust in his backseat, then finally jerked his head toward the door.

I let out a breath I didn't realize I was holding.

Sliding into the backseat, I was immediately hit with the scent of unwashed leather, stale cigars, and something sour—spoiled milk, maybe? The cracked vinyl seat let out a protesting squeak as I settled in, my stomach twisting with exhaustion and the unease of stepping into unknown territory.

A faded license plate sat behind the plastic divider. Earnest, it read, followed by something else in smaller print.

Shifter: Boar origin.

A ripple of awareness coiled through me.

That was...new.

In Chicago, you wouldn't find a taxi service openly advertising its driver's magical heritage. By some unspoken rule, enforced by both Magicals and humans alike, people kept those details tucked away; out of sight, out of mind.

Blakewell was different.

The realization sat heavy in my chest, pressing against the sharp edge of my already frayed nerves.

Across from me, Phontine perched on the narrow ledge of the door, her tiny hands pressed against the window as she took in the city like it was a living thing breathing around us.

"How did you get this address again?" I asked, forcing my voice into something calm, detached.

Earnest's eyes flicked to me in the rearview mirror, suspicion etched into every deep line of his face.

I was ready for it this time.

With practiced ease, I tucked my hair behind my ear, revealing a sleek Bluetooth earbud.

Nothing to see here—just a normal girl talking to totally real, not invisible people.

Earnest grunted and turned back to the road, but something about his lingering stare told me he wasn't fooled.

Not even a little.

Phontine's voice was soft, her excitement tempered by something quieter, something careful. "You know, there wasn't anything in your adoption records."

My spine went stiff.

Phontine never broached this topic lightly.

"It was a closed adoption—nothing about your birth parents was shared. No medical history, no heritage. Just your name and a blank space where their names should have been. Julie and Martin knew you came from Blakewell to Chicago and put in foster care because that was the first time you were given an address. It's safe to assume you lived with...your birthparents until you were one."

A bitter chuckle left my lips before I could stop it. "Tell me something new, Pix," I muttered, using the old nickname I'd outgrown, hoping it would soften the tightness in my throat.

But Phontine didn't smile. She didn't even roll her eyes. Instead, she hovered closer, soaking up a stray beam of sunlight before whispering, "I maybe...broke into the records office."

My head snapped toward her so fast I nearly gave myself whiplash.

"What?"

"There has to be *some* paperwork," she pressed on, unapologetic. "Even with a closed adoption, you don't just vanish into a system without a trail. So, I did some digging."

My stomach clenched. "And?"

She hesitated, then landed delicately on my shoulder, voice dropping low. "They took you to a hospital. That's where it started. And not just any hospital—it had a juvenile office."

"That's how you got their last known address?" My breath hitched around the words.

Phontine nodded. "They were members of the Mage House we're heading to."

My pulse slammed hard against my ribs.

She continued, voice now as careful as glass on the edge of a table. "They were living in the House, like a lot of Mages do. If they were members, why wouldn't they still be there?"

"And if they're not?" My throat was dry, like I'd swallowed dust.

"They're still registered," Phontine said, her tone both gentle and unrelenting. "And if they're not there anymore? The House Matron will know where they are."

I turned toward the busy street, watching the city move past in a blur of light and motion, letting it distract me from the storm inside my chest.

The taxi rumbled through Blakewell's winding streets, the weight of the conversation pressing down on my shoulders. I turned toward the window, forehead resting against the cool glass as Old Town unfurled before me—a labyrinth of history built on worn brick and whispered secrets.

Here, the city felt alive in ways I hadn't expected. Magic didn't just exist in Blakewell—it lingered, thrived, breathed.

The buildings leaned together like old friends sharing secrets, their brick façades softened by time, smog, and a stubborn refusal to be anything but what they were. Between them, narrow alleyways twisted and turned like veins of an ancient beast, pulsing with stories only the city could tell. Firelight flickered from doorways and street corners, where alchemists brewed remedies in copper kettles and magicians wove illusions for anyone willing to toss a coin their way.

A Shifter in a scuffed leather jacket strolled past a lamp post, his glowing eyes flashing with mischief as he tipped an imaginary hat to a trio of Vampires perched on a fire escape, their laughter spilling onto the street below. A group of Trolls crowded around a food cart, their deep, rumbling voices carrying over the sizzle of skewered meat. Nearby, a Goblin vendor gestured animatedly to a human couple, enticing them with trinkets that shimmered under the neon glow of a buzzing sign—part spell, part electricity, all charm.

Here, magic didn't whisper—it sang. It curled through the air in lazy tendrils, woven into the cobblestones, humming beneath the city's heartbeat. In Old Town, Magicals and humans moved together in a chaotic, unpolished harmony, the kind that could only come from years of shared streets and unspoken understandings. It was rough around the edges, sure—but there was something undeniably alive about it, something real.

Blakewell was a collision of myth and modernity, of neon lights and forgotten legends. The streets hummed with an undercurrent of power, a constant push and pull between the magical and the mundane.

Despite the exhaustion dragging at my bones, despite the uncertainty clawing at my chest, I felt it—the undercurrent of possibility.

Blakewell was a city built on what ifs, on lost things found, on questions whispered into the dark.

Maybe—just maybe—it had answers, too.

Phontine settled on my shoulder, sensing my thoughts.

"Thank you," I murmured. The words felt fragile, like something breakable.

"Of course, Sonia."

I swallowed. My voice wavered, but I finally asked the question that had haunted me for as long as I could remember.

"What were their names?"

Phontine hesitated, then softly, carefully, she said, "David and Grace."

Ordinary names.

For people who had left me behind.

My chest tightened, but the moment passed as the city gave way to New Town—where the Mage Houses stood like sentinels against time.

And then, the shift happened.

It was subtle at first. A softening. A quietening.

The tangled streets widened, pulling apart like unraveling thread. The architecture lost its jagged edges, the haphazard layering of old and new giving way to deliberate precision.

Old Town faded into the background like a half-forgotten dream, and New Town rose before me—sleek, modern, carefully curated.

The roads here were too smooth, too pristine, without a single pothole or jagged crack to betray the city's age. Even the streetlights cast an artificial glow, their cold blue hue a stark contrast to the warmth of Old Town's flickering lamps.

The people changed, too. The hustle of the supernatural gave way to a different kind of power—controlled, orderly, restrained.

Mages moved with quiet purpose, their long coats sweeping behind them as they strode down sidewalks lined with shops selling refined magical wares. No alleyway vendors hawking stolen relics. No illicit spellbooks sold from the backs of carts.

New Town was a sanctuary for the elite. For the Mages who belonged.

And I—a Mage with no House, with a gift no one could explain—did not belong.

As the taxi drifted deeper into New Town, the city stretched into the suburbs, and even the magic seemed to soften into something quieter, tamer.

Here, the glass and stone buildings melted into elegant brownstones, each lined with polished steel fences that gleamed in the twilight. Ivy curled around charm-protected gates, subtle spells woven into their roots to keep out unwanted guests. The sidewalks were spotless, the air untouched by the smog of Old Town.

A woman stepped out of a Mage-run café, her long coat cinched at the waist, a House Crest pinned above her heart—a sigil of belonging. Of power. She didn't even glance at the taxi as it rolled past.

New Town wasn't just different from Old Town.

It was another world entirely.

And somewhere, within its manicured streets and gleaming Mage Houses, the answers I had been running from were waiting for me.

I tightened my grip on my suitcase as the taxi pulled to a stop.

This was it.

Blue Lane.

My stomach pitched with a sensation that had nothing to do with the ride.

Blue Lane was actually blue.

The asphalt was impossibly smooth, unmarred by cracks, potholes, or even a stray pebble. It was unnatural, pristine—as if magic had been woven into the very fabric of the road itself.

Blakewell let Mages work their magic on the streets?

That seemed insane.

Humans knew Magicals existed—entire history classes were dedicated to them—but they didn't want magic paraded in front of them every day.

This wasn't Chicago.

This was something else entirely.

Earnest, the cabbie, grunted for payment, his expression unreadable beneath the brim of his faded ball cap.

With a sinking feeling, I dug into my bag and handed over the last of my cash.

Twenty-five bucks.

That was it.

If Phontine had warned me that New Town was on the far edge of Blakewell, I would have walked instead of handing over a small fortune in taxi fare.

My fingers curled around the handle of my suitcase, heart hammering against my ribs as I stared up at the glass and stone façade of the Mage House.

Somewhere beyond that door, in the depths of this place, laid answers I never thought I'd seek.

I took a breath.

And stepped forward.

"Ready?" Phontine's voice was a whisper against my ear, her shimmering blue wings folding around my shoulder like a weightless shield.

No.

I wasn't ready—not for this, not for whatever waited for me beyond the pristine glass doors of the Mage House. And yet, my feet refused to turn back. I lifted my gaze to the towering structure before me, a marvel of impossible design.

The entire House—if it could even be called that—was carved from a single, seamless sheet of crystal clear glass, its three stories bending and curving as if shaped by magic itself. Light fractured and scattered through its walls, casting shifting prisms across the cobblestone street. Through the transparent façade, I glimpsed a cozy sitting area lined with plush, white, fur rugs, towering wooden bookshelves brimming with ancient tomes, and sleek, low-backed chairs arranged around a massive marbled egg resting on a pedestal. Heavy, intricately woven curtains partitioned the space beyond, their deep blue fabric the only thing offering a shred of privacy.

The entire street mirrored the same strange, unsettling transparency—houses of glass standing side by side, their interiors visible to the world. A neighborhood where nothing was hidden. Where even secrets had nowhere to go.

A cold shiver worked its way down my spine.

"Let's get this over with," I muttered, gripping the handle of my rolling suitcase like a lifeline. My steps echoed against the pristine pavement as I approached the golden doorbell embedded in the glass.

My reflection stared back at me—travel-worn, cheeks hollow from stress, black, uncombed hair escaping my messy bun that I somehow thought my bob would stay in. My fingers trembled as they pressed the bell, the soft chime barely audible over the pounding in my chest.

The moment stretched, each breath dragging slow and heavy. Then, movement—a shift in the curtains. A figure emerged, gliding toward the door with effortless grace.

She was about my age, maybe a year or two older, with sun-kissed tan skin and curling hair as dark as mine, but it was her eyes—an unnatural, luminous green—that held me captive.

The door swung open with a soft thud, and for a heartbeat, she simply stared.

"Hello," she said, her voice smooth, warm—welcoming. "Sorry, the door sticks sometimes."

I nodded, swallowing against the lump in my throat. "Hi." My hand twitched in a pathetic wave, heat rising to my cheeks. *Real smooth, Sonia.*

She didn't seem to notice my awkwardness. "Are you looking for someone?"

"Yes," I managed, shifting my weight as Phontine perched invisibly on my shoulder, an anchor in my storm of nerves. "I'm looking for a member of your Mage House."

The girl tilted her head, considering me. "What's your name?"

"Sonia Byrd."

Her lips quirked up in a half smile. "I'm Calypso," she said, offering her name like a piece of something sacred. "Come on in. Let's see who we can find for you."

She stepped aside, and I hesitated only for a second before slipping past her, the threshold humming faintly as I crossed into the House.

Inside, the glass walls gave the eerie illusion of standing in a world without barriers. The ceiling arched high above, chandeliers suspended as if by invisible strings, their candlelight refracting against the transparent walls in golden ribbons.

"Take a seat." Calypso gestured toward one of the sleek chairs, the kind that looked expensive and wholly uncomfortable.

I lowered myself onto the cool leather, fingers knotting together in my lap. "I'm looking for—"

"Grace and David," Phontine finished for me, her small voice barely audible, yet it rang like a bell in my ears.

"Grace and David," I echoed, my throat tight, my pulse thundering against my ribs.

Calypso studied me for a moment, her glowing green eyes sharp with something unreadable. Then she nodded. "I'll see what I can do."

I exhaled a shaky breath, watching as she disappeared beyond the curtains, her silhouette swallowed by the House's depths.

The silence that followed was unbearable. My fingers gripped the armrests, my body tense with the urge to run. I could leave now, slip out before they returned, before I had to face the people who had given me away.

"Sonia," Phontine murmured, a tiny hand pressing against my shoulder. "Breathe."

I barely had time to listen before the soft whisper of fabric drew my attention back to the curtained hall.

A woman stepped forward.

She was draped in white silk, silver threads woven through the fabric, catching the light like strands of moonlight. Her platinum hair cascaded over her shoulders, smooth and shining, each strand too perfect, too ethereal. She moved like a ghost—like a vision plucked from some forgotten dream.

For a moment, my breath caught.

I had imagined my birth mother a thousand different ways—Asian, like me, with straight black hair and soft dimples in her cheeks. A woman who looked like she belonged to me.

But this woman—this glowing, untouchable creature—was nothing like the birth mother I had dreamed of.

She was a stranger.

And she was looking at me like she knew exactly who I was.

"I'm looking for Grace...um," I stammered, suddenly hyperaware that I didn't know her last name. I'd spent my entire childhood thinking about who this person was, and now, standing here, I didn't even have a full name.

The woman before me arched a perfectly sculpted brow. "Guen," she supplied smoothly. "Grace Guen." A knowing pause. "You do look a great deal like her. A family relation?"

I swallowed hard. If this wasn't my birth mother, then why would Calypso have brought me her?

"Yes," I admitted, voice tight. "She's my birth mother."

Something flickered in the woman's dark eyes. Not surprise. Not recognition. Something deeper, something calculating. Then, without breaking my gaze, she lifted a delicate hand and snapped her fingers.

Phontine materialized midair with a startled squeak, nearly colliding with my hair.

"I'm Matron Black," the woman said, as if she had all the time in the world. "Everiss Black."

My stomach twisted. I'd only met a Mage House Matron once before, and that encounter had left me with more wariness than anything else I'd ever experienced.

"Calypso told me your name. Sonia Byrd," she continued, as if tasting the weight of my name on her tongue. "I'm afraid you will not find Grace or David here."

"What?" The word was ripped from me, raw and desperate.

"They left many years ago."

"Where?" I demanded, every muscle in my body tensing. "Where did they go?"

"They did not say," Matron Black replied, her voice calm, measured—too measured. Like she was peeling apart my desperation, examining it piece by piece. "They grew tired of the tedious ways of Grace's magic and wished to leave the Magical community for good."

"That's impossible." The words barely made it past my lips. It had been drilled into me since childhood—Magicals couldn't outrun their heritage. Even I, raised in a human home, had never truly escaped.

The Matron shrugged, an infuriatingly delicate motion. "Why do you want to find her?" she asked, tilting her head. "Is it to get to know your mother?"

The casual way she said *mother* made my stomach turn. My mother was back in Chicago. My mother was the one who'd raised me, who'd taught me how to cook pancakes, and kissed my forehead every night. Not Grace.

"I have a mother," I shot back, the words sharp. "I want to find Grace so I can learn how to use my magic. Magic is hereditary, and I thought she could teach me."

"Hmm." Matron Black studied me, gaze dark and depthless, as though she were unraveling me thread by thread. "I assume you have the Ghost Whisperer ability, as your mother—Grace—did."

I stilled.

There it was. A name. A definition for the thing that had made me an outcast.

Ghost Whisperer.

It sank into me, the weight of it heavy and unshakable.

Matron Black gestured toward the softly glowing glass walls, light refracting across their endless, seamless expanse. "Grace trained here, in this Mage House," she said smoothly. "If you were to join the House, I could train you. It won't be exactly like having a Ghost Whisperer instruct you, but it will be close."

I blinked. "Join your Mage House?"

The offer felt as impossible as the fact that I'd spent the last of my savings to fly to Blakewell, hunting ghosts of people who had no interest in being found.

Matron Black handed me a sleek card with elegant, looping letters in shimmering blue. "We're hosting a picnic this Saturday in the park. Come, meet the House, see if you like what you see." Her lips curved, but the expression didn't reach her eyes. "Then, go from there."

I took the card, feeling its weight between my fingers as my mind raced.

I hadn't found Grace or David. But maybe I could learn enough magic to contact Dad without ever meeting them.

A win-win.

I forced a tight smile and nodded, tucking the card into my pocket. "Okay."

The air outside felt colder, sharper, as we stepped onto the sidewalk.

Phontine fluttered beside me, her small wings a blur of light. "Are you sure about this?" she asked, voice laced with unease.

"Why not?" I said, my pace quickening. "Matron Black could train me. I'd never have to meet Grace or David."

"Yeah..." Phontine's lips pursed, a rare hesitation stealing across her usual confidence.

"What?" I frowned, pausing to glance back at the towering glass House. "You practically begged me to come here."

She was staring at the House too, her brows pinched. "Didn't you feel like...something was off?"

I followed her gaze, scanning the building again. My eyes traced over the glistening windows, the impossibly clean surfaces. Then—

A shadow.

My breath hitched as my gaze locked onto the uppermost window.

A woman stood pressed against the glass.

Her body was marred with scorched flesh, blackened veins stretching like ink beneath the skin. Her eye sockets were hollow, clawed away as though she had torn them from her own face. Her mouth—gaping, empty—where a tongue should have been, only a dark pit remained.

She raised a trembling hand, pressing it to the glass.

Red smeared in its wake.

A sickening screech filled the air as frost spread outward from where she touched, cracks spider-webbing through the pristine transparency.

A deep, guttural groan rumbled through the building, like the glass itself was protesting.

Then—

She was gone.

The frost remained, ice clinging to the windowpane, as if something had lingered.

Phontine whispered, "The glass...it's frozen."

A chill crawled down my spine.

"That was a—"

"Ghost," I breathed, my pulse hammering. "The Mage House is haunted."

I stared up at the building, my fingers curling into fists, my heart pounding against my ribs.

What was this place?

And why the hell was Matron Black so eager to invite me in?

7

I turned away from the Mage House with resolute steps, my pulse still thrumming from what I'd just seen. Phontine darted onto my shoulder, gripping the collar of my dark blue leather jacket like a wind-tossed tassel, her tiny fingers digging in for stability as I picked up my pace.

"It could be an old ghost," Phontine murmured, shifting behind the curtain of my hair like a nervous bird tucking into its nest.

A dry laugh escaped me. "I think she was wearing pants."

The ridiculousness of it did nothing to soften the icy tension laced through my bones. My eyes locked onto the bus stop sign ahead, the final stretch of this eerily flawless street. The sidewalks gleamed, pristine as untouched snow. The lawns were clipped to uniform perfection, not a single fallen leaf daring to mar their symmetry.

Nothing here felt lived-in.

It was too perfect. Too pretty. Too...sterile.

"If we turn around now, we might still catch a glimpse of the House," Phontine tugged lightly at a loose strand of my hair, her whisper barely audible above the quiet hum of the wind. "If—"

"I'd rather not see that again, thanks," I cut in, angling my rolling suitcase as the sidewalk sloped gracefully toward the bus stop. "Why didn't anyone mention a ghost when they already know I'm a Ghost Whisperer?"

Phontine fell silent, for once.

The last few yards felt impossibly long as I reached the empty bus stop, setting my suitcase against the metal bench. The road stretched wide and vacant. A kind of silence pressed in, thick and unnatural. No city hum. No distant car horns. No muffled voices from open windows.

Only the wind, coiling through this too perfect neighborhood like a breath held too long

"If it's a modern ghost," Phontine spoke again, her voice soft but insistent, "do you think the Mages in that House even know who it is?"

A shiver threaded down my spine.

I turned, meeting her periwinkle eyes as she hovered just close enough that our noses almost brushed. "Why would a ghost be haunting that Mage House?" she asked, her voice barely more than a whisper.

I swallowed, but the lump in my throat refused to budge. "The way she looked...she had no eyes or tongue."

The words felt like iron on my tongue. Heavier, colder, wrong.

Phontine's eyes went wide. A shudder rippled through her tiny frame, her wings flaring in a frantic burst before she forced them still.

Before I could gather my thoughts, a voice shattered the uneasy quiet.

"Sonia!"

A dark figure sprinted toward me, black hair streaming behind her, moving too fast, too urgent. My body locked up in instinctive alarm, heart hammering as adrenaline surged.

Phontine vanished in an instant, her body flickering into invisibility.

I clenched my fists, bracing myself as the figure closed the distance.

Only when she was nearly upon me did I recognize her—Calypso.

The Mage from Matron Black's House.

My age, my build, but the urgency in her expression sent a jolt of fresh unease through me.

Why the hell was she chasing me?

And why did it feel like something had just gone very wrong?

Calypso skidded to a stop in front of me, her breath coming in ragged gasps. Strands of raven-black hair stuck to her flushed cheeks, her glowing green eyes flicking to mine with an urgency that sent a ripple of unease through my chest.

"I'm glad I caught you before the bus," she managed between gulps of air. "I wanted to offer you a ride."

I hesitated. Why send Calypso after me? Was this an order, or was she acting on her own?

"That's okay," I said, forcing a polite smile. "I can manage on the bus, but thanks."

"You sure?" Calypso straightened, flipping her long hair over one shoulder as her breath evened out. "Bus fare's brutal this far out from the city."

That made me pause. My stomach twisted. My flight had drained my savings, and I still needed a motel, food, and maybe even another ticket home.

"Come on," she coaxed, lightly tapping the handle of my suitcase. "I don't mind. Blakewell's a lot to take in on your first visit."

As if on cue, the low growl of the approaching bus rumbled through the silent street. Calypso's gaze flicked from the bus to my face, something unreadable passing through her eyes. "And…" she added, voice softer now, "I overheard what Matron Black told you. I know what it's like—to have too many questions and nowhere to turn."

I inhaled sharply, her words cutting through my guarded exterior. I didn't know Calypso. Maybe she had been an orphan once, too. Maybe she understood what it was like to wonder where you came from and feel like the answer was always just out of reach.

"I just want to help, Sonia," she said, fingers fidgeting against the edge of my suitcase.

For the first time since stepping into this city, the weight of my exhaustion cracked just enough for something small and fragile to breathe. Trust.

"Alright," I murmured. "Thanks."

A relieved grin spread across her face. "My car's back at the House. Come on."

Phontine, still invisible to everyone but me, perched on my shoulder, the warmth of her tiny presence a silent reassurance as we retraced our steps toward the looming glass estate.

Inside Calypso's car—a compact but well-loved Toyota—she buckled in smoothly, exuding an easy confidence, and shot me a bright, fox-like grin—like this was just another casual drive instead of a stranger offering me a ride after I nearly bolted from her Mage House. "So, where to?"

"The cheapest motel in Blakewell," I said, my voice barely above a whisper.

Calypso didn't press me, just nodded and pulled onto the road.

Blakewell shifted around us.

Each house in New Town was pristine—a manufactured beauty of sleek glass and sculpted stone, their perfect yards trimmed like magazine covers. It felt sterile, almost artificial, as though no one actually lived here. I exhaled in quiet relief as we crossed into the outskirts, where the city's pulse began to thrum back to life.

Blakewell was a strange beast. Unlike Old Town, where magic bled through the streets like veins of fire, New Town was a performance of control—polished, restrained, and impossibly clean. Yet, in the distance, where the suburbs met the encroaching forest, the city's careful façade gave way to something wilder.

"This is a lot for one day, huh?" Calypso finally said, breaking the silence.

I gave a small, humorless laugh. "Understatement of the year."

She hesitated, fingers flexing on the steering wheel. "I'm sorry about your mom. I didn't mean to eavesdrop, but...well, when you live in a glass house, you get used to overhearing things."

I let that settle between us before nodding. "Yeah, I suppose you would."

"So...you're staying in Blakewell for a while?"

I sighed, my grip tightening around my arms. "I'm trying to find Grace. She was a member of your Mage House. I thought being here might help me figure out where she went."

Calypso furrowed her brow, clearly puzzled. "How do you not know where your mom is?"

I glanced at her, then back out the window. "She's my birth mother, not my mom," I corrected gently. "I was adopted."

A flicker of something crossed Calypso's face—understanding, maybe even sympathy—but she didn't pry. The silence between us settled into something easier, less sharp around the edges.

Eventually, we pulled up in front of a small, run-down motel on the edge of New Town. The encroaching forest loomed behind it, its shadows stretching long over the cracked pavement.

"You sure you want to stay here?" Calypso asked, eyeing the dimly lit sign with a skeptical frown.

"It's cheap," I said with a shrug. "And safe. I'll manage."

"I could talk to Matron Black—"

I cut her off with a dry laugh. "She made it clear that any help from her comes with strings. I'm not looking to be owned by a Mage House."

Calypso exhaled through her nose but didn't argue. Instead, she popped open the glove compartment, grabbed a pen, and scribbled something onto the back of a receipt.

"Here," she said, tearing it off and handing it to me. "My number. If you need anything—or if you get sick of the smell of mildew—just call or text me."

I hesitated, then took the slip of paper.

"Thanks," I murmured, and this time, I meant it.

Calypso gave me one last searching look before I slipped out of her car. The hum of her engine rumbled through the stillness as she pulled away, her taillights vanishing down the road.

For the first time since arriving in Blakewell, Phontine and I weren't entirely alone.

With a breath, I hoisted my suitcase and stepped into the motel lobby, ready—or at least willing—to face whatever came next.

The motel room was exactly what I'd expected—small, outdated, and clinging to the last shreds of functionality like a stubborn weed growing through pavement. The faded floral bedspread did nothing to make it feel inviting, but it would do. I let my suitcase drop onto the narrow bed, my backpack landing beside it with a dull thud, then exhaled deeply, trying to shake off the weight of the day.

Phontine flitted to the bedside table, her tiny wings barely making a sound as she perched on the old alarm clock. "Well, it's not the worst place we've stayed," she offered, her voice light with forced optimism.

I snorted. "That's a low bar, Pix."

Still, my mind wasn't on the lumpy mattress or the peeling wallpaper. It was back at the Black House—back in that glass fortress where a ghost had pressed itself against the window, its eyeless sockets haunting me more than Matron Black's offer. That House had secrets, but right now, my own were pressing in too hard to think about anyone else's.

I sank onto the edge of the bed, phone in hand, thumb hovering over the call button. I wanted to hear Mom's voice, to let the familiar warmth settle over me like a childhood blanket. But she thought I was still in Chicago, living my normal, restaurant-hopping, ghost-ignoring life. The last thing she needed was the truth—that I was standing in a tiny motel room on the edge of a city filled with the kind of magic she had no place in.

Instead, I sent a quick text to Calypso, my fingers tapping out a message before I could second-guess myself.

Thanks again for the ride. What's the Black House like? Really?

I wasn't ready to commit to anything but learning more wouldn't hurt. And if my birth parents had lived there once, maybe it was my only real shot at learning to control this ability—before it controlled me.

A few minutes later, my phone vibrated.

You're welcome! The House is a good place, I swear. The Black House is under the Shadow Court and we specialize in Illusion, Mentamancy, and Shadow-Weaving magic, but we also teach the basics as all Houses do. The picnic would be a great way for you to meet everyone.

I chewed on my lip as I read the message, rolling the idea over in my head. The Black House being in the Shadow Court didn't mean much to me—not when my magic fell into a category no one ever seemed to talk about. Besides, what did the Shadow Court even mean? The inner workings of a Mage House were so foreign to me; Calypso was using words I'd never heard of before.

Another message popped up.

Calypso: I looked up your name in the Magic Council's database. It looks like you've never been registered with a House before?

My grip tightened around my phone. Of course, I wasn't in the system. No House had ever wanted me. Without active magic, I was a footnote in the magical world, a stray no one knew what to do with. It wasn't news, but seeing it written out stung more than I had expected.

Before I could answer, my phone screen went black.

The overhead light flickered, then sputtered out.

Darkness swallowed the room.

A beat of silence passed, thick and unnatural.

Then the air changed.

Goosebumps erupted across my skin as the temperature dropped—sharp and sudden, like stepping into a freezer. The hair on my arms stood on end.

No.

I bolted upright, eyes darting to the shadows curling in the corners of the room. The motel was old, sure, but that didn't explain this. My phone should have had enough charge left to last the night. The lights shouldn't have cut out so fast.

Phontine reappeared in a shimmer of blue light, her tiny form glowing faintly in the dark. "That wasn't normal," she said, voice barely above a whisper.

No kidding.

I reached for my phone again, pressing the power button repeatedly, but the screen remained dark. A low hum filled the air—not quite a sound, more like a vibration in my bones.

The floor creaked.

I stilled.

Phontine darted toward the door, her glow barely illuminating the space in front of me. "Sonia..."

I swallowed hard, forcing myself to breathe through the spike of adrenaline.

The creaking stopped.

Silence.

Then—

A whisper.

Not a voice. Not even words.

Just the distinct sensation of something unseen moving, brushing against the edge of reality.

A ghost.

My stomach twisted.

The whispering grew louder, slithering through the darkness, wrapping around me like unseen fingers.

Then, just as suddenly as it started, it stopped.

The light flickered back on.

The room was empty.

I let out a shaky breath, my heart hammering against my ribs. My phone screen blinked back to life, notifications popping up as if nothing had happened.

Except something had happened.

Phontine landed on my shoulder, pressing close, her wings twitching. "We need to get out of here."

I nodded. I had come to Blakewell to find answers.

But it seemed like something—someone—had found me first.

"How am I supposed to keep Mom from getting suspicious if I can't even get her messages?" My voice came out sharper than I intended, frustration crackling through me like a live wire. Perfect. Just freaking perfect.

Phontine didn't reply right away, but I could feel her tiny presence shift, hovering just over my shoulder, wings beating in slow, measured flutters.

I yanked open the zipper on my suitcase, the rasping sound slicing through the tense silence. Digging through the mess of clothes and travel essentials, I muttered, "You know how she's been lately. Ever since the accident…" My hands stilled over the bristles of my toothbrush. "We like to keep tabs on each other." My voice faltered, quieter now. "If—"

"I know."

Phontine's small, cool hand settled gently on my finger. A simple touch, yet it carried volumes—of understanding, of shared sorrow, of everything we had never quite said aloud.

I turned away, blinking hard.

Because if Phontine started crying, I would, too.

And I couldn't afford to fall apart. Not tonight.

I should be focusing on figuring out how to control my magic.

Bless the Wood—I wasn't about to tie myself to a Mage House in a city I didn't even live in. If Matron Black refused to let her Mages train me without pledging myself to her House…well. I'd figure something else out.

Shaking off the frustration knotting my spine, I focused on something simple—mundane. The rhythmic squeeze of toothpaste onto my brush, the way the bristles scraped against my teeth, the cool tile beneath my feet, grounding me.

A drop of water landed on the back of my hand.

I ignored it.

Then another.

And another.

Drip. Drip. Drip.

A slow, uneasy chill coiled through me. My gaze lifted—first to the bathroom mirror, then beyond my own reflection.

And my breath locked in my throat.

A specter loomed behind me, its body contorted in unnatural ways, as if twisted by something far worse than death. Its ragged, striped shirt clung to its form, torn and worn, and its wide, empty eyes—whole this time—were locked on mine. Pleading.

The scream tore from me before I could stop it. I whirled, toothbrush clenched like a weapon—prepared to defend myself, to do something.

But the space behind me was empty.

No ghost. No whisper of movement. Just the dim, flickering light above the sink, buzzing faintly in the silence.

What the hell?

"Sonia?"

Phontine's voice was tight, her wings fluttering in the doorway.

I stood frozen, my chest rising and falling in erratic, uneven breaths. The air had shifted—thicker, colder, pressing down on me with an almost physical weight. It was the kind of cold that didn't just cling to skin—it sank into the marrow, into the space between ribs, curling deep in the hollow of my spine.

"I saw..." My voice failed me. I turned back to the mirror, expecting—needing—to see something. But there was nothing.

Not even a whisper of her presence.

Ghosts were a part of my reality. I'd seen them for as long as I could remember—spectral figures drifting at the edges of existence, orbs pulsing with echoes of lives long past. But this? This was different.

She had been solid. More than just a lingering soul clinging to the Living Lands.

And then...the cold shifted.

Not away from me. Not fading. But pressing closer.

A phantom weight settled on my shoulder. A touch—cold fingers wrapped around me.

I stilled.

Slowly—so, so slowly—I turned my head toward the mirror.

She was there again. But closer now. Too close.

Her mouth opened, but no sound escaped. No wail. No whisper. No desperate plea.

But I heard her anyway.

A single, rasping word curled around my mind like a breath of winter air:

"The forest."

The ghost's fingers tightened, ice biting into my skin.

And then—she was gone.

The weight lifted, the air snapped back to normal, and I staggered against the sink, gripping the porcelain edge so hard my knuckles ached.

Behind me, Phontine hovered, her small hands clenched against her chest. "Sonia." Her voice was softer now, shaken. "You—you heard her, didn't you?"

I nodded, too rattled to speak.

Her next words sent a slow, creeping dread crawling up my spine.

"The ghost was able to speak to you?" Phontine's wings fluttered faster, "You know I can't hear ghost, or see them, so you got to tell me what happened."

My heart hammered against my ribs, the silence stretching between us like a taut wire ready to snap.

And then I remembered.

The Mage House. The upper window. That ghost had been there.

"If you don't tell me, Sonia, I can't help—"

"Phontine." My voice barely rose above a whisper. "She's the same one. The ghost from the House."

Phontine's eyes widened. "But how? Ghosts don't just...follow people."

Not unless they had unfinished business. Not unless they were bound to someone.

Not unless they were connected to me.

And yet, I had never met her before. Had never been to Blakewell before.

Except...

I swallowed, the bitter taste of realization hitting the back of my tongue.

"...I lived here when I was a baby," I whispered. "She want's me to follow her into the forest."

Phontine's wings faltered.

I had always assumed my ghosts were strangers—lost souls that simply drifted near me. But this one had *found* me. Sought me out.

That meant she had unfinished business.

And it had something to do with me.

A distant chill prickled across my skin.

A new, heavier silence settled over the room.

And then—

A sudden violent gust of air blasted through the motel.

I stumbled back as the lights flickered—once, twice—before dying completely.

The darkness was instant. Complete.

And across the room, through the frost-laced window, she stood at the edge of the trees.

Waiting.

"I know that look," Phontine's tiny voice quivered with concern from beside me. "Sonia, no. You're not actually about to follow a ghost into the forest, are you?"

The cold air burned my lungs as I inhaled deeply, steadying myself. I knew Phontine had a point. Every rational part of me screamed that this was reckless—maybe even suicidal. But something about this ghost felt different. More urgent. More personal.

"If I don't, it might not leave us alone," I murmured, barely able to admit the next part out loud. "And what if she knew my birth parents?"

A jolt of unspoken tension passed between us.

"Not all ghosts can have conversations, you know," Phontine reminded me sharply, clinging to my sleeve as though she could physically stop me. "Remember that dead girl from high school? You had to put the pieces together yourself—she didn't exactly give you a neat and tidy answer."

"This one already spoke," I countered, lifting her off my shoulder and gently placing her on my suitcase. She folded her arms, pouting. "The sooner I learn how to control my magic, the sooner we can go home."

"But the ghost—"

"I deal with ghosts all the time, Phontine," I cut her off, my voice firm, steady. Lying. Because the truth was, I'd never dealt with a ghost quite like this.

Grabbing my jacket, I shoved my motel key into my pocket and Phontine fluttering by my shoulder I stepped outside. The forest stretched before me, a darkened mass of towering trees and tangled undergrowth. Something in its depths called to me, like a whispered secret curling through the cold night air.

The ghost that had once lingered at the forest's edge had moved. Deeper now. Waiting.

I hesitated only for a moment before stepping into the shadows.

Each step muffled by damp leaves, my pulse thundering against my ribs. The air grew heavier, thicker, as if the forest itself was pressing down on me, trying to keep me out. Or maybe...trying to keep something in.

Twenty paces in, the spirit flickered ahead—a pale shimmer against the dark. Her presence pulsed like a beacon, guiding me forward with an urgency that sent ice slicing through my veins. I swallowed hard, fighting the unease pooling in my gut. I was a city girl through and through. Woods? Forests? Places without streetlights and emergency exits? Not my scene. And yet, here I was, following a ghost through a thickening tangle of trees.

Phontine clung tighter to my collar, her tiny breath warm against my skin. "I don't like this, Sonia."

Neither did I.

And then the ghost stopped.

I stepped into a clearing—and my breath caught in my throat.

The scent of iron hit first. Thick. Rotten. The kind that clung to the back of your throat. The ground was littered with damp leaves, but beneath them, something wrong bled through.

Blood.

Parts were dried. Others were dark liquid pools.

Wet, congealing clumps of crimson smeared the earth, soaking into the roots of the trees. Dark scorch marks clawed up the bark, their jagged edges pulsing with the remnants of a spell. The sheer violence of it made my stomach churn.

A ragged, agonized wail ripped through the night.

Phontine flinched violently against me, her tiny fingers digging into my jacket. I felt it, too—that visceral, gut-deep fear that ghosts had never stirred in me before.

Something terrible had happened here.

The ghost let out another keening cry before vanishing, leaving nothing but the blood-stained ground and the suffocating silence of the trees.

No body.

Just blood. Just magic. Just...wrong.

Why wasn't there a body?

A chill crawled up my spine, and for the first time since stepping into the woods, I wanted out.

Then—footsteps.

Distant at first, then closer. Purposeful. Measured.

I went completely still.

Phontine's tiny fingers dug into my collar, her wings fluttering in a silent panic.

Someone—or something—was coming.

And I was standing in the middle of what looked an awful lot like a crime scene.

Fear surged like wildfire, every instinct screaming at me to move. To run. To hide.

But it was too late.

A shadow loomed just beyond the tree line.

And then—the footsteps stopped.

Right at the edge of the clearing.

8

I bolted.

The second that dark figure stepped out of the tree line into the blood-soaked clearing, pure, mindless terror seized me. My body moved on instinct before my brain could catch up. *Run. Just run.*

My heartbeat pounded in my ears, drowning out everything else—my breath, Phontine's panicked squeak, even the snap of twigs beneath my feet as I tore through the undergrowth. My limbs burned, but I pushed forward, shoving aside branches that clawed at my jacket, my pulse a wild drumbeat of *get away, get away, get away.*

The stranger's footsteps thundered behind me, closing in. Too fast. Too relentless. He called out—words lost to the sheer panic surging through my veins.

Then—a hand clamped around my arm.

I twisted, kicked, fought like hell. My body was a blur of thrashing limbs, my breath ragged and desperate. My foot caught on a root, and in an explosion of motion, we went down.

We hit the ground hard—a tangled mess of limbs and force. My elbow cracked against something solid, sending a shock of pain up my arm, but I didn't stop. I scrambled, nails clawing at dirt, at him, anything to break free—

Then his grip tightened.

Iron-strong, unyielding. A vice around my wrist. And suddenly, I wasn't moving.

A voice, low and commanding, cut through the frenzy.

"I'm the police."

The words stopped me cold.

My body still trembled, breath heaving, as my brain caught up. I blinked hard, trying to focus, to see him—not just as the looming threat I'd imagined, but as someone real.

Dark eyes, intense and unwavering, locked onto mine. A storm churned behind them—controlled, unreadable. His brow furrowed just slightly, his jaw set with the kind of practiced restraint that said he'd handled worse than me, that he wasn't easily rattled. That he was used to being in control. But there was something else.

Frustration? Suspicion? Amusement?

I couldn't tell.

Heat flared in my chest, a mix of defiance and something I couldn't name, something sharp and dangerous curling beneath my ribs. I sucked in a breath, my lungs tight, my entire body wound too taut, too aware. The space between us—too close.

Who the hell was he?

Before I could process, before I could breathe, the cold kiss of metal snapped shut around my wrists.

Handcuffs.

"You're under arrest," he said, standing fluidly and yanking me up with him.

I stumbled, my heart still a riot of adrenaline, and blurted out the first thing that came to mind. "Who—who are you?"

His grip was firm, but not cruel. His voice, steady and sharp. "Detective McDara."

The name hit like a gunshot, rattling through my already fried nerves.

He pulled a polished badge from his belt and flashed it in front of my face. My mind scrambled, processing, questioning, rejecting.

A badge meant nothing if I didn't know how to tell a real one from a fake.

I shook my wrists at him, the handcuffs clinking sharply. "Seriously? Is this necessary?" My voice came out edged with frustration, but beneath it, a thread of something more vulnerable—uncertainty.

McDara's dark gaze never wavered. "I found you standing in a crime scene." His tone was even, unshakable. "Then you ran when I identified myself as an officer."

My cheeks flushed hot.

Gods, had he been calling out to me? I hadn't heard a thing beyond the sound of my own terror, my own reckless heartbeat.

For a fleeting moment, something in his expression shifted—just a flicker. Something softer. Then, just as quickly, it was gone.

I swallowed, the weight of it all crashing down. The blood. The scorch marks. The ghost. And now, standing in the presence of this too-steady, too-intense detective, handcuffed like a criminal.

This day was just getting better and better.

I forced down the lump in my throat and scanned him. Dark denim jacket, black T-shirt, definitely not a uniform.

"If you're a cop, why aren't you dressed like one?" I demanded, narrowing my eyes.

McDara arched a brow, like he actually couldn't believe I was questioning him right now. "I'm a detective. It's on the badge."

Wow, thanks. Super helpful.

"I was in the area when the call came in," he continued, his voice gravel and steel. "Decided to check it out. And what do I find? You, standing in the remnants of blood and dark magic."

I exhaled sharply, my pulse still erratic. Blood and dark magic.

Yeah. That sounded about right.

McDara yanked me forward, his grip unyielding, and my panic surged all over again. The handcuffs dug into my wrists, every step jarring, each movement a reminder of just how exposed I was—helpless, trapped. I dug my heels into the forest floor, refusing to be dragged like a criminal.

"How do I know I can trust you?" My voice was sharp, edged with defiance, but the pounding of my pulse in my ears betrayed my fear.

His dark eyes locked onto mine, steady and unwavering. "I found you at the scene of a crime." His tone was clipped, no patience for argument. "I showed you my identification, which, I might add, you've yet to do."

"A cop that just happens to be wandering the woods?" I shot back, breathless. The trees whispered around us, cold wind threading through their twisted limbs like unseen hands reaching in.

McDara hesitated, a flicker of something unreadable passing through his gaze—then gone, shuttered away. "I got an anonymous call," he said finally. "With coordinates. Directing me here."

A convenient excuse.

My chest tightened. The night was too silent, too dark, the forest pressing in like a living thing. Every breath felt wrong, and I could almost sense the weight of something watching—something older than the trees themselves.

McDara must have seen the panic creeping back into my expression, because his voice dipped lower, rough but measured. "You're not in danger." A pause. "I'm not going to hurt you. More officers are on the way."

In the distance, the faint wail of sirens cut through the night. If he wasn't a real cop, would he be leading me toward them?

Phontine's voice slipped into my ear like a silk thread through a needle, her tone taut with urgency. "Do you want me to trip him? Pull his hair out? Bite his ear?"

I kept my gaze forward, biting the inside of my cheek to keep from reacting. If McDara had sensed dark magic at the crime scene, he had to be a Magical of some kind. I couldn't risk him catching on to Phontine, not yet. Not until I knew exactly what I was dealing with.

"I'll go where the other cops are," I said evenly, hoping she caught the hint. McDara's grip tightened, just slightly, as if testing whether I was about to bolt again.

"Then walk." His voice lost whatever trace of patience it had left—now pure steel. Without warning, he hauled me forward, his hand a firm weight on my arm, pulling me through the tangled underbrush.

My pulse battered against my ribs, my mind spinning. I should have fought harder. I should have demanded answers. I should have done something. But in that moment, I could feel it—something pressing in from the darkness of the woods, something deeper than fear.

Blakewell was wrong. This city, this place, was wrong.

Coming here might have been the worst mistake of my life.

The moment we broke through the tree line, it was like stepping from one world into another. The suffocating hush of the forest fell away, swallowed by the pulse of red and blue lights flashing against the cracked pavement of the motel lot. The air, thick with damp earth and the ghosts of whatever horror I'd just stumbled into, was now tainted with cigarette smoke and the faint metallic scent of exhaust. Three cop cars idled with their sirens mercifully silenced, but the sheer presence of them sent a sharp twist through my gut.

The motel owner stood off to the side, wrapped in a bathrobe that had definitely seen better days, cigarette dangling from his fingers like this was just another Thursday night. His face was carved from equal parts annoyance and resignation.

McDara's grip on my arm loosened just enough for me to yank against the cuffs, rattling the metal. "Still necessary?" I muttered, shooting him a sharp look.

His jaw ticked, but he didn't dignify me with an answer. Instead, he guided me toward one of the cop cars—his, I assumed—where another officer leaned lazily against the hood, watching us approach with all the amusement of someone who had nothing better to do.

The moment his gaze flicked over me—disheveled, haunted, cuffed—something in his reflective golden-brown eyes sharpened. My gut clenched at the almost imperceptible twitch of his ears beneath his close-cropped hair.

Shifter.

Lion, if I had to guess.

"She give you trouble?" he asked, voice mild, but there was something in the way his tail flicked behind him that made me bristle.

McDara exhaled sharply, shaking his head. "Found her at the crime scene."

The Shifter let out a low whistle, his grin slow and sharp. "Damn, and here I thought Blakewell had gotten boring. You sure know how to make a first impression, sweetheart."

I narrowed my eyes. "Yeah? And you sure know how to make someone feel *real* safe around law enforcement, officer."

McDara muttered something under his breath, but his partner only chuckled, golden eyes gleaming with barely contained amusement. "She's got a mouth on her. I like her."

McDara ignored him. "Anonymous tip sent me straight to the scene. She was already there when I arrived. Then she ran."

I scoffed, yanking against the cuffs again for good measure. "I didn't run—okay, *technically* I ran, but you chased me! Maybe next time lead with, 'Hey, I'm the police' instead of charging out of the woods like some horror movie villain."

McDara's partner barked a laugh, tail flicking. "She's got a point."

McDara shot him a glare that could have withered crops. "Not helping."

I huffed, shifting my weight. "So, what? I just happened to be in the wrong place at the wrong time, and now I'm the one in handcuffs? What if I was the one who called in the tip?"

McDara arched a dark brow. "Did you?"

I snapped my mouth shut. *Okay, fair.*

His partner grinned. "You planning to book her?"

McDara ran a hand down his face, looking more exhausted by the second. "Taking her in for questioning."

"Questioning?" I echoed, disbelief lacing my voice. "Seriously?"

"You were at a crime scene," McDara said flatly. "*Running.*"

"Alleged running," I corrected.

The Lion Shifter let out another amused huff. "I really like her."

McDara, utterly done with the entire conversation, yanked open the car door. "Get in."

I hesitated—not because I had a choice, but because stepping into that car felt like crossing a threshold I didn't want to acknowledge. I was in trouble. In a city I didn't belong to. And I had zero people to call.

McDara sighed, rubbing the bridge of his nose like he could feel my internal breakdown happening in real time. "Relax, it's a ride, not a prison sentence."

"Forgive me if I'm not eager to be shoved into a cop car like a criminal," I snapped.

His gaze pinned me in place, dark and unreadable. "You cooperate, and I'll get those cuffs off sooner rather than later."

I chewed the inside of my cheek. Fine. Whatever.

Climbing in, I felt the cold seat press against the backs of my legs, the door shutting with a solid, final thunk behind me. McDara and his partner exchanged a few more words outside before the engine rumbled to life, and we pulled out onto the main road.

I cast one last glance at the motel—the irritated owner already wandering back inside, the dark forest stretching behind it, clutching its secrets.

Then we were heading toward Old Town, and somehow, I knew—my night was far from over.

The police station loomed ahead—a squat, weatherworn beast of a building, its stone façade scarred by time and trouble. Streetlamps cast an anemic amber glow across its face, flickering neon barely clinging to life above the entrance. Even from inside the car, I could see the restless movement within—officers pacing, paperwork shuffling, low voices threading through the night air like the hum of an overworked machine.

Blakewell's nightlife, it seemed, offered more than just ghosts and murder scenes in the woods.

McDara pulled into the lot with practiced ease, cutting the engine in one smooth turn. The locks popped open with an audible click, and my stomach twisted, the sound carrying a finality I wasn't ready for. He didn't yank me from the car, but his grip was firm enough that I knew running wasn't on the table.

Not that I had anywhere to go.

The moment we stepped inside, the station swallowed me whole. The air was thick with caffeine and exhaustion, the weight of too many cases pressing against the walls. The bullpen was a living thing, a restless tide of overworked officers and the steady clatter of keyboards and ringing phones. Near the front desk, a slurring drunk was putting on a show for a thoroughly unimpressed cop, while another officer leaned against a desk, nursing a cup of coffee like it was the only thing keeping him upright. The room thrummed with tired voices, the kind that carried the sharp edge of a long night with no end in sight.

McDara moved through it all like he belonged there.

Me? I felt every set of eyes drag over me as I passed.

I wasn't from here. I didn't belong. And in my travel-worn clothes, still streaked with dirt and the unmistakable stains of actual blood, I might as well have had *suspect* stamped across my forehead.

Murmurs followed us, low and questioning. A few raised eyebrows. A curious glance or two. *Who's the girl McDara dragged in from the woods?* But no one stopped him. No one questioned him. He was a known entity here—one of them—and I was the wild card he'd brought into their midst.

McDara led me to a smaller processing station before the interrogation room, where a bored-looking officer handed him a sleek, rune-etched scanner. Without a word, he took my wrist, pressing my fingers one by one against the smooth surface. A faint glow pulsed beneath my skin before the device beeped in confirmation. Then, before I could protest, he pulled out a sterile lancet and pricked my finger, letting a single drop of blood bead onto a glass plate lined with intricate sigils. The magic flared to life for a brief second, then dimmed as the sample was absorbed.

"There," McDara muttered, setting the scanner aside. "Now we'll see if the Mage Council has anything on you."

I frowned as McDara set the scanner aside, rubbing my thumb over the tiny prick on my finger. "Okay, hold on—if I weren't a Mage, the Mage Council wouldn't be able to help you. How do you know I'm not a Shifter?"

McDara leveled me with a long, unreadable stare, like he was genuinely wondering if I was serious. "Because the Mage Council database has information on most Magicals, Mage or not," he said flatly.

I blinked. "Since when?"

His brows ticked up slightly, like he wasn't sure if I was playing dumb or if I really didn't know. "Since forever," he said, voice edged with something I couldn't quite place. "What, you think the Council only keeps tabs on Mages?"

That was...unsettling. "I mean, yeah?" I said, the words more uncertain than I liked. "That's kind of their whole thing. The Mage Houses, the hierarchy, the—"

McDara sighed, rubbing the bridge of his nose like this conversation alone was exhausting him. "The Mage Council regulates all Magicals, not just Mages. Shifters, Fairy, Vampires, Troll, Goblin even the odd Fae—doesn't matter. If you were born Magical, they have a record of you."

I clenched my jaw, barely managing to keep my expression neutral. "Well, that's creepy."

McDara didn't argue. Just grabbed the scanner and my blood sample and gestured toward the hallway. "Come on. Interrogation room's this way."

We reached a hallway lined with doors, their chipped paint and dim lighting doing little to make them seem less ominous. McDara stopped at one—unmarked, lifeless, like every other door here—and pushed it open, gesturing for me to step inside.

I hesitated, but only for a second. Like I had a choice.

The interrogation room was as bleak as I expected—gray walls, a steel table, and the kind of one-way glass that sent a prickle down my spine. The stale scent of burnt coffee and something faintly metallic clung to the air, the room steeped in an atmosphere of weary tension. The single chair scraped against the floor as I stepped closer, hands still cuffed.

Behind me, the door closed with a dull thunk, sealing us inside.

McDara didn't speak as he reached for the cuffs. No snide remarks, no half-bored warnings. Just the quiet click of metal unlocking, followed by the weighty thud of the cuffs landing on the table.

I flexed my fingers, rolling my wrists, resisting the urge to rub at the sore, reddened skin.

I wasn't stupid. The real interrogation was just beginning.

I leaned back in my chair, crossing my arms in a mirror of McDara's posture, letting the silence stretch between us like a taut wire. The fluorescent light hummed overhead, casting sharp lines over his face, making the angles of his jaw and cheekbones seem even sharper, like they'd been carved from stone.

His dark eyes didn't waver. Didn't blink. He was waiting for me to slip—to crack—like I was just another suspect he could wear down with the weight of a heavy pause and an unreadable stare.

Too bad for him, I'd spent my whole life hiding the truth.

"Where's your partner?" I finally asked, voice light but deliberate. "What, he's just gonna let you go all bad cop on me by yourself?"

McDara exhaled, slow and measured, like he was debating whether I was worth the patience. He didn't bother shifting position, just nodded toward the one-way glass. "He's watching," he said, tone flat. "Don't worry. You've got an audience."

I scoffed. "Fantastic. Always dreamed of headlining my own interrogation."

Still, I let my eyes flick to the mirror for the briefest moment. I knew his partner was watching. Probably enjoying himself, too.

McDara didn't take the bait. He just moved, finally, unfolding his arms as he leaned forward, resting them on the cold steel table between us. The air in the room shifted, the easy back-and-forth evaporating in an instant.

"You were trespassing on private property," he said, his voice edged with quiet authority. "You ran from a cop. You resisted arrest. And now you're going to tell me what the hell you were doing in the middle of the woods, standing in a blood-soaked clearing like you belonged there."

I held my ground, fingers curling against the metal table. "I didn't know it was private property. There was no sign," I said carefully, my voice steady. "I did nothing wrong."

McDara's brows lifted just slightly. "You were standing in a blood-soaked clearing in the middle of the night. That doesn't exactly scream innocent tourist."

I clenched my jaw. *There wasn't a body.*

The thought pulsed behind my teeth. That crime scene—if it even was a crime scene—had been drenched in blood and dark magic, but there was no corpse, no sign of a struggle beyond the sheer violence of the magic remnants.

McDara rubbed a hand down his face, the motion weary but calculated. "This isn't about pinning a crime on you, Byrd."

Hearing my name from his mouth made my stomach knot, like it carried the weight of something heavier than just an investigation. I wasn't stupid—I knew how this looked. And I hated sitting here, powerless, knowing I couldn't just call my mom and ask for help.

Knowing that if I told McDara the truth, I'd either end up in an overnight cell or a psych ward.

McDara was watching me closely, reading the way I hesitated, the way I was choosing my words instead of just handing them over. I could feel his attention, sharp as a blade pressed against my throat.

Fine. He wanted answers?

I just had to decide how much of the truth I was willing to give him.

Tapping my fingers against the table, I tilted my head. "You dragged me in here like I committed some grand offense, so you must already have some idea of what happened out there."

McDara didn't react immediately. Just the briefest pause—like he was deciding whether or not I was worth entertaining.

"We're still sorting that out," he said finally, his voice indecipherable.

I let out a slow, exaggerated breath. "Okay. Let me be more direct—you mentioned dark magic when you arrested me."

There it was.

The shift. The flicker of something in his expression. It wasn't huge—just a tightening around his mouth, a slight narrowing of his gaze—but I saw it.

He noticed the dark magic.

Which meant he wasn't just some human detective who'd stumbled onto a magical crime scene by accident. A human would feel that something was off but not immediatly flag it as dark magic. He'd felt the magic. He'd walked into that clearing and recognized it for what it was.

I leaned in slightly, keeping my voice light but deliberate. "So, if you saw it," I said, tilting my head, "are you investigating this as a cop...or as a Mage?"

McDara's expression didn't shift, but the flicker of tension in his jaw told me I'd struck something close to home. He exhaled slowly. "You don't strike me as the type to stumble into dark magic by accident. How do you know what it looks like?"

"You're not answering my question."

"You're not answering mine," he shot back, voice sharp but controlled. "Dark magic is illegal in Blakewell."

I shrugged. "Yeah, I know. So, I assume you're taking this very seriously, then? Since, what was it? Maleficaria or Hexcraft? Even I know both schools of magic are illegal everywhere."

That got him.

It wasn't much. Just a subtle shift in his posture, a moment of silence that felt heavier than it should have.

But it was enough.

He knew exactly what kind of magic had been used in that clearing.

I had him.

I already knew he wasn't a Shifter—I'd have smelled it on him or noticed the reflective nature of his eyes. His partner had been easy to guess with his eyes and *tail*. And if he had no idea what dark magic felt like, he wouldn't have reacted at all. Which left one obvious conclusion.

Detective McDara was a Mage.

And now, the real question: Was he sworn to a House? Or was he a rogue Mage playing by his own rules?

McDara exhaled sharply, pushing off the table and leaning back. "I don't have time for games, Byrd," he said, voice low. Warning.

I held his gaze, pulse still thrumming in my ears. This was the moment.

I had to decide.

Lie. Or tell him everything.

I exhaled slowly, fingers drumming against my wrist, measuring the weight of my next words. "You want to know why I was out there?" I met his gaze without flinching. "A ghost led me to that clearing."

Silence.

McDara didn't scoff. Didn't blink. Didn't even shift in his seat. He just stared.

Then, dragging a hand down his face, he muttered, "A ghost."

"Yep."

"And it just so happened to lead you to a blood-soaked clearing."

"Yep."

His exhale was slow, controlled—the kind of breath people take when they're deciding whether or not to lose their temper. "You expect me to believe that?"

I tilted my head. "You expect me to believe someone just so happened to send you an anonymous tip with the exact coordinates to that clearing? Feels a little too convenient, don't you think?"

His gaze darkened, but I didn't give him a chance to cut in.

"Look, if you think I'm lying, don't take my word for it." I folded my arms, keeping my voice even. "Go to Matron Black's Mage House. Ask about me. They'll tell you exactly what I am."

There.

I expected hesitation. Some prodding for more details. Maybe a smirk, a snide remark. What I didn't expect was the way the second Matron Black left my lips, something in him changed.

The patience in his expression vanished.

His whole body went rigid, his shoulders snapping tight, his jaw locking like he was biting back something sharp.

His next words came out like steel. "You're part of the Black House?"

The sudden shift in his tone—borderline accusatory—sent my stomach into a freefall. "No," I shot back, shaking my head. "I'm not with them."

He wasn't buying it. He leaned in, the air between us sharpening, his dark eyes cutting through me like he could flay the truth right out of my skin. "Then what the hell were you doing in their House?"

My throat felt tight, but I forced the words out. "I was looking for my birth parents."

That made him pause.

His brows drew together, the tension in his jaw lessening just enough for confusion to slip through the cracks.

I could've stopped there, let him stew in it. But if I didn't explain, he'd fill in the blanks himself—and from the look in his eyes, I didn't want to know what assumptions he was already making.

"I was adopted," I said, my voice quieter now, the fight momentarily drained from me. "I didn't grow up in a Mage House. Didn't even know what I was for a long time. But I have magic—something—and I don't know how to use it. So, I came to Blakewell to find my birth parents and see if they could help me."

McDara studied me, his dark eyes picking me apart like I was a puzzle missing too many pieces. Like he wasn't sure if I was lying or just...pathetic.

"They used to be part of the Black House," I admitted. "But they left a long time ago."

His hands curled into fists against the table, tension radiating from his frame. "And you thought getting involved with dark magic was a good idea?"

Frustration snapped through me like a live wire. "I didn't get involved with dark magic," I shot back, sitting forward, pulse spiking. "I went there looking for answers. I wasn't planning on joining them."

McDara didn't flinch. Didn't even blink. "You were at their House."

"I had nowhere else to go!" The words burst out of me, sharp and unsteady. I sucked in a breath, forcing my fingers to loosen their death grip on the chair. "I was trying to figure out where my birth parents went. That's it."

The room went quiet. Too quiet.

McDara stared at me, gaze searching, weighing something unspoken between us.

Then I frowned, a thought slicing through the haze of my anxiety. "Wait. Does the Black House study dark magic?" I asked, skeptical. Matron Black seemed too rigid, too by-the-book for that.

McDara exhaled sharply, the sound almost a scoff. "No. But a Mage trying to understand her magic—desperate enough—could fall into learning Maleficaria. Or worse—start using corporal enchantment to force another Mage to train her."

I froze. "What?" The accusation sent ice down my spine.

McDara's expression didn't waver. "Did you find your birth parents at the Black House?"

"No," I said quickly, shaking my head so hard my whole body felt like it was vibrating. "But I would never enchant someone."

McDara's jaw ticked. "We'll have to test your hands for magical residue."

Panic flared like a spark in my chest. Magical residue. A test that could prove I hadn't touched Maleficaria—but also confirm exactly what kind of magic clung to me. If my abilities weren't already under scrutiny, they were about to be.

McDara didn't seem concerned about my reaction. He barely even looked at me as he turned toward the one-way mirror behind me. "You get one phone call."

I huffed a bitter laugh. "I don't have anyone to call." The words burned on the way out, but they were true.

McDara turned back to me, and for the first time since this whole mess started, something in his expression cracked. It wasn't much—just a flicker of something behind his sharp, guarded eyes. Something human.

Recognition.

Like he understood more than he wanted to admit.

I didn't know what to do with that. Didn't know if it made me feel better or worse.

Finally, after what felt like forever, McDara let out a slow breath, dragging a hand down his face. "This just keeps getting better."

I wanted to argue, but honestly?

I couldn't blame him.

Without another word, McDara turned on his heel and left, broad shoulders stiff as he disappeared through the door, leaving me alone in the too-quiet, too-sterile interrogation room.

My back ached from the hard chair, the chill of the forest still clung to my skin, and the weight of everything pressed down on me like a slow-moving avalanche.

I wasn't sure if it was the ghost's lingering presence or just the suffocating reality of what I'd gotten myself into.

Either way, I wanted out.

Minutes crawled by, heavy with the weight of exhaustion and the lingering chill of the interrogation room. When the door finally creaked open, I half expected McDara, but it wasn't him.

A woman strode inside, sharp and efficient in a dark uniform, a sleek black case in one hand. Her expression was pure stone—unreadable, uninterested, like she had long since run out of patience for whatever nonsense she dealt with on a daily basis.

"Hands," she said. No preamble, no warmth.

I blinked. "Wow. Straight to the romance? At least buy me dinner first."

Nothing. Not a twitch of amusement. Just a stare so flat it could have crushed my soul where I sat.

With a sigh, I held out my wrists, watching as she unclipped a slender, wand-like device from her case. It hummed softly as she ran it over my skin, searching for traces of magic. I already knew what she'd find—nothing. No whispers of a spell, no lingering traces of

Maleficaria, no proof that I had done anything except stand in a bloodstained clearing, trying not to have a full-blown existential crisis.

A few, long sweeps later, she clicked the device off, frowning faintly. "No dark magic."

"Just boring old me," I muttered, but she was already packing up and heading for the door, her business with me clearly finished.

The second it shut, Phontine burst into existence in a frantic blur of wings and lavender light.

"Sonia!" she hissed, her tiny hands clutching at my sleeve. "You're still in here! I thought you'd be out by now! Do you need me to bust you out? I can short out the lights, maybe sneak a key off one of the guards—"

"Phontine."

"Or I could go tiny and crawl into the lock! I saw it in a movie once—"

"Phontine."

She froze mid-flutter, her wings twitching.

I exhaled through my nose, scrubbing a hand over my face. "I appreciate the chaos energy, but I don't think we need to escalate this to a jailbreak."

Phontine crossed her arms, scowling. "Fine. But if they try to throw you in a cell, I am breaking you out. No arguments."

A tired half smile tugged at my lips. "Duly noted."

Then came the waiting. Again.

Two hours. Two long, mind-numbing hours of staring at the interrogation room walls, replaying everything that had happened tonight, every mistake, every second of that eerie encounter in the forest. I debated whether I should just bolt. If Phontine could short out the lights, maybe I could—

Before I could go full fugitive, the door swung open.

McDara's partner—the Lion Shifter—strolled in, hands in his pockets, looking far less grim than his brooding counterpart.

"You're free to go," he said, his voice as casual as if he were commenting on the weather.

I blinked. "Seriously?"

His smirk was all sharp amusement. "Seriously. We ran your background, found nothing, and your story checks out. You're weird, but not a criminal."

"Wow. Flattery and freedom? What a night." I stood, stretching out my arms with a sigh. "Thanks, though. I'd rather be a weirdo than in cuffs."

"Some would argue that's the same thing." His grin widened, then he jerked his head toward the door. "I'm Detective Ashford, by the way. Dom to friends and beautiful people." A wink. "Come on, I'll drive you back to the motel."

I didn't argue. I just followed. Anything to get out of here.

The parking lot was mostly empty, bathed in the flickering glow of old streetlamps. I cast a glance around, half-expecting McDara to materialize from the shadows, but he was nowhere in sight.

I slid into the passenger seat of the police SUV, the quiet hum of the road filling the space between us as we left the station behind. The city blurred past—streetlamps glowing against the dark, storefronts closing for the night, the neon signs of late-night diners flickering like ghostly beacons.

Then, as we neared the motel, the Shifter glanced at me, something more serious in his expression now. "Word of advice?"

I turned toward him, wary. "Do I want to hear this?"

"Stay in Blakewell," he said, his voice lower now. "At least for a little while."

A cold weight settled in my stomach. "Should I be worried?"

He didn't answer right away. Just gripped the wheel a little tighter. Then, after a long beat, he said, "Just...stick around."

Not exactly reassuring.

We pulled into the motel lot, the *VACANCY* sign buzzing faintly overhead. I unbuckled, ready to bolt for the safety of my room, but something nagged at me.

I hesitated. "Why didn't Detective McDara tell me himself?"

The Shifter smirked, all teeth. "Probably off somewhere brooding like the cryptid he is."

I rolled my eyes but said nothing. He was avoiding me. And I wasn't sure why that bothered me so much—but it did.

Climbing out, I didn't look back as I made my way up the walkway, Phontine fluttering onto my shoulder, her tiny presence grounding me more than I cared to admit.

The second I stepped into my room, I locked the door behind me, kicked off my shoes, and collapsed onto the bed with a groan.

I should leave.

I should book the next flight out of this cursed city.

But I couldn't.

Because no matter how badly I wanted to run, I still had unfinished business.

And more than that—

I still needed to see my dad.

9

I woke up in the same damn clothes I'd found the blood-soaked clearing in. The same clothes I'd sat in that interrogation room in. The same clothes that clung to me like a second skin, steeped in dried sweat, stale fear, and something worse.

The moment my mind caught up with my body, a wave of revulsion crashed over me. My jeans had blood on them.

I was out of bed in an instant, Phontine yelping as she tumbled from my pillow in a sleepy blur. I shoved the jeans to the farthest corner of the room, like they might lurch back toward me if I looked away. My shirt wasn't stained, but it reeked of exhaustion, of fear, of the suffocating weight of last night.

I needed a shower. I needed out of this skin.

The motel's tiny bathroom filled with steam as I scrubbed myself raw, the water scalding, relentless. I could still *feel* it—the phantom slick of blood against my legs, the cold weight of the ghost's presence pressing against my skin.

I turned the water hotter.

It didn't help.

By the time I stepped out, my skin was pink, my mind still tangled in the night before. I yanked on a pair of ripped black jeans, layered a deep blue velvet top under my oversized leather jacket, and looped a few silver rings onto my fingers before double-checking my bag. Phone, wallet—essentials. Anything that could get me out of here if I needed to run.

Phontine stirred as I slung the bag over my shoulder, stretching her iridescent wings. "You're going somewhere?"

"Anywhere but here."

She studied me, unusually quiet. "Are you thinking about leaving?"

I hesitated.

I *should* leave. That was the smart thing to do. But logic wasn't exactly winning the battle these days.

Instead of answering, I shoved open the door and let the morning air slap me fully awake.

The motel sat at the edge of New Town, just before the forest that sprawled around Blakewell like an old secret. Even in daylight, the trees loomed, their tangled canopy devouring the sky, shadows stretching long across the empty road.

I didn't trust that forest.

It *watched*.

Or maybe I was just paranoid. Either way, the silence gnawed at me. No city noise. No sirens, no honking cars, no distant hum of life. Just the occasional rustle of leaves and the crunch of gravel under my boots.

Too still. Too empty.

Blakewell might have been a city, but out here? It felt like a ghost town.

Phontine must've felt it too. She clung to the neckline of my leather jacket, unusually still. No snark, no teasing about my overthinking.

Just the quiet.

And the feeling that something—*or someone*—was watching.

By the time I spotted the diner—a squat, retro-looking thing with a gleaming silver exterior and neon-blue signage—my legs were screaming.

Walking everywhere in Chicago was normal. Here, though? In a place where the land stretched wide and empty, where the mountains loomed like silent sentinels, and the roads felt endless? It was something else entirely.

The moment I stepped inside, warmth swallowed me whole, thick with the scent of home-cooked food and fresh coffee. The kind of warmth that seeped into your bones, made you forget the cold had ever existed.

The diner was a time capsule. Red vinyl booths. Chrome accents. A jukebox humming softly in the corner, crooning some oldies tune that barely registered over the quiet murmur of customers trading secrets over plates of eggs and toast.

A place like this didn't change. It had probably seen decades pass, storms roll through, maybe even the rise and fall of the Mage Council, and still—it served the same pancakes, poured the same bottomless coffee. Like a heartbeat. Steady. Familiar. Comforting.

I slid into a booth, the vinyl giving under me. Phontine tucked herself beside me, nearly swallowed by the squishy cushion.

A waitress appeared, silent as a ghost, pouring coffee into the cup in front of me before I even had the chance to ask.

She arched a brow, her voice rich with dry amusement. "You look like you need it."

She had no idea.

I took a sip—hot, bitter, grounding—then actually looked at her.

And froze.

Holy freaking Wood.

A Troll.

Not a textbook drawing. Not a flickering image in some outdated Magical Awareness PSA. A real, breathing Troll—standing right in front of me, balancing a coffee pot in one massive hand like it weighed nothing.

Trolls didn't live in cities. They avoided human settlements for a reason. Ever since the Three Woods appeared and humans started teetering on the edge of World War III over Magicals, creatures who couldn't hold glamours—or couldn't hold them for long—had learned to stay hidden.

But here she was.

She was big. Not just tall—though she easily cleared six feet—but big in the way mountains were big. In the way ancient, immovable things were big. Like she'd been carved straight from the same stone as the cliffs outside Blakewell.

Her skin was rough, uneven, like weathered rock, mottled with deep earthen hues—soil-rich browns, glimmers of mineralized green, the cool undertones of un-touched stone. In the dim lighting, it caught just enough of a shimmer, the way cliffsides did when the sun hit just right.

And her face—gods.

Heavy brow ridges cast deep shadows over sharp, dark eyes—intelligent eyes, the kind that measured and calculated. Not cruel. Not kind. Just...*aware.* A broad nose, ridged like natural armor, took up the center of her face, and when she grinned—because she knew I was staring, could feel it—her lower canines jutted just past her upper lip. Not quite tusks, but enough to make me think twice about getting on her bad side.

And then there was the hair.

A bee-freaking-hive. Vintage, blonde, and so perfectly styled it had to be a wig. The clash between the take-no-shit glint in her eye and the retro hairdo was so absurd that I kind of loved it immediately.

Ancient magic radiated from her. The kind that had existed long before humans carved roads into the earth, before cities swallowed the wild places whole. And yet—there was a sharpness to her. A modernity. Like she had one foot in the past and one in the now and saw exactly how much of a mess both had become.

I had the distinct impression that, if she wanted to, she could break me in half like a dry twig.

And yet, as she studied me with those deep, knowing eyes, I got the feeling she wouldn't.

Not unless I gave her a reason.

Or, you know.

Kept staring.

I snapped the menu up like a shield, my voice sharper than necessary as I rattled off food items—anything to fill the silence.

Eggs. Toast. Bacon. Crispy enough to almost make me forget I was running on three hours of sleep and sheer spite.

The waitress nodded, disappearing with the order, and I exhaled, trying to will the tension from my shoulders.

It helped.

A little.

At least until I looked up.

And saw her.

The ghost sat across from me.

Silent. Staring.

Same tattered stripped shirt. Same haunted eyes. Same sadness pressing in, thick as fog, curling invisible fingers around my ribs and squeezing.

A shiver crawled up my spine, slow and insidious.

Phontine stiffened beside me. I barely noticed, my fingers tightening around my fork like it could do anything against the dead.

My throat felt raw. Dry as dust.

"What do you want from me?"

No answer.

The ghost just watched.

Unblinking.

Too still.

Wrong.

I forced a breath past my lips. "That place you took me to…" My voice was quieter now. The diner had emptied out, the hum of conversation thinning, leaving only the distant clink of dishes and the low croon of the jukebox.

"In the forest—there wasn't a body. Why did you take me there?"

I waited.

Barely breathing.

For a whisper. A sign. A reason.

Nothing.

My pulse kicked hard against my ribs. "Was that where…you died?"

The air around her flickered.

Like static on a broken screen.

Like reality itself was rejecting her presence.

And then—

Gone.

Vanished into the space between one breath and the next.

I swallowed hard, my heartbeat a dull roar in my ears.

Beside me, Phontine let out a sharp breath, muttering a curse.

"I need to go." My voice was hoarse. Hollow. I was already reaching for my wallet, already shoving crumpled bills onto the table.

My appetite was long gone.

The moment I stepped outside, the cold air hit like a slap. Brisk, sharp, like it could cut through the fog in my head.

It didn't.

I was so tired.

Tired of running in circles.

Tired of waiting for answers that never came.

Tired of ghosts staring at me like I was supposed to *do something*.

No more.

Without another word, I turned and started back toward the motel.

It was time to stop waiting.

It was time to act.

The moment the lock clicked into place, a shiver crawled down my spine—slow, deliberate.

It had nothing to do with the cold.

This was something deeper. Older. The knowing that I was about to do something reckless. Something irreversible.

I yanked the bed sheets off and threw them over the single window, pressing the fabric against the frame, sealing myself in. Darkness swallowed the room.

Heavy. Oppressive.

The only light came from the motel's neon sign outside, bleeding through the fabric in fractured streaks of red. It pulsed—slow and rhythmic—like the heartbeat of something watching.

I needed the dark.

I needed to strip away every distraction, every tether to the waking world.

From my suitcase, I pulled out the candles—small, white, their wax warped with past use. Memories of old flames. Old attempts to mimic what me and Valier had done. I placed them in a loose circle around me, their wicks waiting, expectant.

Then, from the deepest pocket of my bag, the pouch.

Pixie dust.

A gift from Phontine, given with a warning and a wing-snap. A substance finer than sand, finer than sugar—but it held weight. Too much weight for something so small. It clung to the air, hovered between the seen and unseen, between magic and memory.

I was done being a stranger to my own power.

I sank onto the floor, the motel carpet scratchy beneath my crossed legs, my breath steady but shallow. The wellspring inside me—the thing I had spent my life ignoring—waited.

I reached for it.

It resisted.

Like a door swollen with rain, stuck in its frame.

I pressed harder.

My mind flitted, restless. My father. The ghost. The frost curling on the diner's window, reaching like fingers. The blood staining my shoes. The Mage House I had barely set foot in before turning away.

All of it churned.

A storm. A spiral. A whirlpool dragging me down, down, down.

And then—beneath it all—

A breath.

Not mine.

Not human.

Cold. Vast. Endless.

A presence lurking just beyond my senses, waiting, watching—*hungry*.

I latched onto it.

Fingers digging, clawing, grasping.

And I pulled.

Crack.

A jagged, brutal fracture—like ice splitting under too much weight.

The world lurched.

My lungs emptied.

Gravity forgot me.

Air thickened, condensed, pressed—a crushing weight, unseen hands testing my shape, my edges, my right to exist.

The motel was gone.

The floor beneath me was gone.

I was nowhere. Weightless. Unmoored. The space around me twisting in on itself, rewriting the laws of reality.

A slow, crawling dread curled in my gut.

I forced my eyes open.

And froze.

The world was wrong.

Not broken. Not shattered.

Just—wrong.

Black and red stretched endlessly.

Not just colors—something alive.

The darkness pulsed, slick and ink-drenched, veins of molten crimson threading through like smoldering embers under charred skin. The sky—or what should have been the sky—twisted, churned, bled into itself. Clouds spiraled, restless, shifting but never settling.

And the worst part?

The silence.

Not quiet. Not hushed.

A hollow, all-consuming void.

A silence that didn't just exist—it devoured.

I wasn't in my motel room anymore.

I wasn't even in my world.

A sharp breath razored through my lungs as I took a step forward, but my body moved like I was wading through oil—thick, slow, wrong. The weightlessness that had first gripped me was fading, but in its place, something worse settled in.

Heaviness.

A slow, creeping force, pressing into my skin, sinking into my bones. With every step, it grew, like gravity was stitching itself back together inch by inch, reasserting its dominion over me.

I clenched my teeth, pressing a hand to my stomach, fighting the rise of nausea. The air here—if it even was air—felt wrong. Heavy with something unseen.

The world around me shifted.

Black and red convulsing. A heartbeat in the dark.

I had stepped into the threshold of something vast.

Something waiting.

And then—

I was inside.

The shift was instant. A jarring, soul-snapping drop through an unseen barrier. One second, I was weightless, hovering in that liminal space—the next, gravity slammed back into place.

Hard. Brutal. Unforgiving.

I hit the ground—knees colliding with something cool, something rough.

Dust kicked up. My breath punched from my lungs.

Beneath me—grit, dark as midnight.

I swallowed, pushing myself up with shaking arms, my pulse a thunderous roar in my ears.

And then—the edge.

A sheer drop.

The kind that didn't just fall—it swallowed. Endless. Abyssal. A void stretched beneath my hands, deeper than shadow, deeper than anything that should exist.

A slow, creeping terror curled up my spine.

I scrambled backward, my breath ragged, raw.

Then I looked up.

And froze.

I was standing on a cliff.

And beyond it—

An impossible landscape.

I pushed to my feet, my breath locked in my throat, and stepped to the edge.

And froze.

Beneath me, the world bled.

A vast, endless desert—red as crushed garnets, dark as fresh-spilled wine. The color stretched forever, an ocean of dust and ruin, shifting with the whisper of unseen winds.

And through it, carving a path like a wound torn into the earth's flesh, a river.

Wide. Glimmering. Black.

Not the reflection of night. Not the ink of deep water. This was absence—a liquid so dark it consumed light instead of reflecting it. It moved like molten shadow, thick and hungry, twisting toward the distant mountains like it had somewhere to be.

And the sky—gods above, the sky.

Not blue. Not gray. Not even night.

Silver.

Not soft or muted, not the gentle light of a rising moon, but a searing, molten glow, alive and shifting, thick clouds rolling like mercury across the endless expanse.

And the lightning.

Violent. Beautiful. Unrelenting.

It didn't flash—it tore. Veins of white-hot fury ripped across the sky, arcing down with merciless precision. Each strike detonated against the desert floor, sending up plumes of red dust, the earth shuddering with the impact.

Thunder rolled like war drums.

I stood there, heart hammering, lungs tight, a terrible weight pressing into my ribs.

What the hell was this place?

The air—thick, electric, alive—hummed with a presence I couldn't name.

A presence that curled around me. Watching. Waiting.

The weight of it pressed against my throat, against my chest, sinking in.

This wasn't a dream.

This wasn't a vision.

This was real.

The realization crashed over me like a rogue wave—merciless, absolute.

I wasn't in some in-between space, some fractured pocket of my own mind.

I was here.

In the Deathscape.

My breath hitched as I stared out at the vastness before me.

The black river cut through the land like a scar, winding toward jagged obsidian mountains, their peaks piercing the storm-churned sky.

Lightning lashed through it, streaks of raw power exploding into the ground, over and over and over again.

I squinted.

But it wasn't lightning.

Not really.

Each strike sent smoke spiraling into the air, twisting, writhing—vanishing before it ever touched the sky.

And as I watched, as I stood on the precipice of something too vast to understand, a terrible, razor-sharp clarity sliced through my awe.

That wasn't just energy.

Those were souls.

I swayed on my feet, nausea and fascination snarling together like twin beasts in my gut.

This was where the dead came.

And the smoke—the delicate wisps rising and dissolving into nothing—was what was left of them.

What was left of the newly dead.

What was left of their last breath.

The Deathscape.

And I was standing in the heart of it.

I knew of it.

Every Magical did.

Death is threefold. Named The Bone Veils.

The first lesson drilled into every child born even adjacent to the magical world.

The Deathscape—where all souls come first, ruled by Death himself. *The Everdark*—where souls find their final rest. Where they truly, completely end. And then...the third.

My throat tightened. My hands curled into fists.

The last realm.

The one no one talked about.

Not even in whispers.

A place worse than damnation.

A purgatory so consuming, so unknowable, that even the most powerful Magicals feared it beyond reason.

I had never heard its true name. No one had.

But the Magicals who had spoken of it—those foolish enough to entertain the thought—only whispered its substitute name: *Abyssus Votum.* Abyss of Oaths.

A place where souls weren't granted passage. Not yet.

A place for souls that needed to redeem themselves before they could pass on. But to Magicals, that redemption was closer to punishment. Some souls made it out, but some...some never did.

A shiver lashed down my spine, sharp as a blade.

And then—a thought, cutting through my haze like a knife through silk.

My dad.

A sharp, shuddering inhale. My lungs squeezed tight as my eyes snapped to the horizon.

Was he here?

Was he somewhere in that desert, lost among the thousands of drifting souls?

Had he been judged yet?

I didn't stop to think.

I moved.

Before reason could root me to the spot, I lunged forward—boots scraping, slipping against the sheer black rock as I half-ran, half-stumbled down the cliffside.

The cuts on my hands barely registered as I gripped jagged edges for balance.

I didn't stop.

I didn't think.

I had one thought.

Find him.

The second my feet slammed onto the red desert, I was running.

The cracked ground beneath me wasn't just dead earth.

It pulsed.

Not with heat—but energy.

The Deathscape was alive.

The air was thick, cloying—breathing felt like a battle, something I had to earn.

But none of it mattered.

Not the weight of this world. Not the thick pull of its gravity.

Because I wasn't sure how much time I had here, and I needed to search each wandering spirit for my dad.

The ghosts were everywhere.

Drifting like mist, their faces frozen in a trance.

They weren't lost.

They weren't aimless.

They were waiting.

For judgment.

For something to pull them deeper into the Deathscape, toward the river, toward their final destination—whichever that would be.

Their expressions were eerily calm. Detached. Like life had already forgotten them, and they had forgotten it in return.

But my dad—

Panic slammed into me, raw and violent.

I searched. Scanned every face. Every shadow. Every drifting form.

I couldn't see him.

"Dad! *Martin Bryd*!" My voice cracked. Sharp. Desperate.

Swallowed.

The Deathscape ate the sound whole.

Nothing.

The ghosts didn't stir. Didn't react. Didn't even seem to acknowledge I was here at all.

I kept moving.

Kept searching.

Heart hammering. Lungs burning.

Where was he?

Was I too late?

Or had he never been here at all?

Did humans come to the Deathscape?

"Please." A ragged breath. My hands clenched at my sides. Spinning. Spinning. Searching.

"Dad!"

I shoved through the ghosts, their half-formed bodies curling away like smoke, barely tangible, barely there—

But then—

I tripped.

Over what, I couldn't tell—a jagged rock, a crack in the earth, my own desperation.

I hit the ground, knees scraping black stone.

The river rushed beside me.

Depthless. Roaring. Violent.

Like it knew I was a trespasser.

And then—

The air changed.

The Deathscape shifted.

Thickened.

Like ink spilling into water, dark and spreading.

The cold was no longer just cold.

It was something deeper.

Something ancient.

Something watching.

And I knew I was no longer alone.

10

I turned.

And froze.

A figure. A man.

Not a ghost. Not some half-there spirit, flickering at the edges of existence.

No—he was solid. Real.

And he was watching me.

Not like someone noticing a stranger walking into a room.

Not even like a predator eyeing prey.

Worse.

Like he had been waiting.

Like he had all the time in the world to unravel me, thread by thread.

He leaned against a jagged outcrop of black rock, utterly at ease, like this place bent to him. Like the very air coiled around him in reverence.

He was tall—elegantly, impossibly so.

Silver hair, slightly too long, framed a face so devastatingly beautiful that my mind stalled.

Like something sculpted by divine hands and left untouched by time.

And yet—something was wrong.

Not human. Not even close.

His eyes—silver with flecks of onyx, like the heart of a dying star—swallowed light instead of reflecting it.

His mouth—a cruel, knowing curve—looked made for nothing but amusement and destruction.

The kind of beauty that made your instincts war—run or step closer, just to see if he was real.

He was smiling.

At me.

"Well, well."

His voice slid through the air, rich and smooth, like velvet pulled over a blade.

He straightened from the rock, slow, unhurried, as if he were indulging in this moment.

"Not often do Mages come to sight see among the dead." A pause. A smirk. "Unless, of course, they want to join them."

The air tightened.

A weight settled over my lungs, pressing—testing.

As if this place—*his* place—was deciding whether I was worth keeping intact.

His gaze flicked downward.

To my shoes.

His smirk deepened.

"You ran through the desert, didn't you?"

He tilted his head slightly, studying me. Measuring.

"How very...desperate."

A taunt. A tease.

A game I hadn't agreed to play, but somehow, I was already losing.

I forced myself to breathe. To think.

Who is he? What is he?

I knew. I *knew*.

But my mind refused to fully wrap around the enormity of it.

My throat was dry, but I managed, somehow, to ask, "Who are you?"

A chuckle.

Soft. Low. Indulgent.

Like I'd asked something truly foolish.

"You already know."

I did.

But I needed to hear it. Needed to be sure.

Please—let there still be some luck left in my life.

Let him be just a reaper.

Maybe. *Maybe.*

His smile sharpened.

Something dark flickered in his gaze—something that promised nothing good.

He stepped forward, slow, deliberate.

Testing the air between us.

Watching for my reaction.

And when I didn't move—when I couldn't—

He murmured, "I am Death."

The words sank into me, curling around my ribs, settling into my bones like ice.

Luck was a lie. A cruel mirage whispered to children.

And Death stood before me.

Not a story. Not a myth. Him.

Watching. Smirking. Like this was all some grand joke.

My heart slammed against my ribs, each beat a frantic war drum. My fingers twitched at my sides, my mind caught between the crushing weight of where I was and the growing, terrifying certainty that he was enjoying this.

His gaze flicked over me—brief, sharp. As if seeing something I couldn't.

As if peeling me apart, layer by layer.

His silver eyes—flecked with onyx, like blackened stardust—held something mocking, something entirely too knowing.

"You're not supposed to be here," he said, his voice rich and smooth, wrapping around me like velvet pulled over a blade.

A pause.

Then, lazily, "But you already knew that, didn't you?"

I swallowed hard.

Tried to breathe.

Tried to speak.

"I—"

Nothing.

No words.

No air.

He stepped closer, unhurried. Measured. Closing the distance with a predator's patience, stopping just short of touching me.

The air between us hummed.

Like the charge before a storm.

Like the world itself was holding its breath.

"Tell me, little Whisperer," he murmured, his words coiling like smoke around my throat, sinking into my skin. "What exactly are you hoping to find in my realm?"

The realization hit like a spell gone wrong—too fast, too deep, burning through every nerve.

I was standing before *Death*.

Head tilting in lazy amusement, as if he had all the time in the world.

Maybe he did.

Maybe time meant nothing to him.

Maybe *I* meant nothing to him.

The weight of that thought suffocated me.

Because if I was insignificant here, in this place of endings, then I had truly wandered beyond reason.

I had put myself in the hands of something ancient. Something vast.

Something that did not play by the rules of the living.

Something that, if it wanted to, could keep me.

The black sand beneath my feet suddenly felt too soft.

Like it might swallow me whole.

I sucked in a breath, but the air wasn't right.

It had no taste but was too heavy—like breathing in a void.

The world was too still.

And he was the only thing in it that felt *real*.

And he was waiting.

I swallowed down the sharp, primal instinct to run.

That was prey thinking.

And I had a feeling prey didn't last long here.

So, I squared my shoulders and met his gaze.

"I'm looking for my dad."

The amusement in his face fractured.

Not completely.

But the teasing curve of his mouth faltered.

And something flickered in his silver-black gaze—something deep, unreadable.

Something dangerous.

"And when you find him?"

His voice lost its lilt, smoothed out, sharpened.

Like a knife before it pressed against your throat.

"What exactly do you plan to do with him?"

A shiver ripped through me.

I forced my feet to stay planted, though my body screamed to step back.

He hadn't moved.

Hadn't so much as shifted his weight.

And yet—

The air had changed. The entire world had changed.

I forced my voice to stay steady. "I just want to talk to him."

And just like that—

The storm passed.

Death exhaled something like a laugh.

Shaking his head, as if I'd just said the most ridiculous thing imaginable. The danger was still there—coiled, waiting—but now it wore a smirk.

"Well, that's refreshing."

He clasped his hands behind his back, the sleek lines of his dark clothing shifting as he took an unhurried step toward me.

"A daughter seeking the dead for conversation instead of resurrection." A smirk. A pause. "How...quaint."

I didn't let myself react.

Didn't let him see how much I wanted—no, *needed*—this.

"Can I see him?"

The words were barely a whisper.

But he heard them.

Of course he did.

Death's smirk remained but he didn't answer.

He circled me.

Slow. Measured.

Like a wolf appraising its next meal.

Like he was considering what to do with me.

The air tightened, a force unseen and absolute, wrapping around my ribs, making every breath feel stolen.

And then, with a purring sort of amusement, he said, "You do realize what you've done, don't you?"

The words slithered over my skin, wrapping around my throat, pressing deep into my bones.

A chill licked down my spine.

"What?"

His grin sharpened—all teeth, all wicked delight.

A thing made to devour.

"You came into my realm, little mortal."

He stopped just in front of me, looking down from some impossible height, his head tilting in mock thoughtfulness.

And then, like he was giving me a gift, he said, "Which means...I have a claim to you now."

My stomach dropped.

"Claim?" My voice was too high, too breathless.

His smile was a weapon.

"Mm." A hum of satisfaction. "You walked in willingly. Which means...you belong to me now."

The words punched through me, sharp and undeniable.

No. No, that—

"That's—that's not how this works."

He only watched me.

Still smiling.

Still reveling in my horror.

The Deathscape curled around me—cold, endless, sentient.

Hungry.

I forced my lips to clamp tight as my entire body began to tremble.

"We can make a deal." Even, pleasant words like a noose tightening neatly around my neck.

"For what?" I forced out.

"Your freedom."

A measured shrug. As if this meant nothing. As if *I* meant nothing.

And yet—

The Deathscape shifted with him.

Like the world itself was waiting on his response.

"Or something else," he murmured, "should I desire it."

The bottom fell out of my stomach.

I stepped back.

Or tried to.

I barely moved an inch before the world itself—the Deathscape itself—folded around me.

Holding me in place.

Like a cage. Like a mouth about to close.

My breath hitched. "I—I need to go back."

The words were fragile, frantic.

"Right now. I wasn't supposed to—"

"Ah." Soft. Almost mocking. "But there's the problem."

He leaned in—not touching, but close enough that I felt him.

The weight of his presence. The static crackle of his power.

A whispered warning against my skin.

"You handed me your own free will when you stepped foot in my realm, Sonia Byrd."

His voice was velvet and iron, folding around my name like he owned it.

Like he owned me.

And then—a pause.

Deliberate. Drawn out.

A knife's edge waiting to bite.

"And now...I might not let you leave."

The air vanished from my lungs.

A cold, creeping horror wrapped around my ribs, digging in, sinking deep.

And for the first time since stepping into this godsforsaken realm—

I realized.

I had made a terrible mistake.

No.

No, no, no.

I couldn't be stuck here.

I wouldn't be.

My pulse slammed against my ribs, a wild, frantic thing caged in hollow air. My limbs locked up, my stomach twisting inside out, but I couldn't shut down. Not here. Not now.

Not when he was watching me.

Like a cat, waiting for its mouse to run.

Death stood too close, his silver eyes glittering with wicked delight, drinking in every fracturing piece of me. He was enjoying this.

Fine.

Watch this.

I clenched my fists and reached.

For what, I didn't know.

But I had done it before—somewhere deep inside myself, I had found my magic, followed it straight into the Deathscape.

If I could find my way in…

I could find my way out.

Get out.

I grasped for it, clawing through the storm of fear and logic, hunting for that same strange pull. I didn't know what I was doing.

I was flailing in the dark, grasping at smoke, at fog.

Nothing.

Come on.

Come on.

My breath hitched, panic snowballing. My lungs locked up, my nails dug into my palms.

The Deathscape felt me struggling.

And it pressed down harder.

Like a beast curling its claws around its prey.

And he was still watching.

"Desperate, aren't we?"

His voice was low, edged with something dangerous.

Admiration.

Or curiosity.

Like I was a puzzle he was halfway to solving.

I ignored him.

Out.

Get out, out, OUT.

Something inside me *tore*.

A crack, like whipcord snapping through the dark, like a seam splitting open—

My magic surged.

Wild. Untamed. Furious.

It ignited beneath my skin, bright and burning, filling my chest, demanding.

A wind roared to life, tearing through the Deathscape.

The ground shuddered.

A pulse of power rattled my bones.

A doorway began to open—

I was *so close*.

The force inside me *pulled*.

Tearing me backward, clawing me free.

Almost—

The air shifted.

Not the Deathscape.

Him.

Death moved.

And then—

His presence collided into me like a tide, thick as smoke and cold metal and storm-washed stone.

I didn't move.

I couldn't.

He didn't touch me.

Not yet.

But he was there, surrounding me, sinking into my bones.

And then—

A fingertip.

Tracing along my collarbone.

Barely there.

Just a ghost of a touch.

Enough to send a sharp thrill up my spine.

Enough to make my breath falter.

His hand curved around my throat.

I froze.

His fingers weren't tight. He wasn't choking me.

But his palm pressed lightly against my pulse.

Holding me there.

Every nerve in my body stilled.

Fire.

That was what it felt like.

Not heat. Not warmth.

White-hot fire, rushing through my veins, surging beneath my skin.

I gasped, but there was no air here.

Only him.

My magic *screamed*.

It fought.

The burning spread outward, spiraling down my arms, sinking into my fingertips, curling beneath my ribs, coiling around my spine like a snake ready to constrict.

And still, he held me.

No kindness in his harshly beautiful face.

His touch was like a mark being left.

Like a brand searing into place.

His thumb skimmed beneath my jaw, tracing something unseen.

And then—

A single, whispered word.

Dark.

Knowing.

"Mine."

My gaze snapped to his.

And for the first time—

I saw something different.

Not amusement.

Not teasing cruelty.

Something older.

Something knowing.

He flexed his fingers, just barely releasing the hold he had on me and then—

The world shattered.

My magic—wild, raw, furious—ripped me away.

A force like a thousand storms slammed into me, tearing me backward, tumbling, spiraling through darkness—

My body splintering apart. Then snapping back together.

Over and over until I slammed into myself.

11

The world lurched.

I gasped—a sharp, ragged sound that tore up my throat like glass.

Too fast. Too shallow. Too real.

I was back.

The motel ceiling spun above me.

The candles flickered wildly, shadows dancing on peeling wallpaper. The air reeked of melted wax, cheap detergent, and something human.

Too human.

But I didn't feel human.

Not anymore.

"Sonia?" Phontine's voice shook.

I jolted upright, breath hitching, my body shaking like it didn't belong to me. The floor was hard beneath me, a reminder that I was back in the world of the living—

And it felt wrong.

Too bright. Too loud. Too shallow.

My skin itched. Too tight. Too raw.

Like I'd been flayed and stitched back together with something that wasn't mine.

And my neck—

I yanked down my collar, heart slamming against my ribs.

Nothing.

No mark.

No bruise.

But I could feel it.

Right where he touched me.

A smoldering ember buried under my skin.

A phantom brand.

Still burning.

I swallowed, hard. My hands clenched. My breath stuttered.

And all I could think—

Was how he let me go.

How I'd been ripped from the Deathscape, flung back into my body like a comet smashing into the earth—

A thousand stars collapsing into my chest.

And I could still feel him.

Even now.

Even here.

Death.

His touch, his presence, his voice—all of it had followed me.

Branded into my bones.

Etched into the rhythm of my pulse.

And that—that was the most terrifying part.

Because whatever he did to me—whatever mark he left—it wasn't fading.

What the hell did Death do to me?

And why—when he could have stopped me, when he could have kept me—

Why did he let me leave?

For the past week, I had done everything I could to pretend none of it happened.

The Deathscape. The ghost. *Him.*

If a shadow flickered at the edge of my vision, I didn't flinch. If the forest whispered—soft and insistent—beckoning with a glowing white figure just beyond the tree line, I didn't follow.

I ran.

Straight into the noise. Into the city.

My candles stayed locked in my suitcase, like relics I didn't dare touch. My phone calls with my mom stretched too long, my voice molded into something steady.

Something fake.

And I clung to her words like a drowning girl gripping a nightlight—pretending they could hold back the dark.

It worked.

Until it didn't.

Last night, not even my mother's voice—warm, familiar, threaded with love and the distant chaos of my aunt's barking dogs—could keep me from staring at the ceiling.

Eyes wide.

Heart thudding.

Because today was the Mage House picnic.

And he still hadn't left me.

Calypso's text was still sitting on my phone, unread. But the preview haunted me.

I hope to see you at the—

I swallowed hard, dragging a hand across the back of my neck.

My fingers paused—hovered.

Right over the spot where the heat still pulsed. A phantom brand. A warning. A promise.

I refused to think about why.

Instead, I tried to anchor myself in the now.

My nearly drained bank account. The Blakewell police department still watching me like I might explode. And—most damning of all—

The fact that I had fallen into the Deathscape completely by accident.

No control. No plan.

Just raw instinct and terror and a kind of magic I didn't understand.

I could pretend all I wanted.

But that didn't change the truth.

I needed help.

And if walking into a Mage House—a den of politics, secrets, and eyes that saw too much—was the only way to get it?

Then so be it.

I pulled up the park's address Calypso had sent me, the screen glowing cold in my hand.

Then I changed direction.

Turned down a side street, my boots hitting the pavement harder than necessary as I wove through New Town.

My breath was shaky. My resolve worse.

But I moved forward anyway.

Because sometimes, pretending wasn't enough.

And sometimes—you walked straight into the fire just to prove you could survive the burn.

Even if you already knew you wouldn't.

Blakewell's New Town didn't look real.

It looked like a dream someone had designed in a lab.

Or a lie polished until it gleamed.

Glass rose in towering, geometric marvels, sharp edged and flawless, reaching toward the sky like the city was trying to cut heaven open. The sunlight hit everything with surgical precision, blinding off mirrored surfaces until I had to squint, teeth gritted against the glare.

Every surface shimmered.

The streets were translucent—not just clean, but unnaturally immaculate. Not a leaf out of place. No gum stuck underfoot. No oil slicks or cracked concrete.

No graffiti.

No history.

Nothing real.

Just perfection. Cold. Manufactured. Curated.

And that made my stomach twist.

Because a place this flawless?

It was hiding something.

A veneer this polished could only mean there were cracks beneath the surface. Cracks they didn't want anyone to see.

The few people I passed looked like they belonged in this dream. Or maybe like they were part of it—Mages and Fairies, glossy and untouchable.

Every outfit was a flex. Tailored jumpsuits in moonlight silk. Linen robes that rippled like water. Sleek monochrome layers that looked effortless but screamed power.

They didn't just look good. They looked *untouchable.*

Like nothing in this city could break them.

Like they had never been dragged to their knees by grief or fear or magic they couldn't control.

Unlike me.

I caught a few glances as I passed—curious, mildly disapproving, like they were trying to figure out where I fit into their perfectly curated ecosystem.

Spoiler: I didn't.

And I could feel it in every step I took.

Every breath of too-clean air.

New Town wasn't just different from Old Town.

It was the opposite.

Old Town pulsed with chaotic life—Vampires laughing in alleyways, Shifters arguing at street vendors, Goblins leaning against time-worn stone buildings that had seen war and magic and blood.

It was messy. Loud. Real.

New Town was a glass coffin.

And the biggest difference?

I hadn't seen a single Fairy in Old Town.

But here—they were everywhere.

Fairies weren't like the stories.

They were tall, willowy, strange.

Their skin shimmered like crushed pearl, their movements too fluid, too quiet. Their eyes caught the light like a predator's—too bright, too sharp.

They made my skin crawl.

Because they were beautiful. And inhuman.

Because they didn't blink like normal people. Didn't breathe like normal people.

And now, standing here, surrounded by all of it, I realized—

Old Town's lack of Mages and Fairies wasn't a coincidence.

It was a boundary.

One I was about to cross.

My steps slowed as I neared the park, the air shifting with the scent of fresh-cut grass and conjured flowers.

I could still feel the ghost of Death's touch at my throat.

Still feel the heat, buried just beneath the skin.

I shook it off.

Pushed it down.

Because I wasn't here to break.

I was here to walk into the fire and come out something brand-new.

The park was wedged between two glass monoliths, hidden like a secret the city only shared with its own.

It didn't look grown.

It looked engineered.

A patch of green carved out with mathematical precision.

The grass was unnaturally perfect—too trimmed, too green. Not a single weed. Not a single fallen leaf.

Even the trees looked suspicious, like they'd been selected from a catalog and positioned for optimal aesthetic balance.

It was beautiful.

And it made my skin crawl.

At first glance, the picnic looked...normal.

Blankets spread across the grass. Laughter. Sparkling drinks floating in midair. Kids giggling as they chased illusion-spells that flickered like fireflies.

The scent of grilled food hung thick in the air—sweet, smoky—twisting with something floral and faintly magical.

It was casual.

Welcoming.

Fun.

Until I walked into it. And everything shifted. Just a little.

But enough.

Conversations dipped.

Eyes flicked toward me—sharp, assessing, too knowing—then turned away a moment too fast.

Not rude.

Just...precise.

They all knew.

Of course they did.

I was the long-lost daughter of a Mage that left their House.

The outsider who had clawed her way back to the edge of their world.

And now I was standing in the middle of it.

Pretending I belonged.

I swallowed the instinct to bolt. To vanish.

Then I spotted her.

Calypso, waving from a checkered blanket like she wasn't surrounded by razor-edged gazes and politics dressed in picnic clothes.

Some of the pressure in my chest eased.

She wasn't alone. Two others sat with her.

One was a girl who looked like a reflection—an uncanny twin, brushing invisible lint off cream-colored wide-leg pants that looked expensive enough to have their own bank account.

The other was a guy built like trouble.

And not the "missed curfew" kind.

The kind that smiled at you and made you forget your own name.

Calypso shot to her feet the second I reached them, beaming. "Sonia! You made it!"

I shoved my phone into my black backpack purse, suddenly painfully aware of my chipped electric-blue nail polish and combat boots that hadn't been shined in...ever.

I didn't belong in this curated meadow.

Calypso grabbed my hand, pulling me closer like she hadn't noticed the shift in the air around me.

"Let me introduce you! This is my twin, Pandora—"

Pandora stood, smoothing nonexistent wrinkles from her linen pants and giving me a smile that didn't quite reach her eyes.

Polished. Controlled. Deadly.

She had Calypso's cheekbones, her full lips, her waterfall of black curls, and the exact same shade of green in her eyes—but where Calypso sparkled, Pandora was ice with a pulse.

"—and this is Elias."

Elias unfolded himself from the blanket like a cat stretching in a sunbeam—all lazy confidence and deliberate slowness.

His shirt hung open just enough to catch the sunlight on the gold edge of his collarbone, and his tousled dark hair looked like he'd just rolled out of someone's bed and hadn't seen a reason to apologize.

"Nice to finally meet you," he said, voice low and gravel-edged, like it had been dipped in bourbon and secrets.

The kind of voice that could wreck you.

And make you say thank you.

Fantastic.

Twins who looked like fallen goddesses and their best friend who could probably charm the shadows off the moon.

I shoved my hands into the pockets of my jacket and gave a crooked smile that felt more like armor than greeting.

"Yeah. Nice to meet you, too."

Calypso looped her arm through mine like I wasn't one wrong move away from cracking.

"Come sit. We've got food, and I need to hear everything about how you've survived Blakewell without a car."

I let her pull me toward the blanket, trying not to shrink beneath the lingering stares.

They weren't cruel.

Just...careful.

Like they were waiting for me to reveal something.

To prove myself. Or fail.

And then—

I saw her.

Matron Black.

Standing several yards away, silver silk cascading around her like she'd dressed for a coronation instead of a picnic.

Her gaze swept the gathering like she owned it.

Like she'd summoned it from the ground with a flick of her hand.

Something cold twisted in my gut.

Because this wasn't just a picnic.

This was a test.

And I had no idea if I was passing.

I adjusted the strap of my bag, fingers curling tight around the fabric like it could anchor me—like it could keep me from unraveling beneath the weight of the trio in front of me.

They looked like they'd stepped straight out of a curated feed—the kind with cool-toned filters and captions about moon phases and third-eye alignment.

Effortless. Unreachable. Sharp.

Even dressed for a picnic, they looked like they belonged on the cover of Modern Mage Monthly.

Maybe it was just a Mage thing.

That quiet, smug certainty that the world already belonged to them.

I stuffed my hands into my jacket pockets, trying to ground myself in something real.

"So, not to sound completely out of the loop," I began, my tone deceptively casual, "but why is New Town just...Mages and Fairies? And Old Town has everything else—but no Fairies?"

Calypso's green eyes flicked toward Pandora and Elias. A flicker of calculation.

Then: Smooth, polished diplomacy.

"New Town was designed to be a hub for high-tier Magicals," she said, her voice like glass over silk. "Fairies and Mages tend to work in government, education, magical sciences—places where structure and knowledge are prioritized."

A practiced smile. Too perfect. Like a line she'd been trained to recite.

"Old Town is more...free flowing. More communal."

Communal.

Right.

That was a pretty way of saying all the Magicals they didn't want in their glass sanctum got shoved into the cracked cobblestones and flickering neon grime of Old Town.

A kingdom for the unpolished.

Pandora snorted, tossing her dark hair over one shoulder like a weapon. Her movements were crisp, surgical—everything about her was honed.

"It's class segregation with extra steps," she said, her voice cool and precise. "They don't want Goblins or Shifters messing up their perfect little streets."

Calypso shot her a look, but didn't argue.

Of course she didn't.

"Sounds like there's an unspoken rule about who gets to exist where," I said slowly, watching their faces.

Elias shifted against the edge of the picnic blanket, arms crossed, chin tilted—every inch of him exuding lazy authority.

"It's not unspoken," he said, voice velvet and smoke. "It's just the way it works. Mages and Fairies sit at the top. We control magic at its purest."

He gave a shrug that said he didn't care whether I agreed.

"The other Magicals are..." A flick of his fingers, like dismissing a gnat. "Messier. Harder to regulate."

"Regulate," I echoed, raising a brow. "That's a pretty word for control."

Elias didn't blink.

"Magic requires discipline. The more raw or instinctual the magic, the more unstable it becomes. That's why Old Town exists. It's controlled chaos."

He looked at me like I was slow. Like he was being generous by explaining it at all.

Pandora rolled her eyes. "Careful, Eli. Keep talking like that and Sonia's going to think you've got plans for magical world domination."

Elias smirked. "Not domination. Just...stability."

Stability.

Right.

The kind that came with cages.

I shifted my weight, the ground beneath me suddenly feeling thinner than it had moments ago.

Calypso, ever the peacekeeper, stepped in with a quick smile. "It's really just different philosophies of magic. Mages and Fairies tend to work well together. The others—" She hesitated. "They have different strengths."

A pretty nonanswer.

Wrapped in ribbons and left to rot.

So, I changed tactics.

"What about the humans?"

Three sets of eyes turned to me.

I gestured around the park. "No offense, but this is a big deal. The rest of the world is terrified of magic. Trying to ban it, suppress it, pretend it's not real. But Blakewell's just...cool with it?"

Calypso smiled. Not fake. But rehearsed.

"Blakewell has a long history of cooperation between Magicals and humans."

Uh-huh.

"That's your polite way of saying, 'We're not going to tell you, so stop asking,' isn't it?"

Pandora's smirk curled like smoke.

"See? I like her."

I looked at Elias, expecting another hit of condescension. But he didn't speak.

He just watched me.

Head tilted. Eyes narrowed.

Curious. Calculating.

Like he was trying to decide what I'd taste like if he sank his teeth in.

"You'll figure it out eventually," he murmured.

And gods help me—

That made my stomach twist.

Because something in his tone said when I did figure it out, I wouldn't be the same.

12

Even with the cryptic half-answers and the polished-glass edges of privilege, I found myself...liking this trio.

I didn't want to. Didn't plan to.

But here we were.

They were sleek and curated, sure. Born into a world that had been gilded long before they took their first breaths.

But underneath the careful styling and that Mage-level confidence, there was something else.

Something genuine.

They didn't look at me like I was a sideshow.

Didn't flinch at the word ghost.

Didn't recoil like I was a disease in human form.

And that?

That was more than I could say for most of the magical world.

I let out a breath and rolled my shoulders, forcing myself to relax.

For now. But deep down, I knew this moment—this slice of sunshine and levity—was just the surface.

Just the top layer of a city that bled secrets.

And I wasn't leaving them buried.

Elias swirled his lemonade like it was an extension of his mood—lazy, sharp, deliberate. Then his eyes locked on mine.

"So, Sonia..." A slow smile. "What exactly does a Ghost Whisperer do?"

The question didn't surprise me. I'd spent most of my life dodging conversations like this. Most people stared like I was a curiosity. A curse.

But Elias's gaze wasn't hostile.

It was something worse.

Curious. Hungry.

Like he was studying me, cataloging every detail.

Still, it was better than fear.

"I see ghosts," I said simply, grabbing a fruit tart like it was a shield. "Some talk. Some just...linger. Like echoes of who they used to be."

Pandora leaned in, chin balanced on her fist, studying me with that sharp-edged interest that felt like it could cut if you got too close.

"Do you summon them?"

"Nope." I took a bite, then gestured vaguely. "They find me. Apparently, I give off a vibe."

Elias let out a thoughtful hum, clearly not satisfied. "So, you're a walking spirit magnet."

"That's one way to put it."

"What do they look like?" Calypso asked, her voice lighter, trying to ease the weight that was building. "Are they like...full apparitions? Or more like creepy, static-photo energy blobs?"

I shrugged. "Depends. Some look exactly how they did when they died. Some are just orbs. And sometimes..." My voice dipped, the words snagging. "Sometimes they decay."

I set the half-eaten tart down.

"They lose pieces. Faces. Voices. They fade. They...rot."

Pandora frowned. "That sounds unsettling."

You have no idea.

"You get used to it." Lie.

I would never get used to it.

Elias was still watching me. Still dissecting. His fingers tapped a slow rhythm against his cup, then stilled.

"Have you ever tried controlling it?"

I stiffened.

There it was.

The question.

The one that always came next.

"I don't have active magic," I said, picking at a pastry flake like it held the answer. "No spell circles. No enchantments. No fancy elemental flares."

Elias didn't blink. Didn't believe me.

"You're sitting here telling us you see and interact with spirits. And you think that's not magic?" He lifted a brow. "Sounds like magic to me."

Calypso cut in with a practiced ease, her tone warm. Reassuring.

"What he means is—your magic's different. It's innate. A part of you, not something you cast."

"Right," I said with a tight smile. "The polite way of saying I have a weird little niche power no one knows what to do with."

Pandora laughed. "She's not wrong."

The sound was unexpected—sharp and bright.

And just like that, some of the tightness in my chest unraveled. I hadn't even realized how tense I'd been until that moment.

They weren't treating me like I was fragile.

They weren't looking at me like I might break something just by existing.

They were just...curious.

Interested.

It was a nice change. But still, curiosity is a blade.

One that starts light. And ends deep.

So, I reminded myself:

Don't get comfortable.

Not here. Not yet.

Because every pretty smile hides something.

And I was just beginning to understand what Blakewell was really made of.

My gaze flicked toward the half-circle of Mages a few yards away—glittering power on full display.

They moved with casual arrogance, spinning spells like it was second nature.

Wisps of gold and silver energy danced between their fingers, shifting into intricate shapes—birds with feathered wings, blooming vines, fractal stars—only to dissolve into smoke.

An older woman transformed a pile of sticks into glittering crystal shards, catching the sunlight like she'd just conjured the gods' crown jewels.

Another Mage coaxed petals to bloom and rot in the same breath.

Life. Death. Life again.

Magic, bent to will.

I felt it hit in my gut. Sharp. Twisting.

Jealousy. Longing.

Or maybe something deeper. Something darker.

But the feeling snapped apart as my own voice slipped out, quieter than I intended.

"Did any of you know my birth parents?"

It landed like a dropped blade. All three of them froze.

Their silence was brief—but loud.

They exchanged looks. A silent shuffle of roles.

Who's going to lie first?

Pandora was the one to take it, her voice cool and carefully neutral.

"No."

Calypso followed smoothly, the diplomat to the end. "They left before we were old enough to remember them."

Elias?

He just shrugged and sipped his drink like this was a trivia question and not my entire life unraveling.

But it wasn't just what they said. It was how they said it.

Too smooth. Too rehearsed. Too careful.

They were lying.

I opened my mouth, about to press—

But then a shadow fell across the table.

And the air turned cold.

"I see you've been making friends."

I didn't have to turn to know who it was.

Matron Black.

Her voice was soft. Smooth. Deadly.

She hadn't been there a second ago.

But now she stood at the head of the table like she'd always belonged there—tall, immovable, and blinding.

She was dressed in silver that caught the light too perfectly, her gown flowing like liquid metal. Her skin was porcelain-pale, veined faintly with power. And her eyes—

So dark they swallowed the sun.

Everyone else at this picnic looked like summer. Matron Black looked like winter carved into a woman's bones.

And I hated—hated—that I hadn't noticed her sooner.

Had she been listening?

Calypso straightened, posture flawless. Pandora stopped swirling her lemonade. Elias looked vaguely entertained, like he couldn't wait for someone to bleed.

"Welcome to our gathering, Sonia," she said.

Her voice was glass.

And just as cold.

Calypso folded her hands in her lap. Pandora plucked at a thread on her sleeve. Elias leaned back, one brow raised like this was a game and I'd just been handed the rules.

"I trust you're enjoying your time here," Matron Black said, gaze pinning me like a butterfly to glass.

The way she phrased it—*your time here*—set my teeth on edge. Like I was a guest she could eject at any moment. Or a variable she was still deciding whether to keep.

"Yeah," I said, clearing my throat. "It's been...enlightening."

A smile ghosted across her lips. Not warm. Not kind.

Calculated.

"Good."

She turned to the others. "Calypso, thank you for making our guest feel welcome."

"Of course," Calypso said, her voice bright and smooth. "Sonia's great company."

Matron Black's gaze slid back to me, unreadable.

"I do hope you'll spend more time with them," she said. "The right company makes all the difference."

The words settled like a weight in my stomach.

That wasn't a suggestion. That was a test. A warning wrapped in a velvet ribbon.

Be with them. Or be watched.

I didn't get a chance to respond.

"Oh, she's definitely spending more time with us," Pandora said suddenly, stretching like a cat.

My stomach twisted.

"She's coming to our favorite pub. And she has to come. Because I already decided for her."

"Wait—"

"Done deal."

Calypso laughed, bumping her shoulder against mine. "You'll love it."

Elias arched a brow. "You sure she's ready for that?"

"She survived a week in Blakewell without getting eaten," Pandora said, tone flippant. "She's earned a drink."

I blinked. "Eaten?"

"Figure of speech." She grinned. Then she hooked her arm through mine like it was already settled.

It was.

"Come on, new girl," Pandora said with a wicked smile. "We're going out."

I should've known.

Of course, Pandora's idea of a "pub" wasn't anything close to what I'd imagined.

No flickering neon. No sticky floors. No mismatched chairs or hand-scrawled chalkboard menus.

This place?

It didn't belong in a city.

It belonged in a dream.

Or a trap.

The building sat wedged between two towering glass and metal giants—piercing structures that caught the sky and bent it. Reflected it like molten silver.

But the place we were walking toward didn't glimmer.

It shimmered. Unreal.

I slowed, instinct prickling at the back of my neck.

Before I could take it in—before I could breathe—something glinted in the sunlight. Sharp. Cold. Wrong.

My gaze snagged on one of the tall, metallic poles lining the street.

It looked like titanium at first. But it wasn't.

It pulsed.

Not light—magic.

A subtle shimmer beneath the surface, like it wasn't reflecting the sun but absorbing it.

No lamp. No wires. No markings.

Just…there.

I frowned, slowing my steps. "What is that?"

Elias glanced over, like he'd been waiting for me to notice. "Veil Tower. One of the originals. There are twenty eight of them scattered across the city."

I kept staring. "What does it do?"

He shoved his hands into his coat pockets, letting the twins walk ahead of us. "Releases the mist. Think of it like… magical anesthesia."

I squinted at the tower. "Anesthesia?"

"For humans," he said, eyes still fixed ahead. "They still see the magic. They just don't panic about it. Don't protest. Don't riot."

He paused, then added, quiet enough that only I would hear, "It's still in prototype, though. The mist's influence isn't precise yet. Doesn't just blur things for humans—it messes with Magicals too. That's why most people don't remember the towers. Even we'd forget them without—well, nevermind that."

I stared harder. The air above the tower shimmered faintly—like heat rising off pavement, but colder. Wrong.

"They say it soothes fear," Elias continued. "Eases the hostility between humans and Magicals. Blakewell's the first test city. If it works here, they'll roll it out everywhere."

I turned to him. "That sounds—"

"Sonia!" Calypso called from up ahead, waving.

I looked toward her—

And the thread snapped.

I blinked once. Twice.

What was I just...?

The word tower brushed the edge of my thoughts, but it drifted away like fog at sunrise. I felt—off. Like I'd walked through a conversation and forgotten to collect any of it on the way out.

I shook my head and jogged to catch up with the others, telling myself it didn't matter.

But the weird feeling stayed with me. All the way down the block.

Like I'd missed something important.

Like something was watching.

But before I could chase it, Pandora yanked me forward.

"Here we are," she announced, far too cheerful.

She threw open a pair of golden doors. Not brass. Not paint.

Gold.

Real. Heavy. Spell-etched.

The moment they parted, the world shifted. And I stepped into something else entirely.

The air changed—warmer, darker, charged.

The sound of laughter echoed from deeper inside, but it was low, decadent, threaded with something wicked.

This wasn't a place for casual drinks.

This was a place for secrets. For shadows. For people who didn't need to ask the price before they paid it.

The scent hit me next—spiced wine, old wood, smoke, and magic.

Thick and heady, curling down my throat like a promise I hadn't agreed to.

I froze just inside the threshold.

And behind me, the golden doors clicked shut.

If New Town had a heart, this was it.

Not a pub. Not really. A sanctum. A shimmering illusion.

The air inside buzzed—sharp, alive, threaded with the kind of magic that clung to skin like static before a storm.

Glass orbs hovered along the walls, glowing with soft, pulsing light. Not flickering. Breathing. Casting the space in a haze of silver-blue luminescence, like moonlight seen through deep water.

And the magic here?

It didn't hum. It thrummed.

The walls practically exhaled it.

There was no scent of spilled beer. No frying oil hanging heavily in the air.

Instead—coolness. Fresh. Herbal. Faintly floral. Like the room had been scented with carefully designed spells.

And the people—Bless the Wood. The people.

Mages and Fairies. Only.

Not a single human. Not even a half-blood.

Magic shimmered around them like a heat haze, invisible but unmistakable. They looked like they belonged in portraits, not real life—impossibly composed, sharp-boned, too symmetrical to be anything but dangerous.

The Fairies were worse. Their wings shimmered with iridescence, catching the enchanted light and reflecting it like jeweled daggers.

They didn't walk. They drifted. Glided. Commanded.

And I, with my chipped electric-blue nail polish and thrift-store jeans, felt like I'd walked into a dream where I didn't exist.

Like I'd already been erased.

Elias smirked, watching the realization dawn on my face.

"Something wrong, new girl?"

"I—" My voice caught. I blinked at the opulence, the precision, the sheer wrongness of calling this a pub. "This isn't a pub."

Pandora didn't blink. "It is to us."

She slid into motion like she owned the place and waved me forward. "Now sit. We're getting you a drink."

I obeyed—because what else was I going to do?—and sank into a chair at a table smooth and black as obsidian, veined with faint glimmers of starlight.

I exhaled, trying to shake the unease coiling in my ribs.

This wasn't just a bar.

It was a curated space of power, a crucible in glittering disguise.

And whatever was in those glasses behind the bar? I doubted it was just alcohol.

My fingers drummed against the table. Restless. Unsettled. Watching.

Then—movement in the back.

A shimmer. A shift. A pulse of something...darker.

That's when I saw it.

The gambling tables.

Not hidden. Just...subtly set apart. Like only the right eyes were meant to see them.

Mages and Fairies clustered around the games, murmuring low over cards and dice etched with runes.

There was laughter—sharp and indulgent. One of them had just won big.

I expected money. Maybe coins. Something tactile.

Wrong.

The winnings glittered—vials of Fairy dust.

Not symbolic. Not decorative.

Currency.

Stacks of them, carefully aligned, each vial glowing with a soft, iridescent shimmer that made my vision blur if I looked too long.

The winner—a Fairy with wings like spun moonlight—collected his haul with a grin sharp enough to draw blood.

I stared.

Fairy dust.

I knew it had value. Sure. It powered spells, strengthened enchantments, enhanced magic in ways few things could.

But this?

This wasn't use.

This was desire. Obsession. Addiction.

And the Mages?

They were leaning in, eyes sharp, hands twitching—hungry.

For the vials. For the power. For the rush.

Something cold slid down my spine.

Because if Fairy dust was currency here...

What else could be bought?

And what did that make the people willing to bleed for it?

A shiver coiled up my spine.

I didn't belong here. I'd stepped into something sharp edged and velvet lined and far too beautiful to be safe.

Before the thought could anchor, Elias leaned in.

"You look like you're about to bolt."

My gaze snapped to his, heartbeat stuttering.

"I don't bolt."

His mouth curved—half smirk, half challenge. "Alright. Then you look like you're plotting your escape."

I let out a breath and dragged my gaze from the shimmering gambling tables and the vials of Fairy dust glinting like currency made from dreams.

"It's just..." I paused, chewing on the truth like it tasted wrong. "I don't exactly fit in here."

The words landed heavier than I meant them to. Like admitting it gave it power.

But it was the truth. Here—surrounded by impossibly beautiful Mages and Fairies with magic stitched into their skin like silk—I felt like a scribbled margin note in someone else's epic.

Elias tilted his head, something unreadable flickering in his dark eyes.

Then he said, softer than I expected, "You're a Mage, Sonia. You have every right to be here."

It should've been nothing. Just a fact.

But it wasn't the words—it was the way he said them. Like he meant them. Like he needed me to mean them, too.

It slipped beneath my ribs and curled there.

"Yeah, well...you're the first person to say that."

His expression didn't change. But his voice dropped to something silk wrapped and razor edged. "Then you've been talking to the wrong people."

Before I could respond—before I could unravel the knot he'd just left in my chest—Pandora and Calypso reappeared, drinks in hand.

"Alright, newbie," Pandora announced, sliding into the seat across from me. "First drink's on me."

She pushed a glass toward me with a grin that dared me to say no.

I picked it up. Hesitated.

The liquid inside shimmered—a light lavender hue threaded with glittering strands that caught the enchanted light and pulsed faintly.

This wasn't just alcohol.

"What is this?"

"Something that won't kill you," Pandora chirped, already sipping hers. "Probably."

Calypso settled beside her, her voice smoother. "It's just a mild enchantment. Nothing heavy. Makes you feel good. Warm."

I wasn't sure *mild* and *enchantment* belonged in the same sentence.

But tonight, I didn't want to overthink.

I took a sip.

And the world tilted.

Not badly. Not dangerously.

Just...softly.

Warmth bloomed behind my ribs, slow and golden, unraveling the knots in my spine.

I hadn't realized how tightly I'd been wound until I started to melt.

Pandora smirked like she'd won something. "See? Told you."

Elias gave her a lazy glance. "Trying to get her drunk already?"

"She needs to loosen up." Pandora twirled her straw. "She's already a lightweight—I can tell."

"You don't know that."

"I know you've never had a drink like that before."

She wasn't wrong.

Calypso leaned forward, elbows on the table, eyes curious. "So?"

"So what?"

"What do you think?" She gestured around the pub. "New Town. The House. All of it."

I hesitated.

Because if I was honest?

It was intoxicating.

The magic. The power. The glittering edges of everything. Like I'd been invited into a secret world carved from moonlight and control.

And for the first time in a long time, I wasn't just surviving.

I was seen.

But that kind of belonging came with a cost. And I wasn't sure I could afford it.

I took another sip. Let the warmth carry me somewhere safer.

And did what I did best when the truth got too close—

I dodged.

"It's...different."

Pandora snorted. "That's an understatement."

Elias leaned back, his chair creaking just slightly under the shift of his weight. He watched me over the rim of his glass, dark eyes unreadable.

"You'll get used to it," he said.

I couldn't tell if it was a promise—or a warning.

At some point, I lost track of how many drinks had appeared at our table.

Which was a problem. Because I was absolutely feeling them.

My cheeks were on fire. My skin pulsed with heat, glowing under the enchanted lighting like I'd swallowed the sun.

And yep—there it was. The dreaded Asian Glow.

Fantastic. Another parting gift from the birth mother I barely remembered.

Calypso clapped her hands together like she'd just solved an ancient riddle. "I'm ordering food!"

Food sounded like salvation.

I thrust both fists into the air. "Food!"

The room tilted in response.

The floor slanted slightly to the right. The ceiling stretched upward like it was trying to escape. And the walls?

Breathing. Definitely breathing.

Okay. Maybe I was drunk.

Just a little.

I stood.

And the entire world decided to spin.

Elias's hand caught my elbow before I could face-plant into oblivion. His grip was steady. Warm. Frustratingly smug.

"I think you should sit back down," he said, voice slick as midnight silk.

"Nope." I peeled myself free with stubborn grace. "Bathroom."

He raised a brow, like he was placing bets on whether I'd fall. "You sure you don't need a chaperone?"

I narrowed my eyes, wobbly but fierce. "Watch me thrive."

I took a step.

Didn't fall.

Victory.

"See?" I gestured broadly—and nearly knocked over an entire chair. "Totally fine."

Pandora chuckled, pulling out her phone. "If you're not back in five, we send in a search party."

"Duly noted."

The flickering light orbs blurred as I stumbled toward the restroom, their glow stretching into halos that kissed the air like falling stars.

And that's when I noticed it.

The change.

The gambling tables were still going, cards flicking and chips clinking in hypnotic rhythm.

But the Mages were gone.

All of them.

The room that had once been a perfectly curated mix of power and elegance now felt...skewed. Off-balance.

Only Fairies remained.

They still looked the same—otherworldly, effortless, terrifying in their beauty.

But the energy had shifted.

Heavier. Hungrier. Like the air itself had turned to glass—fragile and waiting to shatter.

I frowned, the thought wobbling like the rest of me.

Then it slipped. Gone. Like so many things in this city.

I shoved through the restroom door.

Inside, the pub's strange warmth vanished.

Silver tiles. Clean enough to reflect light like mirrors. The scent of citrus and amber. Too elegant. Too pristine. No pub bathroom had the right to look like a spa on steroids.

The walls were lined with mirrors—oval, rimmed in a soft white glow.

I did my business, still half-giggling, the drink making my thoughts foggy and ridiculous.

"The Fairies have taken over the pub," I whispered to myself, grinning at my reflection like I'd just uncovered a conspiracy.

I stumbled to the sink. Braced both hands on the counter. Turned on the water.

The cold helped.

It grounded me. Pulled me back from the edge of the spinning.

I scrubbed my hands, inhaling the sharp scent of amber and citrus soap.

Then—

The temperature dropped.

Not slowly. Not subtly.

Like a hand had clenched around the entire room and squeezed.

The lights dimmed. The air grew still.

And something shifted behind me.

The air collapsed. Not a draft. Not a breeze.

A full-bodied, bone-deep collapse.

Cold sliced into me like a blade, gutting the warmth from my flushed skin and leaving nothing but ice and fear behind.

My breath hitched. My pulse thundered—a jagged, stuttering rhythm that didn't feel like it belonged in my body anymore.

I looked up.

And she was there.

The ghost.

Still as a portrait. Standing at the far end of the bathroom like she had always been there—like I had stepped into her world and not the other way around.

But this time...she had eyes.

And gods, I wished she didn't.

Twin voids, bottomless and black, leaking something thick and ink-like—molten obsidian bleeding down her cheeks in viscous, warpaint streaks. Her lips were cracked open, too wide—like she'd screamed for centuries and still wasn't done.

The sight carved a hollow in my chest.

Something deep inside me curled. Tight. Instinct. Magic. Memory. Terror.

I swallowed the scream clawing its way up my throat. "Are you serious?" I exhaled, breath fogging in the freezing air. "You're haunting a bathroom now?"

No answer.

She didn't move. Didn't blink.

Just stared. Sad. Hollow. Expectant.

I gritted my teeth. The alcohol surged in my veins, lending me a kind of boldness I hadn't earned.

"No. Listen to me." I pointed, snapping the faucet closed with a sharp twist. "I'm not here to solve your murder."

The ghost tilted her head.

A sharp, mechanical movement. Wrong in every way.

Like she wasn't just listening. Like she was measuring me.

"I don't have the training for that," I said, voice wavering but steady enough to hurt. "I barely have training to be anything. Mage, Ghost Whisperer—whatever the hell I'm supposed to be."

Still no movement.

Still those endless, dripping eyes.

A chill spidered down my spine, webbing cold into my lungs.

"I came here to control my magic," I whispered, words slurring around the edges. "I need to see my dad again. That's it. That's all. I don't have time for this."

My fists clenched. Fingernails bit into my palms. "So, stop following me."

The silence snapped.

The air thickened. Sparked. Cracked.

The ghost's face changed.

The grief dropped away like a mask sliding from rotted bone.

And what was left—was rage.

Unfiltered. Unholy. Unleashed.

She lunged.

And I didn't even have time to scream.

She slammed into me with the force of a spell gone wrong—Magic collided with magic, pain detonating in my chest.

Agony ripped through me.

Not fire. Not frost. *Both.*

Like I was being torn apart from the inside out, frozen solid and set aflame in the same breath.

The handprint Death left on my throat ignited. Not a burn—A brand.

My skin blistered. Peeled.

The scream never made it out.

The mirrors exploded.

Glass shattered in every direction, raining down like razor-edged snow. A hundred versions of me fractured and fell in silence.

Then—

Blackness.

My knees buckled. My body followed.

And I was falling.

Into nothing.

13

The world returned in stutters. Like a glitching signal, like something broken trying to remember how to be whole.

Light pulsed behind my eyes. Sound crashed in disjointed waves. My skin prickled with cold.

Everything felt wrong.

My brain was packed with cotton. My ears rang like I'd stood too close to the detonation point of a spell.

I was sprawled on the floor—cold tile, slick with something wet. And above me—

Two faces. Blurred. Too perfect. Too close.

"Sonia?" Calypso's voice cracked through the static—sharp, breathless, frantic. "Sonia, can you hear me?"

I groaned. Everything hurt. But I was here. I was alive.

How?

I blinked hard, the world sharpening in jarring snaps of clarity.

Glass shimmered across the floor like frozen rain. And Calypso and Pandora were crouched beside me, their elegance shaken into something real.

Worry. Fear. For me.

Pandora exhaled like she'd been punched. "Sweet Woods, you scared the hell out of us."

She was still holding my arm like I might evaporate.

That did something brutal and unfamiliar in my chest. It had been a long time since someone had worried about me like that.

"What...happened?" I rasped.

My voice was wreckage. My throat burned. Like I'd screamed through fire and swallowed the smoke.

"You tell us," Pandora snapped, but her voice trembled beneath the frustration. "We found you on the damn floor covered in glass!"

Calypso's green eyes scanned my face, wide with alarm. "You don't look hurt, but—Sonia, that was so much glass. You should be bleeding."

I flexed my fingers.

No cuts. No blood. No pain except the ghost of cold curled beneath my skin.

The ghost.

My mouth was dry. "It was...a ghost."

That landed like a dropped stone.

The sisters exchanged a glance.

"A ghost?" Pandora echoed, all sharp disbelief.

Calypso leaned closer. "Here? Now?"

"She's gone." I dragged a shaking hand through my hair, my breath catching on the edges. "But yeah. Ghost. Very pissed off ghost."

Pandora cursed under her breath—something sharp and ancient-sounding. Then she was gripping my arm tighter, yanking me up with the force of someone who didn't care about dignity, only survival.

"We're getting you out of here." Calypso was already at my other side, her tone firmer than I'd ever heard it. "Come on."

They hooked their arms through mine—warm, steady, and furious with purpose.

The pub didn't blink as we emerged.

The music still pulsed through enchanted speakers, syrupy and slow. Fairies still lounged in golden light, sipping glittering drinks like nothing had happened. Like the air hadn't turned to ice. Like a girl hadn't nearly been torn apart two rooms over.

No one looked at us. No one saw.

The twins moved like a unit, like the girls they'd been before were gone and replaced with something harder, faster, focused.

They didn't pause. Didn't hesitate.

Outside, the air snapped colder—biting, real, sharp with the aftertaste of whatever the hell I had just survived.

A black cab with a bold orange stripe shimmered into existence at the curb, gold runes glowing along the trim.

"In." Pandora yanked the door open like she was breaking into battle.

"But—"

"None of that. In." Pandora's eyes narrowed.

"Elias…" I tried, to turn and look for him but my body was starting to feel the fatigue of everything that happened. "He was at our table."

"He got a call." Calypso cut in with a voice too tight to be soothing. "He had to go to the House."

I wanted to argue more.

Wanted to tell them I'd be fine. That I didn't need babysitting. That I wasn't about to shatter.

But the lie died on my tongue. I didn't have it in me.

Not tonight. Not after her.

So, I slid into the cab without a fight, the leather seat cold against my still-throbbing spine.

The door clicked shut behind us, sealing the night out. Or maybe locking something else in.

The vehicle hummed to life, gliding silently through the sterile perfection of New Town. Glass buildings bled starlight across the pavement. The streets were too clean. Too quiet. Too unreal.

"Sonia." Calypso twisted in her seat, eyes sharp, voice low. "What actually happened in there?"

I sighed, rubbing my arms like I could erase the cold she'd left behind. "Like I said. Ghost."

Pandora's gaze cut to me, hawklike. "Ghosts don't usually obliterate an entire wall of enchanted mirrors, do they?"

I didn't answer.

What was I supposed to say? That I'd pissed off a spirit so thoroughly she tried to drag me out of my own body?

That I still felt her rage crawling beneath my skin like static?

"This town is getting weirder." Calypso exhaled, dragging a hand through her hair with the grace of someone who never looked out of place—and still somehow looked undone.

A dry laugh cracked in my throat. "Tell me about it."

The silence that followed wasn't awkward. Just heavy.

Like we were all waiting for the next disaster to introduce itself.

When the cab finally pulled up in front of my run-down motel, its peeling paint and buzzing sign felt like an insult. A reminder. Back to reality. Back to nothing.

They both turned to me before I could open the door.

"Come to our place," Pandora said. Her voice wasn't demanding. It was...protective.

"Just for the night," Calypso added, softer. "You don't have to be alone after—"

"I need space."

My voice wasn't strong. But it was final.

"But, um, thanks."

And they knew better than to argue with a girl who looked like she was holding herself together with borrowed thread.

Pandora pressed her lips together but didn't fight me. "We're checking on you tomorrow."

The cab sped off before I could respond.

And for a moment, I just stood there. Under the neon buzz and a sky that felt too big.

I turned toward my door, exhaustion crashing into me like a second haunting. All I wanted was to collapse. To sleep. To forget.

But fate wasn't done with me yet.

"Sonia!"

I jolted.

Phontine.

She burst into view like she'd been flung from another dimension, her tiny wings fluttering in a frantic blur. Her lavender eyes were wide with something close to panic.

"Phontine?" I staggered back, heart lurching. "What the hell—"

"I tried to follow you into New Town, but I couldn't!" She gasped, voice pitched high. "Something blocked me! It tasted like a spell—I couldn't even see the boundary—"

She whirled midair and pointed toward my motel.

"Then he showed up."

The words sank into me like cold metal. My stomach flipped.

"Who?"

She didn't answer.

Because she didn't have to.

My eyes locked on the figures gathered outside my room.

Detective McDara. His Lion-Shifter partner. And the motel owner.

The door to my room was open.

Wide.

McDara's partner was inside, rifling through my things like they belonged to him.

And McDara?

He wasn't watching the room.

He was walking toward me.

Eyes locked. Expression unreadable. Power curling around him like a second skin.

And this time, I wasn't sure if he was coming as an ally—or something far more dangerous.

He looked worse than he had a week ago.

The kind of worse that sank into your bones. Eyes ringed in shadows. Shoulders weighed down by something he hadn't said yet. A man unraveling by degrees. Like he'd been chasing ghosts of his own and wasn't winning.

My stomach twisted, heat knotting low behind my ribs.

McDara didn't waste time. "Do you know what this is?"

His voice was low. Somber. Like it had already delivered bad news and was bracing for more.

I followed his gaze.

The evidence bag in his gloved hand.

Inside: A long silver chain.

And something dark clung to it.

Wet. Thick. Crimson-black.

It looked like blood. Old. But not completely dry.

My breath stuttered. My head shook on instinct.

"No."

His jaw clenched. A muscle ticked once. "It's covered with the same blood we found at the crime scene."

The words hit like a spell with no warning—blunt, heavy, and merciless.

I swayed.

"Does that mean..." My voice broke. "You found the body?"

McDara exhaled, slow and heavy. His eyes—those dark, unreadable eyes—never left mine. "Not yet." A beat. "But you can help us find it."

The floor dropped out from under me. "What?" I stepped back. "How would I—"

He didn't blink. Didn't flinch.

He lifted the bag higher. The chain glinted under the buzzing motel light like a noose. "Because this was found in your bathroom vent."

My body went cold.

"No."

A whisper. A denial wrapped in panic.

No. No. No.

"That wasn't there. It wasn't in my room—"

I stumbled back again, my voice too thin, too raw. "I didn't put it there—"

McDara was already moving. And I knew. *I knew.*

He didn't believe me. Or maybe he didn't want to.

He sighed.

A tired, broken sound. Then the click of steel.

Cold metal snapped around my wrists. The cuffs locked into place like truth.

I stared at him—wide-eyed, horrified.

He looked back with something that wasn't anger.

It was worse.

Regret.

"Twice now," he said quietly. "Twice, I've met you, and I've had to put you in cuffs."

He guided me toward the car, his touch steady but careful—like he wasn't sure if I'd crumble or combust.

As I was shoved gently into the backseat, I turned. One last look at the motel. At the room I had thought was mine. Safe.

And there—

In the doorway—

The ghost.

Her face was carved from something awful. Twisted with something more than rage.

And just as the car door slammed shut—

She smiled.

14

The room wasn't the same.

It wasn't just the layout—though this one was larger, colder, with walls set farther apart like they were trying to make me feel small. It was the air. The way it pressed in around me, thick and still, too silent to be anything but intentional.

The first time I'd been here—what, a week ago?—it had been a sterile little box that looked like a prop from a crime drama. A quick slap on the wrist. A warning. This room felt different. Permanent. Like a verdict already written.

My hands were cuffed to the metal table bolted into the floor, as if someone thought I might break through the concrete if given half a chance. But where would I run? Everything was closing in. The past twenty-four hours. The past week. My whole damn life. All of it pressing down like stone—weight I could barely hold up anymore.

If it wasn't for Phontine, I might've already crumbled.

She perched invisibly on my shoulder, her tiny hands twisted in the collar of my jacket like she could anchor me to myself. Only McDara seemed to notice. His gaze flicked to her once—brief, unreadable—but he didn't say a word. He just sat across from me, arms folded, his expression carved from stone.

The silence stretched, heavy and long. Then, at last, his voice cut through it.

"Pixie," He said, "You need to leave."

"What?" I rasped as Phontine popped into visibility and made a sound that was more hiss than anything else.

"I will be speaking to Miss Byrd alone." McDara cast a look at Phontine, all dark eyes and hard edges. No compromise in sight. "Wait outside or I will use magic to remove you."

This time Phontine did hiss at him in a rare show of the creature she really was. With one last look at me, her lavendar eyes wilting from rage to worry, she disappeared.

Silence reined and any steadiness that Phontine had provided me was gone.

"Twenty-four's too young to be facing a murder charge."

My breath didn't just catch—it stopped. The words hit with surgical precision. Cold. Clean. Brutal.

I stared at him, numbness crawling beneath my skin like frost spreading through my veins.

McDara leaned back in his chair, the motion deceptively casual. His tone remained even, almost detached, like he wasn't talking about my life unraveling. Like it was just another entry in a case file.

"The item we found in your motel room is a pendant. A charm." His gaze stayed steady on mine. "We're still testing it, but the blood on it is laced with dark magic."

The phrase echoed. Dark magic.

My mind seized around it, a slow recoil I couldn't stop.

"Do you know what that means?" His voice wasn't cruel, but it wasn't gentle either. It was the voice of someone used to people breaking across from him. The voice of someone who expected me to.

I didn't answer. I couldn't. My lungs refused to work properly. My vision blurred at the edges.

Then his tone shifted—lower, sharper. A blade, not a question.

"The use of Soul Enchantment alone could get you thirty years."

Thirty. Years.

Something inside me fractured.

It wasn't a clean break. It was the kind of shattering that didn't make sound at first—just silence. Then came the collapse.

The tears struck without warning. Not soft, not pretty. Not something you could wipe away and pretend hadn't happened.

This was grief that had been waiting to explode.

My body convulsed with it. Shoulders heaving. Hands trembling against the cuffs. Breath after breath that refused to come smoothly.

I wasn't crying just because of the charge.

I cried for my dad. For how much I missed him. For the stupid, desperate hope that maybe he was still out there and somehow all of this was leading me to him.

I cried for my mom, for every lie I'd fed her over the phone. For every "I'm fine" when I hadn't been fine in days.

I cried for the version of me who'd walked into this week with nothing but a dying savings account, and a hunger for answers I didn't understand.

And now...now I was just a girl in cuffs. A girl in a room too big and too cold, with a murder charge pressing down on her like a noose made of magic and blood.

A shift.

The scrape of his chair echoed louder than it should have in the stillness, sharp against concrete. Then—the soft thud of boots. Measured. Unhurried.

Warmth followed.

It approached slowly, curling into the cold void I hadn't realized had rooted itself in my chest.

I didn't want to look. But I did.

McDara crouched beside me, silent and steady, his dark eyes level with mine. His expression gave nothing away—just the same unflinching calm he always wore like armor. Controlled. Contained.

And gods, I hated it.

Hated that he looked at me like I might break. Like I hadn't already.

I wanted to scream. To shake him. To demand why the world kept dragging me down, burying me under the weight of things I didn't understand and didn't ask for.

But all I had were tears. Hot, silent, suffocating.

Until he reached for me.

I flinched—instinctive, sharp.

Not because I didn't want it. But because it was too much.

His hand, rough with callouses, brushed against my cheek with a tenderness I hadn't earned. A thumb moved slowly beneath my eye, collecting a tear as if it belonged to him.

Then another.

His skin was warm. Real.

And it made something inside me shatter again—not from pain, but from the sheer unfamiliarity of it. Because no one touched me like this. Not in comfort. Not in quiet. Not in kindness.

Death had touched me. His hands had branded me, claimed me, burned his presence into the soft skin of my throat with otherworldly fire and whispered that I belonged to him.

But this—

McDara's touch didn't sear.

It didn't possess. It didn't devour.

It steadied.

It tricked me into believing—for just one trembling breath—that I might be okay. That maybe I wasn't lost. That maybe someone saw me through the grief and the fear and the blood and still thought I was worth anchoring to this world.

That was the lie of it. That was the danger.

Because I didn't know which man's touch haunted me more now. The one that burned. Or the one that soothed.

McDara didn't speak. Didn't look away. His thumb brushed just beneath my jaw in one final pass, slow and deliberate.

And I hated how badly I wanted him to do it again.

My breath hitched—too loud in the silence. My wrists were still cuffed to the table, metal biting into my skin like a reminder.

I couldn't move. I couldn't run. I could only feel.

His hand. His gaze. His presence.

Every inch of me trembled—not from fear, not even from pain. But from the weight of the moment. From the quiet understanding passing between us.

I was still drowning. Still falling apart.

But for the first time in days, I wasn't doing it alone.

And I wasn't sure which was more dangerous. Being alone with my ghosts.

Or being seen by him.

"It knows where its body is," I said, my voice raw from crying, my throat torn by silence and swallowed screams.

McDara's brow furrowed. Not in confusion—calculation. "What?"

I swallowed, forcing breath into lungs that still didn't feel like they belonged to me. "The ghost," I said again, clearer now. "It knows where its body is."

Silence pulsed between us. Thick. Pressurized.

He didn't move. Didn't speak. But something about him shifted—something behind his eyes. A flicker. Like he was reassessing everything he thought he knew about me.

Then, slow and deliberate, he leaned in.

One hand braced on the table, the other curling around the back of my chair. Too close.

His scent wrapped around me—leather, clean rain, something darker beneath, something that was distinctly *him*. It made my pulse stutter. It made me ache.

He was too close. And I couldn't move.

His voice came low, threaded with steel. "Explain."

Not a challenge. Not disbelief. An order.

And gods help me, I wanted to obey.

I dragged a breath into my chest and started talking. Piecing it together through the fog and the fear and the ever-growing noise in my head.

I told him everything.

The ghost. The diner. The shifting shape of her. The way she stared at me like I was already hers. The restroom. The frost that crashed into me like a tidal wave. The rage in her face before she struck.

McDara didn't interrupt. His gaze locked on mine, absorbing every word, cataloging each detail like evidence—like I was both a suspect and something else entirely.

When I finished, his mouth twitched. The smallest movement. A flicker of something I couldn't quite name.

Then, with maddening calmness, he said, "So, just to be clear...your official story is that the ghost is framing you?"

The words landed with infuriating amusement.

I glared at him, heat rising to the surface like lava. "It makes sense."

His tone sharpened, mocking. "Oh, does it?"

"Yes!" My hands jerked—cuffed. Chained. My fury stuck in place. "What else makes sense?"

His smirk vanished. That smooth mask of his cracked just enough to let something colder slip through. He straightened slowly, his arms crossing with military precision.

"You used Soul Enchantment to kill a Mage."

I blinked. The disbelief cracked into a bitter, sharp laugh. "Right. That's what we're going with?"

McDara didn't flinch. His words came sharp, clipped. "You tell me. There's dark magic all over a crime scene you were found at. A Mage is missing. A silver charm soaked in soul magic and blood shows up in your motel room." He stepped closer. "What part of that doesn't track?"

"Maybe the part where I don't have active magic?" I snapped. My voice was too loud, but I didn't care. "I'm a Ghost Whisperer. I see things. Hear things. I don't cast spells. I don't even know the Mage who died—or vanished—or whatever you think happened."

His expression didn't waver. But something else did.

The air shifted.

Quieter now, he said, "You've been here before."

I stilled. Then, softly—"I was one when I left."

McDara's jaw tightened. A beat passed. He gave a short, begrudging nod. "Fair point."

For one breath, the pressure around my chest loosened. A crack of hope—small, fragile. I clung to it like it might save me.

"I don't know where the body is," I said. My voice steadied. "But I can find it."

He raised a brow. All skepticism. All steel.

"If I find the body, you can test it." I pushed forward. "It'll have dark magic on it right? I can't case *any* magic. Including dark magic. You'll see. Run your tests. The magic won't match mine."

His stare burned into me. Flickers of something unreadable passed through it—doubt, anger, maybe the faintest thread of reluctant belief.

And then—he muttered under his breath, low and sharp, "Gods save me."

I couldn't tell if it meant he believed me. Or if I'd finally broken him. Maybe both.

McDara stepped back, scraping his hand down his face like he already regretted the next five decisions he was about to make. The sharp line of his jaw clenched. His shoulders tensed.

But I saw it.

The shift.

Not in the case. Not in the magic. *In him.*

Something inside him had cracked open—just a little. And for the first time since I sat in this room, shackled and shaking, I wasn't the only one coming apart at the seams.

"Alright," he said at last, his voice a low growl of command—sharp edges dressed in steel.

He wasn't asking. He was about to lay down the law.

I crossed my arms, or tried to, considering the whole still-cuffed-to-the-damn-table thing. "Do I get a say in this?"

McDara didn't even blink. Both hands pressed flat against the cold metal table as he leaned in—closer than was necessary. Close enough that I could see the shadows beneath his eyes, the faint scar slicing through the left side of his hairline. Close enough that I felt the heat of him, even as he looked carved from winter stone.

"First rule," he said, voice flat and unyielding, "you do not go off chasing ghosts alone."

I blinked. "That's oddly specific."

No smirk. No sarcasm. Just that wall of stone, standing tall between us.

"You don't follow leads without me. You don't speak to that ghost unless I'm there, hearing exactly what you say."

The command in his voice was a blade—thin and cold, sliding just beneath my skin.

I scoffed, pushing against the edge of my restraints. "What, you don't trust me?"

A beat. Then a single, sharp laugh—humorless and bitter. "Nope."

The word sliced something deep.

I told myself I didn't care. That trust didn't matter. That he didn't matter. But gods, something inside me still bristled like a live wire. I didn't even know why. Maybe because some feral part of me wanted to be trusted. To be believed.

I looked away before I said something I'd regret. Something like, *Why does it bother me so much that you don't trust me?*

He straightened, arms crossing again like armor. "Second rule—I'm leading this investigation. Not you. You listen. You follow orders. You do not make this harder than it already is."

I tilted my head, tone syrupy and razor sharp. "Define 'harder.'"

His jaw clenched. That muscle at the corner of his mouth ticked. "You know exactly what I mean."

I gave him my best innocent-little-mage look. He didn't buy it.

"Third rule," he said, voice dropping lower, colder. "If we find anything—*anything*—that even hints you're connected to this murder...I bring you in. Again."

The weight of his words settled around my shoulders like shackles I hadn't earned.

He was giving me a shot—but it came bound in thorns. One misstep, and I was done.

"Got it." I nodded stiffly.

His gaze held mine for a long, electric second. Then he reached into his coat pocket, pulled out a small key, and slid it into the cuffs.

With a sharp click, they popped open.

I flexed my fingers as the pressure eased, rubbing at the angry red marks circling my wrists. The metal had left its imprint—but so had the words.

"Any more rules?" I asked, flexing my hands, voice barely above a whisper.

He didn't smile. Not really. But something flickered in those storm-dark eyes. "Yeah." His voice dropped to a near-growl. "Don't die."

I stilled.

Not at the words. At the way he said them.

Not as a threat. Not as protocol. As a warning. A plea wrapped in stone. Like some part of him meant it. Like some part of him couldn't stomach the thought of dragging my body out of the forest.

I swallowed hard. "I'll do my best."

He nodded once. That was all the softness he'd allow himself.

Then—without a word—he turned and strode toward the door, his coat snapping around his legs like a shadow.

"Wait—what? Now?"

He glanced back over his shoulder, unreadable gaze pinning me in place. "You said you can find the body, right?"

I opened my mouth. Closed it. Right. That was what I'd said.

He smirked.

The barest curve of a mouth that could be cruel or kind, depending on the day.

"Then let's go find ourselves a corpse."

15

I followed McDara out of the station, expecting him to lead me to the same soulless cruiser I'd already been cuffed and tossed into—twice. The kind of vehicle that reeked of cold authority and leftover fast food.

But he didn't head for the lineup of black and white regulation boxes.

The moment I stepped into he parking garage Phontine materialized. She was faded, a clear sign that she had chosen to appear invisible to everyone but me. She looked grim and glared at McDara with such force I was surprised lightening hadn't struck him down.

McDara veered left—toward the employee lot.

And stopped.

My steps faltered. Because parked in front of him was not a cop car.

It was a red vintage sports car—sleek, low to the ground, with curves that practically purred under the streetlights. The paint job gleamed like blood in moonlight.

I blinked. "You have got to be kidding me."

McDara didn't look at me, just opened the driver's side door with the ease of someone who didn't need to explain himself.

"What?"

I drifted closer, fingers skimming the hood. The car was smooth, cool, every inch of it humming with restrained power. I could feel the engine like a second heartbeat.

"This is so not what I expected from you."

He arched a brow, the barest hint of amusement ghosting across his features.

"Yeah? And what were you expecting?"

I circled to the passenger side, still slightly stunned. "I don't know…maybe a black SUV with muddy tires and emotional damage?" I motioned broadly at the car. "This? This is bold. Flashy. You're practically flirting with the road."

McDara sighed, the sound long-suffering but threaded with restraint. "Get in, Byrd."

I smirked as I dropped into the passenger seat, the leather creaking beneath me—worn, expensive, lived-in. The entire car smelled like him—leather, cedar, rain.

Danger in a tailored package.

"So…" I buckled in. "Midlife crisis?"

The engine purred to life with the smooth, throaty growl of something ancient and barely leashed.

He didn't glance at me. But the corner of his mouth twitched.

"First of all," he said as he backed out of the space, "I'm thirty-four. Not midlife. Not even close."

I grinned. "Right. *Early* midlife crisis. Got it."

McDara let out a quiet groan—equal parts irritation and amusement. But I saw it—the twitch at his jaw, the almost-smile. It was quick. Fleeting.

But real.

I leaned back, watching the city blur by as we drove—Old Town bleeding into New Town like ink into water.

Old Town pulsed with life—neon lights buzzing overhead, shopkeepers calling out last-chance discounts, the smell of roasted meat and diesel curling through the air. A Troll woman stirred something enormous in a cauldron the size of a kiddie pool. It caused a small crowd to gather, waving green money and calling out orders. A pack of Shifters laughed, beer bottles in hand. Vampires in streetwear slinked past, eyes gleaming like onyx.

It was loud. Messy. Gloriously alive.

It was the kind of place where things happened. Where secrets lived in the alleyways, and nobody walked in a straight line.

But the second we crossed that invisible line into New Town—

Everything changed.

The sound dimmed. The light cooled.

Buildings gleamed like teeth. Perfect. Polished. People moved in single-file lines like clockwork. No shouting. No music. Just the faint hum of magical wards and carefully manicured civility.

Only Mages and Fairies walked these streets—elegant, glittering creatures with sharp eyes and smoother smiles. Their conversations were quiet. Their footsteps barely audible. The power that rolled off them was like perfume—refined, intentional, suffocating.

Even the air smelled expensive.

Phontine shivered where she perched on my shoulder, then tucked herself into the edge of my hair like a child hiding from a thunderstorm.

I didn't blame her.

Something about New Town made my skin crawl—not because it was dangerous, but because it pretended it wasn't.

I shifted, suddenly aware of how loud my heart felt in my chest. Of how real I was in a place built on illusion.

McDara didn't speak.

He didn't have to.

His presence filled the silence like smoke. Heavy. Lingering.

And I couldn't help but wonder—was I heading toward answers?

Or deeper into something I wouldn't be able to crawl back out of?

As if sensing the nerves thrumming under my skin, McDara said, "You know your Pixie doesn't have to stay invisible."

Phontine, still nestled against my collarbone, tensed. Her claws curled tighter into the fabric of my jacket—not enough to pierce, but enough to make her point.

"I know," she murmured. But she didn't appear.

McDara didn't press. Just sighed through his nose and kept driving.

The motel loomed ahead like a bad memory waiting to repeat itself. He pulled into the lot and parked in front of my room, killing the engine in a quiet finality that made my stomach twist.

Everything looked the same.

Door closed. Blinds drawn. The flickering *VACANCY* sign casting tired, red light across the pavement.

Nothing out of place.

Except for the cold sinking into my gut like a warning.

McDara stepped out first, moving like a man with ghosts of his own. He reached the door before me and gestured—*After you.*

So gallant.

I rolled my eyes but said nothing, pushing the door open like it might bite. The air inside hit me like a memory made physical—thick, heavy, wrong. The kind of stillness that wasn't silence but a held breath.

Nothing moved. Nothing stirred.

But I could feel it.

The motel room remembered everything. My panic. My tears. The phantom of Death's touch, still smoldering like a brand at the base of my throat.

"Um..." I cleared my throat. "Hello? Ghost?"

My voice sounded thin, stupid in the too-quiet room.

I turned slowly in place, eyes sweeping across the familiar shadows. It should've been here. It had haunted me relentlessly, trailing me like smoke, shattering glass, whispering fury in frostbite and silence.

But now? Nothing.

I took a shaky breath and braced myself. "I need a minute," I said over my shoulder, forcing the words to come out even. "Maybe it'll come if I'm alone."

McDara didn't move. His arms were crossed, his expression stone. "Not a chance."

Right. Rules. No wandering off. No solo ghost whispering. No dying.

I closed my eyes anyway, searching for that strange place inside me that felt too open lately. The space where the veil was thin. Where things came through.

"I'm sorry," I whispered to the room. To the air. To the space between worlds. "I shouldn't have said what I did. I was scared. I am scared. But I'm trying. I'm trying to help you."

The words echoed softly—and then were swallowed by stillness.

Until the temperature dropped.

A breath. A bite. A bloom of frost across my skin.

Behind me, McDara swore under his breath at the drop of temperature. "Rutting Woods."

I opened my eyes.

She stood less than a foot away—closer than before.

The ghost.

Eyes sunken and sorrowful. Black tears streaking like wax down pale, broken skin. Her mouth didn't move. But she looked at me like she heard me. Like she understood.

The silence stretched, taut as wire.

Then—without sound, without fanfare—she turned.

And vanished.

I spun, heart pounding, only to find her again.

Outside. Standing at the edge of the forest. Waiting.

My mouth went dry. Relief tangled with dread in my gut, both clawing for dominance. She wanted us to follow. And this time, I wouldn't have to go alone.

"You're pressed so tight against that window it looks like you're about to jump through." McDara cursed again, dragging a hand down his jaw. "Guess we're going for a walk."

I looked at him, the corner of my mouth twitching into something that could almost be called a smile. "Hope you wore your hiking boots."

His only answer was a glare—and the click of his gun being holstered.

We left the motel and walked to the edge of the forest in silence. Holding our breaths, we stepped into the dark.

The forest swallowed us the moment we crossed the tree line.

Behind us, the city's glow vanished—devoured by the dense canopy above, like the trees were desperate to cut us off from the world we knew. Shadows clung to everything, stretching long and sharp between the trunks, flickering like they might peel away from the bark and become something else entirely. The scent of pine and loam filled the air—rich, wild, damp. Alive.

And laced with something colder. Something watching.

The only light came from the ghost ahead of us. Not that McDara could see her. I would be his only guide.

She glowed faintly—less a person, more a will-o'-the-wisp in a tattered striped shirt. Her pale luminescence painted the underbrush in washed-out hues, casting just enough light to show the way forward. A flickering flame guiding us deeper into the unknown.

Each step I took felt like trespassing.

Behind me, McDara's footfalls were deliberate, even. A steady rhythm that pulsed against the ragged beat of my heart. He didn't speak. Didn't ask if I was okay. He just watched. Measured. Studied. Like I was a live wire he didn't quite know how to disarm.

Phontine's tiny fingers curled into my jacket collar like she was expecting something to lunge from the dark.

She turned, very slowly, and looked at McDara.

It wasn't a casual glance.

It was the kind of stare that could curdle milk and set fire to curses mid-spell.

McDara didn't blink. His gaze flicked to her—calm, unflinching—then back to the path ahead. "Am I supposed to feel threatened?"

Phontine's wings snapped behind her, crisp as a blade. "That depends. Have you wronged her?"

He exhaled through his nose, like he wasn't sure if he found that funny or exhausting. "No."

Phontine narrowed her periwinkle eyes at him. "You *arrested* her."

The tension between them crackled like a storm building in a bottle. And somehow, it made me want to laugh. Because yes—this was my life now. A murder charge, a judgmental Pixie, and a detective who looked like sin in boots and had the patience of a coiled predator.

Phontine didn't let up. She stared at him like she was trying to decide which internal organ would hurt the most to hex.

McDara arched a brow. "You're looking at me like I'm dinner. And not in a fun way."

A startled laugh slipped from me. Sharp, unguarded. "Fun way? That's what you're going with?"

"Depends on who's doing the eating," he said, dry as bone dust. That ghost of a smirk haunted the edge of his mouth again—dangerous and impossible to ignore.

Phontine sniffed, thoroughly unimpressed. "You are not funny. You are not trustworthy. And I do not like your face."

"I don't think you're winning her over," I added.

McDara gave me a sidelong look. "Yeah, I got that from the death glare."

Phontine huffed and disappeared back into my collar like a dagger sliding into its sheath, muttering something about "dull humans and their oversized egos."

The absurdity of it all—the murder investigation, the damn ghost, the cold crawl of the forest—softened under her indignation. Just a little.

But the moment was brief.

The deeper we walked, the tighter the woods seemed to close in. The air grew heavier, and the dirt beneath my boots started to feel...familiar. Too familiar.

I knew this place. This stretch of forest. I'd been here.

The memory slammed into me like a punch. Blood. Soaked earth. The way the ghost had stared at me that night—desperate. Ruined.

And now here I was again. With a man who didn't trust me, and a Pixie who trusted no one, following a dead woman deeper into the dark.

McDara's voice broke the silence. "You okay?"

I almost said yes. Reflex.

But I swallowed the lie and gave a truth so quiet it barely made a sound. "Not even close."

He didn't answer. Just stepped a little closer.

Close enough that I could feel his presence brushing mine. Solid. Warm. Real in a way the rest of this world didn't feel anymore.

I didn't lean into it.

But I didn't pull away either.

And for now...that was enough. Because the forest was still watching. And the ghost was still waiting.

The trees loomed like sentinels—tall, skeletal things with gnarled limbs clawing toward a moonless sky. No wind. No sound. Just the low, pulsing hum of magic soaked into the soil and the too-long shadows writhing at the edge of my vision, as if the forest itself had teeth.

Every breath felt stolen. The air was thick, dense with the kind of energy that raised every hair on my body. Wrong. This place felt wrong.

Like we were walking into something ancient's mouth—and it was waiting to close.

McDara's voice came low, pitched to the hush the forest demanded. "You sure you're alright?"

I exhaled, trying to make the tremble in my lungs sound like sarcasm. "Oh, totally. Creepy woods, vengeful ghost, nightfall murder vibe? Living the dream."

His gaze flicked to me, unreadable in the dark—but I felt it. The weight of it. The way his attention lingered, not out of concern, but calculation.

Noticing. Cataloging.

It should've made me uncomfortable.

Instead, it made heat slide low in my stomach.

Phontine stirred on my shoulder, wings giving a nervous flutter. My eyes snapped forward.

The ghost had stopped.

She hovered ahead of us—no face, no voice, just a flicker of cold light pulsing like a heartbeat at the edge of a thick, tangled wall of trees. The forest darkened there, unnaturally dense. And beyond that?

A gaping black maw in the earth.

Not a cave.

A wound.

The mouth of something that had never known sunlight, carved out of the world by claw and shadow. The stone around it jutted in unnatural angles, like bone broken from the inside. Cold bled from it. A deep, bone-deep chill that whispered, *you are not welcome here.*

Every instinct in my body screamed to turn around.

And without thinking, I reached for McDara.

My hand found his arm—solid, warm, and so real it nearly buckled my knees.

For a second, I just...froze.

Because gods, the man was built like sin and stubbornness had teamed up and forged him by hand. Corded muscle coiled beneath his leather jacket, heat seeping through the worn fabric and into my skin like a shock.

I didn't mean to hold on. Didn't mean to lean just slightly into him. But I did.

And when I breathed in?

Leather. Rain. Smoke and cedar. And something deeper, something uniquely him—dark and grounding and steady in the storm.

My heartbeat kicked hard against my ribs, and for a single, traitorous second, I imagined what it would feel like to turn fully into him. Let him hold me there. Pretend I was safe. That *he* was safe.

I yanked my hand back like I'd touched fire.

McDara didn't move. He didn't tease or speak. Just watched me—still as the trees, sharp as the blade of a knife. But I saw the flare in his eyes. The tension that rolled through his frame. The way his jaw clenched, like he'd felt it too.

Like he'd wanted it just as much.

I cleared my throat, willing my voice not to shake. "Should we, uh...call for backup? Maybe before we walk into the setting of everyone's collective nightmares?"

McDara dragged his eyes from me to the ghost. She drifted just inside the cave now, a glowing specter swallowed by shadow.

"That where she wants us to go?"

I didn't want to answer. Didn't want to be the one who opened this door. But the ghost had chosen me. Again.

I nodded once, voice barely audible. "Yeah. She's waiting."

He looked back at me—and something shifted in that gaze. No longer the detective. No longer the man dragging me through a case he didn't want. There was something darker there now.

Protective.

Predatory.

Possessive.

Then he turned toward the cave and said, "Stay close."

And gods help me...

I wanted to.

"So, back up?"

McDara made a noise low in his throat—a sharp exhale that vibrated with disdain. The kind of sound a man made when he was too smart to say what he was really thinking but too annoyed to hide it.

"Having a Mage who can talk to ghosts help in a murder investigation," he said, tone flat and cold, "isn't exactly protocol."

I stopped walking.

Stopped breathing.

Just—froze.

Had he really just said that?

Like I was some delusional amateur fumbling through trauma. Like my magic—my existence—wasn't real enough to register on his polished, logic-drenched checklist of acceptable realities.

Heat surged through me.

Not the prickling edge of embarrassment. Not even the cold fire of fear that had been my constant shadow these past few days.

This was fury. White-hot and rising.

"I'm a Ghost Whisperer," I said, the words slicing clean through the air between us. "Not a theory. Not a myth. Not some unhinged girl in need of a psych eval. A. Real. Thing."

My voice echoed slightly, swallowed by the forest, but the power in it stayed, vibrating beneath my skin like static.

McDara turned.

His face—his whole damn body—was carved in restraint. Jaw tight. Eyes unreadable. Like he hadn't expected me to bite back and wasn't entirely sure what to do with it now that I had.

Something flickered across his face. Regret, maybe. Recognition. It was gone too fast to catch.

He exhaled through his nose, opened his mouth like he was about to say something— I didn't let him.

"No," I snapped, stepping into his space. "You don't get to roll your eyes and dismiss me like I'm some conspiracy theory in boots. You brought me here because you need me. So, if this has to be some off-the-books mess, then fine." I jabbed a finger toward his chest, my magic crackling under my skin like a live wire. "Call your partner. Loop him in. Or don't. But I'm not walking into that cave just so you can pretend I'm a liability instead of your best damn lead."

McDara stared at me.

Not blank. Not cold.

Just...watching.

And gods, it was maddening. Because his silence didn't feel like indifference.

It felt like tension.

It felt like the kind of quiet that builds before something breaks.

And I wanted to see what McDara looked like when his carefully crafted control *broke*.

Then—without a word—he pulled out his phone.

The glow of the screen painted the sharp lines of his face in white-blue light as his fingers moved in clipped, precise motions. A message sent. Nothing more.

But the way his jaw clenched, the tight grip of his hand around the phone—it said everything.

He was rattled.

And trying very hard not to be.

"Stay close," he said, the words low, gravel-edged. But there was something else layered beneath the command now. Not annoyance. Not obligation.

Concern.

Possession.

He hesitated just long enough for me to feel the weight of it.

And then he turned toward the cave.

The dark swallowed the ghost as she drifted ahead, her pale glow vanishing into the black like a candle dropped into a well.

I followed, my heart a drumbeat of rage and fear and something sharp that had his name tangled in it.

McDara held the cave entrance open with his body, waiting for me to pass. Not chivalrous. Just precise.

But when I moved past him, our arms brushed.

The contact was brief.

Too brief.

But it lit something under my skin. Heat. Real heat.

Not the ghost's cold. Not Death's fire.

His.

I didn't look at him. I couldn't.

Because if I did, I knew I'd see it reflected back.

That thing building between us.

That thing I wasn't ready for.

And then we stepped into the dark.

16

The darkness swallowed us like a tide.

Not just the absence of light—but something deeper. Heavier. A presence that pressed in from all sides, cold and clinging, like the cave had a heartbeat and it was pulsing against my skin.

I could barely breathe.

Each step deeper into the tunnel was like walking through molasses, my boots crunching on damp stone that felt too slick, too soft. The air turned wet and metallic, thick with a scent I couldn't name—something sharp and mineral, laced with rot.

It was wrong.

Every part of this place whispered that we shouldn't be here.

Behind me, McDara moved like a shadow—solid, unyielding. I could feel the weight of him at my back, every step deliberate, careful. He didn't speak. Didn't fill the silence with reassurance or bravado. Just moved beside me like he'd done this before—walked straight into something that reeked of death and dared it to touch him.

Then I heard it.

A low string of words, murmured under his breath—ancient, guttural, too fluid to be common—and then light.

White-blue flame unfurled in his palm like a breathing star, flickering just enough to cast jagged shadows along the walls.

The cave lit up in flashes.

The stone glistened with moisture. Stalactites hung like icicles from the ceiling, sharp and close. The walls themselves were clawed—long, deep gouges trailing through the rock like something had been trying to crawl its way out.

I swallowed hard.

McDara didn't react. He held the light steady, face unreadable. His magic didn't glide, didn't shimmer like the Mages back at the Black House. It struck. Clean and brutal. No flourishes. No theatrics. He spoke, and the magic bent. It was raw. Elemental.

Dangerous.

We moved in silence, deeper into the tunnels, the walls narrowing until the path began to spiral. The ghost drifted ahead, pale and flickering, casting just enough glow to guide us—but not enough to soothe the storm building in my chest.

The deeper we went, the worse it smelled.

It wasn't decay, not quite. It was something more unnatural—like the very air had been leeched of life, drained and left to stagnate. My stomach rolled. Phontine trembled against my collar, her tiny wings twitching with unease.

Then, the tunnel widened. Just ahead, the walls opened into a chamber.

And that's when we saw it.

A figure—cloaked, hunched—knelt in the center of the room, motionless except for the slow curl of their gloved hands over something sprawled beneath them.

Not something.

Someone.

The body was skeletal, twisted into an unnatural sprawl. Skin stretched over bones like parchment over kindling, mouth frozen in a silent scream. Eyes—if it had any—were sunken, blackened. Like the life had been scraped out one breath at a time.

My blood ran cold.

I recognized that look. I had seen that kind of death. On the ghost's face. On the inside of my eyelids when I woke gasping at night.

McDara reacted first.

His arm snapped up, his stance shifting. Gun drawn. Finger steady.

The light in his palm flared brighter, throwing the whole chamber into relief—and that's when the figure moved.

Its head snapped up like a beast scenting blood, the hood stiff, like magic held it in a vice grip.

And then—

That hooded head turned to me.

The air in the chamber thickened, turned electric. Like every atom in the space had caught fire but didn't know how to burn.

The figure froze, something twitching beneath its skin, like it recognized me.

My heart pounded. I didn't know why, but I could feel it—that whatever this thing was, it hadn't expected me.

Which meant whatever was about to happen...

Was personal.

McDara's voice cut through the tension, low and lethal. "Step away from the body."

The figure didn't move.

The ghost flared brighter—screaming without sound—and vanished through the cavern wall.

And then all hell broke loose.

The reaction was instant.

A guttural incantation ripped from the cloaked figure's throat—vile, spit-laced, ancient. The cavern erupted with light as green flames ignited, roaring across the space like a living inferno. It wasn't fire. It was corruption, pure and seething, magic warped and rotted, hunger in spell form.

And I knew it.

Not because of some Mage's sixth sense. Because of the way it felt.

Like the air had been infected. Like it was crawling down my spine, gnawing into the marrow of my bones.

Maleficaria.

The same kind of twisted magic that had killed the ghost...was now coming straight for me.

I didn't even scream. Didn't have time. My body froze, instinctively throwing my arms up, useless as they were.

Then—McDara moved.

He stepped in front of me like a damn wall of steel, his hand carving the air in a jagged, brutal motion. No hesitation. No chant. Just command.

A shield ignited between us—a wall of iridescent light, pulsing like a living thing. The green fire collided with it in a violent crash, an explosion of energy that tore through the cave like a thunderclap. The air shattered. Dust rained down. My ears rang as I stumbled back, slamming into the jagged rock behind me, breath knocked from my lungs.

Phontine screamed and vanished into my collar, trembling so hard I could feel it in my bones.

McDara didn't budge.

His feet were braced, eyes locked on the enemy like he was already calculating how to destroy them.

He threw another spell—this one fast, hard, brutal. A bolt of raw energy, pure white-blue, spiraled from his palm and struck toward the cloaked figure like lightning with purpose.

They moved.

Too fast. Inhuman.

The blast hit stone, exploding into shards of rock and blinding light.

The figure lunged to the side, their cloak a smear of shadow as they flung more dark magic, not flames this time but tendrils—writhing, venomous coils of black smoke. They hit McDara's shield again, and the surface cracked.

A splintered, spiderwebbed shatter of light. Too thin. Too weak.

He couldn't hold it forever.

McDara snarled something under his breath, low and furious. A different spell, something harsher. I couldn't catch the words—but I felt it when he slammed his boot into the cavern floor.

The entire earth answered.

With a tremor that shook the cave to its bones, the ground erupted beneath the cloaked figure—jagged spears of molten energy shooting upward like roots forged from lightning and rage. The shockwave nearly knocked me off my feet.

But the figure wasn't caught.

They twisted again, too fast, ducking under the arcing blast, one gloved hand snapping up. The magic that gathered then was wrong. Not flashy. Not wild. It was focused. Surgical. Old.

My heart stuttered.

Whatever that spell was—it wasn't meant for McDara.

It was meant for me.

I felt it like a noose tightening around my throat, like claws digging into the base of my spine. Something ancient and vile clawed toward me, and I knew in the pit of my soul—it would rip me apart.

McDara felt it, too.

His stance shifted, wide and defensive. Magic surged around him, cracking against the stone, lighting the walls with violent bursts. His hand flared with runes, his voice cutting like thunder.

"Sonia—move!"

I didn't need to be told twice.

My body obeyed before my brain could, launching sideways just as the spell cracked toward where I'd stood—carving through the air with a sound like screaming steel.

I hit the ground hard. Pain spiked through my shoulder, dirt and blood in my mouth.

But I was alive.

And the fight was only beginning.

McDara moved in a blur, both hands slamming into the space between us and the oncoming magic. The shield erupted again, brighter this time—angrier. The barrier quaked under the force of the dark spell, light cracking along its edges like lightning caught in glass.

A single bead of sweat slid down the sharp line of McDara's temple.

And for the first time, I saw it.

Not fear.

But doubt.

"McDara—" I gasped, voice raw.

"I've got it," he snapped, his teeth clenched so hard I could see the tension vibrating through his jaw.

The cloaked figure raised a skeletal hand—the glove couldn't hide that its body was wasting away—and the air fractured around it. Shadows deepened unnaturally, swallowing the light, pulling at the cavern like it wanted to collapse reality itself.

McDara's magic flared.

His lips parted, and the air around us shuddered.

"No," he growled, voice low and violent. "You don't."

He twisted his hands sharply.

The shield didn't just hold—it imploded. Condensing inward like it had weight, power, mass—and then it detonated, blasting outward in a rippling shockwave of pure, blistering force.

The cloaked figure flew back, slammed into the cavern wall with bone-jarring violence.

We hit the ground hard. I felt the sting of stone through my jeans, the cut of air in my throat as I scrambled upright.

McDara was already up. Already moving.

He surged forward like a weapon unleashed—shoulders squared, magic crackling at his fingertips, ready to end this.

But then—The figure whispered something.

The shadows responded.

Darkness twisted, collapsed inward—and swallowed the cloaked figure whole.

Gone.

Like they'd never been there at all.

My pulse echoed like war drums inside my skull. I couldn't move. Couldn't breathe. The silence that followed was unnatural, thick with the residue of magic and the weight of what we'd just witnessed.

Drip.

Drip.

Water echoed from somewhere deep in the cave.

The ghost was gone.

So was the enemy.

But the body remained.

McDara lowered his hands slowly, as if expecting another attack. His frame vibrated with tension, shoulders still coiled tight. Not fear. Not exhaustion.

Readiness.

He turned toward me, and when our eyes locked, I saw everything he wasn't saying—fury, adrenaline, questions he wasn't ready to ask.

"Tell me," he said, voice tight, dark with disbelief, "that you just saw that."

I swallowed hard. "Oh, I saw it."

And gods, I wished I hadn't.

McDara crouched beside the body, careful, precise—but I saw the way his hands shook as he reached out. Just barely. Just for a second. He masked it well, but not from me.

Phontine clung to my shoulder, her wings twitching so fast I could feel the wind off them.

I didn't look at her.

I couldn't stop staring at the body.

The woman.

She wasn't just dead. She was emptied. Her limbs twisted in unnatural angles, her face hollow, skin drawn so tight she barely looked human anymore. Magic clung to her in flickering ribbons—dark magic—like a sickness too stubborn to die.

A wound carved through her abdomen. Deep. Intentional.

It hadn't been a fast death.

It had been ritual.

My throat closed.

McDara exhaled—low, almost reverent—and lifted his hands. Then he spoke.

Not a spell. Not a chant.

A sentence. A command in a language I didn't know but felt in my blood.

The air around us tightened. Vibrated. The cave itself responded like a living thing, groaning with power.

Light sparked from McDara's hands—bright and burning. The tendrils of dark magic recoiled like they were screaming, writhing before snapping away from the corpse one by one, curling into ash midair.

Gone.

The silence left behind felt haunted.

McDara flexed his fingers once, then brushed them together like he was scraping something off—like the magic left a taste.

I stared. "Did you just—did you remove the dark magic?"

Before he could answer, the cave answered for him.

The temperature plummeted.

The walls groaned.

And from the far corner of the cavern, something watched.

The cold hit me first. Not the kind that pricks at your skin, not the kind that makes you shiver. This was the kind that dug in. That reached past muscle and bone and tore into the soul. I staggered as the breath left my lungs in one ragged, ice-laced gust—and then I saw her.

The ghost.

No longer hollow. No longer screaming behind eyeless sorrow.

She stood at the mouth of the cave, her features softened into something whole, radiant even. For the first time since she'd started haunting me, she looked...free. Her gaze found mine—and she smiled.

That fragile, aching smile hit harder than any spell. Not warmth exactly, but something like it spread through me. A release. She was thanking me.

Then—she vanished. A blink of pale light and she was gone. Was she...did this mean she had moved on? A tightness in my gut kept me unsure.

I exhaled, slow and shaky, shoulders sagging as the chill seeped from the air.

McDara stood nearby, brushing dust from his fingers, the low flare of his magic still dancing faintly beneath his skin. When he turned, his eyes were unreadable—dark, steady, simmering with something more than just residual adrenaline.

And then he said it.

"Why was that cloaked Mage trying to kill you?"

The question landed like a blade to the chest.

I straightened instinctively. "Excuse me?"

His tone didn't shift. Controlled. Crisp. Dangerous. He stepped toward me, every inch of his presence like a wall bearing down.

"That Mage didn't try to flee. It didn't hesitate to attack. Not you and me—you." His voice dropped. "I was just in the way."

I blinked. "You're serious?"

McDara's arms crossed over his chest, the stretch of his jacket pulling tight over his broad frame. His gaze locked on mine, unyielding. "That wasn't random. It was an execution."

And something in me snapped.

"Why do you think I know that?" My voice cracked the air, sharp as the echo of gunfire. "Do you think I've got a list somewhere? That I just keep a cute little journal labeled People Who Want Me Dead?"

I threw my arms out, gesturing to the cave, to the rotting stench of what we'd just survived. "Because this?" I bit out. "This is not normal! I didn't ask for this! I didn't summon a ghost or ask a murderous Mage to show up and ruin my week!"

McDara didn't flinch. Of course he didn't.

He just stared at me, the tight line of his jaw giving nothing away. "I think someone wants you dead," he said evenly. As if it were a statement of weather. As if it were just true.

"Oh." I laughed. Barked it. Ugly and unhinged. "You think that, huh? Should I make you a gold star?"

"Sonia—"

"Maybe I'll stitch it on the sleeve of my jacket. Right next to *Fell into the Deathscape Like an Idiot and Can't Control Her Magic to Save Her Life*." The breath he took was slow—calculated. But it was too late. My mouth kept going, even as my mind screamed at me to shut up.

"Hell, maybe I should get it tattooed. Right over my heart. Just so the next Mage who tries to kill me doesn't have to dig too hard to find a target."

McDara's head tilted. "Wait. Fell into the Deathscape?"

Shit. The words hung between us, loud and jagged.

I turned away before I could see his face. "Just another thing for you to arrest me for."

"Sonia—"

"Well?"

"My job is to solve murders," McDara's voice was hard and his body too warm next to mine. "I'll leave the Mage Council to police their rules themselves." A beat. "Unless, it becomes connected to the case."

I looked at him, at the dark intensity of those eyes and the grim line of his lips. I didn't know what to say. My frantic thoughts were quickly becoming to jumbled to sift through.

Phontine—bless her—zipped off my shoulder with a flare of magic, tossing a glare over her shoulder at McDara before conjuring several soft orbs of lavender light. They hovered between us, illuminating the blood-streaked walls, the twisted shadows.

I turned on my heel.

And walked.

"Sonia," McDara growled, a warning buried under my name.

I didn't stop.

I didn't care.

Let him glare. Let him dissect me with those cold, cutting eyes. Let him throw his rules and his suspicions around like they were gospel. Because right now?

I needed to get out before the cracks inside me turned into something worse.

Before I said something I couldn't take back.

Before I begged him to touch me again—and lie to me with the warmth of his hands. Tell me I'd be okay.

When we both knew I wasn't.

The cave pulsed around me, alive with shadows and cold. Every step I took crunched over gravel-like bones, and I could still hear McDara's voice echoing behind me—low, clipped, sharp with command. Probably barking orders into his phone like nothing had just tried to kill us.

How did he even have reception down here?

I didn't care. Magic, probably. Whatever.

I just needed space. I needed to be away from him and his questions and that look in his eyes like he was about to take me apart piece by piece.

I was halfway through a furious thought about how I could find my own damn way back when it happened.

The laugh.

It wasn't McDara.

It wasn't human.

It slid through the air like smoke, like silk over bare skin. It wasn't loud—it didn't need to be. It sank its claws into my chest, curled itself behind my ribs, and waited.

My throat burned. The mark—*his* mark—flared to life, a searing brand across my skin.

No.

Not here. Not now.

But before I could even breathe, he was there.

He stepped out of the shadows like they belonged to him. Maybe they did.

Long black coat flowing behind him, silver hair catching the cave's faint light like spun frost, and those eyes—those deep, endless eyes—fixed on me like I'd just wandered into his cage. Or maybe he'd wandered into mine.

My breath caught. My body locked. Seeing him again was like falling off a cliff I hadn't realized I was standing on. My skin remembered his touch. My blood remembered the burn. My heart remembered the danger—and how close I'd come to wanting it.

He was beautiful in that wrong kind of way, the kind that made your instincts scream *run* even as your feet stayed planted.

Behind me, McDara's voice echoed through the tunnel.

"Byrd!"

I didn't answer. Couldn't.

"Sonia!"

That made Death smile—just the barest twitch of his lips. Like he enjoyed hearing my name.

Then he leaned in.

Slow. Measured. Inevitable.

I didn't move. I couldn't move. My body had gone still in that way prey did when a predator stepped close.

His scent wrapped around me—cold rain, spice, something menacing and impossible. Something not of this world.

"What are you doing," he murmured, voice like velvet over broken glass, "running in dark caves, Little Bird?"

Little Bird.

The nickname hit hard. Too hard.

It curled into my spine and shivered there.

I clenched my fists, fighting to breathe like a person again. "You shouldn't be here," I said. Or tried to. It came out low, too rough.

He tilted his head like I was amusing, or disappointing, or both. "Neither should you. But you came anyway."

I forced steel into my spine. "Why are you in the Living Lands?"

His smile deepened. Slow. Dark. Like something blooming in poison.

"I didn't come looking, Sonia." He said my name like a possession. "I didn't need to."

My throat tightened.

Then his hand lifted—not touching, just there, hovering inches from the place where the mark still burned like a phantom brand.

"You're bound to me."

The world tilted.

The cave, the body, McDara's voice—they all blurred into static. Everything shrank down to him, to those words, to the horrible, beautiful finality in his voice.

Bound.

"No," I breathed. "You're lying."

His smile turned razor sharp. "I don't have to lie. You felt it, didn't you? When I touched you."

I had.

Gods, I had.

And now it made sense. The ghost's death—the way her magic was ripped apart. The cloaked Mage. The way the dark magic had come straight for me, like it already knew exactly who it was looking for. It wasn't random. None of it was. This wasn't just something I walked into.

This wasn't over.

This was only just beginning. And Death?

Death had plans.

17

McDara's voice cracked through the cave again—low, gritted, and laced with something sharp beneath the surface.

"Byrd!"

The sound scraped against my spine like a blade. Not just commanding. Not just irritated.

Worried.

I turned to run. I had to. Away from the noise, the questions, the too-intense stare of a man who kept trying to crack me open like I was some riddle he was owed the answer to.

But Death was already there.

He moved like the dark itself—never quite walking, never quite still. His body eclipsed the path before me, shadow-wreathed and patient, like he'd been waiting for this moment to unfold exactly as it had. The way his gaze pinned me, the way his presence pressed into the space around me—it was a touch without contact, a weight I couldn't shake.

"Do you need an escape from your detective?" he murmured, voice soft as smoke, silk wrapped around something jagged. It wasn't a question, not really. More like a challenge wrapped in velvet. His lips curled slightly, his tone laced with a dark delight that made my skin prickle. "You look like a girl dying to be free."

"He's not my detective," I snapped.

Too sharp. Too fast.

But I couldn't take it back.

My pulse roared in my ears, thrumming high and wild, as if my body knew what my brain refused to admit—that I was standing on the knife's edge of something irreversible.

Death smiled wider.

Like he tasted the panic on my breath.

He moved again, slower this time, a subtle shift that made the shadows bend unnaturally. His hand lifted, a single finger pointing to a side tunnel cloaked in pitch. No light. No sound. Just a gaping corridor into deeper dark.

"I can show you the way out," he said smoothly. "For a price."

I tensed. "I'm not paying you anything."

The words snapped like ice in the air.

And yet—he didn't strike. Didn't vanish me into some cruel realm. He simply tilted his head, eyes narrowing like I'd just said something particularly fascinating. The pressure in the room changed, coiling tighter. Thicker. Every atom in my body screamed to run, and still I stood there, caught in his gravity.

"Are you certain, Little Bird?" he murmured.

That name again. Little Bird.

It should've sounded condescending. Mocking. But it didn't. It felt personal. Like a tether pulling taut.

"Everything," he said, stepping infinitesimally closer, "has a price. Even freedom."

Behind me, the echo of boots—McDara, close now, his presence a different kind of weight. Grounded. Steady. Real.

And yet—I looked into the eyes of Death and didn't blink.

"Show me," I said, breath shallow. "Show me the way out."

A pause. And then—

That smile.

The kind that said, *You'll regret this, but I'll enjoy watching it happen.*

He gestured again. And this time, the motion left a tear in the air, like his hand had sliced through the edge of this world. Beyond that invisible line, only shadows waited.

I ran.

My boots slipped on the uneven stone, gravel crunching beneath each frantic step. The tunnel swallowed me whole. Behind me, I felt him watching—always watching.

Phontine clung tighter to my jacket, her tiny voice vibrating against my ear. "This is a mistake."

I didn't respond.

I couldn't.

Because part of me—the terrified, rational part—agreed with her.

But the other part, the deeper, darker part of me that had touched the Deathscape and lived to tell the tale?

It wasn't so sure.

The tunnel twisted, and I ran harder.

The air pressed down, thick and bruising, like it was trying to claw its way into my lungs. Every breath came ragged. My ribs burned. My heart thundered a war drum beat against my chest, drowning out everything—McDara's voice, my own frantic thoughts, the world behind me.

All I could hear was out.

Out. Out. Out.

And then—

The world broke.

The ground beneath me wasn't stone anymore. My boots slammed onto cracked pavement. The damp cave air was gone, replaced by the sharp, acrid bite of exhaust and rain-slick concrete. The shadows around me shifted from natural black to neon-stained grime.

I stumbled forward, crashing to my knees, skin scraping raw on the rough street. Pain flared, hot and sharp, but it grounded me.

Phontine shrieked, wings buzzing in frantic, chaotic bursts as she tumbled free from my collar.

I lifted my head, lungs heaving. The city pressed around me—Old Town, but not the version I knew. This wasn't the cozy chaos of Trolls cooking street food or Shifters laughing outside pubs. No. This was something else. Hollow. Predatory. Watching.

The cave behind me? Gone.

Just a stretch of dark alley, flickering signs, and the electric hum of a city that never really slept—just shifted into something hungrier at night.

"Sonia?" Phontine's voice trembled, thin and sharp. She darted beside me, a flickering blur of lavender light. "What just—how did we—?"

I didn't answer. I couldn't. My pulse was still lagging behind the fact that I'd somehow been ripped from one part of the world and thrown into another.

No. Not somehow.

Him.

Death.

He'd twisted the world around me, like it was a thread he could pull. And he'd dropped me here. Out of the cave. Out of reach of McDara. It had to have been Death.

But not for free.

And I had no idea what it had cost me.

A prickle worked its way up my spine.

Something was wrong.

Deeply wrong.

The street should've been alive at this hour. The taverns. The music. The chatter.

Instead, it was empty.

Too empty.

Until it wasn't.

Three figures emerged from the far end of the alley, moving with a grace that didn't belong to mortals. Too smooth. Too precise. Their eyes caught the light—red flash. Predator's glint.

Vampires.

I didn't flinch. Didn't freeze. But my hand was already gripping my phone, fingers shaking as I pulled up the map of Blakewell.

No sudden moves.

No worry. No panic.

They could smell both.

I kept my head down, footsteps even, and pretended I didn't feel them watching. Pretended they weren't enjoying the way my heartbeat echoed too loud in the alley.

"Hey, sweetheart," one called, his voice rich velvet slinking across the pavement. "You look a little...lost."

The second one laughed, low and amused. "Want a guide?"

Nope. No, thank you. Not in the mood to be drained dry tonight.

I didn't answer. I didn't look.

I just walked faster.

Not running. Never running.

Running meant weakness.

Running made you prey.

The silence stretched long behind me. Then—

A shift.

Not sound. Not movement.

Just pressure.

Like the air warped. Like the shadows changed their mind.

A presence bloomed at my side—effortless, seamless.

He didn't step out of the shadows.

He *was* the shadows.

I didn't have to look.

I *knew*.

Death.

His presence slid against mine like silk over bare skin, cool and ancient and too familiar. I didn't breathe. Couldn't. Because if I did, I might inhale the scent of him again—night rain, smoke, and something more.

Something not of this world.

And when I finally looked—

He was already watching me.

No words. Just that smile.

Like he'd never left me at all.

Like he was only ever a step behind.

Like I'd just walked into his waiting hands.

Again.

His presence devoured the air.

Not just the warmth—everything. Sound. Motion. Thought.

The Vampires, bold just seconds before, fell into silence so complete it felt unnatural. They didn't retreat so much as dissolve, their confidence curling into the shadows like ash in wind. Death didn't speak. Didn't move.

He didn't need to.

He *was* the answer to every unspoken threat, the quiet at the end of all things. And from the sudden wariness on the Vampires faces they noticed. They might not have been able to see Death but they felt the wrongness, the danger that had just sprouted around me.

My pulse thundered in my ears, deafening. I forced my voice to work. "Why'd you make the tunnel spit me out here?"

He turned.

Slow. Effortless.

His eyes locked on mine—bottomless, silver-lit voids filled with truths no mortal mind should ever see. There was no emotion on his face. Just stillness. As if the concept of urgency had never applied to him.

His head tilted.

I stared him down anyway. I had to.

One breath. Then another.

I wasn't going to let him shake me. Not more than he already had. Not when I still didn't know what kind of game I was caught in—or if I was already checkmated.

The bus stop sat at the corner of the next block, tucked under a flickering streetlamp like a forgotten thought. Faded bench. Cracked glass. A map so weathered it may as well have been a relic.

I dug into my bag, fingers fumbling through receipts and cards and—

No cash.

Of course.

The bus required exact change. Not enchantments. Not whispered apologies to ancient powers. Just cold, mortal cash.

I let out a low groan. "Great."

No answer.

I turned—already braced for some smug response—but he was gone.

A tight, broken sound slipped from my throat—half growl, half whimper.

I was so tired.

Tired of ghosts. Of monsters. Of magic. Of the unrelenting weight of being hunted by things I couldn't name.

Phontine huddled closer to my collar, silent for once. Her wings barely stirred the air. I was grateful. Words would've shattered me.

I walked.

The city changed around me with every step, like slipping between pages in a book someone else was writing. The grit and neon of Old Town bled into the eerie perfection of New Town, seamless and jarring all at once.

No boundary. No sign. Just otherness.

Too clean. Too quiet.

The kind of quiet that didn't mean peace.

It meant control.

"Almost there," I whispered, mostly for myself. Phontine didn't answer. She just tucked her head deeper beneath my hair.

The stretch of road between New Town and the motel was a dead man's bridge—suspended between two lives. On one end: Sterile glass, lifeless order. On the other: Cracked stone, reckless magic, chaos.

And me.

Stuck in the middle.

My thoughts spiraled, looping back to the cave, the corpse, Death's handprint still burning on my throat. I half expected him to step out of the shadows again, to say something devastating in that voice like midnight and funeral smoke. Maybe he already had. Maybe he was still watching.

Maybe he was always watching.

But it wasn't Death who appeared next.

It was light.

A sharp glare split the night.

Headlights.

The low, smooth purr of an engine pulled me back into my body. Tires slowed. Stopped. A door swung open with surgical precision.

Red.

Vintage.

McDara.

His silhouette cut through the light like a blade—broad shouldered, coat swinging, tension radiating from him in slow, measured waves.

No words. Not yet.

Just the sound of the engine ticking as it cooled.

And the sharp, echoing thud of my heartbeat as I realized I had no idea what version of him was about to step into the night.

The detective?

The Mage?

The man who had dragged me out to a cave, touched my face like it mattered, and looked at me like I was unraveling something inside him?

Or the man who still thought I might be a killer?

"Just keep walking," Phontine huffed. "He deserves to chase you if he wants to talk."

So, my legs kept moving. Step after step. Hollow. Mechanical. If I just kept walking, he'd get the message.

Leave me alone.

I couldn't do another round of questions. Of accusations. Of him.

But of course, McDara only needed three strides to catch up. His hand closed around my arm—firm, not rough—and I froze.

Heat bloomed where his fingers touched me. Sharp. Immediate. Overwhelming.

I hated that.

"Byrd." His voice was low, frayed at the edges. The nickname landed like a tether, soft and heavy around my throat. "Please. Just...stop."

Please.

That one word almost unraveled me. Almost.

I didn't look at him. My jaw locked tight. "If you're here to cuff me again, save it. I'm fresh out of murder scenes to get framed for."

His hand dropped.

I heard the breath he dragged in, saw the way his fingers scraped through his hair, leaving it a mess of dark waves. The kind of mess you only get from frustration—or regret.

When he looked at me, something in him cracked open.

"I don't think you did it." The words landed like a blow. Heavy. Raw. A confession more than a declaration.

"The murder," he clarified, quieter now. "I don't think you're involved."

My heart twisted, caught between disbelief and something sharp edged I didn't want to name. "Great. Should I frame that? Maybe put it on my résumé?"

He almost smiled. Just barely. But it vanished as fast as it came.

"I mean it, Sonia. I...I messed up. You didn't deserve that." His voice caught at the edges. Uneven. Like it wasn't used to carrying the weight of guilt.

For a second, I didn't know what to do with that—this version of him. Not the cop. Not the interrogator. Just...a man trying to undo something that couldn't be undone.

Then he stepped closer.

The heat of him curled into the cold around me, driving it back inch by inch.

"But you are involved." He wasn't accusing this time. He was…unraveling. "Somehow. Maybe you don't know how. Maybe it's not your fault. But there's a connection. I need to find it."

His eyes burned into mine. "And I need your help."

I wanted to stay angry. I wanted the fury. It had kept me warm this long.

But something deeper cracked in me.

Because beneath the anger, beneath the exhaustion, was that same feeling I'd carried since this all started.

Alone.

And I was so tired of walking into the dark with no one beside me.

I inhaled. The night air was sharp as glass in my lungs. "What happens if I say I'm done?"

McDara's expression shifted.

Not pity. He was too careful for that.

Understanding.

"Then I keep looking," he said. "But I'd rather do it with you. Not against you."

His words pressed in like a second heartbeat, filling the space between us.

For once, he wasn't trying to play detective. He was just…asking me to stay.

The silence between us was fragile. Unspoken things crackled inside it.

I let out a long, slow breath. "Fine. But I'm not promising anything."

Something in his posture eased, just a little. Relief flickered in his eyes like the first light after a long night.

He nodded toward the car. "Come on. You need food. And I'm guessing you've had enough of this road for one night."

I didn't move right away.

It wasn't the offer that made me hesitate. It was the look in his eyes.

Not suspicion. Not calculation.

Recognition.

Like he saw me—not the Ghost Whisperer, not the girl with a curse, not the maybe-suspect.

Me.

And gods help me, that look made something in me unravel.

Still, my limbs were heavy. Exhaustion coiled tight around my spine. I needed warmth. I needed food. And maybe, just maybe, I needed to not be alone tonight.

"Alright," I said, the word barely more than a whisper. "Lead the way."

18

McDara opened the passenger door without a word. I slid in, the cold leather biting against my skin, but the car's warmth—already humming from the vents—was a quiet balm. He climbed in beside me, the engine rumbling to life like a low growl. Shadows danced across his face as streetlight spilled through the windshield.

I turned toward the window, forehead against the glass. The strip of road between New Town and the motel darkening with every minute we headed away from that shining glass prison.

McDara didn't speak. No clipped questions. No tension-laced accusations. Just silence. Solid. Steady. The kind that stretched and curled between two people who didn't know what to say—but somehow knew speaking would break something.

So I let myself unravel.

Just a little.

I let my shoulders sag, my spine uncoil. The chaos in my head was a storm I couldn't hold back anymore. And if he noticed me unraveling in the passenger seat, McDara didn't mention it.

The diner's neon sign buzzed ahead—rosy, pink, bleeding into the misty night, flickering like a heartbeat. I followed him inside, the door's chime cutting through the stillness like a blade.

The booth creaked beneath us as we sank into the cracked red vinyl. The smell of fried food and burnt coffee hit me like a memory I couldn't place, warm and grounding in a way that made my throat ache. My fingers curled tighter around the edges of my jacket.

McDara handed the waitress his menu without glancing at it. "Black coffee. Full breakfast. Extra bacon." A beat. Then his eyes flicked to me. "You?"

My stomach twisted. I wasn't hungry. I was still half stuck in that cave, in the shadows, in *him*—but McDara raised a brow like he wasn't going to let me get away with skipping a meal.

"Pancakes," I muttered. "And hot chocolate."

He nodded once. "It's on me."

I didn't argue. Couldn't. The warmth curling from the kitchen was too much, too tempting. And free pancakes were still free pancakes.

Once the waitress left, McDara leaned back—but not relaxed. Never relaxed. His body was all tension and unreadable edges, like he was wired too tightly and didn't know how to unwind without snapping.

"They recovered the woman's body," he said finally, his voice low and gravel lined. "Forensics is in the cave now."

I didn't respond. Just stared at my reflection in the silver napkin holder. The warped metal made my face look like it was melting. I felt like that. Like someone had lit a match inside my chest and left it burning.

McDara leaned forward, forearms braced on the table. "How'd you make it out of the cave, Sonia?"

My head snapped up. His tone was soft, but the question had weight. Heavy and sharp.

My spine straightened. "What, you think I used dark magic? Or sprouted wings?"

His sigh wasn't annoyed—it was tired. "No. I'm not accusing you. I just..." He paused. His eyes, dark and storm-wrecked, met mine. "I thought you were still in there. I heard you—and then you were gone."

It hit different, hearing it like that. Not detective-speak. Not suspicion. Just—concern. Real.

But I couldn't tell him the truth. That it had been Death who plucked me from the darkness and spit me back out into Old Town like a discarded coin. How else could it have happened? So, I lied. Told a version of the truth, anyway.

"One of the tunnels had a portal, I guess," I said, shrugging like it was no big deal. "Dumped me in some alley in Old Town."

His jaw locked. "Where in Old Town?"

I rubbed my forehead. "Vampire district. Lots of alleyways. Shadows. A few leeches tried following me, but they got the message."

The air shifted.

McDara's gaze sharpened. "Are you okay?"

"I'm fine."

His eyes said he didn't believe me, but he let it go.

"That must be why it took you so long to get back near the motel," he said after a beat. "I've been driving around looking for you."

I blinked. The words weren't dramatic. Just quiet. Honest. But they stole the breath right out of my lungs.

He'd been looking.

Not because he had to. Because he wanted to.

Something cracked open in my chest. Just a little.

I didn't know what I was to him. A suspect? A Mage with a curse? A headache? But maybe, just maybe, I was also something else.

The silence thickened, heavy with things neither of us knew how to say. The waitress returned with plates and mugs and steam and syrup—and the moment burst like a bubble.

But under it all, something lingered.

Not spoken. Not acknowledged.

Just there.

Waiting.

The sun dragged low across the sky, bleeding gold across the rooftops of the Mage neighborhood. Shadows spilled long over manicured lawns, stretching like fingers across pavement that was too clean, too perfect.

Each step I took sent another jolt of pain up my spine. My legs were lead. My back ached. My brain? A knot of static and questions I couldn't shake. I was two seconds from screaming just to hear something real.

Maybe that would summon him—Death had a habit of appearing when I was about to fall apart.

Phontine shifted against my collar, her wings a faint whisper on my skin. "Are you sure about this, Sonia?" Her voice, soft and worried, cut through the thick afternoon air. "You passed out for like, maybe, three hours. You look like you might drop dead—uh, again."

"Appreciate the vote of confidence," I muttered. "But yeah. I'm sure. I need to figure out how to control this...thing inside me. I can't just fall into the Deathscape again."

Or keep waking up with that silver-eyed menace burned behind my eyelids. His hand-print still ghosted across my throat, an invisible brand that itched like a warning.

"And," I added, voice dropping to a whisper, "I still want to see my dad."

That part stayed unspoken most days. But it lived inside me like a second pulse. I didn't care what kind of magic it took—I'd crawl through fire and shadow if it got me even a second more with him.

The truth was, I didn't want to be here. Not at the Black House. Not anywhere near it. But want had nothing to do with survival. The Mages here were my best shot at controlling whatever magic was buried in my blood. And maybe, just maybe, if I could master it—I could break the bond.

Break *him*.

Phontine's wings faltered. "McDara didn't want you coming here."

"Exactly why I'm here," I said, a little too sharply. "He practically short-circuited when I brought it up. That kind of reaction? Makes me think there's something worth finding inside."

But even as I said it, doubt coiled tight in my chest. McDara wasn't the type to panic. The kind of fury I'd seen in him when I'd mentioned at the diner about going to the Black House—that had been personal.

"Maybe he knows something I don't," I murmured.

"Maybe you should listen," Phontine replied. "He hasn't steered you wrong yet."

"Coming from the Pixie that wanted to hex him into tomorrow for arresting me." I said. "Twice."

"Oh, I'll always hate him on principle when it comes to that but"—Phontine flitted high enough to catch my eyes—"he doesn't seem like the type to do something without a reason."

I didn't answer. Because I wasn't sure I wanted to believe he was right.

Ahead, the Black House rose like something out of a fever dream. A mansion carved in angles too clean, too cold—its glass walls gleamed under the dying sun, bone-bright beneath a skin of reflective glass. The wrought iron gate curled like vines twisted in on themselves, casting spiderweb shadows across the polished path.

It was beautiful. In the same way a blade was beautiful—elegant, sharp, and absolutely made to cut.

I stepped up to the gate and reached for the bell.

The door opened first.

Calypso.

She stepped out into the light, her silhouette framed in glass and shadow, ink-dark hair cascading around her like a halo of night. She didn't glide so much as arrive, like she belonged here.

"Sonia!" she called, smile lighting up her face like we weren't standing in the most haunted, cursed-feeling House in Blakewell. "I thought that was you. What are you doing here? We were worried when you never called back after that incident at the pub."

I hesitated, the lie catching behind my teeth.

Phontine tightened her grip on my jacket.

Breathe.

"I... I'm fine." I forced the words out, steady and slow. "I thought I'd take you up on your offer. About showing me around."

There was a flicker in Calypso's eyes—curiosity, maybe surprise—but then her smile softened.

"Well then," she said, stepping aside. "Welcome to the Black House."

And just like that, I walked through the gate.

Into the lion's den.

Into the shadows.

Into whatever the hell came next.

Calypso's face lit up like I'd just handed her the sun, and gods help me, something in my chest unknotted at the sight. "Come on in. Pandora and Elias are here, too. We were just about to have some tea."

Tea. Of course. Because nothing screamed murder investigation like a dainty cup of floral regret.

Still, I stepped through the threshold.

The shift was immediate—like walking through a veil. The air turned cooler, heavier. The world outside dimmed, and all that remained was this: The scent of ancient parchment and something electric humming beneath the silence. Magic—sharp, alive, laced through the walls like veins. And underneath it all, buried like bone beneath silk, was the echo of something darker. Something watching.

I followed her deeper into the House because standing still felt more dangerous.

Because the motel was a coffin with fluorescent lighting.

Because I couldn't keep wandering a city filled with ghosts, Mages, and secrets carved in shadows.

And because waiting for Death to show up again—with his silver eyes and that damn smirk like he knew exactly what I tasted like when I was afraid—wasn't an option.

Tea was...anticlimactic.

No secrets poured from porcelain cups. No whispered truths floating in the steam. Just over-steeped jasmine and tension clinging to the corners of the pristine room like cobwebs no one bothered to sweep.

Phontine's tiny, invisible, body was about to topple from my shoulder while she dozed. Ten minutes into our little tea party and the lack of gossip had practically put her to sleep.

The twins guided me through a hallway so sleek it belonged in a futuristic cathedral. The outer walls were pure glass, clean and perfect as a mirror—and just as deceptive. New Town's skyline stretched beyond, a gleaming mural of power and polish. Curtains hung at the ready, thick and slate-gray, but no one reached for them.

Because here, privacy was either irrelevant—or a weapon no one wanted to admit they wielded.

The Black House didn't feel like a home. It felt like a performance.

Marble floors veined with silver. Chandeliers like frozen spiderwebs. Abstract art that twitched at the edges of my vision, shifting subtly when I wasn't watching.

It was a dreamscape dressed in wealth. Beautiful. Chilling. A trap disguised as an invitation.

"What's through there?" I asked, nodding to a pair of dark wooden doors at the end of the hall. The brass handles were shaped like intertwined serpents—detailed, coiled, and unmistakably threatening.

Elias glanced over, a lazy smile tugging at his lips. "That's the sanctum. I've got work to do in there."

The sanctum. That had Phontine perking up on my shoulder. The word landed heavy on my tongue, like it already knew its own meaning. Like it didn't care if I understood it or not.

"That's where we learn all the bad magic," Pandora said, dry as sand and just as cutting. Her voice slid down my spine and left a chill behind.

I laughed. Or tried to. "Is that where you hide the bodies, too?"

"Only on Tuesdays," Calypso chimed, looping her arm through mine like we were skipping toward a picnic instead of a magical nexus built on secrets. She pulled me gently away before I could linger too long in thought—or notice how neither of them had actually said they were kidding.

The rest of the ground floor unfolded like a palace made for watching, not living.

A library with shelves taller than most buildings I'd lived in. Sitting rooms dressed in velvet, firelight flickering inside crystal hearths. A dining hall with a chandelier that looked like it belonged in a cathedral built for gods.

Everything whispered wealth. Legacy. Power.

And just beneath that, the promise: *You are either welcome here—or you are prey.*

Other House members passed us now and then. Smiles came easily. Their gazes lingered just a second too long, eyes gleaming with the kind of curiosity that didn't feel innocent. Like they were wondering what kind of creature I was. Like they were already deciding if I would break.

We climbed the winding staircase to the second floor, the banister warm beneath my fingers despite the cold settling into my bones. Offices. Meeting rooms. Quiet, polished corridors where conversations died in the air and the walls held more secrets than stone.

At the end of one hallway stood a row of doors. Closed. Heavy. Final.

"The House Leaders work down there," Calypso said, her voice lighter now. But I could feel the tension ripple through her arm. "They don't love surprise visits."

I stared at the ornate portraits lining the walls. Silver-framed. Faces too poised, too perfect. And every one of them felt like it was watching.

Because maybe it was.

I paused in front of a gap in the lineup—one empty space where a silver frame had once hung. The wallpaper behind it was darker, a ghost-print left behind. A hollow outline of someone erased.

Phontine slid from my shoulder and flitted closer to the photo. Her lavender eyes met mine for a split second before my fingers brushed the void. "Lost one?"

Pandora didn't flinch. But her eyes went sharp, like glass left out in a storm. "Sometimes people leave the House. When they do, their picture comes down."

"Where do they go?" I asked, keeping my tone breezy. Useless attempt.

Calypso answered, voice velvet-smooth but laced with something brittle beneath the surface. "Not everyone belongs here forever."

I kept moving, my hand trailing the row of frames like they were tombstones—until it landed on one that stopped my heart cold.

Her.

Even frozen in black and white, her face held the same hollow sorrow. The same haunted eyes I'd seen in the motel mirror. In the forest. In the bathroom at the pub.

The ghost.

"Sonia?" Calypso's voice was soft behind me, but it still made me flinch. "That's Orlla."

My fingers pulled back like I'd been burned. Phontine dart back to my shoulder and clung there. "Orlla?"

"She works at Veritas University," Calypso said. "She's one of the best. Specializes in folklore and occult studies. Brilliant."

"What happened to her?" I asked, though every bone in my body already knew.

"She left the House," Pandora said. Her tone was cool. Detached. But the words hung heavy, the air frosting around them. "Almost two weeks ago."

My phone buzzed.

I dragged my gaze away from Orlla's sad, too knowing eyes and checked the screen. It was from McDara:

DNA results are back. The victim is Orlla Kane. Used to be part of the Black House. Worked at Veritas University. Call me.

My breath stuttered.

The ghost. The cave. The dark magic. The body.

All of it tied to her.

And I was already tangled in the center of it.

"Sonia?" Calypso's voice again, gentler this time. She was watching me closely now. Her brows pulled together, her concern real. "You okay?"

I nodded, mechanical. "Yeah. Just...a lot to take in."

She and Pandora exchanged a glance—something unspoken and sharp. Before I could peel back the layers of that look, Calypso slipped her arm through mine again, her touch cool and grounding.

"Let's get some fresh air," she said softly, pulling me away from Orlla's photo. But the image followed me. That face. That ache. It lingered in my chest like a ghost in its own right.

We barely made it halfway down the hall before a door opened with a sharp, deliberate click.

Matron Black.

She stepped into the hallway like the hallway itself had summoned her. The ethereal silver of her gown shimmered like smoke clinging to bone, the light from the glass walls throwing jagged shadows across her face.

Her expression was carved from marble, but her eyes...her eyes burned cold.

"Sonia," she said, voice like crushed frost. "In my office. Now."

Calypso's hand tightened on my arm. "We were just showing her around, Matron. She—"

"Enough." The word cracked like a whip, slicing Calypso's protest in half. "I will not ask again."

Pandora shifted beside her sister, her defiance barely veiled behind narrowed eyes. But she didn't speak. Didn't move.

Neither did I.

"Leave your Pixie."

I stared at Matron Black's cold dark eyes and swallowed. How the hell had she'd known Phontine was there? But, after all, McDara and Calypso had seemed to notice when she was around. Was it just humans that were completely clueless to a Pixie when they were invisible? This was the most time I had spent around Mages, so I wasn't sure.

With one gentle tap on Phontine's leg, I got her to raise. Hollowly she beat her wings next to me.

"Sonia," Phontine began but I jerked my head once. I did not want Phontine anywhere near Matron Black. I watched my oldest friend, my eyes demanding until she blew an angry snort through her nose and puffed out of existence.

Then I turned to Matron Black.

I pulled free from Calypso's grip, nodded once to both of them—though I had no idea if I looked brave or like I was walking to my execution—and turned toward Matron Black's open door.

She stepped aside, letting me pass.

The office beyond was shadow and dark wood, a stark, unnatural contrast to the House's glittering glass exterior. Like I'd stepped behind the curtain of something much more ancient, much more dangerous.

The door closed behind me with a whisper and a click that echoed all the way through my bones.

And I was alone with her.

19

Matron Black's office was a different world.

Gone were the sleek glass walls and curated elegance of the House beyond. Here, the air thickened like smoke, steeped in shadows and old secrets. The walls were paneled in obsidian-stained wood, the only light filtered through candle sconces and the soft, eerie glow of runes stitched into the jet-black tapestries. Magic pulsed in the floorboards, slow and seething—ancient and aware.

Matron Black stood behind a hulking desk carved from wood so dark it drank the light. Her silver gown poured like molten starlight around her feet, but there was nothing soft about her. Her fingers gripped the edge of the desk, tendons flexed, like she was one breath from snapping it in half.

"Come. Join me, Sonia."

I looked back at the door.

The lock clicked into place, and the temperature dropped like a guillotine blade. Cold soaked into my bones. I forced myself forward, step by step, even as every instinct screamed to *run*.

Matron Black didn't move. She didn't have to. Her fury radiated in slow, coiled waves. Her eyes, black and sharp, pinned me in place.

"Do you want to explain to me," she said, voice still soft, "why the chief of police called me this morning to inform me that one of my Mages has been murdered?" She tilted her head, gaze slicing deeper. "And that *you* are the prime suspect?"

The words hit like stone dropped into water—sinking, spreading, drowning.

"I didn't—"

"*Don't.*" The word cracked like a whip, and I flinched. It *hurt.* The air split, pressure slicing across my cheek like a slap without touch. Her magic was alive in here, hungry.

"I gave you a chance, Sonia. I opened my House to you. And this is how you repay me?" Her voice sharpened, each word a blade. "You think you can waltz into my halls, murder one of my own, and soil the sanctity of this House with *dark magic?*"

The shadows twisted behind her—real, living things. A picture frame exploded on the wall. Glass hit the floor like shrapnel.

Then—

The cold shifted.

It wasn't her magic this time.

It was *him.*

Death stood in the far corner, half swallowed by the dark, but there was no mistaking that grin—sharp, knowing, wicked. His hair spilled across his coat in mercury waves, his silver eyes fixed on Matron Black like she was a fire burning just for him.

Quite the predicament, Little Bird. His voice curled through my mind, velvet and teeth. *Should I rescue you again...or watch you squirm?*

I didn't flinch. Didn't look at him. If she saw me react, I was done.

My fingers slipped into my jacket pocket. I unlocked my phone without looking and dialed the last number that had called me. The screen buzzed faintly. One ring. Two.

Please pick up. Please.

Matron Black stepped out from behind the desk. The wood creaked beneath her heels like it feared her. "You think this is a game? That you can *hide* behind innocence while bringing *corruption* into my House?"

"I didn't kill Orlla."

The name dropped into the silence like a detonator.

She stilled.

The expression on her face shifted—just slightly—but I saw it. Something cracked. Something *real*.

"Orlla," she repeated, the word coming from between gritted teeth. "She was a *loyal Mage*. Brilliant. Dedicated. She was *one of us*."

My pulse kicked hard. "From what I know she left the House two weeks ago."

"She did. She wanted space for her work—"

Her voice wavered. For just a moment. Then it snapped back into steel.

"What do you know about Orlla?"

I lifted my chin, breath sharp in my lungs. "I know she's been haunting me since I got to Blakewell. That she led me to her body. That someone used Enchantment magic to kill her." My voice trembled, but I didn't stop. "And if you weren't so busy accusing me, maybe we could *actually* figure out who murdered your Mage."

Matron Black's eyes narrowed into slits of pitch. Power surged through the air again, taut and crackling like the seconds before a storm.

Behind me, my phone buzzed. Still connected.

McDara was listening.

And Death...Death smiled wider.

Like this was his favorite kind of show.

A gust tore through the office like a scream held too long. Papers scattered, candle flames flailed, and shadows surged across the walls like they were alive—writhing in time with the fury radiating off Matron Black.

And through it all, Death laughed.

Oh, I do love a good storm, he murmured, voice like crushed velvet and broken glass. *Tell me, Sonia...how many lives will you collect for me before this is done?*

His words slithered under my skin, but I didn't turn. Not now. Not with Matron Black watching me like I was a cornered animal, and she was deciding which part of me to break first.

Then—footsteps. Shouting. The twins' voices, sharp and breathless beyond the door.

And then it *burst open*.

Detective McDara filled the frame—broad, dark, furious. His hand hovered near his holstered weapon, but his eyes were locked on *me*. Not on Death, not on Matron Black. *Me*.

A muscle ticked in his jaw. "Sonia," he said, and the way my name landed in the space between us was a shield.

He stepped forward, slow and deliberate, inserting his body between mine and Matron Black's like a wall of stone. The room shifted around him—light skewed, magic recoiled. His presence didn't just challenge the atmosphere, it *rewrote* it.

"Everess." His voice was ice over fire. "You and I are going to have a conversation about your *accusations*."

Matron Black's smile curled like smoke, slow and venomous. "McDara. Still rushing to the aid of tragic little girls. You always did have a weakness for strays."

The air grew tighter.

What the hell?

McDara didn't move, but the storm behind his eyes built—silent, brewing, *dangerous*.

"Don't," he said, low and lethal. Even Death, lounging like a shadow stitched to the wall, stilled to savor the moment. "You were informed about an ongoing investigation. *Not* handed authority to pronounce judgment."

Matron Black clicked her nails against the desk—sharp, precise, like counting down to something inevitable.

"I am responsible for this House. When one of my Mages is murdered, I *will* protect what's mine. And forgive me if I don't trust your judgment. We all know how your last investigation involving this House ended."

The hit landed.

McDara flinched—barely—but I saw it. His mask fractured for a single heartbeat. A ghost of pain, buried deep, flickered through his expression before it vanished beneath the armor again.

"Leave her out of this," he said, voice gravel-edged and cracking with something raw. "Sonia is *not* involved in Orlla Kane's death. She's been cleared and will not get caught in this House like others have."

"We'll see." Matron Black's smile widened. It was a predator's grin—slow, deliberate, cruel. "Your sister is safer with me than she ever was with you, *Cillian*. The House gives her purpose. Discipline. *Family*. Something you threw away."

That name—*Cillian*—struck me like lightning. My breath hitched. I barely managed to keep my knees locked.

Cillian McDara.

He didn't even blink. His jaw clenched tighter, voice cutting like a drawn blade. "She stays because she doesn't know what you've done. You feed her lies and chain it in the name of loyalty. You never cared about her—you just needed a puppet. Just like you're trying to do with Sonia."

The air crackled. My name between their fire felt like kindling. I wanted to speak. To tell them to stop *using me*. But my throat locked. The pressure in the room was too much—Death's eyes on me, McDara's tension coiled like a sprung trap, Matron Black's power stretching like frost across my skin.

"You always did struggle with loyalty, McDara." Her words were silk stretched over steel. "But don't worry. I'm *very* good at handling Mages who forget where they belong."

The magic in the room shifted.

Not just charged—*constricting*.

It crept along the floor like spilled ink, curled up the legs of chairs, pressed against my chest. Not quite dark magic...but close enough to leave the taste of blood on my tongue.

My hand curled around the edge of the desk, grounding myself. The scent of smoke and something *wrong* filled my lungs.

And Death?

He just smiled.

Watching.

Waiting.

And I realized in that moment—whatever this was between McDara and Matron Black...it wasn't over.

It was *only just beginning*.

McDara didn't flinch. Didn't so much as blink. His voice came low and lethal, the kind of calm that promised disaster. "If you threaten her again," he said, "I'll make sure every Mage in your perfect little house of glass hears exactly what you did two years ago. The Council might still bow to you—but your Mages? They'll turn to dust beneath you." Magic cracked under his skin like lightning held back by sheer will.

Silence descended, deep and suffocating.

Even Death went still, his ghostlike form draped in shadows at the edge of the room, watching like a patron of the theatre enjoying his favorite act.

Matron Black's expression didn't shift. But the power that had swelled thick in the room recoiled—drawing back like something wounded or calculating. A vacuum replaced it, cold and empty. "You've overstepped, Detective," she said, voice smooth as a dagger's kiss.

"Then arrest me," McDara spat, the threat wrapped in steel. "Otherwise, get the hell out of my way."

A beat.

Her jaw tightened. Hands smoothed the silver folds of her gown, graceful as ever, but the silence beneath it was venomous. "Fine," she said. Every syllable a scalpel. "But I expect to be kept informed. I won't let this House get dragged into your chaos again."

McDara didn't dignify it with a reply. He turned to me, expression unreadable but sharp as flint. "We're leaving."

I didn't argue. My feet moved before I fully processed it, and as I passed the threshold, I felt *him*. Death. Close. He leaned in, so close I could feel the cold bite of his presence against my skin—like the air around him forgot how to breathe. Then his breath ghosted over my ear, a whisper only I could hear.

Little Bird, it seems your detective has a story of his own. I wonder which of you will break first.

A chill rooted itself in my spine.

McDara's hand gripped the door, and as he opened it, the pressure in the room snapped—like a cord pulled too tight finally giving way. He didn't look back.

I did.

Matron Black stood in the fading light like a statue carved from moonlight and judgment, her eyes fixed on my back. And in her gaze, I saw it—the promise of war.

This wasn't just a murder. It was a bloodline of secrets, cracked open and bleeding. And we were standing in the spill.

We passed through the hall like fugitives. Calypso stood near the stairwell, her face pale, wide-eyed. Pandora was carved from stone—rigid, unreadable.

Hurry, Little Bird. Death's voice curled in my mind, thick with anticipation. *It seems you have a murder to solve.*

We pushed through the glass doors of the Black House. Sunlight cut across the manicured lawn in long, deliberate blades. McDara moved like he wanted to put the entire House behind him, each step stiff with fury.

But Calypso slipped up beside me—silent as mist—and her fingers found mine. Cool. Delicate. Real.

"Sonia," she whispered, darting a glance at McDara's back. "Are you...are you using your Ghost Whisper abilities? To talk to Orlla?"

The question hit like a blow to the chest.

I stumbled. Calypso caught me, fingers tightening, the press of her nails anchoring me to the now. "What?" I breathed. My voice cracked, barely audible over the rustle of the wind threading through the hedges.

"Orlla. Her ghost. Are you communicating with her?" Hope and fear braided through her voice, pulling tight.

My mind whirled. *How much does she know?* And worse— *Did she believe I was innocent?*

McDara's voice cut through the stillness like a whip. "Sonia. *Now.*"

No time.

I turned to Calypso, throat tight. "Yeah," I whispered. "I am."

Her expression shifted—shocked, yes, but *relieved,* too. Like she hadn't been sure if she believed me, or what she'd heard Matron Black say.

Her fingers squeezed mine one last time, grounding me. Then she let go. There was something in her eyes. Not fear. *Warning.*

Before I could ask, McDara's hand closed around my arm.

Not rough. Not gentle.

Just final.

And without another word, he pulled me toward the car and away from the House that was unraveling behind us—one secret at a time.

McDara yanked open the passenger door, and I slid in without a word, my body a puppet strung together by exhaustion and adrenaline. Through the window, Calypso stood motionless on the stone path, her black curls a sharp silhouette against the glowing glass bones of the Black House. She didn't wave. Didn't move. Just watched—arms wrapped tight around herself like she was holding something in.

Like she was holding something back.

McDara dropped into the driver's seat beside me, the door slamming shut hard enough to rattle the frame. The engine roared to life, a low growl that vibrated through my bones. His hands gripped the steering wheel, knuckles bone-white, tendons pulled tight beneath his skin like he was holding back a scream.

We pulled away in silence.

The world outside blurred—immaculate lawns, gleaming marble, and glass walls vanishing behind us like a mirage. And still, I couldn't shake it. That something was unraveling behind me. That whatever I'd left back there hadn't stayed behind.

I clutched my phone like it might splinter if I let go, the screen still dimmed from the last call I hadn't ended. Calypso's question echoed in my skull, whisper-soft but unrelenting.

Are you using your Ghost Whisper abilities to talk to Orlla?

She'd known.

She hadn't been afraid.

But she hadn't looked surprised, either.

What did that mean? Had Orlla reached out to others? But that was impossible. Had she only chosen me? And if Calypso believed me...what else did she know?

Beside me, McDara said nothing, but the air in the car was thick with barely leashed tension. His magic buzzed faintly beneath the surface, sparking like static in the tight silence. Every tick of the turn signal felt too loud. Every second stretched thin enough to snap.

And still, neither of us broke the silence.

We didn't have to.

Because whatever line we'd crossed back there in the House...there was no uncrossing it.

20

McDara drove like the road had personally offended him.

His grip strangled the steering wheel, knuckles bone-pale, the leather groaning beneath the pressure. Jaw tight. Eyes forward. Every muscle in his body wound taut like he was holding back more than words—like if he spoke, he'd unravel.

I sat in silence, my hands knotted in my lap, fingernails carving half-moons into the denim over my knees. The air inside the car was heavy—thick with everything we weren't saying. I felt the weight of him, the sheer intensity of his presence, pressing into me from the driver's seat.

I thought about saying something. *Sorry Matron Black is a raging nightmare, maybe next time we'll bring sage?* But my throat locked around the words. I didn't think I had the kind of magic it would take to soothe a storm like McDara.

When we turned off the main road and pulled into a narrow parking lot tucked between towering glass buildings, I blinked.

The Obsidian Quill.

The soft glow of fairy lights danced along the awning, warm against the sterile chill of New Town's skyline and Old Town cozy grunge. The café looked like it had stepped out of a storybook and refused to apologize for it—wooden trim, crooked charm, and the kind of magic that didn't need to announce itself to be felt.

It didn't escape my notice that The Obsidian Quill was on a street that hovered between the two different sides of Blakewell.

McDara killed the engine and climbed out, wordless. I followed, my limbs slow, the chill of Matron Black's office still clinging to my skin like a curse. The shop door opened with a soft chime, and the smell hit me instantly—coffee, sugar, ink, and the faint ozone of magic.

It was the first time I'd felt remotely safe all day.

Inside, The Obsidian Quill pulsed with quiet magic. Floating orbs lit the space with a slow, dreamy flicker. Shelves brimming with spellbooks and dog-eared poetry lined the brick walls. Tables mismatched. Chairs lovingly worn. Everything felt...lived-in. Like the shop itself knew how to hold you when the world outside was too sharp.

At the counter, a tall barista with pale pink hair and the unmistakable gleam of the Fae grinned like McDara had just walked in wearing a clown nose.

"Back already, Detective? I swear you're one cup away from a caffeine curse."

McDara grunted—his version of *shut up, you know I like your coffee*—and ordered his black. No cream. No sugar. No small talk.

I tried to pretend I didn't find it absurdly attractive.

When it was my turn, I ordered a lavender latte and a cinnamon roll that looked like it could resurrect the dead. The barista added a perk-up charm after just one look at me. McDara paid before I could even reach for my wallet, sliding his card across the counter with the same unthinking authority he used to pull a weapon. Like protecting me—even from a pastry bill—was just a reflex.

We settled into a corner nook, tucked away from the windows. McDara chose a low armchair, sprawling in a way that should've looked casual, but didn't. He was all coiled tension, shadow, and stone in human form. I curled into the couch opposite, pulling my legs beneath me, the plush cushions swallowing me whole.

A light breeze fluttered my hair then Phontine materialized before me. Her eyes radiating worry.

"Thank the Wood, your still in one piece!" And she tucked herself against my collarbone like it was home. "Tell me everything."

The demand was muffled by my hair but I could feel McDara still looking at me so I peeled my gaze form my own coffee cup and settled it on him.

McDara took a long sip of his coffee. Steam curled around his face, but his eyes never left mine. "What did Calypso ask you?"

The question cut through the quiet like a blade.

"What?"

"Outside the House," he said, voice low, rough. "I saw her say something."

I stared into my latte, watching the foam swirl. "She asked if I was using my Ghost Whisperer abilities. To talk to Orlla."

His eyes narrowed, all sharp edges and storm clouds. "How would she know to ask that?"

I picked at the lace trim of my napkin, trying to sound calmer than I felt. "Everyone in that House knows what I am. Matron Black made sure of it. It's not a stretch to think I might be speaking to the ghost of one of their own."

"You think Calypso's involved?" His voice didn't rise—but it didn't have to. The quiet way he said it was worse.

"I don't know." I took a bite of the cinnamon roll and chewed like it might keep me from unraveling. "She seemed...worried."

"You trust her?"

I looked up, locking eyes with him. "Do you trust anyone?"

The question hung there, brittle and bright like a struck match.

A muscle ticked in his jaw. "Not in that House."

I didn't respond. Didn't need to. Because that—right there—was the crack in him. And I didn't know if it meant he was trying to protect me...or protect himself from caring.

But either way, we were both too far in to walk away clean.

I leaned forward, letting curiosity override caution. "What happened between you and Matron Black?"

His fingers curled tighter around the ceramic mug, his grip white-knuckled. For a second, I thought the cup might crack under the pressure. "Not your business."

The words were blunt. Final. A wall thrown up without warning.

I sank back into the cushions, but I didn't retreat entirely. "Okay," I said softly. "But if you want me to help, you need to stop keeping me in the dark."

He didn't look away. Didn't blink. Just stared at me like he was weighing the risk of letting me in—and the danger of not.

"I'm being honest when I say the only reason I haven't taken you back to the station is because I believe you." His voice was low, firm, each word deliberate. "But if something comes up—something that affects you—I'll tell you."

It wasn't everything. Not even close. But it was a thread. And right now, I'd take it.

"Fine," I breathed, the word more fragile than I wanted it to be.

Something in his expression shifted—not a smile, but the barest softening, like the tension had loosened just slightly beneath his skin. "Now that we know who the victim is," he said, "we have a place to start. We'll figure it out."

He hesitated. Just for a heartbeat. Then he added, "Together."

The word hit me like an anchor in a storm.

Together.

It shouldn't have meant as much as it did, but bless the Wood, it did.

"Okay," I whispered.

"Oh boy," Phontine whispered to me. "Do I need to get used to the Mage being around?"

The atmosphere shifted again.

Not with tension this time, but with something warmer. Something I wasn't prepared for.

Because just then, the quiet magic of the shop seemed to bend——and a woman walked in.

The first crack in McDara's lone-wolf armor came not with a word, but a smile—and it wasn't his.

It was hers.

The woman stepping into The Obsidian Quill was like sunlight breaking through a storm cloud—graceful, warm, and impossibly calm, as if the chaos of the world simply bent around her. The shop's soft shadows bent around her, the floating lights overhead seeming to glow a little brighter in her presence. She didn't belong to this world of half-spoken truths and bloodstained secrets. She belonged to something softer. Kinder.

And yet—she came straight to him.

"Or not." Phontine hopped from my shoulder to the table and began gulping handfuls of my coffee.

"*Cillian!*" Her voice was honey and home, warm enough to chase the cold from my bones.

McDara—no, *Cillian*—stood.

I blinked. He *stood*.

The man who barely spoke unless pressed, who met fire with steel and rarely looked anything but battle-worn—stood. Towering and stiff as a tree that didn't quite know what to do with affection. And yet, when she wrapped her arms around him, he didn't pull away. He didn't even hesitate.

He let her hold him.

And gods help me; he *patted her shoulder*—like a man trying to pretend he hadn't forgotten how to be touched.

It did something to me. Something tight. Something sharp and uninvited, curling just beneath my ribs.

Because hearing her say his name—*Cillian*—was like stumbling across a secret I wasn't meant to find. Like watching a lock turn in a door I wasn't allowed to walk through. He wasn't just the closed-off detective anymore. He was *this*, too—this softer, warmer version hidden beneath layers of leather and scowl.

And I hated that I wanted in. I wanted to *know* him. Not as a case. Not as a suspect's handler. But as someone who *could* call him Cillian. And mean it.

A door opened somewhere deep in him when she said it, and I wasn't inside it. I was just watching from the hallway, uninvited.

I couldn't help myself. "Cillian?" I teased under my breath, raising a brow as I grabbed my cup and sipped from my lavender latte. Phontine grumbled at loosing the coffee but quickly went for a muffin on another table. "And here I thought you were a one-name wonder. Like Rihanna."

He shot me a glare over his shoulder—sharp, exasperated, but faintly amused. I counted it as a win.

The woman turned to me then, her smile so warm it nearly knocked the breath from my lungs. She looked at me like I mattered. Like I wasn't just another name caught in the middle of a murder investigation, but someone worth seeing.

"You must be Sonia," she said, sliding into the seat beside me with that easy, graceful poise only someone born of magic and firelight could carry. "I'm Keyleth. I've heard so much about you."

My eyes flicked to McDara, who was already back to brooding into his coffee like it held the answers to the universe.

"From *McDara*?" I asked, lifting an eyebrow. "That doesn't sound like him."

Her laugh was bright and honest. "Well. Not in so many words."

And just like that, the air shifted again. Lighter. Charged. Like maybe the storm hadn't passed—but for now, we were breathing in the eye of it.

"Well, now I'm dying to know what *exact* words he used," I said, voice low and teasing. "Let me guess—'she's irritating, stubborn, possibly cursed, and keeps attracting ghosts like flies to honey'?"

I took a sip of my latte, then added, deadpan, "I'd be flattered, really."

The woman—Keyleth—laughed, a sound like wind chimes in summer air. "Not quite," she said, tapping the side of her nose. The gesture was light, playful, but her gaze shimmered with quiet power. "I hear all sorts of things."

Magic. That's what she meant—I was almost certain. But it didn't hum off her like Mage magic usually did. It was subtler. Softer. Like a different current altogether. Maybe I was just off...or maybe she wasn't a Mage at all. Not exactly. "You've been making quite the impression."

I didn't know how to respond to that. Praise? Warning? A veiled threat dressed in honey? I took a sip of my lavender latte and offered a noncommittal, "Yeah, I guess that's one way to put it."

Keyleth leaned back, fingers drumming a soft rhythm against the table, her posture relaxed but watchful. "I'm closing up soon," she said, already halfway to the next topic. "You two are staying for dinner, right? I've been setting aside the uneaten pastries and sandwiches. We always have more than we need."

McDara muttered something into his coffee that sounded like a protest and a curse tangled into one, but she just patted his shoulder, utterly unfazed. "I run The Obsidian Quill." She added, for my benefit. "Dom and Deidre are on their way. Rafe and Malchom are out of town. Short notice." Then her eyes snapped to mine, gleaming with mischief. "I'm guessing this is your first Friendsdinner?"

"Friendsdinner?" I echoed, wary but intrigued.

"It's not official," McDara cut in, dry as a desert wind. "She just thinks every meal deserves a name."

"Life deserves celebration," Keyleth shot back, her voice like sunlight warming chilled skin. Then she turned to me with a smile that melted right through my guard. "Once a week, whoever's still breathing and halfway stable shows up. Sometimes here, sometimes somewhere else. It's not formal, not even planned. But it's ours. A place to be real. To breathe."

"Relatively stable," McDara muttered, but his voice lacked its usual edge.

"Deidre's bringing dessert," Keyleth added, ignoring him, "and Dom said something about wine. Whether or not he remembers is another matter."

I found myself nodding before I even thought about it, the warmth in her words weaving around something cold and knotted inside me. "I'd love to stay," I said, quieter than I meant to.

McDara looked at me then. Really looked. The weight of his stare pressed against my skin—not judging, not annoyed. Just...watching. Taking me in like he was trying to decipher why that simple admission mattered.

Keyleth beamed. "Perfect. You'll fit right in. We've been short on women, anyway."

The words were casual, tossed like a stone into still water, but they sent ripples through me all the same. I glanced at McDara again.

Did he bring me here on purpose? Did he know they were gathering tonight?

He didn't say anything. But he didn't tell me no either. That felt like something.

He looked different here. Not softer—but steadier. As if the jagged edges of his anger had dulled slightly, the weight he carried set down for a moment beside his coffee. The silence between us wasn't empty anymore. It felt lived-in. Like a room I could maybe sit inside for a while.

I watched him, the way his shoulders relaxed against the chair, how his fingers skimmed the rim of his mug in slow, thoughtful circles. For the first time, I saw not the detective, not the enforcer—but the man. Cillian.

And gods help me, I wanted to know more. What kind of man he was when no one was looking. What it meant to be someone he let stay.

"You've got good friends," I said, softer than I meant to. The words slipped out wrapped in something fragile—longing, maybe. Or envy.

McDara's gaze met mine, dark and steady. "Yeah," he said, slow and careful, like he wasn't sure what admitting that might cost him. "They're alright."

I let out a short breath, somewhere between a laugh and a sigh. "It's nice. You all getting together like this."

His eyes lingered—too long, too direct. The weight of it settled over my skin, brushing the raw edges of something I didn't want to name. His fingers tapped absently against the side of his mug, a steady rhythm like he needed something to hold on to.

Then, like he'd been waiting for the right moment to breach the silence, he asked, "What was life like in Chicago?"

The question hit different. Not small talk. Not just curiosity. It felt like an invitation—a door cracked open, his hand on the knob.

"My parents and I had a rhythm," I said quietly. "My mom ran a rescue, before she had a stroke the year after I graduated high school—only, not for animals. For abandoned magical kids. She would only take one or two at a time because she said she wanted to give the kids that came to our house the support they needed, not just a place to sleep and eat. That led to her coordinating a group of foster homes for magical kids because she wanted to help as many as she could. Mom still helps out with that part. When kids would stay with us it was loud, full of tiny disasters and weird magic flare-ups. One time, a kid set the laundry on fire just because they didn't want to fold it." I huffed a breath of laughter. "She was able to open up an official foster system just for magical kids six years ago."

I glanced down at my mug, fingers tightening around the warmth.

"How did she get into that?" McDara asked, real curiosity painting his deep voice.

"She started it years after she adopted me. Back then, it was just us and whatever magic-related disaster I brought into the house. But after a while...after seeing what the foster system did to me—how broken it was for kids like us—she couldn't ignore it anymore."

I took a breath, the memory thick in my throat. "They didn't know what to do with a kid who saw ghosts. They wanted to medicate it out of me. Suppress it. Label it as something broken instead of something magical."

McDara didn't speak, but his gaze held mine, steady and burning.

"She saw what that kind of neglect did," I whispered. "And she decided if no one else was going to protect kids like me—she would."

McDara's voice was low, warm with something that sounded suspiciously like respect. "She sounds like hell in a fight."

"She is," I said with a quiet laugh. "But she fights for the right things."

He nodded once, slowly. "And your dad?"

"My dad was the quiet one. A professor. Books piled everywhere, chalk dust on everything. He used to say our home was where theory met reality. He'd lecture in the living room and then get interrupted by a three-year-old Shapeshifter throwing juice boxes."

My throat tightened. "I loved it. All of it."

McDara's voice cut gently through the hush between us. "What did he teach?"

I blinked, surprised by the softness in his tone. "Magical anthropology. Mostly ancient magical civilizations. He could talk about forgotten blood rituals and cultural ethics in the same breath—and make it sound like bedtime reading."

A silence stretched between us. Not heavy. Just...full. Like he was giving the memory room to breathe.

"He sounds like someone I would've liked," McDara said.

"Yeah." I smiled faintly. "You would've."

His mouth quirked. Not quite a smile, but something softer. "What did you study?"

"Culinary arts," I said, and for a heartbeat, the answer made me feel like myself again. "Wanted to open a place of my own someday. Something small. Cozy. Big flavors."

"Impressive," he said, like he meant it.

I looked down at the chipped edge of my mug. "Yeah. I tried getting into some top kitchens after graduation. Figured if I could survive a few years of screaming chefs and hundred-hour weeks, I'd learn how to really run a place." I exhaled slowly. "But...ghosts don't care about your nine to five."

McDara blinked. "They showed up at work?"

"Oh yeah." I cleared my throat, heat rushing to my cheeks. "Apparently 'haunted sauté station' doesn't look good on a résumé."

His brow creased, the concern in his expression flickering like a low-burning flame. "That's a lot."

"I'm thinking of trying something else." My voice thinned. "My mom needs help now. And the medical bills from her heart attack..." I trailed off, my throat tightening, and suddenly the words felt like too much.

I pressed my hands to my face. "Oh my god, why am I trauma dumping right now?"

Out of the corner of my eyes I saw Phontine glance over at me, half buried in a muffin, like she knew I was distressed.

"It's okay, Sonia." My eyes locked back on McDara, his voice—low, steady—landed soft against my nerves. Then a weight settled against my knee. His hand. Warm. Steady. Real.

I lowered my hands, blinking through the heat in my eyes, trying not to dissolve under the gentleness of that single touch. I didn't crawl into his lap for comfort, but bless the Wood, I wanted to.

"Maybe starting over somewhere new isn't the worst idea," I said, quietly. "My mom would love Blakewell. Or she'd be terrified. Either way, she'd be fascinated. And Phontine would like living in a place she wouldn't need to be invisible all the time."

His fingers stilled around his mug, knuckles flexing once. "And friends? You leave any behind?"

I huffed, avoiding his gaze. "Not really. It's hard to drop the whole 'I see dead people' conversation over brunch. And Mages in Chicago weren't exactly eager to befriend a Mage with no active magic."

His expression hardened at that, something flaring in his eyes. "Because of what you are."

"Yeah." I tried to smile. Failed. "Turns out being rare doesn't mean you're valued. Just...strange."

Silence settled between us. Not empty—dense. Like we'd stepped into a different current, one where every word mattered too much.

He didn't look away from me. His attention stayed locked, focused, unrelenting. It made me want to look away and lean closer all at once.

"I had Phontine, though," I added, my voice quieter now. "She's been my constant since I was a kid."

Somewhere near my collarbone, I felt the faint flutter of her wings. That quiet, glowing presence that had always been there when no one else was.

And still, McDara watched me—like he was seeing something new beneath the cracks. And maybe...I was letting him.

Phontine chose that moment to flit over, dusting off muffin crumbs along the way. She perched on my shoulder with practiced ease, one tiny hand resting on my collarbone like a claim and a challenge all at once.

"And aren't you lucky I exist?" she drawled, her voice full of unimpressed affection. "Without me, you'd be halfway into another haunted forest, or worse—trusting the wrong broody detective."

A laugh escaped me before I could swallow it. A real one—unforced, sharp, bright. McDara's gaze snapped to mine, the corners of his mouth twitching into something dangerously close to a smile. Not quite. But enough to make my stomach flutter.

"I take it your hands are full?" he asked Phontine dryly, though the warmth in his voice betrayed him.

Phontine lifted her chin with all the self-importance of a pocket-sized queen. "Full-time job, Detective. You'd be amazed at how often she nearly dies."

McDara's chuckle was low and rough, like gravel smoothed by rain. "Not as amazed as you think."

His eyes met mine, and something passed between us—quiet, electric. It left the air just a little thinner, the world just a little louder.

And then the door swung open with a chime and a gust of cold night air.

21

Dom strolled in like he owned the place, his grin a crooked blade, two bottles of wine clutched in his hands like prizes from a war no one remembered fighting. "Well, well," he announced, eyes landing on me. "Didn't expect our favorite grump to show up with company. And not just any company—but *the* Ghost Whisperer herself."

McDara shot him a glare sharp enough to skin bone. "Dom. Don't."

"Don't what? Compliment your social development? You brought a girl to Friends-diner. This is character growth." He slid onto the couch beside me with too much charm and too little space. "Sonia, blink twice if you're being held hostage."

I smirked, playing along. "He bribed me with caffeine and carbs."

"Classic seduction technique," Dom said, elbowing McDara. "Didn't know you had it in you, Cillian."

The name hit like a secret whispered too loud.

McDara didn't flinch, but the heat that flared in his gaze promised payback. "Don't you have someone else to annoy?"

"Not when dinner's this promising." Dom leaned back, utterly at ease, his arm draped across the back of the booth like he'd known me for years. "Besides, I'm here for emotional support. For you, mostly."

Before McDara could retort, the warm scent of toasted bread and something buttery wrapped around us. Keyleth appeared, balancing plates piled with food like a benevolent goddess of carbs. Her glow seemed to hum brighter in Dom's presence, like sunlight sharpening on metal.

"Look at that, you actually remembered the wine," she said, clearly surprised. "Six dinners in a row, and we were starting to lose hope."

"I contain multitudes," Dom said, already uncorking a bottle and pouring into mismatched mugs.

Keyleth rolled her eyes but beamed at him, then turned to me. "I'm so glad you're here, Sonia. We don't always get new faces. You holding up?"

There was something in her voice—sincere, steady—that loosened a knot I hadn't realized I'd been carrying. I nodded. "Yeah. This is...nice."

"Nice," Dom echoed, grinning. "Give it five minutes. Once she brings out the leftover egg salad, you'll start praying for an early death."

"A delicious death," Keyleth corrected, shooing him to another chair so she could sit next to me. "And don't think I won't make you eat every last sandwich."

Dom mock gagged. "You're a monster."

But there was laughter in the air now—bright, bubbling, and real. McDara hadn't said a word in minutes, but I didn't miss the shift. His shoulders had dropped, the tension easing from his frame like melting ice. He nursed his coffee like he wasn't guarding himself with it anymore. Like this was familiar. Safe.

And maybe, just maybe, I was starting to understand why he didn't walk away from this chaos.

Because it wasn't chaos at all. It was something else. Something that looked suspiciously like home.

I took a sip of the wine Dom poured, the flavor rich and surprisingly bold—dark cherry, something herbal, something ancient. It slid warm down my throat, spreading through me like a protective charm. For a breath, the world outside—the cold caves, the ghosts, the chilling imprint of Death's voice—fell away.

Then the door swung open.

A gust of cool night air curled through the shop as a woman stepped inside, and the entire energy of the room shifted. She moved like mist, quiet and sure, wrapped in soft layers of cream and pale gray. Her skin was porcelain-pale, hair thin but long and chestnut-dark, falling in gentle waves over her shoulders too thin shoulders. The amber light caught the shimmer in her hazel eyes, casting her in something otherworldly.

I didn't recognize her, but I didn't need to.

Because McDara's reaction said it all.

"Dee," he said—his voice unrecognizable, warm, open, and *alive*. He stood fast, the legs of his chair scraping back, and in a blink, he crossed the room, reaching for the box in her arms with a kind of care I'd never seen in him before.

"You should've called," he said. "I would've helped."

"I'm fine, Cillian." Her smile was small, but it broke something open in him. "It's just a box."

Cillian. That name again. His real name, not the badge-worn McDara I knew. And he didn't correct her.

My mouth tightened. I turned back to the table, forcing my attention on the half-eaten cinnamon roll like it held the answers to the universe. I had no claim on him. I knew that. But knowing didn't stop the twist in my stomach—the low, burning ache I couldn't quite name.

Bless the rutting Wood, what was wrong with me? Keyleth, and now this woman? I needed to chill out.

She was beautiful. Ethereal. And he was *soft* with her. Gentler than I'd ever imagined he could be. The gruff detective, undone with a single look. I hated how much I noticed.

"She's his sister," Keyleth murmured beside me, her voice warm and amused.

Relief hit me like a splash of cold water. I exhaled so hard my shoulders slumped.

"Oh," I breathed, probably a little too loudly.

Across from me, Dom caught the whole thing. His smirk was slow and knowing, the kind that could dismantle someone with nothing but a look. He didn't speak, but the glint in his eyes said, *busted*.

McDara returned, hand still resting lightly on Deidre's shoulder, and I understood now—why he was like iron around everyone else and something else entirely around her. That was affection born in the marrow of what it meant to be a big brother, and he had to be older. She looked close to my age, maybe a few years older, but still that protectiveness screamed big brother now that I knew they were related. Family.

"Sonia," he said, his tone a touch hesitant. "This is my sister, Deidre. She's...she brought dessert."

I lifted my gaze to her. "Hi."

Deidre's eyes widened just a little, like she was studying me. Her smile was soft, hesitant. "It's nice to meet you. I've heard"—she glanced at her brother—"Cillian mentioned you."

"He did?" The words slipped out sharper than I intended.

He cleared his throat, suddenly interested in the floorboards. "In passing. I said you were helping."

"Helping," Dom echoed, practically purring now. "That's what we're calling it?"

Keyleth swatted him with a napkin, but laughter threaded her scolding.

I barely heard them. My gaze had locked on McDara again—no, *Cillian*. There was something unguarded in his face, the barest flicker of vulnerability that only surfaced when his sister was near. His walls hadn't crumbled, but I could see the cracks now. And I wanted to know what lived inside them.

Deidre set the box on the table and flipped it open, revealing delicate macarons and raspberry-glazed tarts, each one a tiny work of art. "You've been working too hard," she said. "Thought you could use something sweet."

McDara—*Cillian*—smiled. Not the rare, reluctant smirk I'd seen before. This one was real. It broke over his face, slow and genuine, and something in me unraveled.

"Thanks, Dee," he said.

The way he said it...

The way her presence softened him, grounded him, *revealed* him—it was like watching a storm lose its teeth. And maybe that's what gnawed at me the most. Not jealousy, exactly. But longing. To know him like that. To be the person who could reach past the steel and the silence and pull something beautiful into the light.

I bit into a lavender macaron, letting the sugary crunch distract me from the riot of feelings inside me.

But the sweetness did nothing to numb the ache.

When McDara nudged the plate of pastries closer to me, his fingers brushed mine—barely there, a flicker of contact—but I didn't pull away.

His eyes found mine.

Dark. Steady. Unreadable. But beneath the storm, something flickered—something quiet and unfinished, like the echo of a word never spoken. It wasn't an invitation. But it wasn't indifference either.

I bit my lip, a pulse of heat blooming in my chest, low and slow and traitorous.

Whatever *this* was, whatever delicate tether stretched between us, it scared me. Because I didn't know if it was real, or if I was just too hollow to tell the difference. Starved for something steady. Something that saw me. And here was McDara, looking at me like I wasn't a problem to solve or a danger to contain—but something else entirely.

And in this moment, wrapped in the golden hum of The Obsidian Quill, with Deidre's laughter catching in the light like chimes, Keyleth's calm nature and Dom's voice a low rumble of jokes, I let myself believe—just for a heartbeat—that I could belong here.

That maybe *I* didn't have to be the haunted girl. The one caught between worlds.

McDara's fingers lingered, just a second too long, skin brushing skin.

And I let myself feel it.

The warmth. The possibility. The whisper of something that could become everything—if I was reckless enough to reach for it.

"Deidre, come over here and join us," Keyleth called, her smile glowing. She patted the sofa beside me. "We're having girl talk, and I need backup. These two are impossible." She tilted her chin toward Dom and McDara, who were mock arguing over the last tart like it was sacred.

Deidre hesitated, then crossed the room and slipped between Keyleth and me, her movements graceful despite her lanky frame. As she settled in, her boney hand brushed mine, a fleeting touch as she adjusted the box on the coffee table.

A chill swept through the coffee shop, and I drew a sharp breath, and the room seemed to exhale frost. Something bone deep. Supernatural. Wrong.

I gasped. A breath that burned.

The warm amber light flickered. The enchanted orbs overhead pulsed once—twice—then crackled with a web of frost. My vision swam.

And I knew that cold.

Knew it like trauma. Like memory. Like nightmare.

Orlla.

Her ghost didn't shimmer at the edges of the room this time.

She was beside me. *On me.*

Her apparition rippled into existence with a sickening clarity—closer than ever before. Her figure was sharp, solid, too solid. Skin stretched tight over bone. Eyes black and bottomless, burning—not with grief this time—but with *rage*.

The kind that scorched worlds.

I tried to speak. Tried to scream. But I was frozen. Paralyzed.

Then she moved.

She didn't pass *through* me.

She went *in*.

A spike of ice drove through my chest.

And then I was *gone*.

No breath. No body.

Just cold.

Just *her*.

I was Orlla.

And Sonia Byrd disappeared.

22

The world snapped into focus—but it wasn't The Obsidian Quill.

It was a palace of shadows and quiet power. The Black House.

Only, it wasn't *now*.

I was Orlla.

The knowledge lodged deep in my bones like a splinter that had always been there, waiting to surface.

The hallway stretched before me, long and narrow, its gilded walls gleaming like teeth. Light bled in through crystal sconces, sharp and silver, too polished to feel real. Every step felt wrong—too quiet, too slow—like the floor itself was holding its breath.

Beneath me, the intricate rug pulsed with magic, its patterns slithering like serpents. I felt the tension in my limbs—the same tension Orlla had felt. I wore her fear like a second skin.

Ahead: The door to Matron Black's office.

It loomed at the end of the corridor like a mouth carved from midnight, waiting to devour. Power leaked from the cracks like smoke, acrid and burning, leaving a sting in the back of my throat.

Voices clawed from the other side—sharp, fractured. An argument wrapped in magic. Then—silence.

A vacuum.

The kind that makes the soul tighten.

The door *snapped* open.

And Deidre stumbled out.

She looked like a ghost of herself—pale, trembling, undone. Her hazel eyes were wild, her breath ragged, as if she'd just clawed her way out of something terrible and barely held herself together with the threadbare strength of hope.

We locked eyes.

And the world narrowed to the space between us.

I stepped forward, every inch of me caught between Sonia and the woman whose skin I now wore.

"If you want to know more about the forbidden magic...if you're desperate enough...call me."

My voice rang out soft and low—so quiet, it should have vanished.

But it didn't.

It slid between us like a blade, thin and gleaming.

Deidre froze, the purse in her hands trembling. "How did you...?"

Her voice broke on the last word. Not confusion. Not fear.

Recognition.

The sickness coiled behind her eyes. The secret she wore like a noose. I could feel it, crawling beneath her skin. The way magic twisted inside her. Fractured. Failing. And I—Orlla—knew the truth.

Matron Black wouldn't heal her.

Wouldn't help her.

Wouldn't *save* her.

"I know," I said.

Two words, barely a breath. But they landed with the weight of a thousand unspoken things. The ache of being abandoned. The shame of needing what others refused to give. The temptation to reach for darkness when the light shut its doors.

For a heartbeat, Deidre didn't move.

Then her face cracked.

Not fully. Just enough.

"I can't. I—", she whispered, so quiet I almost missed it.

And then she turned, her pale form gliding back down the corridor like a dream receding into sleep.

I—Orlla—watched her go.

Watched the shadows swallow her whole.

And then—like a shudder through the marrow of the world—the vision broke.

The hallway rippled into nothingness.

And I was back in the Black House, but it was evening.

The air was colder now. Thicker. The light through the tall windows had turned violet-dusk, low against the horizon.

My—*Orlla's*—footsteps cracked across the marble like thunder in a cathedral.

The Black House stretched wide and yawning, the entrance hall too vast, too ornate. Shadows clung to the corners, curling behind bloodred drapes and gold-threaded tapestries that whispered of ancient victories and darker sacrifices. The chandeliers dripped light like melting ice, casting fractured rainbows that danced like spirits on the floor.

I moved quickly. Purpose bracing every breath, fear coiled beneath it like a second spine. The halls blurred—identical turns, endless arches, every corridor a looped mirage of silver trim and glass. Glass everywhere. And I could hear them.

Mages. Hushed voices like knives behind velvet curtains. Their words bled from half-open doors and shadowed alcoves—whispers of power, control, leverage. Of Matron Black and the grip she kept wrapped around Blakewell's throat.

I pushed forward.

There was something I needed. Something hidden.

A door appeared ahead—recessed into the stone like it didn't want to be found. The wood was dark, almost black, the edges shrouded in unnatural shadow. It pulsed.

My—*Orlla's*—hand reached out, fingers brushing the icy brass of the handle. It burned like frostbite. I didn't stop. The door creaked open on a whisper that scraped against the back of my teeth.

The room was small. Plain. But alive.

Magic lived here.

The walls were lined with tomes, their spines embossed with glimmering sigils that shifted when I blinked. The air was heavy, drenched in old spells and older secrets. Every breath tasted of parchment, candle wax, and dust laced with danger.

Then I saw it.

A chest beneath the desk. Wooden. Locked.

My fingers fumbled over the latch. It groaned open with a sound like splintering bones.

Inside—

A vial.

Small. Delicate.

Its contents: a storm trapped in glass.

Swirling black smoke and glinting silver dust moved like it was alive. The liquid pulsed in rhythm with the beat of my heart. It wasn't just magic. It was *enchanted essence.* The kind of spell that tore open souls and stitched them back wrong.

Forbidden. Corrupted.

My gasp cracked the silence.

The air snapped tight.

I spun—and froze.

A figure filled the doorway.

Cloaked. Hooded. Faceless in the dim light. A void where a person should be.

They stepped forward—slow, deliberate—trailing shadows like spilled ink. The very walls seemed to recoil.

A voice cut the air clean through.

"You shouldn't have come here."

Cold. Measured. Laced with promise.

I backed away, but the room felt smaller now, the air too thick to breathe. Then I was racing through a darkening forest.

The figure raised a hand as they chased me, and green fire bloomed to life in their palm—vicious, writhing, *hungry.*

The flame surged toward me—

And everything *exploded.*

The world snapped sideways.

I hit the floor of The Obsidian Quill with a sickening *thud.*

Pain flared through my ribs, sharp and immediate. My cheek met cold tile, grounding me in the now—but only barely. The air smelled of sugar and spice and burned-out magic.

My limbs twitched like they didn't belong to me. Like they were still trapped in Orlla's nightmare.

A ringing howled in my ears. The room spun.

Voices bled in—distant, frantic, *wrong*.

Then—

"Sonia!"

McDara's voice shattered through the fog.

Boots. A blur. Then his face—too close, too sharp. His eyes were fire and fury, cutting through the haze.

"Call a healer!" Phontine's voice shouted, too close and too shrill.

"Let me see her." The ever calm voice of Keyleth came, and the sharp beating of Pixie wings receded. "I can help."

I blinked, and sparkling lavender swam with a gold so white it looked like my vision was sparking.

McDara dropped to his knees beside me, his hand reaching out—not touching yet—but *there*, radiating heat like a beacon in the dark.

"Sonia, talk to me." His voice was rough. *Scared.*

I tried to answer. My tongue stuck to the roof of my mouth and the copper taste told me I'd bitten my lip. My hands trembled against the floor, nails dragging across cool tile as I tried to remember how to *move*.

"I—I saw..." My voice cracked, raw and fraying. "I was *her*. I was Orlla."

McDara's breath caught. I felt his hand press gently, firmly, against my shoulder.

"You're here now," he said, like a promise he didn't know how to keep. "You're safe."

But we both knew better.

Because Orlla wasn't done.

I couldn't focus on McDara.

Because above him, draped in shadow like it belonged to him alone, was Death.

He leaned over me, his silver hair falling like moonlight through mist, his eyes dark and glinting with something too ancient to name. Amusement danced at the edges of his mouth, but underneath—colder, deeper—was something sharper. A flicker of possessiveness. Hunger.

Well, well, Little Bird, you do have a knack for needing rescue, he murmured, voice like velvet lined with frost. *I might have to stay closer than I thought. At this rate, you'll become quite the regular in my domain.*

His tone was light, teasing—but it coiled around my spine like smoke. His gaze pierced through the fog clinging to my mind, heat and chill bleeding together until I didn't know if I was burning or freezing.

I couldn't move.

Couldn't breathe.

Death's face hovered so close I could see the subtle shimmer of power beneath his skin, like starlight trapped behind glass. The mark on my neck throbbed, seared and electric. His magic. His *claim*.

His fingers twitched.

For one terrifying, impossible second, I thought he might touch me. And the Wood damn me—I didn't know if I wanted him to.

"Get *back*," McDara barked, his voice cutting the air like a blade.

I flinched. But he wasn't talking to *him*. Of course he wasn't. He couldn't see the figure kneeling just inches from me, couldn't feel the abyss crawling under my skin. He was speaking to Dom and Keyleth, who hovered nearby, faces pale, unsure whether to approach or flee.

But Death—he didn't flinch. Didn't blink.

He just smiled.

Something sharp. Something private.

And then he leaned in, his breath a whisper against my ear.

I'll be seeing you, Sonia, he purred, and I felt my name sink into me like a hook.

And just like that—

He vanished.

No sound. No swirl of shadow. Just *gone*.

The world roared back.

Sound crashed into me—Dom's voice low and frantic, Keyleth murmuring something soft as her fingers brushed the damp hair from my forehead. McDara's hand gripped my arm, solid and grounding, the weight of him dragging me back from the edge.

"Sonia." His voice was softer now. Steady. Desperate. "Can you hear me?"

I forced a swallow. It burned. "Yeah," I rasped, my voice shredded silk. "I'm...I'm here."

But even as the word left my lips, I knew it was a lie.

Because part of me was still there—in the cold, in the dark, in the gaze of Death.

And somewhere deep inside, Orlla's scream still echoed.

Scraping.

Clawing.

Trying to get out.

23

I surfaced from unconsciousness like being dragged through glass—every pulse of pain behind my eyes a jagged flash of white. My skull throbbed, a war drum in my temples, and my body felt like it had been wrung out, twisted, and stitched back together with the wrong thread.

The room around me was unfamiliar—half guest room, half storage, with mismatched furniture and cardboard boxes stacked in the corner. The bed I was in felt too big, the sheets cool against my skin, and the quilt over me was the kind of scratchy comfort only found in childhood homes and thrift shops. The silence too sharp.

I was pressing the heels of my palms into my eyes, trying to hold my skull together, when a voice—low and velvet—brushed the air like silk pulled across a blade.

"Good morning, Little Bird."

I froze.

My heart punched against my ribs. Slowly, I turned my head.

Death lounged in an absurdly floral armchair straight out of the '90s in the corner of the room, the roses on the fabric practically wilting under the weight of his presence. He didn't belong here—he never did—but that didn't stop him from looking completely at home. Legs crossed. Fingers steepled. Darkness pouring off him in lazy waves.

His black suit melted into shadow. His silver eyes gleamed like starlight trapped in obsidian. He was terrifying and beautiful in the same way fire was—hypnotic, inevitable, and fatal if you stepped too close.

I sat up too fast. The room lurched sideways.

"What are you doing here?" My voice was sandpaper dragged across glass.

Death's smile tilted, more predator than prince. "Is that any way to greet the one who saved you from spiritual implosion? I expected swooning. Gratitude. Maybe even a kiss."

I shot him a glare. "Sorry. Ghost hijacking tends to kill the mood."

The smile faded.

Just like that, the temperature dropped. His expression calcified into something cold, sharp, and unreadable—like marble carved by grief.

"You almost died, Sonia." His voice scraped low, like a whisper from a crypt. "Letting a spirit into your body without control, without wards...It's suicide. Most who try become echoes—hollow husks, lost between worlds."

I swallowed the lump in my throat, raking fingers through damp hair. "She didn't exactly ask for permission."

Death tilted his head. His hair moved like smoke, like shadow given breath. "Which is precisely why you need training. You're drowning in power you don't understand. And I..." He leaned forward, shadows stretching from him like wings. "I don't want you dead. Not yet."

A bitter laugh caught in my throat. "You really know how to comfort, don't you?"

But my pulse wouldn't settle. Because behind the sarcasm, behind the thrum of magic under my skin, I remembered.

Orlla's scream.

Her memories—buried under my own, like coiled wires sparking against the edges of my sanity. The hallway. Deidre scared and sick. The forbidden vial. The cloaked Mage with dark magic.

What was she sick with? What could Matron Black—so powerful, so revered—*refuse* to heal?

And why did Orlla have forbidden magic in her possession?

My thoughts turned sharp. Fast.

McDara.

His fury with Matron Black. His sudden arrival at the crime scene in the forest. He'd said he received an anonymous tip, but what if he hadn't? What if he was already there—already cleaning something up?

Would he kill for his sister?

Would he *lie* for her?

The world tilted. I needed air. Space. *Answers.*

The quilt hit the floor in a heap as I stumbled from bed, my feet cold on the hardwood. The door creaked under my hand, and I eased it open. Warmth spilled in from the hallway, along with the smell of herbs, garlic, and something savory.

My stomach growled like I hadn't eaten in days.

"Your...Pixie left right before you woke." Death said, still lounging in the floral chair. "She looked tired. She was panting like her wings were too heavy to fly. I don't remember Pixies being so delicate but it has been a millennium since I visited the Living Lands."

For a second panic clogged my throat. Was Phontine okay? Yes, of course she was. Pixies needed to recharge their magic every few days. That's where she went. Just to recharge. She would be back soon. I forced myself to swallow and try to ground myself in this unfamiliar setting.

I crept into the corridor, the ache in my skull flaring with every step. Light bled from the kitchen at the end of the hall, golden and soft—and then my brain simply *shut down.*

McDara.

Shirtless.

Standing at the stove like a walking contradiction, dark hair a mess, steam curling around him like a damn spell. A tattoo slashed across his shoulder blade, part of it visible beneath his shoulder—runes, maybe. Scars lined his side like old memories written in pain.

I froze. Stared.

I *couldn't not* stare.

His back was a study in temptation—broad, powerful, every muscle shifting beneath golden skin like poetry made flesh. Shadows traced the defined line of his spine, dipping into the curve of his waist where his sweatpants sat scandalously low, clinging to his hips like they'd been stitched by sin itself.

A scatter of freckles dusted his shoulders, a constellation across a battlefield. Too soft for someone like him. Too human. Too real.

My fingers dug into the doorframe as my pulse stuttered. I should've looked away.

I didn't.

His hair was still a mess—dark, unruly waves curling at the nape of his neck, wild in a way his strict, storm-born energy never allowed. It made him look younger. Bare. A little unmade.

And the Wood help me, I wanted to keep watching him like that.

He moved with that same maddening, quiet efficiency, flipping something in a pan like it was second nature. The air filled with the warm scent of butter and peppered sausage, and something else—earthy, herbal. Comfort layered over heat. It was too much. Too domestic. Too *intimate*.

This wasn't the gruff, guarded detective with the blade-sharp voice and cold eyes.

This was Cillian.

And that truth hit me harder than I expected.

I'd seen him furious. I'd seen him dangerous. I'd seen him carved from stone and lightning, standing between me and the world like a fortress. But this? This was something different.

This was the man who got up early to cook breakfast for people who scared him half to death the night before.

And gods, my heart couldn't handle it.

My breath hitched.

My gaze dipped—dragged, really—down the ridges of his back, to the curve of his waist, to the way those damned sweatpants clung like a challenge. I was caught. Drowning in thoughts I shouldn't have, feelings I shouldn't want. My body was still ringing from what Orlla had done to me, still shaking from the kiss of Death's magic—

And yet, here I was, staring at McDara like he was the most dangerous thing in the room.

A low sound drifted from the shadows behind me. Dry. Annoyed.

Death.

"Careful, Little Bird," he murmured, his voice a blade sliding through silk. "You might just burn your wings."

I stiffened. The air went colder, and I felt him before I heard him move. Always a breath too close, always where I didn't want him to be.

"You do realize staring won't make him yours?" he added, softer this time. A whisper curled against my ear, invasive and intimate. "But by all means—keep looking. He is...so very mortal."

"Go away," I hissed, but it came out broken. Breathless.

Because he was right.

I stood there barefoot, looking like hell—yesterday's clothes twisted around my frame, hair matted from sweat and sleep and stress. I probably smelled like ghost dust and fear. I wasn't some seductive mystery. I wasn't even coherent.

And McDara?

He looked like sin carved from morning light.

My stomach knotted, hot and sick and wanting. I hated how much I cared. How badly I wanted to be something other than what I was in this moment—messy, broken, haunted.

Death's chuckle ghosted down my spine. "How very *human* of you," he drawled. "Afraid he won't want you once he sees the cracks?"

I clenched my jaw. But I didn't answer.

Because maybe...maybe I was.

And still—I couldn't look away.

"Tell me if I'm wrong," Death practically purred.

I scoffed—quiet, dry, an involuntary crack in the silence—but it caught him anyway.

McDara turned.

Slow. Intentional.

And when his gaze landed on me, it wasn't just a glance—it was gravity. The curve of his mouth lifted just slightly, as if my presence was something he felt down to the bone.

"You're up," he said, voice low and rough, like gravel soaked in honey. The kind of voice that could wind around your spine and stay there.

"Yeah." My throat scraped over the word. "I, uh—yeah."

Brilliant, Sonia. Absolutely dripping with charm.

His lips twitched at the corners, as if he was amused by my inability to function around six feet of shirtless detective. He set the spatula down, the movement measured, deliberate, and every muscle in his back shifted like a promise beneath golden skin.

"How's your head?" he asked, voice softer now. Almost careful.

"Like someone's hosting a rock concert behind my eyes." I winced, rubbing my temples. "What...happened? How did I get here?"

A flush crept up his throat, staining his collarbones. He rubbed the back of his neck, and for the briefest second, he wasn't the intimidating detective with the too-quiet magic and the unreadable eyes—he was just a man, uncertain and standing in front of a stove in sweatpants.

"You passed out," he said, looking anywhere but at me. "I didn't want to leave you alone, so...I brought you back here."

"How very chivalrous," Death whispered from the shadows behind me, his voice a phantom breeze brushing over my neck. "Though, I must say...you could've stayed with the blonde. She seemed quite nurturing. All soft smiles and tragic eyes."

I didn't look at him. Didn't breathe for him. All my focus was on McDara.

And his? It was on me.

There was something bare in his expression—unarmored. His gaze held mine like a question neither of us had the words for. Like he was looking at me differently now. Or maybe I was just desperate to be seen.

The quiet between us wasn't empty. It was charged. A slow-building storm humming beneath the surface.

"If you want a shower," he said finally, his voice quieter now, throatier, "I laid out some stuff for you in the bathroom. I'm about to start on pancakes. Thought you might need something warm."

Something in the way he said it—*thought you might need*—unraveled me a little.

"Okay," I murmured. But it didn't sound okay. It sounded like breathlessness. Like want.

I turned before I could embarrass myself further, practically fleeing into the hallway with Death's silent laughter curling behind me like smoke.

McDara's bathroom was its own world—dark marble, rich wood, silver accents gleaming like moonlight against deep jade tiles. A storm-hued sanctuary. Cool and luxurious and quiet in all the ways that man wasn't.

I ran my fingers along the sink's edge. He'd made this place into something sacred. A retreat carved out of chaos.

For a detective in a city like Blakewell, a city that hummed with dark magic and whispered secrets, I couldn't blame him. It must be an escape from the chaos, a way to wash away the grit of his job.

The hot water hit my skin, and I exhaled, steam curling around my body like a blessing. The scent of cedar and spice rose from the soap, earthy and grounding. I let it anchor me, let it strip away the terror, the ghost-ache, the lingering shudder of Death's voice in my ear.

But even with the water pounding against me, I couldn't stop thinking about what was just outside this door.

McDara.

Standing barefoot in a kitchen, flipping pancakes in sleep-ruffled hair and nothing else but low-slung sweatpants and that maddening stillness he wore like a second skin.

I tried not to imagine him waiting for me.

Tried not to imagine his eyes when I walked out of here.

Tried—and failed.

Because the air between us was no longer just tension. It was the edge of something sharper. Something that could break skin and leave you breathless.

And gods help me, I wasn't sure I wanted to stop it.

The towel clung to my damp skin, heavy with heat and steam, as I caught sight of the clothes folded neatly on the counter. A worn gray T-shirt—soft, oversized, clearly his—and a pair of faded, acid-washed jean shorts. My fingers brushed the hem, the fabric rough and frayed, and my chest went tight.

The shirt was obviously his. The kind of lived-in cotton that held warmth and scent and the ghost of someone's touch. But the shorts...they weren't. Too feminine. Too fitted. Not his.

A slow burn unfurled in my chest.

A girlfriend? An ex? Someone who'd been here enough to forget her clothes in his drawer?

I shook the thought off, but it didn't go quietly. It clung, a jealous, little thorn twisting just beneath the skin.

I slipped the shorts on—snug, but passable—and pulled the T-shirt over my head. It swallowed me whole, brushing mid-thigh like a second skin spun from memory and scent. Woodsmoke. Warm spice. Something unnameable that was *him*. The kind of scent that made your heart misstep, that made your throat tighten for no good reason at all.

I knotted the hem at my waist, a small rebellion against the flutter in my chest. I didn't want to feel delicate. I wanted to feel like I had control.

I opened the door—and the warmth of the bathroom fled, chased off by the cooler air outside.

McDara sat at the table, his long body folded into a chair that looked too small for him. He'd pulled on a shirt—black cotton stretched across his chest, sleeves rolled just enough to bare the muscle of his arms. And still, I mourned the loss of skin like something precious had been taken from me.

He looked up, his eyes meeting mine with an intensity that stole the air from my lungs. "Shirt's a bit big on you," he said, voice low, rough-edged. A flicker of something unreadable danced in his expression. "All I could find were those old shorts Deidre left behind."

Relief broke through the tight knot in my ribs.

Deidre's.

Not a lover. Not some woman with a claim on his space, his scent, his shirt.

Just his sister.

"Right," I said, too quickly. I swallowed and tried again, lighter. "Thanks for the loaner wardrobe."

His eyes dragged over me again, lingering a beat too long. "Looks better on you."

It hit like heat pooling low in my stomach.

He gestured toward the table—pancakes stacked high, eggs fluffy, fruit glistening in a bowl like it had been kissed by magic. The scent of maple syrup and fresh-brewed coffee wrapped around the room like a spell meant to disarm.

"I hope you're hungry."

I slid into the chair across from him, the cold metal biting my thighs. His shirt shifted against my skin, soft and intimate, and I bit the inside of my cheek to keep from reacting. It felt too much like wearing a piece of him.

"I could eat," I murmured.

But food was the last thing on my mind.

McDara watched me. Not like I was fragile. Not like I was trouble. He watched like he wanted to understand me, wanted to know what was running through my head as I sat there in his clothes, at his table, in his quiet orbit.

My hand hovered over the fork, and I felt it, the air shifting.

A sudden draft of cold. A phantom hush that crawled across my skin.

Death.

He appeared in the empty chair beside me, all shadow and smirk, draped in dark elegance. The illusion of comfort with none of the warmth.

"Domesticity becomes you, Little Bird," he murmured, voice a silk blade. "But don't let the scent of syrup and flannel fool you. Even wolves pretend to be tame—until their teeth sink in."

I didn't flinch. Barely breathed. McDara's gaze was still on me, waiting.

And I couldn't afford to let either of them know how off-balance I truly was.

Not yet.

Suddenly Death leaned forward but his attention wasn't on me or McDara.

His gaze stayed locked on the breakfast plate in front of me, unmoving and ravenous. Syrup bled into scrambled eggs, berries glinting like garnets, steam curling from the fresh coffee. And still, his expression remained carved in longing, not quite hunger, not quite grief. Something deeper. Emptier.

What do you eat, Death? What does the end of all things crave?

I almost asked. Almost whispered it into the thick quiet, just to hear him say something impossible.

Instead, I cleared my throat, the sound too loud in the hush. It fractured the moment like a dropped glass. McDara stilled. His fork hovered midair. His eyes—those sharp, storm-dark eyes—found mine and held.

"About last night," I started, and already my voice cracked under the weight of what I needed to say. I took a sip of coffee, the bitterness a small, grounding pain. "I didn't just pass out."

His fork lowered. The metallic clink against porcelain was a gunshot in the silence.

"It was Orlla," I said, slowly, every word pulled from some raw, vulnerable place inside me. "She didn't just show me something—she took me. Jumped into me. Possessed me. And I saw things. Her memories. Not like a dream...it was real. I *was* her."

McDara went utterly still. Like a beast sensing a trap about to spring.

The tension stretched between us, a live wire humming just beneath the surface. I could feel Death's presence beside me, not speaking, not even looking now—just *there*, like a pressure in the air. Waiting. Listening.

"What did you see?" McDara asked. His voice was too careful. Like he already knew he wouldn't like the answer.

I hesitated, the words tasting like ash. "She was at the Black House. With Deidre. She offered to help her—with forbidden magic. She told her that if she got desperate enough, she could call her."

The effect was immediate.

McDara's jaw flexed, hard enough that I thought something might crack. His fingers curled around the coffee mug, white-knuckled and shaking. The heat radiating off him wasn't magic—it was *rage*. Contained, reined in—but barely.

"And you're sure it was my sister?" he asked, quiet, like a man already halfway to breaking.

"I'm sure," I whispered. The words felt like a betrayal. "She was pale. Shaking. Scared. I think...I think she was sick. And Matron Black wasn't helping. Orlla wasn't trying to pull her into something dark—she was trying to *save* her."

McDara's shoulders bowed. Not in defeat—but in weight. The weight of too many truths too long buried. He didn't speak, didn't even blink. He stared down at his plate like it had betrayed him.

Death's voice slid against my neck, low and velvet dark. "Eat, Little Bird. You'll need the strength—truth has a taste sharper than any blade, and your detective is about to bleed for it."

I ignored him. But the dread was already blooming in my chest.

I leaned forward. "What is she sick with, McDara? What's so bad that Orlla thought *dark magic* was the only option?"

His gaze lifted, and it hit me like a blow.

Pain. Real and raw and shining behind the cracks in his armor. No mask. No shield. Just him—and the truth clawing its way up.

And still, he said nothing.

I didn't realize I was holding my breath until my lungs burned.

"Deidre has brain cancer."

McDara's voice was low, frayed—like it had been dragged across gravel just to reach me. "A tumor. Deep. Inoperable. They said if we tried to cut it out, she wouldn't survive the surgery. And every treatment we've thrown at it?" He shook his head. "Nothing touches it. Nothing even slows it down."

His hands were wrapped around his coffee mug like it was the only thing keeping him tethered. The ceramic creaked beneath the pressure. He didn't look at me as he spoke, like saying the words out loud might make them real again. Might shatter him.

"She's my baby sister," he whispered. "And I can't save her."

His pain spilled into the room like floodwater—quiet, suffocating, unstoppable. I'd braced myself for something dark, for some twist of magic or monstrous secret. But this...this was cruel in a way that made my bones ache. Not a curse. Not some eldritch horror.

Just cancer. Just the slow unraveling of someone you loved while the world watched and did nothing.

I didn't think. My body moved on instinct.

The chair scraped back, and then I was around the table, wrapping my arms around him like it might help hold him together. My cheek pressed against his shoulder, the heat of him bleeding into me, and still, it didn't feel like enough. He was solid beneath me—stone and storm and skin—but there was a fracture running through him now, and I could feel it.

For a beat, he didn't move. His breath was caught somewhere between his lungs and his heart, like even that was too heavy to carry.

Then his arms came around me.

Strong.

Desperate.

His face buried against my neck, stubble scraping my skin, and his breath stuttering warm across my collarbone. The rawness of him cracked something inside me. This wasn't just pain—it was guilt and fury and helplessness balled into something too big to hold alone. So, I held it with him.

My fingers slid into his hair, combing gently through the strands at the nape of his neck. He shivered. The kind of full-body tremor that made me pull him closer. I wanted to press every part of me into him, to give him shelter in a storm I couldn't stop.

He didn't cry. Not really. But I felt the wet heat of something unspoken where his cheek pressed against my skin.

"Thank you," he breathed, the words featherlight and broken.

I didn't answer. Just held him tighter. Let the silence say the rest. Let it blur the lines between detective and suspect, protector and haunted girl. Between the man who wanted to save his sister and the girl who might not survive saving herself.

Across from us, Death lounged in a chair like a king at court. His expression unreadable. His fingers drummed against the wood—slow, deliberate. A rhythm older than time. He tilted his head toward McDara, eyes narrowed in consideration, like he was deciding how much grief a man could carry before it snapped his soul in half.

The air thinned. Magic pressed at the corners of the room. And still I held on.

"Why wouldn't Matron Black help her?" I asked, voice barely above a whisper. The question tasted like ash. But I had to know. Even if it cracked whatever fragile peace this moment had gifted us.

McDara tensed.

I felt it ripple through him, the question striking a vein. His breath hitched against me before he slowly pulled away. And just like that, the warmth disappeared. He left me cold and aching and alone in the space he'd just filled.

I sank back into my chair, arms wrapping around myself to chase the echo of his embrace. My skin still remembered him. Still burned from the place where his grief had bled into mine.

He sat like a statue now. Silent. Sharp edged. A man rebuilt in seconds from raw to ruthless.

"Matron Black wouldn't risk her reputation for a 'lost cause,'" he said. His voice was jagged, brittle with venom. "Her words. Not mine."

The fury behind his eyes was cold. Controlled. Deadly.

I wanted to say something. Anything. But the words died in my throat.

Deidre. A lost cause.

To *them*, maybe. But not to him.

Never to him.

And now I understood why he carried that rage like armor. Why he looked at that House like it had swallowed everything good and spit out something cruel.

Because it had.

And he was the one left holding the pieces.

24

"Do you think..." The words trembled on the edge of my lips. "Do you think Deidre would use dark magic?"

McDara's head snapped up like I'd struck him.

"No." One word. Sharp. Immediate. A blade hurled across the table. "She wouldn't." The second came quieter, but no less forceful. "She *couldn't.*"

His jaw flexed, muscles clenching beneath the stubble, but it was his voice that betrayed him—tight, frayed at the edges. Not certainty. Not truth.

Hope.

I swallowed, hard. His denial wasn't just conviction—it was *need*. A desperate tether holding his world together. Because if Deidre *could*, if she *had*...then the sister he'd fought so hard to protect wasn't who he thought she was. Maybe never had been.

But I couldn't forget the way Orlla had looked at her. Or the way Deidre's eyes had shimmered with something raw and hollow. Not guilt—something worse. *Need.* And fear.

I forced a small nod. A show of agreement. A lie made of mercy.

Across from me, Death slouched deeper into his chair, legs stretched out, hands drumming on the wood with a slow, deliberate rhythm. Like he was keeping time for a song only he could hear.

"It's always the ones we love the most, isn't it?" His voice curled through the air like smoke. "The ones we'd bet our lives on...who end up setting the fire."

I didn't look at him.

I couldn't. Not when McDara's gaze was still pinned to mine like a brand. Something between betrayal and disbelief flickered in his eyes, and my stomach twisted with the weight of what I'd said. Of what I *hadn't* said.

My fork hovered over my plate, hand trembling. The eggs had gone cold. Tasteless. The scent of syrup and spiced coffee now cloying, heavy. The air itself felt wrong. Too still. Too quiet.

I didn't dare move. Not yet. Not while he was still looking at me like that. Like I was someone who could destroy him with a single sentence.

But if we were already standing on the edge, teetering above something that could break us both, then I had to ask the question that had been clawing at my insides since I woke up.

"If we're talking about hard truths," I said, voice lower now, steady despite the storm inside me, "then I have one more."

McDara didn't blink. But something in him shifted—his body tensed like he was bracing for impact. "You haven't held back this whole conversation, Byrd." A beat. "Don't start now."

There was something almost bitter in the way he said my name. Like it tasted different now.

I let the silence draw tight for one more breath. Then—

"Did you know Orlla offered to teach Deidre dark magic?"

The words hit like a punch. "And if Deidre was considering it—if she was even *thinking* about it—that would've given you motive to kill Orlla. Wouldn't it?"

The room went still.

No music. No wind. Not even Death moved.

Only McDara. Or rather, the way he *didn't* move. The stillness that stretched across his frame was too precise, too quiet.

Like the calm before detonation.

I watched the fissures form across his expression—his composure fracturing hairline by hairline. His fingers flexed on the table, slow and deliberate, as if restraining something that wanted to rip through the room and *burn*.

Then he stood.

No words. Just the scrape of the chair against the floor.

He walked to the window, spine straight, shoulders squared, and for a moment, I thought he might say nothing. Just let the silence crush me. Let my own question carve me open.

But when he turned, his eyes were dark fire. And his voice—his voice was death by a thousand cuts.

"You think I killed Orlla."

Not a question. A verdict.

"I think," I said quietly, "if you believed she was pulling your sister into something that could kill her—something that would damn her—you'd do just about anything to stop it."

Another silence. This one colder. He took one step forward. Then another.

My heart thudded in my chest, not from fear—but from the *weight* of him. From the grief and fury and love braided in the tension between us. His presence filled the room, a storm barely leashed beneath skin and bone.

"And you think *murder* is on that list."

I stood too. Slowly. My knees a little shaky. "I don't *want* to believe it." My voice caught. "But I've seen people do worse for less."

His jaw ticked. His eyes—those eyes—locked on mine, and for a second, I saw it all:

His pain. His fear. His need to protect what little he had left.

And something else. Something that had nothing to do with Deidre or Orlla. *Me.*

The look he gave me wasn't just hurt.

It was betrayal. It was heat. It was *want* tangled up in grief and fury.

The silence stretched between us, no longer a pause but a battlefield. Every second loaded with the weight of what I'd just said—*what I'd accused him of*. Trust balanced on the edge of a blade, and I could feel it tipping. Tilting.

McDara's face hardened, the planes of his features turning to carved stone. Beautiful. Cold. But it wasn't anger I saw first—it was disbelief. And under that, something deeper. Something *worse*.

Hurt.

His lips parted, a breath caught on the edge of speech. But no words came. He just *looked* at me—like he didn't recognize the person sitting across from him anymore. Like I'd become something dangerous.

And maybe I had.

But I kept my chin lifted, my voice steady even as my ribs felt like they were caving in around my heart. "You said you got an anonymous call the night Orlla was murdered," I said, each word deliberate. "Said someone reported exact codinates because of strange sounds. But if Deidre was even *considering* dark magic, and Orlla was offering to teach her...then that's motive, isn't it? For you. To stop her. To keep your sister safe."

The silence that followed wasn't empty. It was *crushing*.

Then—

The sharp turn of his body. His movement too smooth, too precise to be calm. His shoulders were tight, his jaw locked like he was holding something back—words, fury, grief—I couldn't tell.

He moved around the table, each step laced with quiet violence, like a storm barely contained by skin.

My pulse slammed against my throat.

He didn't speak. Didn't look at me. Just pulled on his boots, fingers moving fast and sharp. Grabbed his wallet. His jacket. Keys. Movements clipped, mechanical.

Like he couldn't bear to be here another second.

"McDara," I breathed, standing. My voice cracked on his name. "What are you doing?"

He turned.

And the look he gave me—gods help me, it *burned*. Frost across my chest. Ash down my throat.

"I'm taking you to the station," he said, voice low and flat, razor sharp in its control. "You want proof? You want to accuse me of murder in my own home?" His eyes pinned me, dark and furious. "Then come listen to the damn call yourself."

My breath hitched.

He wasn't dodging. He wasn't hiding. He was *challenging* me.

And beneath the fury? That same cracked edge I'd seen when he spoke of Deidre. The heartbreak of a man clinging to control because everything else was slipping through his fingers.

I stepped toward him, heart thundering like hooves on hollow ground.

"Fine," I said, my voice tight. "Let's go."

Behind us, Death let out a long, slow whistle. "Tell me, Sonia," he murmured, leaning in just enough for the air to chill, "do you always look this lovely when accusing men of murder? Or is this little witch hunt your idea of foreplay?"

I didn't dare acknowledge him.

McDara opened the door with a flick of his wrist, letting the cold air rush in. He held it wide, his frame blocking the light like a shadow given shape.

A line had been drawn. And I stepped across it.

Because whatever came next—truth or devastation—I *had* to know.

And maybe...maybe I needed to see what he looked like when the lies were stripped away.

The walk into the station was a slow descent into pressure. Each step behind McDara felt like walking a line of coals—silent, blistering, inevitable. His shoulders were tight as wire beneath his jacket, every movement coiled like a storm waiting for the right pressure point to snap. Not once did he look back. Not once did he soften.

His silence carved a path through the noise of the precinct. Greetings from other officers met a wall of indifference. He didn't answer. He didn't blink. He just kept walking, long strides cutting through the chaos until we reached a glass-paneled door marked *Detective C. McDara*—his name staring at me like a verdict with *Detective D. Ashford* right beneath it.

He threw the door open, and I didn't wait for an invitation. I slipped inside before he could decide locking it behind him was the better choice.

The room crackled with tension. Two desks. One tidy. One a slow-burning disaster. A whiteboard dominated the wall—its surface stitched with red string, newspaper clippings, location markers. Photos pinned like crime scene relics. In the center of it all—Orlla. Her face printed in grayscale; her eyes forever caught in the moment before death.

My breath hitched.

"Well, well, well," came a voice soaked in lazy charm and shadowed bite. Dom sat at the messy desk, boot propped like he owned the place, his grin as easy as it was knowing. "If it isn't our ghost-whispering goddess. How's the head, sweetheart? You gave us all quite the scare."

I tried to return his smile, but it felt cracked. "Still standing. For now."

Dom stretched, arms folding behind his head. "Keyleth's been texting me like a banshee. And Cillian? Won't answer unless you bribe him with black coffee and crime scenes. Brooding bastard." His amber eyes flicked to mine, gleaming. "Good to see you up and glowing. Brings a little warmth to this tomb of a room."

I opened my mouth, unsure whether to flirt back or flinch—but the air shifted.

The door slammed shut.

The blinds rattled from the impact.

McDara stepped farther into the room, and everything about him screamed volcanic stillness—the kind of calm that cracks mountains.

He woke up his computer. All I could see was his face set in stone over the top of his laptop before he angled it toward me.

"Play the recording."

No warmth. No explanation. Just stone.

Dom's grin dropped like a blade. He straightened slowly, tail twitching somewhere behind his chair, boots hitting the ground. "What's going on?"

McDara didn't answer. His eyes were on me—cutting through me. There was no fire, no shouting. Just the low burn of betrayal simmering beneath the surface.

"You think I faked that call the night Orlla died? That I used it to cover her murder?" he asked. "Then listen. See for yourself."

The words were flint. The spark that lit the room.

Dom swore under his breath. "Cillian—what the hell?"

I didn't answer either of them. My body moved before my thoughts caught up. I crossed the room, each step brittle with adrenaline, the charge between us prickling against my skin. His desk was pristine, every object placed with obsessive control. And I could feel both of them watching me—one sharp with disbelief, the other cloaked in icy anticipation.

I pressed the play button.

Static cracked to life. Then a voice—mechanical, low, inhuman:

"Forest edge, 42.1345° N. 88.2345° W…lights, noise…That's 42.1345° N, 88.2—W …hurry."

The message repeated, warped by distortion, disembodied urgency woven through every number.

The recording ended, but the silence that followed was worse.

My blood chilled. The voice was real. But it could've been faked. A manufactured digital ghost meant to manipulate timelines and motives. Nothing about it *cleared* him.

And worse—it didn't clear me.

I stared at McDara.

He stared right back.

Something had shifted.

Trust—whatever flicker had existed—was a match caught in the wind.

And all around us, the storm waited to be named.

I met McDara's eyes.

Still simmering. Still dark.

Still the kind of look that could strip a person to the bone.

My voice didn't tremble, but it felt like a thread unraveling in my throat. "It doesn't prove anything."

He stepped forward—and the air changed. Thickened.

Suddenly, the office was too small. The light too sharp. The space between us too electric. His body eclipsed everything, the heat of him reaching me before his shadow did, his presence overwhelming every other thought in my head. He smelled like cedar and steel and rain-soaked earth—like everything grounding and dangerous all at once.

When he spoke, his voice was rough velvet, low and cutting.

"Are you accusing me because you think I'm guilty...or because you want me to feel what it's like to be doubted?"

The question gutted me.

It wasn't anger behind it. There was something fractured beneath the sharp edges—something that hurt to look at. Like staring at a wound still bleeding.

My skin tingled, every nerve raw beneath the weight of his voice. But I didn't look away.

"If I didn't question you, I'd be stupid," I said, my voice sharper than I meant it to be. "You got an anonymous call—no name, no details—and just happened to show up where Orlla's body was found? And now we know she was offering Deidre dark magic?" I took a step closer, eyes locked on his. "You haven't exactly been forthcoming, Cillian."

His name came out before I could stop it.

It hit the air like a confession.

His eyes narrowed—not in anger, but like I'd just exposed something neither of us were ready to name. And still...he didn't look away.

The space between us crackled.

Then—

"Alright, both of you. That's enough," Dom's voice cut through, steady and grounding, like iron pounded into the heat. He stepped between us, and just like that, the charge in the room broke. "You've got questions, Sonia? Fine. But we're not going to tear each other apart over them."

I swallowed. My chest felt too tight, my pulse too loud.

"When Orlla ghost-jacked me," I began, "I saw her memories. One of them was her telling Deidre she could help—with dark magic. Said it might help with her cancer."

I looked at McDara again. I couldn't not. "If Deidre said yes, and you found out—what would you have done to stop it?"

Dom went still. His easy charm vanished like mist.

"I already knew Orlla approached Deidre," he said slowly. "But Deidre refused. Said she'd rather die than lose herself to that kind of magic."

The floor dropped out beneath me.

Everything I'd pieced together—every suspicion, every thread I'd followed—came undone in an instant. The righteous fury I'd wrapped myself in collapsed, leaving only the sharp edges of guilt.

Dom gave me a look—not unkind, but firm. "You don't know me. But you need to trust that Cillian would never kill someone who could've helped his sister. That's not who he is."

I turned toward McDara again, throat aching. His body was taut, every line a wall. But his eyes—his eyes were the worst. Still that quiet storm. Still that depthless hurt. And I'd put it there.

His voice, when it came, was ice. Controlled. Dangerous.

"Are you finished?" he asked. "Or should I recuse myself from this case too?"

"No." My answer was immediate. Barely a whisper. "I just...I needed the truth."

He nodded, sharp and unforgiving. "Then let's find it. Together. No more accusations."

I nodded back, but it felt like surrender. Because the space between us was no longer filled with suspicion. It was filled with everything we didn't say. With everything I might've broken just by asking the question.

Dom leaned against his desk, arms crossed, his eyes flicking between us like he was watching something that had already begun to fall apart.

Then, after a long beat, he sighed.

"Maybe it's time we tell her everything," he said. His voice was quiet. Grave. "If she's going to stay in this, Sonia needs to know the whole damn truth."

My pulse skittered, a frantic rhythm that thudded beneath my skin as I looked between them—McDara, a wall of storm clouds barely held at bay, and Dom, usually all swagger and ease, now silent and watchful. The weight in the room pressed down like a velvet noose, and I wasn't sure what was more suffocating—the truth they were about to tell me, or the damage I'd just done to whatever fragile thing existed between me and McDara.

Partners? Allies? Something more?

Or just two people bound together by proximity, violence, and ghosts?

Whatever we were, it wasn't simple. And I wasn't sure I could survive unraveling it.

McDara's jaw ticked. The muscle there pulsed like a fuse counting down. He ran a hand over his face, and when his eyes finally met mine, something in them changed. Not softened. Just...surrendered.

"Yeah," he rasped. "She deserves to know."

The words landed like gravel in my chest.

He dropped into his chair, the frame creaking under the weight of everything unsaid. His eyes locked on mine—dark, relentless, as if he were daring me to flinch.

Dom dragged a chair out for me, nudging it with his foot. No grin. No lazy charm. Just a grim nod. I sat, barely breathing, every part of me braced for impact.

McDara's voice came low and rough, like it was clawing its way out of him. "The day Orlla died...she came here. To the station. Asked for me and Dom."

My breath stuttered. "She what?" The words rushed out, sharp and jagged. "Why? What did she want?"

Dom leaned back against his desk, arms crossed over his chest. His posture was all relaxed lines, but his face betrayed him. There was tension there—tight across his brow, coiled in his jaw.

"She wanted files," he said. "On the town west of here. Larkend."

"Larkend?" I echoed, the name foreign and foreboding on my tongue. "What's in Larkend?"

McDara answered, voice clipped and hard. "Nothing. Not anymore."

That answer was worse than silence. My skin prickled.

"Larkend was hit with dark magic," he went on, his tone darkening like thunder rolling in. "Years ago. It wasn't a fire or a storm—it was a purge. Entire families disappeared. No one survived. No one is *left* in that town."

I leaned forward, a cold coil winding through my gut. "You think the same kind of magic that killed Orlla...came from Larkend?"

"No," Dom said. "We think it might have started there."

A chill licked down my spine.

"Damn Malifax Mages." Dom nearly growled. His beast tipping to the surface of his being and making his eyes glow gold.

"Malifax," McDara said, the word like poison in his mouth. "It's what the Council calls Mages who use dark magic. Forbidden stuff. The kind that burns through the soul and leaves nothing behind but ash and screams."

Dom added, quieter, "Or worse—obedience."

I gripped the arms of the chair tighter, trying to ground myself against the rising storm in my head. "And Orlla...she was looking into this place? Why?"

"That's what we don't know," McDara said. "She was asking questions about old case files. Missing persons. Strange activity. And she wanted everything we had on Larkend."

"But you didn't give it to her," I said, not a question.

"No," he said. "She left...frustrated. Said she'd find her own way in."

"And then she died," I said quietly. The words fell flat, but they echoed. "You called her later?"

Dom nodded once. "We found something. A file that'd been redacted, buried so deep even the Council pretends it doesn't exist. We called her to come back."

"But she never answered," McDara said. His voice didn't crack, but the pain was there, raw and just under the surface.

A silence fell between us, heavy and bitter. Orlla had been on the edge of something. Something ancient and rotting. And now she was dead.

I looked at McDara again. Really looked.

He wasn't just a man with secrets. He was a man bound by them. And somewhere between our accusations and the echo of Orlla's scream, I realized something terrible:

Whatever was happening in Blakewell...it had already started.

And none of us were safe from what came next.

"What exactly happened to Larkend?" I asked, though part of me already feared the answer.

Every sound seemed to dim beneath the weight of what McDara was about to say.

He looked at me—and for once, there was no wall in those dark eyes. No shield. No bite. Just bare, devastating honesty.

"Larkend was a thriving town," he said, voice rough with memory. "Almost twenty-three years ago, it started unraveling. People vanished. Not just one by one—entire families. Homes left with meals still warm on the table. Pets starving in locked houses. No bodies. No blood. Just...absence."

His words sank into me like stones.

"The ones who stayed behind?" he continued. "Went mad. Paranoid. Violent. Some swore they heard voices. Others set fire to their own homes. The Council tried to quarantine it, but by then it was already too late. Larkend rotted from the inside out."

Dom's voice cut in, lower now, edged with a kind of haunted reverence. "The dark magic there didn't just kill. It nested. Burrowed into the soil, into the bones of the buildings. You can feel it if you step too close. It hums under your skin, like something alive."

My breath caught. A town turned into a ghost. A wound on the map that never stopped bleeding.

And Orlla—bright, curious, reckless Orlla—had been looking into it.

I tried to speak, but no sound made it past the knot in my throat. My thoughts spun in a dozen directions, none of them safe. Orlla's link to Larkend. Her death. Her ties to Matron Black. Every piece a jagged shard, and none of them fit cleanly.

"What if Orlla figured it out?" I whispered. "What if she found out who caused Larkend...and they followed her here?"

The question fractured the silence. It didn't echo—it sank, heavy and final, like the closing of a tomb.

McDara's gaze was unwavering, the shadows under his eyes darker than I remembered. "Then we find them," he said, each word like a vow etched in stone. "We find out who. And why. Before it happens again."

25

The backseat of McDara's police cruiser had started to feel less like a ride-along and more like a cage made of steel and guilt. I leaned my forehead against the glass, the window fogging faintly with each exhale, watching as Blakewell's fractured soul shifted outside.

Old Town passed in a blur of crumbling charm—ivy-covered stone, crooked chimneys, signs weathered by time and secrets. Then came New Town, gleaming and clinical, all sharp angles and silver towers that reached too far and too fast. The divide between the districts was like a knife-edge—two halves of a city stitched together by grief and magic.

"How you holding up back there, Byrd?" Dom's voice cut through the haze, warm and teasing. He twisted in his seat, flashing a grin over his shoulder. "Starting to get mugshot withdrawal?"

"Maybe," I said, dry as dust. "Might as well start a scrapbook. Add a few glamour shots. Really lean into my criminal era."

Dom barked a laugh, the sound genuine, contagious. Even McDara's mouth twitched, the barest shadow of a smile ghosting his lips before it vanished like mist. The moment passed quickly, but it was enough to ease the coil of dread tightening in my stomach.

"Orlla worked at Veritas, didn't she?" I asked, needing something concrete. Something to anchor me before I spiraled again.

"Occult and Folklore department," McDara confirmed, his tone all business. "She was a research fellow there for the last two years."

"Do you really think we'll find something?" I twisted my fingers in my lap, the memory of Orlla's ghost still scraping along the inside of my skull. "Feels like chasing smoke."

McDara's gaze stayed locked on the road, but his voice softened, just a hair. "Long shots are still shots. And she wouldn't have buried herself in that place if it didn't matter."

The words landed with more weight than they should've. Maybe because they came from him. Or maybe because I wanted them to mean something more.

As the city funneled tighter, the skyline shifted again—old-world façade butted against chrome-clad towers. Wrought iron fences cast twisted shadows against mirrored glass. The heart of Blakewell was a contradiction wrapped in magic and grit, every building humming with stories no one dared to write down.

I leaned forward, eyes scanning the labyrinth of alleyways and sharp corners, when—

A chill slithered down my spine, coiling around my ribs like a ghost's grip.

"Still breathing, Little Bird," Death murmured, his voice curling against the shell of my ear like smoke. "Color me impressed."

I didn't jump—but only because I refused to give him the satisfaction.

He sat beside me, one leg draped lazily over the other, his presence void of warmth in the confined space. Shadows bent toward him, subtle but constant, like the world itself knew he didn't belong here.

"You survived another confrontation with your detective," he purred, sharp teeth glinting in his grin. "I half expected to find your soul dripping through the cracks by now."

I rolled my eyes, but the flutter in my chest betrayed me. His smile deepened, catching it. Of course he had caught it. Death saw everything—especially the things I didn't want him to.

"Careful, Little Bird," he added, his voice a velvet blade. "You keep wrapping yourself in his scent and wearing his clothes, and I might start to think you've forgotten who you really belong to."

My heart stuttered.

He vanished before I could curse him for saying it.

But his words stayed.

So did the heat. And the ache.

McDara eased the cruiser into a visitor slot, the engine growling one last breath before falling silent. Veritas University loomed before us, its Gothic spires knifing into the gray sky like sentinels from another time. Stone towers crowned with ivy and ironwork arched high above the entryway, regal and weatherworn—a cathedral of forgotten power. It looked like it had been plucked from the pages of a spellbook and forced to exist in the real world.

But the illusion shattered the moment we stepped inside.

Gone was the romance of old magic. The halls were sterile and sharp, all steel bones and glass skin, humming with quiet electricity. Light gleamed off polished concrete floors. Modern art installations pulsed with enchantments. The air was too clean, too artificial—like the scent of magic that had been packaged, processed, and sold back as safe.

It was Blakewell in miniature. Magic and mundanity in a delicate waltz. One misstep, and the whole place would shatter.

McDara and Dom went to the registrar's desk. Since I wasn't exactly on the books for this case, and I needed a moment away form McDara's angry glare, I hung back.

The atrium stretched wide, a hybrid of cathedral and tech lab. Exposed beams soared overhead like ribs of an ancient beast. Floating orbs of light drifted lazily through the air, casting soft, shifting halos. Students moved like river currents around us—Magicals and humans, side by side, their voices low, their lives wrapped in books and secrets.

No one noticed me.

I hovered near a glass display case, peering into the warped reflection of ancient tomes and cursed-looking trinkets. The closer I looked, the more I felt like the artifacts were watching *me.*

Behind me, I could feel the weight of Death before I heard him.

"Shouldn't you be off reaping souls? And why do you keep popping up?" I muttered, keeping my tone low, eyes trained on a dusty mirror etched with runes I couldn't read. "It's giving me whiplash."

Death's chuckle brushed my spine like a cold kiss. "If I'd known you missed me this much, Little Bird, I'd have let you summon me properly."

His voice was silk laced with venom—elegant, dangerous. I didn't turn to face him, but I could see the reflection of his sharp grin in the glass: All teeth and beautiful menace.

"I'm trying to focus," I whispered through clenched teeth. "Go haunt someone else."

"That's the problem," he murmured, stepping closer, his voice sliding into my ear like a shadow with hands. "You're so *fun* to haunt. Especially when you pretend I don't make your pulse jump."

I clenched my jaw, heat blooming at the base of my neck. "I don't have time for this."

"Oh, but you *feel* it." He leaned closer, his voice a sin-soaked purr. "The way the air shifts when I'm near. The way your skin tightens. The way you wish you didn't react to me—but you do."

My hand tightened into a fist just as—

"Sonia!"

McDara's voice cracked through the haze like thunder. I jerked upright, blinking away the fog of Death's presence. He and Dom stood near the registrar's desk, Dom leaning casually, McDara sharp as a blade drawn halfway from its sheath.

And both of them were staring at me.

Dom's brow furrowed, his gaze not quite on me—but on the space just behind my shoulder. My skin prickled.

Did he see him?

My heart stumbled against my ribs as I crossed the atrium. Each step echoed in the cathedral hush, and I felt Death's gaze tracking me like smoke curling around flame. He didn't follow, but he didn't fade either. He just stood there. Watching.

Waiting.

Dom tilted his head, his eyes narrowing just slightly. "You good?"

I nodded. "Fine." My voice wasn't convincing. I didn't care.

McDara didn't speak, just held my gaze with those dark, unreadable eyes. But there was a flicker beneath the surface—of concern, of curiosity. Of something far more dangerous if left to bloom.

I wasn't sure if he was staring at me like I was the mystery—or the fire threatening to burn down everything he'd built.

And honestly?

I wasn't sure either.

McDara jerked his chin toward the corridor beyond the registrar's desk. "Faculty offices are this way. Professors Halverson and Dr. Niall Wren agreed to meet. They were the last ones to see Orlla alive."

"Lead on," I said, trying to slip into detective mode—cool, controlled, detached. Anything to mask the electric chill curling down my spine. Death hadn't left. I could still feel him—a shadow breathing too close, an itch just under the surface of my skin. Watching.

We moved deeper into the university, away from the open cathedral spaces and into a winding stretch of corridors that felt more like a forgotten temple than an academic wing. Stone gave way to dark-paneled walls, and the farther we walked, the quieter the air became. It felt like stepping through layers of time. Like the building itself was holding its breath.

The scent changed, too—no longer ozone and magic, but dust and parchment. And beneath that...something faintly metallic. Like blood iron rusted into the bones of the place.

McDara walked ahead of me, his broad shoulders cutting a path through the corridor. He moved like someone who didn't question his place in the world. Every step was confident, grounded—each movement efficient, contained. The kind of control that only came from years of needing to hold back something dangerous. And I felt it again—the magnetic pull of him, the way the air seemed to bend around his body, warping the space between us.

We stopped at a door etched with brass letters: *Professor Halverson — Occult Studies.*

McDara knocked once—sharp, decisive.

The door creaked open to reveal a man who looked like he'd walked straight out of a ghost story. Tall and rail-thin, with a hawklike nose and eyes too sharp for someone his age. His sweater-vest was moth-eaten, his glasses smudged, but there was intelligence in his gaze. Intelligence—and something else. Something wary.

"Detective McDara?" he asked, voice smooth, but laced with unease.

"That's right," McDara said. "This is Detective Ashford and Sonia Byrd. We need to ask you some questions about Orlla."

At the mention of her name, something flickered in the professor's expression. Grief. Or fear. It was hard to tell where one bled into the other.

He stepped aside, and we entered the office.

It smelled of dried herbs and old secrets. Books lined every inch of wall space, sagging under their own weight. Stacks of parchment, rune-etched stones, bones polished smooth by time. One corner held a cluster of candles—unlit, but I could feel the dormant magic soaked into the wax like memory.

Dom leaned casually against the doorframe, but I didn't miss the flicker of his fingers near his belt, near the hidden dagger I knew he carried. McDara stood near the desk, all coiled stillness, like a storm contained in human form.

I sat lightly on the edge of a chair, fingers clasped in my lap to hide the tremor in them. Not fear, exactly. But something colder. Sharper. Like a warning in the bones.

And somewhere, unseen but undeniable, Death lingered. I could feel him standing just inside the threshold, his presence a cold exhale against the back of my neck. His silence said more than words ever could.

McDara leaned against the desk with deceptive ease, his posture relaxed—but I recognized the look in his eyes. Still. Sharp. Dangerous.

"Professor," he began, voice low and unreadable. "Tell us about Orlla. What kind of academic was she?"

Halverson folded his long fingers together, his spine stiff against the creaking leather of his chair. "She was brilliant," he said. "Too brilliant for this place, if I'm honest. She taught Folklore and Mythology, but her real love was enchantment. Not just theory—Orlla believed in the *depth* of it. In the layers beneath spells and sigils. The *intention* behind magic. What we give it. What it takes from us in return."

Goosebumps whispered up my arms.

Dom let out a low whistle. "Sounds like someone who didn't believe in boundaries."

Halverson's gaze snapped to him. "She believed in truth," he said, each word laced with something brittle. "Even when it was dangerous."

My breath caught.

McDara leaned closer, shadows kissing the edge of his jaw. "Was she researching anything dangerous?"

Halverson hesitated.

And that silence? It wasn't just nerves. It was fear.

Real, living fear.

"Depends on your definition of dangerous," he said finally.

McDara's voice dropped into something lethal. "Try me."

And that was the moment I knew—this wasn't just about academic curiosity. Orlla had been digging. And whatever she'd found?

It had teeth.

And it was still out there. Waiting to bite.

"Dark Enchantment?" Dom asked, his voice smooth as ever, but the words hit like flint striking stone.

The air seemed to still.

Professor Halverson's mouth pulled into a thin line, like the very term left a bad taste on his tongue. "Yes," he said finally, the word brittle. "Unfortunately."

He glanced toward the window, where rain misted the glass in delicate rivulets—like the sky itself was eavesdropping.

"She'd always been fascinated by enchantments," he continued, voice low and worn. "But recently...she shifted. Started asking about things that don't belong in polite magical circles. Binding spells. Soul-lock enchantments. The kind of magic whispered about in old tongues and buried in unmarked graves."

The tension in the room thickened, the walls closing in, pressing against my ribs.

"What kind of binding spells?" McDara's tone cut through the air like a blade.

Halverson hesitated. Then, with a breath that looked like it cost him, he said, "The kind that rewires will. That traps people inside themselves. Enchantments that bend autonomy, that take control—permanently. Spells that require...sacrifice."

I didn't realize my fingers had curled into fists until my nails bit into my palms. A shiver whispered down my spine like a promise. The kind of magic he described wasn't just dangerous. It was *unnatural*.

"Did she say why?" I asked, surprised by the calm threading my voice. Beneath it, my pulse thundered. "Why she needed to learn it?"

Halverson's eyes met mine. For a moment, something cracked in his stoicism—something ancient and grieving. "She mentioned a girl," he said. "Never by name. But there was a desperation in her. Like she was searching for a way to fix something that had already unraveled."

Across the room, McDara stilled. He didn't move, didn't blink—but I could feel the change in him, like a storm building behind iron doors.

"What about Larkend?" he asked. His voice was quieter now. Rougher. "We know she was looking into it."

Halverson's expression darkened, shadows carving themselves into the lines of his face. "Larkend," he echoed. "A tragedy the Council would rather bury."

His fingers dragged over his desk, as though trying to anchor himself in the present. "The town was thriving...until it wasn't. People started disappearing. Others—those who remained—turned hollow. Like their minds had been scooped clean, their spirits drained. Some called it a curse. Others said the town itself became sentient. All I know is—whatever happened there, it was Maleficaria. Magic twisted beyond recognition. And it lingers. The air, the ground…it remembers."

Dom swore under his breath, the easy charm stripped from his face. "Malifax Mages," he muttered. "Council's favorite scapegoat—and their worst nightmare."

I swallowed hard. "Why was she looking into Larkend? What did Orlla want?"

"Enchantment magic, in less reputable circles, has been used to rewrite a persons way of thinking. Even alter preexisting spells should that person's spell need to draw on their will to sustain itself."

"Orlla wanted to reverse what happened in Larkend?" Cold spiked down my spine.

Halverson gave a grim nod. "She believed there was a thread connecting Larkend to something happening here. She thought she could trace it, unravel it. But the Mage Council's banned all research tied to dark magic. They shut doors before you even knock."

"Which is why she didn't go through official channels," Dom said, half to himself. "She knew the Council would cut her off."

"There were whispers," Halverson said, leaning in slightly, his voice almost a confession. "Rumors that the Council was involved. That someone high up—maybe more than one—helped create whatever corrupted Larkend. Or benefited from it."

McDara's jaw locked. I saw it in the way his shoulders tensed, the slow flare of his nostrils. The pain etched deep in his silence.

"Did she mention threats?" he asked, voice controlled—but only just.

"She got calls," Halverson said. "Every day the week before she died. Never answered them. She'd look at the screen, then turn it face down. Said she couldn't trust anyone. When I pushed, she shut down completely. Just…worked harder."

The pieces were shifting now, locking into place in ways I didn't like. A girl needing help. A forbidden cure. A Council desperate to erase its sins. And Orlla—caught in the middle, trying to stitch together salvation from strands soaked in rot.

Dom pushed off the wall. "Did she leave any notes? Journals? Something we can work from?"

Halverson nodded slowly, the exhaustion settling back into his bones. "We boxed her things. They're in the storage room down the hall. You're welcome to look."

McDara headed toward the door, and I followed, heart racing, stomach churning with dread and the ghost of magic. The shadows in this case weren't just long now—they were moving. Growing. Watching.

And somewhere, I felt Death smile.

McDara's boots struck the stone floors of Veritas University like war drums—steady, unyielding, each thud echoing between us with the precision of a blade drawn but not yet sheathed. The silence stretched, taut as wire. Dom had gone to storage to retrieve Orlla's effects, leaving me alone with the man I'd nearly accused of murder. Again.

His back was all coiled tension, a living wall of muscle wrapped in a detective's armor. The space between us simmered, crowded with unsaid things. Guilt clung to my ribs like smoke. I followed, pulse skipping like it wasn't sure what rhythm to keep anymore. My throat burned with the words I couldn't quite form.

When we reached Orlla's classroom, McDara unlocked the door with a flick of his wrist, then stepped aside without a word. His face was unreadable—too smooth, too practiced—but his eyes flicked to mine, just once, and the weight of his silence was a blade across my skin.

I stepped through.

Inside, the modern world vanished. The air was thick with old magic, the kind that sank into wood and bone and never truly left. Shelves lined the walls, crammed with tomes older than the city itself. Talismans dangled from hooks. Crystal orbs shimmered with trapped light. In the corner, a skeleton in tattered robes grinned hollowly, a silent witness to secrets long buried.

It felt like stepping into a sanctum. Or a crypt.

McDara moved with sharp purpose, rifling through drawers with the methodical calm of someone who needed to keep his hands busy or risk shattering. I watched the clean lines of his body, the way tension lived in every controlled movement. It was grounding. Dangerous, too.

At the front of the room, a podium stood like a sentinel. Upon it, an open grimoire rested—massive, leather-bound, its pages edged in silver and inked in a shade of shifting, midnight blue. It shimmered with latent magic, each word pulsing like a heartbeat beneath the surface.

I stepped closer, drawn without choice.

The moment my fingers brushed the edge of the page, the temperature crashed.

The windows laced with frost. The orbs of light dimmed to pale ghosts of themselves. I gasped as ice kissed my skin from the inside out. My breath misted in the air—and then I saw her.

Orlla.

Her ghost coalesced between me and the book, her figure no longer the echo of peace I'd glimpsed before. She was twisted now, desperate. Her mouth opened in a soundless scream, her eyes wide with fury—or fear. She reached for me, and the room *shuddered*.

"Sonia."

His voice—*McDara's voice*—cut through the haze like a beacon. Warmth chased the chill as he reached me, his hand gripping my shoulder, solid and real.

I turned toward him, my pulse racing. "She's here. She doesn't want me to read the grimoire."

His hand tightened slightly, his gaze locking onto mine. "Is she trying to hurt you?"

"No," I whispered. "Not this time. She's...warning me."

He didn't let go.

Orlla flickered like a flame about to go out, her hand passing through the podium, through the book, and the surge of magic that followed swept through me like a tidal wave of frost. The scent of crushed herbs and scorched parchment filled the air.

McDara leaned in closer, his voice low, right at my ear. "Tell me what you need me to do."

My heart stuttered. The nearness of him, the quiet command laced with protective-ness, with something deeper—it was a tether I hadn't realized I'd needed. The only thing keeping me from floating into the void Orlla was opening between worlds.

"I need to see what's in this book," I murmured, eyes still locked on the pulsing script. "If she's trying to keep us from it, then it might be exactly what we need to understand what happened to her."

His thumb brushed gently against my shoulder, the smallest touch, but it echoed through me like a vow.

"Then we take it with us," he said. "And we read it together."

Those last words—*together*—settled something fragile inside me. The silence between us no longer felt like punishment but promise. A vow unspoken. A line drawn in the dark.

And even as Orlla's ghost faded, retreating into the cold with eyes full of warning, I knew we had already crossed a threshold.

Whatever secrets this book held...

We would face them side by side.

26

McDara snapped the grimoire shut with a sound like a guillotine blade falling. The crack of it echoed through the enchanted hush of the classroom, and a thin sheen of frost bloomed across the chalkboard behind him, spider-webbing out like fractured glass. The cold still lingered, the kind that wasn't born of temperature but something deeper—residual, spectral.

Orlla's ghost had vanished, but her fury still pressed against the back of my neck like a hand made of ice.

McDara tucked the ancient tome under his arm, every line of his body taut but unreadable. Not even the twitch of a muscle betrayed what he was thinking. Still, I could feel the tension rippling beneath his calm like a fault line—coiled, waiting.

I needed out. Now.

I turned, pushing into the corridor where the artificial lighting didn't quite reach the corners and the walls felt a little too narrow. My breath still fogged the air in front of me. The chill hadn't let go, not entirely. And neither had she.

The slap of my boots against the stone was too loud in the quiet, McDara's footfalls silent but ever present behind me, the sound of him somehow louder in my chest than in my ears.

And then—

Movement at the end of the hall.

A figure—slight, familiar—frozen mid-step.

Calypso.

She stood like she'd walked into the middle of someone else's nightmare, a stack of papers clutched against her chest. Her sea-glass eyes locked on mine first, startled but curious. But the moment McDara stepped beside me, the change in her expression was instant.

Confusion crumpled into panic. Her spine snapped straight, her breath hitched audibly from where I stood, and then she turned—bolted—papers crinkling in her arms as she disappeared around the corner like a ghost herself.

"What—" I started, the word catching in my throat like glass. But before I could move, before I could process what I'd just seen, Dom appeared from the other end of the corridor.

"Good news, bad news," he called, the words bouncing off stone and shadow. "Good news: I found the storage office. Bad news: They've already lost Orlla's research. Misplaced, they said. Like she's been dead for years instead of weeks."

He laughed, sharp and joyless.

But I didn't laugh. I couldn't. My thoughts still lingered on the way Calypso had looked at McDara—like he was a monster she hadn't expected to see again.

McDara came to a stop beside me, his arm brushing mine as he handed the grimoire to Dom. That small, accidental contact lit up every nerve beneath my skin.

"She didn't want Sonia touching it," he said, his voice low, rough. The kind of voice you felt in your spine. "Whatever's in here, it meant something. Maybe too much."

Dom raised an eyebrow and took the book like it might shatter in his hands. "Orlla hiding things from us? I thought she wanted us to find out what happened to her."

McDara didn't respond. His lips had thinned into that tight, unreadable line again. But his eyes—his eyes were storm-dark and burning with something closer to fury than doubt.

And I...said nothing.

I wanted to tell them what I'd seen. That Calypso had been here. That she'd run when she saw McDara. That her panic hadn't been vague discomfort—it had been visceral. But something inside me said, *Not yet*. That truth was a match, and this hallway already smelled like kindling.

We drove back in silence. A silence so thick it made every creak of the car feel like thunder.

Dom's phone buzzed, and he snatched it from his pocket with one hand, frowning at the screen. "It's dispatch." He answered, listening for a beat before muttering, "Of course." He ended the call and glanced at McDara. "We've been called in—emergency meeting at the station. No details yet, but it didn't sound like a drill."

At the motel, the cruiser rolled to a stop. McDara didn't say anything as he got out to open my door. Dom gave me a faint, two-fingered salute from the front seat, but even his usual teasing smile was dimmed beneath the weight of everything unsaid.

"We'll call when the meeting's over," McDara said, and his voice brushed my ear like a memory.

I nodded. Words weren't safe right now. Not with the kind of silence we'd buried them in.

As they pulled away, I stood in the cracked lot, the sun sinking behind the motel like it couldn't quite bear to witness the end of this day. A weak light clung to the rooftops, but the chill from Veritas hadn't faded. It was buried too deep. Beneath my skin, beneath the memory of Orlla's scream, and the way Calypso's fear had felt like a dagger turned inward.

And under it all...the echo of McDara's voice.

She didn't want Sonia touching it.

Like maybe—just maybe—I was already closer to the fire than anyone wanted to admit.

I scanned the empty stretch of the motel parking lot, breath fogging in the cooling air. The sky above was bruised with the last remnants of daylight, and every shadow felt like it might stir. I half expected Orlla's ghost to shimmer into existence with that hollow, aching stare. But there was nothing.

Just me. Alone.

And gods, I had never felt more *haunted*.

The door to my room groaned as I pushed it open, that familiar creak greeting me like an old war wound. I stepped inside, the air stale with motel quiet, the kind of silence that wasn't peace so much as pause—like the breath before a scream. I shut the door behind me and leaned against it, dragging a hand down my face. My mind spun with the echo of too many voices—McDara's quiet hurt, Orlla's ghostly scream, and the whisper of magic that still clung to the edges of everything I touched.

I wanted Phontine. Her sarcastic chirps. Her chaotic energy. Her grounding comfort. But what I got—was him.

"Welcome back, Little Bird."

His voice rolled through the room like black velvet laced with cold steel.

Death.

He sat on the edge of my bed like he'd never left, like this was his place, too. One long leg crossed over the other, his dark coat pooled around him like spilled ink. His fingers traced idle patterns over the sheets—*my* sheets—and his silver eyes glinted with equal parts mischief and menace.

I flinched despite myself. "Seriously?" My voice came out sharper than intended, laced with exhaustion. "Don't you have a realm of the dead to tend to? Or are you moonlighting now as a professional creeper?"

One silver brow lifted. That ever-present smirk curved his mouth like he knew every secret I didn't want to share. "You wound me," he purred, standing in a single, fluid motion. "Is this not our little sanctuary now? You, me, and the ghosts you collect?"

I rolled my eyes, but my pulse betrayed me. Thudding, traitorous. He moved closer, slow and deliberate, like a storm deciding where to strike.

"You were trembling the last time we spoke," he murmured, voice low and velvety. "Now you mouth off. I like this version of you. So much fire behind the fear."

"I'm not afraid of you," I lied.

He laughed, low and rich, like thunder behind a closed door. "No?" he said, leaning in just enough that his breath kissed my cheek. "Then why are your hands shaking, Sonia?"

My spine locked. I hadn't realized they were.

"You've had a hundred chances to drag me into your precious Deathscape," I snapped, stepping back to put a breath of distance between us. "But you haven't. So, either you're bluffing...or you're waiting for something. And I'm starting to think it's the latter."

His smile sharpened. "Careful, Little Bird. You're starting to sound like someone who thinks she understands me. That sort of arrogance tends to get mortals...burned."

"Then burn me," I said before I could stop myself. My voice broke on the edge of it, but the words hung in the space between us, reckless and aching.

For a long moment, he just looked at me. The amusement faded, replaced by something hungrier. Older. *Realer.* The shadows in the room thickened, drawn to him like he was their king. Maybe he was.

Then, slowly, he stepped back. The heat broke, but the tension didn't. If anything, it doubled.

"You amuse me," he said softly, brushing a gloved hand through the air as if wiping dust from the veil between life and death. "And I don't get *amused*, Sonia. Be careful. That kind of attention is the first step to becoming mine."

I opened my mouth, ready to fire back with something reckless—maybe foolish—but the air cracked first.

A burst of electric-blue light shattered the tension. Phontine erupted into view, her wings beating so fast they left glowing trails behind her. She hovered midair, her glow a pulsing, panicked thing. She saw me glaring at thin air and sighed.

"Oh, *great*," she snapped. "He's *still* here."

Death shifted like smoke solidifying. No surprise crossed his face—just a quiet shift, the way predators reacted when they heard a mouse squeak behind a wall.

"The Pixie lives," he said, his tone languid. "I was beginning to think you'd abandoned her."

Phontine zipped toward me, her tiny claws latching onto the collar of my shirt, like she was afraid the world might collapse without warning. "Recharge break, over. Pixies don't run on sunshine and caffeine even if I wish we did. I had to hop to the other side."

Death's head tilted slightly. His voice dropped a note, sharp and quiet. "*The Wood?* The Pixie needs to recharge?"

"Yes," I nearly spat the words. He was eons old and he didn't know how Pixies worked? "Pixie's have a limited amount of magic that gets easily depleted—"

"None of your business, reaper," Phontine snapped, glowing brighter with the effort of her anger. "You should try visiting sometime. Might clear the rot out of your attitude."

His lips twitched at the corners—just a sliver of amusement—but he didn't rise to the bait. Instead, his gaze cut back to me, sweeping over me like a judgment.

"You should rest, Little Bird," he said. "You've got more eyes on you than you know. It would be such a waste if exhaustion blinded you to the ones who are the most dangerous."

Phontine let out a sharp exhale, leaning in she whispered in my ear. "Gods, I thought ghosts were bad. But having Death himself as your live-in poltergeist? You've leveled up into a new kind of cursed."

I managed a dry smile, but my limbs sagged under the weight of the day. I sank onto the bed, every part of me aching—from the pressure of secrets, the cold of Orlla, the searing gaze of the man who wasn't quite a man.

And then the air shifted again. Not loud. Not visible. But real.

No sound. No shimmer. Just *presence*.

When I looked, Death was already lying beside me.

He hadn't walked. Hadn't blinked. He'd simply...*been*, and now he was here, long legs stretched out on the musty motel bed like it belonged to him. He reclined with one arm beneath his head, regal and effortless, as though this run-down room was his throne and I his inconvenient guest.

His proximity was suffocating. Not in the way that closed in, but in the way that took all the oxygen and *remade* it. My lungs forgot how to breathe. The mark on my neck, where his hand had touched me in the Deathscape, throbbed in answer.

He wasn't touching me now.

He didn't *have* to.

"What does the detective want you to do?" Death asked, his voice coiling low and slow like candle smoke rising into dusk. "What's he asked of you, exactly?"

The question curled around me, dark and intimate. My mouth went dry.

"He wants me to help with the case," I said. My voice was quieter than I intended. "He thinks my abilities—what I can do with spirits—might help us figure out what happened to Orlla."

Death's smile was all edge, no warmth. "How noble. You assisting the living in their little games." He turned his face toward me fully, silver eyes gleaming like polished steel. "Or is it *him* you're helping? The detective. The one who broods like he bleeds thunderclouds. Have you developed a taste for him?"

My breath caught. Heat flared in my cheeks, low and treacherous. My heart stammered. And I could've lied. I could've turned away, but instead—

"Maybe I have."

The air changed. The shadows pulled tighter.

Death moved.

He didn't lunge. He didn't speak.

He just *shifted*—and suddenly he was over me, braced with one hand on the mattress. His body hovered above mine, close enough that I could see the way his lashes framed those impossible eyes. Cold light flickered beneath his skin like starlight trapped beneath ice.

And his voice—gods, his voice—was a velvet growl that slid down my spine and tangled somewhere deep in my chest.

"You do *not* belong to the detective."

My pulse kicked. I could feel it in every inch of my body, wild and hot.

I swallowed. "I don't belong to *anyone*."

He leaned closer, just enough for my breath to catch again. For a single, suspended heartbeat, the world held its breath with me.

His gaze pinned me like a spell, fierce and inescapable, burning straight through my skin and bone. I couldn't move. Could barely think. The mark on my neck—his mark—blazed with heat, a wildfire licking up my spine, pulling something ancient and primal from deep within me.

"We are bound."

The words hit like a spell cast in blood.

Shadows curled inward, drawn to the power threaded through his voice. The very air seemed to still, waiting.

"Your magic calls to mine," he murmured, voice low and dark as midnight thunder. "Your life threads through my domain. You walk a line no one else sees...and I will not have you tangled in mortal chains."

I couldn't breathe. Not from fear. From *him*. From the weight of what he *was*—what I was starting to understand I might become. His presence pressed against me, wrapped around me like a tether spun from frost and fire.

And then—something flickered behind his eyes. The wild edge of possession softened, just slightly, revealing the thinnest seam of something...*tender*. As if, for a heartbeat, he wasn't Death incarnate.

He looked at my lips.

The space between us snapped tight, heat and tension winding around every nerve in my body. My heart pounded, a brutal rhythm, and I didn't know if I wanted to run—or grab his coat and pull him into the dark with me.

Then—

Shatter.

Glass exploded inward in a brutal burst of sound and motion. Cold wind whipped through the room as jagged shards rained down like razor hail. I threw myself back, instinct taking over.

A figure landed hard in the room, cloaked in torn, black fabric and humming with wrongness.

The Malifax Mage.

27

S hadows licked off their body like smoke. Magic warped the air around them, thick and oily, and their voice came out a distorted tangle of echoes and venom.

"How much do you and the detective know?"

My pulse shot into overdrive. Every instinct screamed *run*, but I held my ground. Barely.

I forced a breath into my lungs. "If you're this scared," I said, my voice rough, "you should've hired a better clean-up crew."

Their hood twitched. A second later, green fire ripped from their hands.

I dove, the spell searing past with a scream of heat. It slammed into the wall, blasting it apart in a plume of plaster and smoke. My body hit the ground hard, shards biting into my palms.

"Such a smart mouth," the Mage hissed. "Let's see if it still works when I peel the truth from your skull."

Another pulse of shadow-choked energy surged around them.

And still—Death didn't move.

He stood at the room's edge, still as midnight. But the temperature dropped again, frost spider-webbing across the floor. The light twisted around him. His form flickered—solid, then less than real. A myth stepping through a myth.

"Help me," I gasped. I hadn't meant to say it out loud. But the word tore itself from my throat.

Death turned his face fully to me—and something monstrous slipped through.

His pupils were gone, swallowed by black. His features warped just slightly, angles too sharp, shadows alive beneath his skin. He didn't *step* forward—he *unfolded*, space bending to let him through.

"Use your magic, Little Bird." His voice curved around me, soft as silk, deadly as night. "You are not powerless."

"I *don't* have active magic—"

"*Liar.*"

The word wasn't cruel. It was truth, stripped bare.

Before I could blink, green light surged toward me—another strike.

I couldn't dodge.

The blast clipped my arm. Pain screamed through me, hot and blinding. I fell to one knee; breath knocked from my lungs.

"Who are you talking to?" the Mage snapped. "*There's no one here!*"

From the corner, Phontine burst into view, her wings a streak of blue panic. "*I'll get McDara!*" she yelled, and then—*gone*.

I couldn't speak. Could barely move.

The Malifax Mage was in front of me now, a hand outstretched, glove glinting like metal.

It closed around my neck.

No spell. No incantation. Just pure, physical power.

"If you do not have magic," the Malifax Mage snarled, "then I'll use other means to silence you."

I clawed at them, legs kicking, air ripped from my lungs as their magic pressed in around me—coiling, strangling, *invading*.

My vision blurred.

"Call to them!"

Death's roar cracked the air like thunder splitting stone. The room trembled with the sound—walls vibrating, frost exploding outward in spiraling veins over the broken windows. Shadows surged around him like a storm given form, twisting into tendrils, his limbs no longer fully human. Claws unfurled from his fingers. His mouth stretched, fangs gleaming. His eyes—

Empty. Bottomless. A void that remembered every soul it had swallowed.

His power rolled toward me, a tidal wave of *cold and desperation*, crashing into my failing body.

"You are the master of the dead, Sonia. Call to them!"

The Mage's hand crushed harder against my throat. My knees gave out. My vision bled white at the edges. I was unraveling, sinking under.

But through the haze—

A sharp *sting* of cold. *Precision.* Not death—but magic, honed and focused. The mark on my neck flared, searing hot against my skin, and suddenly, I remembered who I was.

Not just a girl caught between monsters.

Not just someone trying to survive.

I was marked by Death.

And the dead—they remembered.

I opened my mouth. The word caught on broken breath.

"Orlla."

A name.

A summoning.

A command.

The world snapped like a pulled wire.

Frost spread faster now, curling in tendrils over walls and ceiling. The air turned razor sharp, biting with the scent of winter storms. And then—

She appeared.

Orlla stepped out of the frost like it had birthed her. Her ghostly form shimmered, not just translucent, but *blazing* with quiet fury. Her eyes weren't empty—they were *knowing*. Her presence filled the room like a bell tolling at the edge of a battlefield.

She moved.

The Malifax Mage never saw her.

Her hands plunged through their back—spectral fingers slicing through shadow and flesh. The Mage's body arched violently. The grip on my throat loosened. I dropped like a marionette cut from its strings, air tearing down my throat in greedy gasps.

But I didn't look away.

Orlla's hands twisted.

The Mage *screamed*—a raw, bone-deep sound that scraped against the walls of reality. Shadows poured from their body, writhing like something alive, something wounded. Orlla pulled harder. The tendrils of magic tore free in writhing streams, unraveling spellwork, soul-bonds, *self*.

The Mage stumbled back.

Cracked open.

And collapsed inward, using the last bit of their dark magic to wink out of the motel room.

Silence.

Not peace—*aftermath*.

Ashes where fire once raged.

The room swayed. My body trembled, but I could feel the magic in me—*under me*—woven through my limbs like threads tugging at the dead. I wasn't just haunted anymore.

I was *anchored*.

To them.

To her.

To him.

Orlla turned. Her expression softened, pain fading into something quieter—sorrow and strength. She looked at me like I had finally understood something she'd been trying to say all along.

She nodded.

And vanished.

The cold receded like breath pulled back into lungs. The room exhaled.

And I—

I was shaking.

Then Death was there, standing over me, still cloaked in remnants of shadow. Not fully human. Not fully gone.

His eyes locked on mine—endless and storm lit.

"Well done, Little Bird," he whispered.

And it wasn't mockery.

It was pride. Reverence.

Possession.

And beneath it all, a promise:

You called the dead—and they answered.

Death moved like smoke given form—fluid, unhurried, lethal. His long frame folded into a crouch before me, and the ruined motel room felt like it had collapsed inward around him. Shadows clung to the torn edges of furniture and fractured glass like reverent offerings, all of it pulled into the cold gravity of his presence.

Silver eyes, no longer sharp with mockery, burned low—*darker*, stormier. The usual glint of cruel amusement had bled into something more dangerous. Something that looked too much like concern.

He lifted a hand. Slow. Deliberate. As though I was something fragile he wasn't sure wouldn't break—or break *him*. His fingers hovered over the angry red burn on my arm, the air thick with unspoken intent. I didn't breathe.

The space between us trembled.

And then his hand passed *through* me.

A rush of cold—not a temperature but a *truth*—cascaded over my skin, like the whisper of winter sliding down the bones. I gasped, blinking hard. It wasn't pain. It wasn't even numbness.

It was *absence*.

He couldn't touch me.

Death's expression cracked, a fissure of raw emotion cutting across his otherwise impenetrable mask. His jaw flexed. His eyes, silver storms, flared with something ancient. Feral. *Wounded.* He withdrew his hand slowly, as if the very act had cost him something. His fingers curled into a fist.

"You can't touch me," I breathed, the words small, but they echoed like a verdict.

"No," he said. Just that. His voice low, rough-edged. That single syllable was both admission and curse.

The room throbbed with stillness. A heartbeat caught between us.

That Death—*the end of all things*—couldn't touch me...and it *bothered* him? That was a truth I wasn't prepared to hold. It coiled around my ribs like a brand-new mark. A twist of power I didn't know how to use.

He looked at me, and gone was the predator's smirk, the reaper's grin. What stared back was a hunger older than bones, older than fire. And beneath that—

Longing.

Not for my soul.

But *me*.

"Why?" I whispered. "Are you even really here? Or are you just some...projection, a ghost in my head?"

His lips curled, but the smile was razored at the edges. "Do I feel like nothing to you?" His voice dipped, low and intimate, coiling like silk across bare skin. "You tremble when I speak your name. You breathe me in like air you're afraid to need. And yet,"—he leaned forward, the space between us drawn taut—"you wonder if I'm not *real*?"

His breath should've been warm.

It wasn't.

It tasted of old magic and cold stars and the spaces between life and death. I wanted to flinch, to lean away. But I didn't. My body wouldn't obey. It *wanted*—gods help me—to stay near him.

"If you can't touch me," I said, my voice thinned but defiant, "then maybe I'm safe after all. Maybe all this time, I haven't been powerless."

Death didn't move.

But the motel *shifted*.

The air pulled tight. The shadows behind him lengthened, grew teeth. The silver in his gaze sharpened to blades. And yet, he didn't strike. He didn't threaten. He just stared.

And in his silence, I realized—

He hadn't denied it.

Not the hunger. Not the wanting. Not the fury that his hands could not reach what he claimed.

And not the terrible, intoxicating truth that I was still his.

Even when he couldn't touch me.

Before I could speak, before I could ask him what the hell this bond between us truly meant, the door exploded inward.

The frame cracked, the hinges shrieked, and the motel manager—Sam? Stan? Something forgettable—stood silhouetted in the chaos. His face was a warzone of shock, fury, and disbelief, every vein in his neck bulging like he might detonate from sheer rage.

"What in the holy *hell* happened here?" he screeched, his voice high and sharp enough to splinter glass. "My *room*! My—my—what is this, some kind of meth lab exorcism?!"

He flailed toward the wreckage. The shattered window. The frost blooming across the walls. The scorched, broken lamp now fused to the carpet. And *me*—bruised, burnt, and crouched on the floor like something had clawed its way out of a nightmare and into my skin.

I tried to rise. My legs trembled like they'd forgotten how to hold me.

Death moved with me. Always the echo, never the anchor. His form slipped from the shadows beside me, solid yet untouchable. And though he didn't offer his hand—couldn't—his presence was a wall against the storm. His silver stare locked on the manager, cool and cutting.

For a terrifying heartbeat, I thought Death might *do* something. There was a flicker in his expression, sharp and ancient, like he was measuring Sam's soul—calculating its weight, its worth.

But he didn't move.

He couldn't help me.

Not *here.*

"I—I didn't—" I started, but the manager's tirade slammed over my voice like a tidal wave.

"You're OUT!" he barked, jabbing a trembling finger at me. "You're lucky I don't call the NHG. I *am* calling the cops! You can explain this to them, lady."

The threat of the NHG (National Human Gaurd) made my heart stutter. They were an international organization that delt with Magicals who commited crimes against humans. their popularity had grown exponentially in the last decade. I did not want to be on their radar.

He spun on his heel, already dialing, his voice rising into a shrill screech as he stalked down the hallway. The door swung shut behind him, catching on its broken hinge and shuddering like it might fall right off the frame.

But it didn't matter.

Because I could hear them now—

Sirens.

Distant but getting closer. A sound that crawled up my spine like a warning. No longer a threat. *A promise.*

I stood frozen in the ruins of my room, breath jagged, blood thrumming with the memory of green fire and ghostlight. My burned arm pulsed in time with my panic. I could feel the shadows stretching at the edge of my vision. And in front of me, Death crouched again, one knee to the floor, watching me with eyes that held galaxies of stillness.

"Well," he murmured, his voice velvet and razor wire, curling low against my ribs. "What will you do now, Little Bird?"

There was no malice in his tone—just quiet inevitability. He knew. That the choices were gone. That the walls were closing in. That the noose wasn't a metaphor anymore.

And *he*—death incarnate—was the one holding the rope.

The sting of antiseptic licked over my skin like fire. I hissed through my teeth, jaw clenched tight as the medic dabbed the bandage against the burn on my arm. My legs hung off the edge of the ambulance, boots scuffed and jeans torn, the grated metal beneath me cold enough to numb.

All around me, Blakewell burned in color—red and blue lights strobing, washing over the cracked pavement and the fractured remains of my motel room. Radios crackled like distant thunder. Boots thudded. Someone barked orders I couldn't process. And somewhere behind the tangle of caution tape and shadows, Dom was talking to the motel manager, who gestured like he was auditioning for a drama he couldn't begin to understand.

But McDara wasn't here. Dom said he got a call after their meeting.

And that fact hollowed out something in me I didn't want to name.

The medic—mid-forties maybe, sharp-boned with the kind of eyes that had watched life leak out of too many bodies—worked in quiet efficiency. Her fingers were practiced, sure. Gentle, but distant, like she'd learned the hard way how to stop caring too much. The burn throbbed under her touch, heat blooming beneath the gauze, the magic still simmering just under my skin.

"Magic's in the wound," she murmured, mostly to herself. "I can clean it. But you'll need a healer to get it out. A proper one. Someone in a Mage House."

I studied her face. Not just her words—her eyes, her tone, the way her hands moved like muscle memory. "What do you think about magic?" I asked, the question strange even as it left me. Too intimate for this moment. Too important not to ask.

She paused. Just for a breath.

And in that breath—something shifted.

A flicker. Barely perceptible.

Her eyes darkened, just a fraction. Like a curtain pulling shut behind her gaze. Then she blinked—slow, unnatural—and her face reset. Smoothed over like a wax mask.

She offered a too-placid smile. "I'll get this burn cleaned up as best I can," she said softly. "But you should have your Mage House take a look at it."

I stared. "That's not what I asked."

She didn't seem to hear me. Or maybe she didn't know *how*. She secured the final wrap of the bandage, the motion too fluid, too polished—like she was playing a role rather than living one.

"I'm all done here, sweetheart." A pat on my arm, impersonal. "Make sure a healer checks that, okay? Don't want to leave any traces of dark magic to fester. You'll lose more than just your arm."

Then she stood, expression unchanged, and walked away—not like someone who'd just helped stitch a person back together, but like a clock winding itself into motion.

A shiver rippled through me. Phontine materialized and zeroed in on me.

"Did you see that?" Phontine whispered at my ear, her voice barely a breath, the flutter of wings brushing my cheek.

"Yeah," I murmured, eyes still locked on the medic's retreating back. "I saw."

But it wasn't just the medic. It was all of them. All the humans.

Something was wrong in Blakewell.

Something unnatural.

McDara's car sliced through the chaos like a crimson omen. The vintage body gleamed under the wash of emergency lights, an anomaly amid the clutter of sirens and shattered glass. He killed the engine, and the silence that followed was louder than the wail of police radios.

He got out—a storm in human skin. Tension coiled through every step he took, his jaw clenched tight, his hands fisted at his sides. The set of his shoulders dared anyone to speak to him. Dom intercepted him, palm flat against McDara's chest, murmuring something low, trying to ground him, but Cillian didn't even blink.

He was scanning the scene like a predator.

And then his eyes locked on me.

The world stilled.

No sirens. No shouting. Just the sound of my pulse thudding against my ribs like a warning bell. His gaze burned. It swallowed everything else—dragged me into it, until the air was too thick, and I couldn't breathe without inhaling him.

Phontine stirred on my shoulder, invisible to everyone but me. "About time. People travel so slow by car, but its good he's here now. It took me forever to find him at the Obsidian Quill. It looked like he was waiting for someone." She whispered. "You looked like you were about to unravel."

I already had.

McDara moved. Each stride purposeful. Unyielding. The crowd parted without needing to be told, as if everyone instinctively understood not to stand between him and me.

He didn't speak. Not at first.

His hands were on me before I could say anything—not frantic, not careless, but with a desperate kind of control. He unwound the bandage from my arm, his fingers gentle, his breath brushing my skin as he examined the burn beneath the lights. The moment his hand touched my wrist, something inside me uncoiled.

"Who did this?" he asked, his voice low and razor-edged. The medic, who had been finishing up her kit, stepped back like she'd felt the shift in the atmosphere—like the heat of a storm rolling in over broken land.

"A Malifax Mage," I breathed. "They broke into the room—I barely got away."

"I'll get someone to take care of this properly." His tone was threaded with fury, but his touch was steady, as if he was holding every piece of me together by will alone. He rewrapped my arm with such focused tenderness it made my throat ache.

Then his hand was beneath my chin, tilting my face toward him.

His thumb brushed the curve of my jaw, and his eyes met mine—dark, deep, and carved with something far more dangerous than anger.

"What happened?" he said, voice like flint striking stone. "All of it. I need to know."

I told him. Not everything—but enough. Enough to make his eyes narrow and his jaw harden. I left Death out of it. Didn't mention how close I'd come to being dragged under. But I told him about Orlla. About calling her. About the way she saved me.

McDara's expression darkened, the edges of control starting to fray. "Is that dangerous?" he asked. "Calling her like that?"

"I don't know," I whispered.

Before he could answer, a voice broke between us like a dropped blade.

"Detective McDara."

An officer approached, Dom trailing behind, tension riding both their shoulders. The clipboard in the officer's hands looked like a weapon barely disguised as paperwork. "We need her statement. Now."

McDara didn't move. Didn't even blink. His hand was still on my face, thumb brushing the corner of my mouth like he was memorizing it.

"After she sees a healer," he said flatly.

The officer squared up. "Protocol requires a statement—"

"She was prematurely cleared from the investigation without being tagged as a witness and given protection. Protocol just got her attacked," McDara snapped, his voice all steel and shadow. "My way now."

Dom stepped in, hands lifted like he was trying to calm two wolves circling the same kill. "Cillian, five minutes. Just a few questions—"

"No." The word landed with finality. McDara's voice was velvet-wrapped iron. "Five minutes is all it would take for another Malifax bastard to finish what the first one started."

The officer's face darkened. "I'll have to report this."

McDara's gaze didn't waver. "Do it."

Dom's eyes flicked to me. He saw it then—the way McDara hovered just on the edge of me, like gravity had shifted and I was the only thing anchoring him. He opened his mouth, closed it, and backed off with a resigned sigh.

Then McDara moved.

One moment I was perched on the ambulance. The next—I was in his arms.

Phontine was knocked from her perch on my shoulder and frantically beat her wings with annoyance.

The world tilted. My fingers clutched his jacket on instinct, and the scent of him hit me—cedar and wind and something that felt like safety even when he was burning alive with fury.

"What—? I can walk," I stammered, even though my body said otherwise, even though some traitorous part of me never wanted to move again if it meant being held like this.

"Not fast enough," he murmured. His voice was gravel and thunder, brushing against my skin like a promise. His arms tightened—protective, fierce. Possessive.

I was wrapped in him—his scent, his heat, the unshakable strength of his body pressed against mine. It didn't matter that the world outside was still on fire, a blur of flashing lights and chaos. Inside his arms, there was silence. Shelter. An illusion of safety that I didn't want to question too hard.

My thoughts spiraled—fear tangled with comfort, panic laced with something deeper. Thicker. Hotter. Something that made my pulse flicker against the hollow of my throat like a secret.

Dom's voice drifted behind us, low and calm as he worked damage control with the officer, but it was background noise, static against the gravity of McDara carrying me through the wreckage like I was breakable and his to protect.

When he opened the door of the car, the cool interior kissed my overheated skin, and then he set me down like I was made of glass.

The door shut behind me with a heavy thunk, not loud, but final. A vow. A line drawn around me in steel and stubbornness, and the raw need carved into the set of his jaw.

McDara slid into the driver's seat beside me, his knuckles pale against the wheel, every line of him pulled tight, like he was seconds from snapping or shattering—or both. He didn't look at me. Not yet. But his presence roared.

The car peeled out, gravel spitting beneath the tires. The motel lights, the sirens, the shouting—all of it fell away like a fever dream behind glass.

I hadn't even taken a full breath when he said it.

"You're staying with me."

No hesitation. Just iron.

"The motel's compromised. It's not safe anymore."

The words hit like another collision—jarring, sharp, inevitable.

I blinked. "Do I get a say in this?"

He turned his head just enough for me to catch the fire in his eyes. That signature McDara glare. Scalding. Unapologetic. Possessive.

"If you'd rather stay with someone else," he said, voice low, laced with something far more dangerous than anger, "they'll need to be vetted. Thoroughly."

He didn't wait for my answer. Just grabbed his phone, fired off a quick message, and shifted gears. The kind of movement that said he was used to taking control—and not used to being questioned for it.

A dry laugh scraped out of my throat. "I don't know anyone else well enough to crash with them."

His hands tightened on the wheel. His voice dropped. "Good."

One word. Simple. Quiet.

But it hit like a thunderclap.

The silence that followed wasn't empty—it was charged. The kind of silence that made the air feel too thick, like if either of us breathed wrong, it would all crack open. I stared out the window, hiding my face in the glass, trying to ignore the way my heart had started pounding all over again.

Not from fear. Not anymore.

From the impossible, undeniable truth unraveling between us—that the man beside me was quickly becoming something more than a shield, more than a partner. That I liked the way he stormed into chaos just to make sure I made it out. That I wanted to reach out, even now, and feel his hand on mine.

But I didn't.

Not yet.

And still—I felt his eyes on me. Just a flicker. Just enough.

The buzz of my skin. The pulse under my ribs. The awareness of him.

And then—

In the reflection of the window, I saw him.

Death. His figure carved from shadow, lounging in the backseat like he'd been there the whole time. His expression unreadable but his eyes—those silver-ringed voids—were locked on McDara.

And for once, they weren't mocking.

They were calculating.

And jealous.

28

McDara's apartment wrapped around me like a storm-worn fortress—all dark wood and steel edges, shadowed light and the faint scent of something warm and leathery. The space was too still, too quiet, as if it had held its breath the moment I crossed the threshold.

He carried me in like I weighed nothing, but when he set me down on the worn, overstuffed couch, it was with the kind of care that made something inside me ache. His hand lingered on my back just a second too long, his fingers pressing into fabric, into skin, into memory.

The burn on my arm throbbed, a slow pulse of pain that reminded me I was alive. Barely. And that something dark still curled beneath my skin—a shadow that didn't belong to me.

He crouched in front of me, elbows braced on his knees, his body a study in controlled tension. Coiled and dangerous, but all of it aimed at the world—not me.

"Your things are being processed as evidence," he said, his voice roughened by gravel and heat. "If anything's left, it'll take time."

I swallowed, the words cutting deeper than I wanted to admit. "So, I have nothing."

His silence said everything. But his eyes didn't. They moved over my face like a storm reading the coastline—tracking the bruises, the shadows, the things I hadn't yet said.

"I'll take care of it," he murmured, like it was already done.

Not a question. Not an offer. A vow.

And something inside me—something tired and raw and wanting—broke open under the weight of that certainty.

I didn't realize I was holding my breath until he rose and crossed the room, the tension of his presence still wrapped around me like armor. "Tea?" he asked. His voice was quieter now, as if it mattered how loud he spoke. As if anything might break the fragile thread between us. "Deidre left some peppermint or lavender blend."

I nodded, the word caught in my throat. Watching him move—shoulders tense beneath the dark stretch of his shirt, muscles shifting with quiet control—did things to my chest that had nothing to do with danger. I wanted to reach across the space and slide my hands beneath the tension in his back, to pull him close until all the unspoken things between us burned to ash.

And just as quickly—a knock shattered the moment.

McDara stilled mid-step. The water in the kettle hissed as he turned toward the door, every inch of him snapping alert. No weapon drawn, no fists clenched. Just stillness—the kind that meant someone was about to bleed.

Then—

"Cillian," Keyleth's voice sang through the threshold as she stepped into the apartment like light through a storm. "Hope I didn't take too long getting here."

She swept in, her energy warm and golden, in direct contrast to the cold, tight coil I'd been holding inside me. She crossed the room in three strides and wrapped me in a hug before I could stop her. And gods—it undid me.

Just for a second, I let myself fall into it. Her arms around me. The quiet understanding of someone who didn't need every detail to know I was not okay.

She pulled back, her gaze sweeping my face like she could see the damage I hadn't even looked at yet. "How are you holding up?"

"I'm..." I tried. Failed. Swallowed the lie. "I'm here."

"She doesn't know why I'm here, does she?" she asked, turning toward McDara.

I shook my head before he could respond. "It's kind of his thing."

He huffed. Not quite a laugh. Not quite not.

"He texted me," Keyleth said, softer now, pulling a small satchel from her shoulder. "He knew you'd need a healer."

Emotion punched into me so fast I had to look away. Of course he did.

She knelt beside me, her fingers already loosening the bandages around my arm. "This will sting," she warned.

I nodded. Didn't care.

Her magic sparked to life—warm and golden, citrus and cedar and starlight—wrapping around my wound like a balm and a blade. The pain hit fast and hard, a burn deep in the nerves. My breath hitched, my jaw clenched, and then—

McDara was there.

Not touching. Just close enough that his shadow slid over mine, his presence anchoring me like gravity. His eyes didn't leave me. Not once.

The magic cooled. The pain eased. The darkness in the wound receded until all that was left was breath and silence and the aftermath.

Keyleth leaned back, her face pale with effort but smiling. "The dark magic's gone. You'll be okay now."

I whispered something like thank you.

But my eyes—my eyes found him.

He hadn't moved. Still standing there, arms crossed, his jaw tight with something far too big for this room.

"Cillian," I said. Quiet. Soft. A name and a lifeline.

It worked.

He stilled. Looked at me. Breathed.

"Sit down," I whispered. "You're making me nervous."

A flicker passed through his eyes—something half amused, half surrendered—and he sat. Slowly. The armchair groaned beneath him.

But he didn't relax.

Because his eyes never left mine.

Not for a second.

And in that gaze, in the pull between us, was a promise neither of us knew how to speak yet.

But we would.

We would.

Keyleth arched a brow, that signature glint in her eyes catching me like a flicker of sun through storm clouds. She didn't speak—but she didn't have to. The look she gave me said everything.

You're safe. He's not going anywhere.

And for the first time since stepping foot in Blakewell, since ghosts and curses and shadowed figures in the mist, I *believed it.*

"I didn't just bring herbs and healing magic," Keyleth said, pulling her oversized bag onto the coffee table. "I brought sandwiches too. You've got that about-to-faint look."

My stomach gave a traitorous growl, and Keyleth's smile lit up the room like a sunrise. Even McDara's mouth twitched upward—just barely—but enough to count.

"What kind of sandwich do you want?" she asked, already unwrapping wax paper.

I woke up wrapped in something impossibly soft. A well-worn T-shirt, loose and warm against my skin, the sleeves brushing my fingertips.

McDara's shirt.

The realization settled over me like the weight of a secret. It smelled like him—cedar, fresh rain, a touch of cold steel—and I curled deeper into the fabric, trying not to let it mean more than it did.

It didn't work.

I blinked into the blanket and realized I wasn't on the couch anymore. Someone must have moved me.

I hadn't meant to pass out. But the world had been too loud, and McDara's apartment was the first place that hadn't made me feel like I was about to come undone.

The couch had been too soft, the blankets too warm. And the shirt…that had been my undoing.

A tiny yawn chirped beside me. Phontine peeked out from the pillow, her wings still drooping from sleep, her hair a glittering mess of bedhead.

"That was the first real sleep I've had since we got here," she mumbled, stretching her limbs like a cat.

I smiled, bleary-eyed. "Yeah. Me too."

There was something about this place—McDara's place—that *held*. A haven carved out of chaos. The shadows here were still, the kind that didn't reach for your throat. The hum of the apartment, the distant groan of pipes and creak of wood, was the first lullaby I'd heard in weeks.

For once, I hadn't fallen asleep wondering if I'd wake to a ghost's scream or a curse burning through my blood. I'd slept...like I was safe.

I stood, the shirt falling to my thighs, and padded into the quiet stillness of the living room. Phontine fluttered up to perch on my shoulder, her wings tickling my cheek as she yawned again.

The apartment was empty, but the space still felt full—with presence, with care, with the soft aftershock of someone who'd been here only moments ago.

My phone was on the coffee table, and beneath it, a note. I unfolded it slowly, the ink bold and slanted, every stroke unmistakably his:

Went to the station to get your phone from evidence. Don't like that you couldn't contact me if you needed. Be back soon. Coffee's made.

Something inside me unraveled—a thread pulled loose by quiet protection.

He didn't say *be careful*. He said *you should've been able to reach me*. Because in his world, I was someone worth reaching.

Beside the note was a sleek, black card. A second note in smaller print explained: *From the motel's insurance claim. For clothes and essentials.* But it might as well have said: *You lost everything. Here's a start.*

My throat tightened.

"Mmm. Coffee," Phontine hummed, nose twitching like a tiny bloodhound. "You know...if McDara's not secretly working with the Malifax Mage, I vote we keep him."

I rolled my eyes and headed for the kitchen, but the smile on my face gave me away. "He's not a stray, Pix."

"No," she said thoughtfully. "He's more like a wolf. Protective, intense. Growly. But he'd rip someone's throat out if they hurt you."

I pulled down a mug and poured the coffee. "You think he's not involved? With the Malifax?"

She fluttered toward the counter, struggling to lift the mug until I pushed it closer. She dipped her hands into the steaming liquid like it was a hot spring and sighed.

"I found him last night at The Obsidian Quill. When I told him you were under attack, he didn't even blink. Just *ran*. No goodbye. No questions. I don't think someone plotting your death panics when you're in danger."

I froze, hand hovering over the sugar jar. My pulse thudded, a low, steady drumbeat against my ribs.

"He panicked?" I asked softly.

"Like he'd already lost you once," she said, her voice gentler now. "And wasn't going to let it happen again."

The silence that followed wasn't empty—it was *heavy*, thick with meaning I hadn't dared put into words. But now they were here. Between us. In the quiet hum of his apartment. In his shirt I was still wearing.

And I didn't know what to do with the way that made me feel.

Not yet.

But I was starting to want to.

I wrapped my hands around the mug, the warm ceramic grounding me as steam curled into the air like whispers I couldn't quite catch. The taste of the coffee barely registered, but it was enough to cut through the haze, to anchor me in the present as the threads of everything tangled tighter around me.

The case. The attack. The Mage who nearly ended me. McDara's hands on me—steady, strong, possessive in ways he hadn't voiced. And beneath it all, the way the Malifax Mage had treated at me like I was a key...or a threat.

The puzzle was still scattered, but something inside me had shifted. I could feel the border taking shape, the jagged edges aligning. The corners were there. All I had to do now was fill in the dark middle.

And figure out exactly where McDara belonged in all of it. Because wanting to trust him and being safe to trust him were two very different things. And in Blakewell, the line between them could be lethal.

The bandaged ache in my arm pulsed, a quiet heartbeat of pain laced with the memory of magic. I set the cup down and stared at the dark liquid, as if it might offer answers. It didn't.

"I can't believe it was only yesterday," I murmured. "I saw Calypso at Veritas. She looked like she'd seen a ghost...and then she saw McDara—and ran."

Phontine, still soaking in her mug like it was a personal hot spring, opened one sleepy eye. "Weird. What would she even be doing there? Is she even old enough to be a professor?"

"Not all college professors are greying and, in their seventies," I muttered, tapping my phone against the counter, jaw tight. "But she definitely didn't want us to see her."

"And the Black House?" Phontine added, stretching her tiny arms with a yawn. "Still gives me the creeps. Orlla was one of theirs, right? Why didn't anyone report her missing?"

"Calypso said she had left the Black house. Two weeks ago, well longer now," I said, trying—and failing—not to let the bitterness seep into my voice. "Two weeks being gone from a House she had spent, probably, most of her life in and then the night before we arrive in Blakewell she's murdered. You're telling me no one reached out to her? No one cared enough to wonder where she went after leaving?"

"Mage House's are like clubs. Maybe after she left no one was allowed to reach out," Phontine offered gently. "People don't really keep tabs after that, do they?"

"So what?" I snapped, heat rising, unbidden. "She didn't have *friends*? People who noticed she was gone? The Black House can't be *that* dead inside."

Phontine floated upward, her wings stirring the air as she hovered just in front of me. Her face softened, serious now. "Then maybe that's the question you need to ask. Who *were* her friends?"

The question sank into the room like a dropped blade. Quiet. Heavy. Sharp.

I opened my mouth, then closed it.

I didn't know.

I knew what Orlla had been researching. What she'd died chasing. But I didn't know who she'd laughed with. Who she trusted. Who she called when her hands were shaking, and her world was coming undone.

And I *hated* that.

I grabbed my phone, my thumbs moving fast over the keys, the thought sharpening with each word I typed. I hit send. My breath caught in my throat as I waited. Seconds passed. Then, my screen lit up with a reply.

A smile curved my lips. Slow. Focused.

"I don't know who her friends were," I said, eyes locked on Phontine and picked up the black card. "But I know someone who might."

Phontine's wings shimmered as she spun in midair. Her grin was mischievous, bordering on dangerous. "We're going shopping, aren't we?"

"With Calypso." I met her gaze. "And if she happens to spill a few secrets along the way...well. Who am I to stop her?"

Phontine tugged at a loose strand of my hair, her smirk smug. "Shopping trip with a side of covert questioning? You really *are* becoming a detective."

I laughed—low and rough around the edges. But it was real. "Better than waiting for another Malifax Mage to kick down the door and ask if I've seen their missing nightmare spellbook."

The phone buzzed again, and I glanced down. Calypso's response glowed bright on the screen—peppered with emojis, exclamation points, and enough enthusiasm to feel like a performance.

She was hiding something. I'd stake my soul on it.

But if Blakewell had taught me one thing, it was that smiles could lie, and glitter could cover up rot. Whatever mask she wore, I was done pretending not to see the cracks.

And I was finally ready to dig beneath them. One step. One secret. One sip of coffee at a time.

Calypso's car was a silver phantom of New Town wealth—sleek, seamless, and far too pristine for the likes of me. The door sighed open, and I slid into buttery leather that still smelled faintly of florals and status. Clean edges. Cool chrome. No room for dust or doubt. A far cry from my ash-streaked motel room.

Phontine fluttered in after me, wings leaving a faint trail of shimmer as she landed cross-legged on the dash. She'd opted to stay visible, her posture deceptively relaxed. But I knew her tension. I felt it mirrored in my chest. Ever since the motel attack, we'd decided that hiding wasn't an option anymore—not when the shadows were already crawling up our backs.

Calypso glanced at her, green eyes narrowing with clinical interest rather than wonder. "You're a Pixie?"

The question hung there, dissecting. Cold. Curious. Like Phontine was some relic under glass.

Phontine's wings twitched—small, but sharp. "Last time I checked," she said sweetly, her voice honey-laced steel.

I jumped in before Calypso could say something that would make things worse. "Phontine's been with me a long time. Kind of a ride-or-die situation."

Calypso didn't respond to *me*. Her gaze lingered on Phontine's wings like they were puzzle pieces. "Do you shed dust like Fairies, or is that something you can control?"

Phontine's lips thinned. I didn't need to look to know she was imagining glittering explosions in the shape of middle fingers. My own irritation sparked hot, but I buried it under a careful smile. "Where are we headed first?"

That broke the spell. Calypso shifted gears—literally—and the car pulled away from the curb with a hum that sounded like secrets being swept under marble floors.

Old Town blurred past in warm hues—brick buildings and ivy-strangled balconies, cracked sidewalks kissed by years of footsteps. But New Town rose like a mirror-world: All steel and shimmer, edges sharp enough to cut, its perfection an accusation. Even the air here smelled more expensive.

Our first stops were full of glass and silence. Clothes hung like museum pieces, too polished to be real. The music was soft, the stares cold. None of it fit. I didn't need armor that shimmered—I needed something I could bleed in without breaking.

Then, finally, Calypso led us through a beaded arch, and I breathed out. This place had color. Soul. A pulse beneath the stitched chaos. Boho-grunge, lush with velvet and attitude. Oversized silhouettes. Textured walls. Scents of sandalwood and sage hung in the air like an invitation.

Calypso lifted a kaleidoscope dress, but my mind was already turning, each click of a hanger a drumbeat under my next move.

"I've been thinking," I said, running my fingers over a rack of vintage band tees, voice light as smoke. "About the Black House."

She perked up instantly—too fast, too bright. "Yeah? What about it?"

I hesitated, just enough to let her lean in. "If Matron Black would still have me...I think I want to join." I bit my lip, injecting a dose of doubt. "I can't get this magic under control on my own."

Something flared in her eyes. A spark. Not quite relief. Not quite hunger. "That's amazing. Matron Black would be thrilled." She smiled, too practiced. "The House is everything. Power, structure. Family."

Family. She said it like a spell. Like it was meant to root me, trap me.

"What's it really like, though?" I asked, pulling a soft cardigan from the rack and hiding behind its warmth. "I mean...when Matron Black isn't around, who runs things?"

"Oh, we have House Leaders." Calypso's voice slid back into silk, all smooth edges. "They handle the day-to-day. Like mentors. It's not as rigid as it sounds."

I tilted my head, just enough to look casual. "Are you close to any of them?"

"Sure." She reached for a necklace, but her fingers didn't land. "Orlla was one. Organized, in control. She had a hand in everything. That's why it was weird when she vanished."

I kept my gaze on a stack of bracelets, voice featherlight. "And no one...looked for her?"

"She kept her personal life personal. Especially at the end. From what I know about her, her job at Varitas University was kind of everything. I think people thought she just..." She trailed off, fingers brushing beads that didn't glitter nearly as much as the lie between her lips. "Left."

Phontine floated past a crystal display, her wings catching the light just enough to look accidental. But her eyes found mine—and in them, a flicker of truth: *She's hiding something.*

"And Matron Black was okay with her job at the university?"

"Of course," Calypso answered with practiced ease. "No one in the House gets a job anywhere unless Matron Black approves."

In other words, as long as Matron Black could use Orlla's job somehow to her benefit she could keep it.

The air grew tighter, thick with perfume and false sincerity. I held Calypso's words like glass—beautiful, fragile, and just waiting to shatter.

And I was ready to break it. Piece by piece. Secret by secret.

I didn't let up. "What about the other House Leaders?" I asked, voice silk-wrapped steel. "Did they notice anything off?"

Calypso gave a soft shrug, all polished grace. "There are always whispers. But nothing solid." Her tone was careful, rehearsed. "Orlla was...intense. Maybe she just needed a break. A reset."

A reset in the woods where no one comes back, I thought, but said nothing.

I grabbed a few oversized tops, all ripped edges and soft cotton, and gestured toward the dressing room. "Mind if I try these on?"

"Go for it," Calypso said, distracted by a display of scarves that shimmered like spun moonlight.

The curtain whispered shut behind me. Dim light flickered overhead, and my reflection stared back, raw and too aware. I leaned in close, whispering to the only one I could trust. "What do you think?"

Phontine landed lightly on my shoulder, her voice barely more than breath. "She knows more than she's saying. Orlla couldn't have been that isolated. If Calypso's lying about that..."

"Then what else is she lying about?" I finished, heart ticking faster.

The curtain rustled. I barely had time to straighten before Calypso's arm slipped through the side, hanging a few more skirts and dresses on the hook. "You never know when you'll want to look cute for someone," she teased, her voice singsong.

Startled, I nearly yelped. *Had she heard us?* My pulse spiked, but I forced a laugh, my fingers brushing soft velvet as I muttered, "Yeah, because clearly the ghosts and I are on a hot date trajectory."

Phontine snorted behind me.

I peeked through the gap in the curtain. Calypso browsed racks with a breezy sort of grace, a carefree sway in her hips. Everything about her was bright, effortless. Friendly.

But that friendliness was a mask, and I knew it—because I was wearing one too.

Even so, it was hard not to feel her light. Hard not to like her.

We made our way to the checkout, the boutique now glowing in the soft gold of early afternoon. Phontine hovered nearby, wings trailing shimmer, while the Fairy cashier rang up our finds with all the enthusiasm of someone stuck between shifts. Magic hummed softly in the air—New Town's version of normal.

Calypso turned to me, a sly smile lifting the corners of her mouth. "So...you and Detective Broody McTall-and-Dark?"

My fingers slipped on my bag, nearly sending it tumbling to the floor. "What about him?"

"Oh, come on." She grinned. "You weren't exactly sneaky. I picked you up at his place."

Before I could deflect, Phontine dove in with zero shame. "Oh, she definitely has a thing for him. You should've seen her the other morning. All swoony and awkward over eggs."

"Phontine!" I hissed, but the damage was done.

She twirled midair, unrepentant. "He was cooking shirtless. What's a girl supposed to do?"

Calypso's laughter rang out, clear and easy. "Well, well. So, the detective has hidden talents. Good to know he's not all temper and scowls."

"He's not as bad as he seems," I muttered.

Even if you looked terrified of him at the University.

Which only made her grin deepen. "Mm-hmm. That's what people say right before they fall hard."

And damn it, I laughed. Genuine, breath-stealing laughter. It felt good. Dangerous, but good.

We stepped back onto the sunlit sidewalk, New Town's glittering towers reflecting the sky like mirrors trying to convince you they were portals to somewhere better. Calypso's bags swung in rhythm with her steps, and that lightness she carried suddenly made me want to tell her everything.

So, I did.

"Last night…" My voice came out softer than I expected. "I was attacked. In my motel room."

She stopped walking. Just—stopped. Her face shifted instantly, her smile vanishing like mist. "What?"

"A Malifax Mage," I said. "They almost killed me."

Her lips parted in shock, the horror in her expression raw and real. "Bless the Wood, Sonia. Are you—are you okay?"

I gave a small nod. "McDara and Dom showed up after I got away. But the room's gone. I'm staying with McDara until I figure out my next move."

She blinked, as if trying to reorder her mental list of me. Her voice was quieter now. More grounded. "I'm glad he was there. I mean that. And…if you ever need somewhere else—my place, anything—I'm here."

"I know," I said, and for a moment, I let myself believe her.

I studied her as we walked toward the car, the weight of what I hadn't said hanging between us. There were still gaps in her story—edges that didn't line up. But there was also kindness. And concern. And maybe, just maybe, something real.

"Hey," I said lightly. "You up for a coffee stop? I know a place in Old Town. The Obsidian Quill."

Calypso tilted her head. "That place with the spiraling book tower and all the weird tea blends?"

"That's the one."

She smiled. "I've always wanted to go." And started down the sidewalk.

Phontine brushed against my cheek, a tiny puff of breath. "She's either hiding something really well...or she's just as tangled as you are."

"Great," I said, slipping into the passenger seat. "Let's see what else today has planned."

Because secrets don't stay buried forever.

And Blakewell? It had a habit of digging things up.

29

The Obsidian Quill shimmered with twilight magic—soft orbs of light floating above tables, the scent of caramel and ancient parchment curling through the air like a charm. It was the kind of place that breathed; alive in the quiet moments, warm against the cold edge of the world outside.

As soon as we stepped through the door, Keyleth spotted us. Her honey-brown eyes lit up, her white-blonde curls bouncing as she darted across the floor like sunlight incarnate.

"There you are!" she exclaimed, sweeping me into a hug that stole the tension from my spine. Her arms were warm, grounding, the kind of comfort that settled too deep to be just skin and bone. "And you brought a friend!"

"Calypso." She introduced herself with a polite smile and a flick of her sleek hair.

They hit it off immediately, like long-lost cousins catching up. Phontine, never one to be left out, landed on Keyleth's shoulder and promptly helped herself to a pinch of scone, chattering between crumbs. For the first time in days, I felt something close to *normal*. Just a girl in a cozy café, hands wrapped around a warm mug, the ghost of fear quiet—for now.

When the afternoon rush crested, Keyleth was swept back behind the counter in a flurry of laughter and glowing drink orders. The hum of life filled the air—clinking mugs, whispered conversations, the occasional spell flickering from a corner table. She moved like a ribbon of light through it all, radiant and untouchable.

Calypso and I sank into the quiet lull that followed. Phontine curled into the nook between my neck and the chair, her tiny presence a steady rhythm against my pulse. The calm was disarming. Dangerous, even. It made room for questions.

I turned to Calypso, voice casual, but edged with something sharper. "I thought I saw you at Veritas yesterday."

She stilled, just a flicker, but it was there—the way her grip tightened on her mug, the way her eyes darted before she masked it. "Oh. You did. I'm a teaching assistant there."

I tilted my head. "Really? You never mentioned you were in school."

She gave a small, sheepish smile. "Matron Black doesn't know. None of the House Leaders do. They've got...other plans for me." Her voice dropped, quieter. More real.

Something in her face cracked open—just enough for me to see the girl behind the perfection. Not the recruiter. Not the polished, Black House Mage. Just a young woman who wanted a future she might never get to claim.

"What kind of plans?" I asked gently, tracing the rim of my mug with one finger.

"They want me on the Mage Council someday. But first, I'm supposed to take on more responsibility within the House. Politics, leadership...all of it." She shrugged. "But I just want to teach."

For a beat, we sat in the silence between should and want, between power and peace. Then she leaned in, voice barely a breath. "I wasn't just there for work. I was looking for something."

My grip tightened around my cup. "In Orlla's classroom?"

A single nod. "She was working on something for the House. When she died, Matron Black and the others couldn't find it. I thought maybe...she hid it."

"What was it?" I asked, tone even, as if my heart wasn't pounding against my ribs.

"Two things," she whispered. "A map—really old. And a spell. One Orlla made herself. Matron Black wanted both. Badly."

A *spell*. My mind flashed to the grimoire, to Orlla's ghost guarding it like a final breath she hadn't yet released. "Did you find them?"

Calypso's mouth thinned. "No. I think Matron Black might already have them, but…I had to be sure." Her hand shot across the table, closing over mine. Her fingers were trembling. "Please don't tell her I was searching. If she finds out…"

Her fear wasn't performative. It was raw. Real. It bled through the cracks in her smile and wrapped around her words like a curse. "She can't know."

"I won't say a word," I said, squeezing her hand in return. And I meant it.

She exhaled like someone who hadn't let their lungs fill in days. "Thank you. I just…I want to find my own path. Not one someone else carved for me."

I nodded slowly, my thoughts already spiraling.

An ancient map. A hidden spell. A House Leader who died with secrets wrapped around her like a shroud. And a girl, bright and earnest, tangled in a game she might not survive.

The question was no longer *if* someone tightened the noose around Orlla's throat.

It was *who* planned to use the same rope on the rest of us.

The car whispered over pavement, soft indie chords threading through the silence like a spell meant to hold the day together. Phontine perched on my shoulder, wings barely rustling, while Calypso hummed along—too sweet, too normal.

For a heartbeat, it felt like a stolen afternoon. Like I could pretend the world wasn't unraveling beneath our feet.

Then we turned a corner.

And everything cracked.

Old Town's streets were choked with bodies—Magicals pressed shoulder to shoulder, their voices raised in a tide of protest that swallowed the quiet whole. Signs rose like teeth above the crowd: *We Bleed Too, The Wood Is Not Yours, Protect Magic. Protect Us.*

Magic clung to the air like mist, charged and volatile, humming with rage and desperation. The crowd didn't buzz—it pulsed, like a living heart on the verge of rupturing.

Calypso's hands tightened on the wheel. Her knuckles blanched against the leather, and I felt the mood in the car snap from calm to coiled in an instant.

"What's going on?" My voice was thinner than I meant it to be.

Phontine's wings trembled against my hair. "This isn't good," she whispered, and for once, her voice held no sarcasm.

Calypso's jaw clenched. "The protests are growing. More cities. More fear."

"Why?" I asked, my breath fogging slightly against the window. "What are they protesting?"

She hesitated.

And in that hesitation, I felt the answer begin to burn.

"Australia," she said finally. Her voice was low, distant, like she didn't want to say it aloud. "They're preparing to send troops into the Wood in Australia. The government wants to eliminate it. The NHG is helping. If the Wood falls...so does everything born of it."

I froze. "Eliminate the Wood?"

"That's suicide," Phontine snapped. "You don't *destroy* the Wood. Nothing manmade can take it out unless they want to try an atomic bomb."

"They might," Calypso whispered. "They think they can rewrite magic with bullets and bombs. That maybe the old rules can be overwritten by new warfare."

Outside, the protesters pressed closer, their eyes sharp with fury, their signs shaking like shields against a world that had turned on them. Fae in leather jackets, Shifters with eyes like predators, Goblins standing firm between their taller kin. The desperation was tangible, almost unbearable.

I swallowed hard. "Why now?"

Calypso's eyes flicked toward me, then back to the road. "Humans are dying. Important ones. Ministers. Celebrities. There's always a magical trace. Fairy dust. Malifax residue. Vampire venom."

The chill in the car wasn't from the AC.

"Vampires aren't even natural-born Magicals," I muttered. "They're a human experiment gone wrong."

"Same with Mages," she said softly. "But the humans don't care. They see magic, and they see the threat. And they want to put it down before it devours them."

The car crept through the crowd, a fragile shell in the center of a brewing storm. Protesters parted slowly, reluctantly, like they had to force themselves not to lash out. Some glared through the windows, their eyes raw with betrayal. Others looked through us like we were already ghosts.

"I didn't realize it had gotten this bad," I murmured.

Calypso's knuckles flexed against the wheel. "Because they've kept it quiet. Behind press conferences and diplomacy. But underneath? It's a powder keg. And it only takes one spark."

My fingers curled against my thigh. "What do you think should happen?"

Her silence was the loudest sound I'd ever heard.

"I don't know," she admitted, her voice cracking like glass under pressure. "I just know we're all standing on a cliff. And I don't know if we're going to fly—or fall."

I turned back to the window, but I wasn't seeing the protest anymore. I was seeing shadows—the Malifax Mage, Orlla's ghost, the slow creep of darkness threading through Blakewell like poison in a vein.

And somewhere beneath all that—McDara, standing alone in the storm, trying to hold back a flood.

The world was changing.

And if we weren't careful, it would break us with it.

30

The apartment wrapped around me like a heartbeat—low and steady, warm and waiting.

It smelled like garlic and rosemary, like heat and home. The kind of scent that lingers in someone's clothes long after they've left. I moved through McDara's kitchen barefoot, sleeves rolled up, surrounded by mismatched dishes and the clatter of silverware that didn't quite go together. Everything had a story here—nothing perfect, but everything purposeful. Lived-in. Like him.

The marinara simmered, a low, bubbling murmur from the stove. Chicken sizzled in the pan, golden and crisp, and a pot of pasta steamed beside it. I stirred. Tasted. Adjusted the salt. Not because I was trying to impress him—okay, maybe a little—but because it kept me from staring at my phone like a lunatic.

Only one text from him all day.

You okay?

That was it. Two words. Just enough to make my heart stutter in my chest, and not nearly enough to calm the storm building inside me.

No follow-up. No update. The news barely acknowledged the protests beyond the sanitized headline, *Rising Magical Tensions.* As if the world wasn't slowly fracturing beneath our feet.

So, I cooked.

One look at my face and the meal I was intending to prepare and Phontine said she needed to "go for a walk". As if the Pixie ever willing walked anywhere but I appreciated her giving me space to...Well I wasn't entirely sure *what* I was doing but I wanted to spend time with McDara. Which was exciting and terrifying all at once, hints the elaborate meal.

Food was grounding. It was something real to offer someone who'd stepped into the fire for me. Someone who made me feel like maybe I wasn't always falling.

I was just placing the last mismatched plate when the door opened with a soft click.

And McDara stepped inside.

The breath caught in my throat.

He looked...wrecked. His shirt was rumpled, dark smudges painted beneath his eyes, and the weight of the city clung to his shoulders like a second skin. But when he saw me—standing in his kitchen like I belonged there, the scent of dinner curling through the air—something fractured behind his eyes.

And then...softened.

His gaze swept over the scene, lingering on me like he couldn't quite believe I was real. Like he'd been bracing himself for something sharp and found warmth instead.

"Hey," I said, voice soft, almost unsure. "I, uh...made dinner. Thought I'd say thank you. For the whole...keeping me alive thing."

Smooth. Real smooth.

He didn't smile right away. Just blinked. Then his mouth curved slowly, a tug of amusement and something deeper. Something that lit a flicker of heat low in my belly.

"You didn't have to do that," he said, voice rasped raw from too many hours without rest. He stepped into the kitchen, opening a cabinet and pulling down two wineglasses like he'd done it a hundred times. "But I'm glad you did."

The space between us was too small. Intimate. Every movement brought us closer—reaching for forks, brushing shoulders, breathing the same air. His scent—cedar and storm light and something that felt like safety—wrapped around me.

He took the wine bottle from the counter. Our fingers grazed.

A spark. Sharp. Immediate. Alive.

He paused, eyes flicking to mine, then uncorked the bottle in one smooth motion. Poured. Handed me a glass. The briefest brush of skin again—enough to make my pulse trip.

He lifted his own. "To not letting you die," he said, a crooked smile teasing at the corner of his mouth.

Gods help me, I smiled back. "I'll drink to that."

We sat; the table between us but barely a barrier. I served the plates, nerves twisting in my stomach, but he took the first bite and stilled—eyes closing for a brief, silent moment. His shoulders eased, a breath slipping from him like he'd been holding it all day.

"This is really good," he said, like it surprised him.

I shrugged, trying not to show how much that meant. "Cooking helps me think."

He studied me across the flickering candlelight—his gaze not the usual guarded steel, but something achingly raw. Quiet. Curious.

And I couldn't help wondering what he saw when he looked at me like that.

Not a Ghost Whisperer. Not a victim. Not even a problem to solve.

Just...me.

And somehow, that was the most dangerous thing of all.

"You could put half the places in Old Town to shame." McDara said around a mouthful of chicken, his voice low with something close to reverence.

Warmth flared in my chest—unsteady, uninvited, but impossible to ignore. I looked down at my plate, cheeks heating like the simmering sauce on the stove. "Figured I'd use my culinary degree before the real world melts it out of me."

He froze mid-bite, his fork suspended in the air. "I didn't ask before but, why culinary school?"

I lifted my wineglass, suddenly shy under his gaze. "My dream is to open a restaurant because... The first time I felt like I had a family was in my parents tiny, kitchen. It had this horrible 90s aesthetic but that's where she taught me how to make pancakes." I blinked quickly to keep the hot burn prickingly my eyes at bay. "She had tried for three weeks to get me to spend time out of my room but back then I was always being shuffled form foster homes and just...couldn't get attached but cooking with her. It's my first memory of having a mom and I want to honor that."

The admiration that flickered across his face wasn't casual. It wasn't pity or politeness. It was genuine—and it hit harder than I expected. He looked at me like I wasn't just surviving Blakewell...like I *deserved* something more.

"That's a big dream," he said quietly.

I gave a small, brittle laugh and swirled the wine in my glass. "Kind of ridiculous now, isn't it? I mean, I can't even go a week here without being cursed or nearly murdered."

McDara set his fork down slowly. The scrape of metal on ceramic was soft but final. He leaned forward, his elbows on the table, his eyes locked on mine like he could see straight through the cracks.

"You could still do it," he said, low and firm. "You *will* do it. You've already survived more than most people could stomach. Don't downplay that. You're tougher than you think."

The words slid under my skin, catching in every fragile place I didn't know was still bleeding.

And gods—he meant it. Not just as comfort. Not as pity. As fact.

I wanted to say something. To thank him. To tell him he didn't have to look at me like that, but that I didn't want him to stop.

Instead, I just nodded. A small motion. But it held everything I couldn't say.

The room settled into silence, the kind that *throbbed* with things unsaid. His foot brushed mine beneath the table, and neither of us moved away. That one point of contact burned. The kind of touch that lingered. That *meant* something.

The quiet wrapped around us, soft and thick as fog. The scent of garlic and rosemary still hung in the air. But beneath it was something deeper. A pulse. A shift.

I didn't know what this was—this thing between us. I didn't know if it was real or if I just wanted it to be. But with McDara watching me like I was something worth protecting, something worth *believing in*—I let myself hope.

When the last bite of food disappeared, he rose and began clearing the dishes before I could move.

"You cooked," he said, not even looking back. "I clean."

No room for argument. His voice was steady, almost gentle, but edged with that quiet authority he wore like armor.

I watched him rinse the dishes, his movements efficient, practiced. The flex of muscle beneath his shirt made my breath catch—and not just from admiration. From safety. From the strange intimacy of it all. This wasn't a battlefield or an interrogation or some near-death adrenaline rush. It was *quiet*. And that made it more dangerous.

I tucked the leftovers into the fridge, pretending not to notice the way his eyes followed me when he thought I wouldn't catch it. When I turned, he was leaning against the counter, arms crossed, a smile ghosting his lips.

"You've got a real system going," he said, nodding at the neat rows of containers.

I shrugged, trying to play it cool. "Occupational hazard. Order matters in a kitchen."

His voice dipped lower. "I get that."

It hit a little too close. I swallowed. Smiled. Reached for something lighter.

"You know," I said, opening the freezer with a dramatic flourish, "I also splurged. Häagen-Dazs."

His brow arched. "What flavor?"

I turned, holding up the carton like it was a prized relic. "Chocolate peanut butter. The best flavor."

He leaned in, challenging. "Debatable."

I gasped. "You wound me."

"Mint chip," he said without hesitation.

I narrowed my eyes. "You mean toothpaste."

He scoffed, stepping closer. "You have *no* taste."

"Fine. I'll eat the ice cream myself. Alone. In dramatic mourning."

He was smiling now—really smiling—the kind of expression that softened every hard edge and made him look just a little less like a man who carried the weight of Blakewell on his back.

Then he said, voice low, lazy, *dangerous*, "How about we split it? Over a movie."

My pulse skipped.

He didn't move, didn't press. Just stood there with the offer hanging between us, charged and quiet and far more intimate than it should've been.

I nodded before I could talk myself out of it. "Yeah," I said, the word barely more than breath. "Sure. Why not."

McDara moved into the living room, his body moving with that effortless confidence that made everything seem deliberate, measured, like a predator conserving energy until it was time to strike. He grabbed the remote, flicked on the TV, and dropped onto the couch with the kind of ease that said he rarely let anyone into this space. And now...I was here.

His apartment was small. Just a few steps separated the kitchen from the couch. But crossing that space felt like something more than distance—it felt like permission. Like I was being let in not just physically, but in all the ways that mattered.

I brought the ice cream and two spoons, ignoring how fast my heart was beating. My hands didn't shake, but they wanted to. I wasn't sure what terrified me more: The proximity or the fact that I didn't *want* to pull back from it.

McDara glanced at me, the flicker of a smirk playing on his lips. "What kind of movies do you like?"

I passed him a spoon and took a bite of ice cream, the cool sweetness grounding me. "Scary movies. Action, too."

His brow arched, skepticism wrapped in amusement. "Seriously?"

I met his gaze and shrugged, casual. "Seeing ghosts every day kind of ruined horror flicks for me. Fake monsters don't really hit the same when you've had Death lounging on your motel bed."

That earned a laugh—a real one. Low and rough and beautiful. The kind of sound that tugged at something in my chest. I wanted to hear it again. I wanted to be the reason he laughed like that again.

"And the action movies?" he asked, still smiling.

I leaned back into the couch with faux nonchalance. "The guys in *Fast and Furious* are hot."

His laugh deepened, resonating from somewhere in his chest. "That's fair. I mean, they do have a lot of cars...and biceps."

I grinned. "Exactly."

He shook his head, but there was something soft in his expression now. "I thought girls were into rom-coms. Emotional endings. Grand gestures."

I rolled my eyes. "Heartbreak already sucks in real life. Why would I want to pay for two hours of it on purpose?"

That sobered him, the amusement fading into something quieter. More sincere. "Yeah," he said, his voice a little rougher now. "You're right."

The way he looked at me then—it wasn't playful. It wasn't teasing. It was *intent*. Like he saw something in me he wasn't sure he deserved but wasn't about to look away from either. My breath caught, chest tightening around something fragile and foolish and *hopeful*.

He clicked the remote. "*Fast and Furious* it is."

The TV filled the space with roaring engines and pulsing beats, but the real tension wasn't on the screen. It was here. In the way our shoulders touched. In the warmth of his thigh pressed to mine. In the hum of awareness that sparked to life every time our hands grazed reaching for the same tub of ice cream.

We didn't talk.

We didn't need to.

The silence between us was thick with things unsaid—desire and doubt and the ache of everything we couldn't admit. The movie became background noise, the forgotten ice cream melting slowly on the coffee table as we leaned in without meaning to. Or maybe we *did* mean to. Maybe we'd both just run out of excuses to pretend we didn't.

At some point, the space between us vanished completely.

His arm was a quiet weight behind me, not quite around me, but close enough to make my skin burn where it hovered. I could feel his breath, warm against my temple. I could feel him watching me, just as intently as I had been watching him.

I turned my head—and found him already looking.

Time didn't slow. It *stopped*.

His eyes were dark and steady, stormy with things he hadn't said and didn't know how to say. The light from the TV painted the sharp lines of his face in silver and shadow. And in that suspended heartbeat, I forgot every reason to hold back.

Neither of us moved.

And yet, somehow, we were closer.

His hand shifted, just slightly, the brush of his fingers a ghost of a touch against my arm. It wasn't a kiss. It wasn't a confession.

But it was enough to burn.

And I wasn't sure what scared me more—that he might kiss me...

Or that he wouldn't.

He didn't move. Didn't blink. Didn't break the fragile thread stretched taut between us, as though even breath could snap it.

His gaze held mine like gravity, unrelenting and silent. I could feel the warmth of him in the space we shared, the way his exhale ghosted across my lips—peppermint-laced from the tea he'd sipped earlier.

My mouth parted, breath catching. And that was when his eyes dropped.

The moment his gaze landed on my lips, everything inside me stilled—then ignited. The weight of his attention was fire and restraint, molten heat barely caged. A burn waiting for permission.

His hand moved, slow and deliberate, as though even the act of reaching for me was sacred. Fingers brushed a loose strand of hair behind my ear, his knuckles skimming my cheek like an afterthought that wrecked me. A barely there touch, but my skin lit up beneath it, nerves blazing, breath faltering.

His thumb trailed the line of my jaw. Featherlight. Reverent. Like I was something precious. Like he didn't trust himself not to ruin me.

Then his hand slipped into my hair, a careful cradle at the nape of my neck. He pulled me an inch closer, and that inch was everything.

My lungs forgot how to work.

Our breath tangled. Our lips hovered. The air between us thinned to a heartbeat.

"Tell me to stop," he said. It was a rasp—fractured and low, threaded with something broken and aching. "Say the word, Sonia, and I will."

But I couldn't.

I wouldn't.

I wet my bottom lip, a nervous flick of my tongue, and his eyes followed the movement like it hurt him. His breath hitched, a sound half swallowed, and then—

I moved first.

I leaned in that final sliver and our mouths met like a match striking flame.

His lips caught mine in a kiss that felt like a fall and a fight all at once—rough and reverent, steady and starved. His hand in my hair tightened, angling my face just right as he deepened the kiss. It wasn't tentative. It wasn't careful.

It was *real*.

A rush of heat surged through me. When I pressed closer, his free hand slid over my waist, his touch warm through the thin fabric of his shirt I wore. His fingers flexed, pulling me closer until there was no space left, only heat and breath and the soft, electric slide of lips against lips.

We moved together like we were built for this. Like every silence, every glance, every charged breath between us had been a prelude to this exact moment.

The kiss was a quiet devastation, a promise and a plea, and I gave myself to it, to him, losing track of where I ended and he began. The movie played on, an irrelevant backdrop to the symphony of our breathing, the soft rustle of fabric, and the quiet, aching sounds escaping between us.

When he pulled back, just enough to meet my gaze, his forehead resting against mine, I opened my eyes. His were dark, his pupils blown wide, a mix of desire and something softer, something that made my chest tighten.

"Sonia," he whispered, my name a rough prayer on his lips. His thumb brushed against my cheek, a gentle counterpoint to the possessive hold he still had on me.

"Yeah?" I whispered back, my voice a ghost of itself.

He didn't answer, not with words. Instead, he kissed me again, softer this time, a quiet vow, and I melted into him, knowing that I could stay like this, tangled up in him, and never need anything else.

McDara's lips were still a warm ghost against mine, the heat of his breath mingling with mine, when the sharp trill of my phone pierced through the heady fog between us. I jolted, the abruptness like a splash of ice water, and blinked up at him. His eyes were dark, unfocused, the kind of dazed I'd never seen on him before. His hand still rested on my cheek, his thumb brushing the curve of my jaw, as if letting go wasn't an option he'd considered.

I could've stayed there forever.

But then—

BRRRRT. BRRRRT.

The shrill ring going off again shattered the moment, the sound slicing through the warmth like ice water. I jolted, startled, and blinked up at him.

McDara looked dazed—like he'd just surfaced from something deep and consuming. His hand was still on my cheek, thumb brushing along the curve of my jaw, reluctant to let go.

Another buzz. *Then another.*

I fumbled for the phone, still breathless, and read the name glowing on the screen.

"It's my mom," I said, the weight of reality pressing back in.

His thumb stilled. His lips parted, like maybe—just maybe—he was going to kiss me again anyway.

But then his hand slipped away, slow and unwilling, like the moment between us had teeth, and neither of us wanted to unhook.

"Go ahead," he said, voice rough and low, scraped raw by restraint. But his eyes didn't release me.

They held me there—strung tight between the ache of what almost was...

And what still might be.

I nodded, forcing my body to move—each step away from him felt like I was peeling myself out of something warm and safe. The space between us stretched like tension in a held breath as I crossed to the window, phone pressed tight to my ear.

"Hey, Mom."

Her voice poured through the line like sunlight after a storm—soft, familiar, and impossibly kind. "Sonia, sweetheart! How are you doing, honey? I know you said not to worry, but you know me."

Bless the Wood. That voice. It wrapped around the bruised parts of me like a blanket I hadn't realized I needed until it was already there. The knot in my chest twisted, tight and painful—grief and guilt braided together.

I pressed my forehead to the rain-specked window, letting the glass cool the burn beneath my skin. Behind me, McDara stayed silent. I could feel him watching. The echo of our kiss still pulsed on my lips.

"Yeah, I'm good," I lied softly. "Everything's...fine."

The word cracked under its own weight.

"That's good." Her voice lowered, gentle and so full of love it made my throat ache. "You'd tell me if you weren't, right? I just worry, you know? Especially with everything...well, with everything."

Especially since Dad died.

My fingers clenched the hem of McDara's shirt where it hung on my body—soft, oversized, his scent still clinging to the fabric like a phantom touch. I breathed in, steadying myself.

"Actually," I said slowly, "I decided to take a little trip."

A pause. Tension braided into silence.

"A trip? Where to?"

I swallowed hard. "Blakewell."

Another silence—this one colder.

"Blakewell?" she echoed. Not angry, but careful. Like stepping into an old wound. "Why did you go to Blakewell, honey?"

I bit the inside of my cheek until I tasted copper. "I needed to learn more about my magic. You know how it is. No Mage House in Chicago would take me. Not without active casting magic." My voice wavered. I forced it steady again. "I thought...if I could find a blood relative, maybe I could get some answers. Figure out how to control it."

The silence that followed was long and heavy. A truth waiting to be spoken.

"You're looking for your birth parents." It wasn't a question.

I turned my face to the glass, breath fogging a soft circle there. "Yes. But it's not about them. Not really. You're my mom. You always will be." My voice cracked, and I didn't fight it. "This is just...about my magic. About figuring it out so maybe...maybe we can talk to Dad again."

Her sigh broke something in me. That mother sigh. Full of love, full of ache. Full of things she'd never say out loud because her daughter already carried too much.

"Oh, sweetheart," she murmured, that same hush she used to soothe nightmares when I was little. "You don't have to do this. Not for me. I know how much you miss him. I do too. But this—this burden—it's not yours to carry alone."

"I want to," I whispered. "I *need* to. If there's even a chance to talk to him again...to hear his voice..." My throat closed around the hope, the desperation I'd been burying under sarcasm and silence. "I need to try."

Another pause. Then her voice, soft and steady. "I understand. Just promise me you'll be safe. No matter what you find, you're my little girl. You always will be. Nothing changes that."

The tear slipped free before I could stop it, burning a trail down my cheek. "I promise. I love you, Mom."

"I love you too, sweetheart. Always. Call me tomorrow, okay? And if you need any-thing—anything—you let me know."

"I will." My voice was threadbare.

We said goodbye. The line went dead.

And I was left with the echo of her love, the weight of my silence, and a truth I still wasn't ready to tell her. That I wasn't just in Blakewell looking for answers. I was in Blakewell running from something I hadn't even named yet.

I wiped at my face with the back of my hand, straightening, and turned—

McDara was still there.

He hadn't moved. He hadn't left.

He just sat in the warm light of his apartment, watching me like I was something breakable. His eyes held no judgment, only quiet understanding. The kind that didn't demand words.

He just held out a hand.

A simple thing. A devastating thing. A vow made with no words at all. A promise that said: *I'm here. I'm not going anywhere.*

And I reached for him before I could think better of it.

I took his hand.

The warmth of his palm wrapped around mine like a tether, pulling me back from the edge of the ache I hadn't realized I was standing on. Just that simple connection—his skin against mine—was enough to quiet the storm still crackling in my chest.

The room had gone quiet, too quiet, the air thick with everything unspoken. I fidgeted, thumb brushing the still warm phone in my hand, my mom's voice echoing like a lullaby laced with guilt.

I curled into his side. His arm came around me immediately, strong and sure, and I let my head rest against his chest. The sound of his heartbeat filled my ear—steady, protective, *present*. I hadn't realized how much I missed feeling that. The reassurance of someone simply *staying*.

"You didn't tell her about the Malifax Mage or the ghost," he murmured, voice a low thrum against my cheek.

"No," I whispered, watching the way my fingers twisted into the hem of his shirt. "She's been through too much already. I didn't want to make it worse."

His thumb brushed slow, steady circles across my shoulder, and it felt like the only thing holding me together.

"Why Blakewell?" he asked, quiet. "Why not anywhere else?"

I exhaled hard, the breath shuddering through me like a confession. "My dad died six months ago. Car crash. One minute he was there, the next he was just…gone." I swallowed. "I've been trying to use my abilities to see him again. Just once. Just so my mom and I could say goodbye. But I don't know how to *do* this. Ghost Whisperers aren't trained with books. And no Mage House would even look at me without active casting magic."

His hand stilled, resting against my arm like he was trying to absorb the weight of my pain into himself. "So, you came here looking for someone who would."

"Someone who *has* to." I blinked back the burn behind my eyes. "My birth parents. They lived here before they left. Before I was put in foster care."

He was quiet for a long moment. But his arm didn't loosen. His breath stayed warm and even against my skin.

"And your adoptive parents?"

"I knew the truth from the start. I mean…" I let out a short, bitter laugh. "I was eight when they adopted me. Before them any family that had fostered me with the intention of adoption bailed once I started acting…wired. Ghost don't make you an appealing option to future moms and dads." My voice softened. "But my parents never made me feel anything less than loved. It didn't matter that I didn't come from them. They told me I *belonged* with them. Always."

I closed my eyes, letting the stillness press in around us like a second skin. I owed Mom and Dad so much.

"But now I'm here. Because if I can find my birth family…maybe I can find a way to control this. Find a way to say goodbye to my dad. Give my mom that peace."

His breath brushed the crown of my head. When he spoke again, his voice was hushed, laced with something rough and reverent. "That makes sense. If anyone could help you, it would be them."

A lump swelled in my throat. "If they're gone now…I don't know what I'll do."

His grip around me tightened—not possessive but anchoring. Like he was wordlessly saying *you're not alone*.

I stayed there, curled into the quiet strength of him, listening to the rhythm of his heart. I wanted to stay like this forever, wrapped in a moment that asked nothing of me but to *be*. To feel without explanation. To exist without defense.

But the truth sat heavy on my tongue. The offer from Matron Black. The pull of the Black House. The dark shadow of everything he *hated*.

I could feel the question unspoken between us, flickering in the space where honesty waited to rise.

And still—I said nothing.

Not yet.

Because for once, I didn't want to feel like a burden. I wanted to feel like *his*. And right now, in the hush between the past and whatever came next…I did.

31

The scent hit me first—garlic, black pepper, and bacon fat curling through the air like a promise. Coffee brewed low and steady, a rhythm that pulsed through the kitchen like a heartbeat. I stepped inside, the hem of my new skirt brushing my thighs, soft fabric against skin that still remembered last night's warmth.

McDara stood at the counter, his broad back to me, muscles tense under a faded, gray shirt. He moved with quiet precision, pouring coffee into a travel mug, his shoulders rigid like he'd braced for battle rather than breakfast.

A flutter stirred low in my chest—stupid and hopeful, reckless and fragile.

I stepped forward and wrapped my arms around him from behind, cheek pressing to the space between his shoulder blades. His warmth radiated through the cotton, and for a beat, I let myself sink into it. Into him.

He stilled.

No lean into me. No shift of comfort. Just...a pause. Then a single, hesitant pat on my arm. Not a touch. A dismissal disguised as one.

I pulled away. The movement felt sharper than I meant it to be, but the cold that swept over me was instant and biting.

McDara turned, face unreadable, all hard lines and guarded silence. He offered me a travel mug like it was a peace offering. "Coffee's ready."

His voice was smooth. Controlled. Nothing like the man who'd held me like a lifeline last night.

"Thanks," I murmured, taking the mug. My fingers curled around it like it could shield me from the chill his distance had left behind.

He was already moving, grabbing his keys, his wallet, his badge. Back to routine. Back to control. "Dom's waiting. You'll give your statement at the station."

I forced a nod, added cream and sugar to my coffee like it mattered. Like I hadn't just watched something invisible but real fracture between us.

"If you're hungry, there's toast. Bacon too."

His voice was polite. Flat.

Like I was a guest. Not the girl he'd kissed like she mattered.

"I'm fine," I said quickly. Too quickly. I drank the coffee anyway, ignoring the way it scalded the back of my throat.

The drive to the station was a graveyard of unsaid words. Phontine popped into existence but one look between me and McDara and not even she spoke. The engine hummed. The city rolled by in muted grays. And he said nothing. No teasing. No glances. Just silence that felt heavier with every mile.

"Is everything okay?" I finally asked, my voice quieter than I wanted it to be.

His jaw flexed. "Everything's fine."

A lie wrapped in steel.

When we reached the station, Dom greeted us with his usual sunshine grin, but even he paused, sensing the freeze between us. He led me into their shared office, Phontine silent on my shoulder, his jokes softer now, his tone edged with curiosity and caution.

McDara sat beside him but never *with* me. Just a wall of shadows, nodding as I described the motel attack in clipped, clinical detail. There were no comforting glances. No warmth in his silence. Just a professional mask pulled tight over the raw truth of last night.

I tried to tell myself I hadn't imagined it. That I hadn't imagined *him*—his touch, his voice, the way he'd held me like I meant something.

But I had.

And this coldness now...it cut deeper because of that.

He stood when I finished, stacking papers like they hadn't just carved my memory open. "I've got work," he said simply. "I'll touch base later."

The dismissal was gentle.

But it still felt like a door closing in my face.

Dom lingered by the door, eyebrows lifting, eyes tracking McDara's retreat like a hawk. Then, with the subtlety of a man who knew *exactly* what he was doing, he turned to me and said, "If Detective Dark and Moody's going to be busy, maybe I'll take you out."

I blinked. "What?"

He leaned against the doorframe, arms crossed, charm weaponized and pointed straight at me. "Lunch. Old Town's got some hidden gems. I know all the best spots. We can even stop by the coffee shop you like."

McDara froze mid-step.

Dom grinned wider. "Unless he's got objections."

"Dom." McDara's voice was low and sharp—lethal as a blade left too long in the fire.

But Dom didn't stop. "Come on, Sonia. Don't you want to see the city through someone else's eyes? I know how to make Old Town *fun*."

A slow, dangerous silence wrapped around McDara like smoke.

His hand flexed against the edge of the desk, knuckles pale, voice tight. "We both have work to do."

And yet he hadn't moved. Not really. His gaze stayed locked on me—not Dom, not the case, *me*—like he was trying to make sense of something he couldn't say out loud.

Something I was still waiting to hear.

And in that moment, with Dom's teasing in the air and McDara's quiet fury simmering beneath the surface, I realized something else: He hadn't pulled away because of me. He was scared.

Of what it meant to want something he thought he shouldn't have? Of what it meant to *need* someone?

But I wasn't sure if I could be patient enough to wait for him to decide I was worth the risk.

Dom didn't flinch beneath the weight of McDara's silence. If anything, he leaned into it, a smirk tugging at his lips like he *thrived* in the storm. "I've got time," he said, voice light but loaded. "Wouldn't be right to let a lady wander the city alone after everything she's been through."

He pushed off the doorframe in a smooth, easy glide, all sunlit charm and reckless defiance. "Or, you know, we could grab that lunch. Let you bury yourself in paperwork, Detective."

The air shifted—sharp, charged. Like a string had been pulled too tight and was ready to snap.

I caught the edge of McDara's jaw tightening, the flicker in his eyes. Not jealousy. Not quite. But something just as dangerous. Something like *claiming* held carefully behind a steel mask.

And I couldn't help it—a small smile curled on my lips, more edge than sweetness. Dom's teasing wasn't just a balm to the ache McDara had left this morning. It was a weapon, and I let it cut.

"Thanks, Dom," I said, my tone smooth as silk over blades. "But I think I'll just go to The Obsidian Quill and bug Keyleth."

The words were light, but the meaning wasn't.

McDara's voice cut through the tension, low and gravel-edged. "Stay in populated areas and go straight to the Quill."

It wasn't a command. It was a warning. One wrapped in something rougher—*fear*.

"The Malifax Mage will probably stay away if your with people." He added. And this time, it wasn't the detective speaking.

It was the man who held me like I was breakable. The man who kissed me like he'd never let me go.

But he had. And now he stood there, acting like I was a stranger again.

I straightened, steel settling in my spine. "I've lived in a city my whole life, McDara. I know how to look both ways before crossing the street."

A flicker passed through his eyes. Something caught between pride and pain.

I forced a smile—sharp, practiced, the kind I'd worn long before he ever touched me. "Besides, Phontine's with me. She's lethal when properly caffeinated."

Phontine, ever the performer, stood to her full four inches of glory on my shoulder. "I bite," she declared solemnly, puffing out her tiny chest.

Dom snorted, muttering something about needing backup for future cases, but I didn't laugh. Not really.

Because McDara's lips twitched...and then didn't.

He stayed quiet, like he didn't trust himself to speak. Like every syllable might shatter the mask he'd so carefully reconstructed.

I couldn't take the silence anymore.

My boots clicked with purpose as I turned, walking out of the office and into the corridor's fluorescent haze. Each step echoed behind me, a clean break from whatever *almost* was.

I didn't look back.

Because if he wanted distance, I'd give it to him. But gods help him—if he came looking later, he'd better be ready to fight for what he let slip through his fingers.

And right now?

That ache in my chest said I might not wait.

I didn't want to waste the day wandering Blakewell's streets like a lovesick ghost, dragging my heart behind me and dissecting every glance McDara hadn't given me. There wasn't time for it. Not with shadows thickening at the edges of the city and a tangle of unanswered questions coiling tighter around my throat. If I was going to survive this—if I was going to *understand* any of it—I needed answers more than comfort. Truth over tenderness.

So, I walked, every step a declaration. Phontine fluttering silently beside me.

Veritas University towered ahead, carved from old stone and secrets, ivy crawling up its weathered bones like the forest itself was trying to reclaim it. The library stood at its heart, a sanctuary of forgotten truths, and I stepped through its arched doors as if crossing a threshold into something sacred and dangerous.

Inside, the air was sharp with dust and magic—old magic, the kind that clung to spines of leather-bound grimoires and whispered from the margins of yellowing pages. Sunlight filtered through high, stained-glass windows, painting slanted shafts of color across the floor like the last remnants of a forgotten spell.

The library, it seemed, was the only part of the original building that was not gutted and modernized.

Phontine fluttered to my shoulder, a weightless presence that still grounded me. "This place gives me the creeps," she murmured. "Too many ghosts whispering about failed finals and broken spells."

My mouth tugged at the edges as I scanned the room.

The deeper I moved into the aisles, the quieter it became—like the books themselves were holding their breath. I ran my fingers across their spines, inked in languages older than Blakewell itself, and finally found what I was looking for: *Magical Phenomena & Enchantments Most Foul*. The section was carved out of silence, darker here, colder. The books were heavier. Bound in cracked leather. Marked with silver runes that glinted as if they recognized me.

I slid one from the shelf. It groaned like it didn't want to be disturbed.

Tucking myself into a shadowed alcove, I let the world narrow to parchment and ink.

The early pages were nothing I hadn't already heard in whispers—basic theories of Maleficaria, the usual warnings that always read more like dares. But then, like a sliver of truth caught in the bones of a lie, I saw it.

Larkend.

The name bled across the page, anchoring the chapter like a wound.

I read slowly, the weight of each word like stones laid across my ribs. Larkend had been a sanctuary once. A hidden town tucked near the edge of one of the three Wood. Until something tore through it—a battle, a ritual, a rupture in the weave of magic so violent that even the ground refused to forget. The air itself had turned to mist, thick with wild enchantment. The survivors were not *whole*. Those who didn't vanish...changed.

Twisted.

"It's cursed," I whispered, my breath catching cold against the page. "Avoided by Magicals and humans alike."

Phontine stirred on my shoulder, wings rustling like dry leaves. "That's where Orlla was digging, right?"

"Yeah," I murmured, tracing the edges of a diagram—Larkend's layout, jagged and incomplete. "She wasn't just researching it. She was looking for something *inside* it. Maybe this raw magic the book mentions."

The words *raw magic* vibrated on the page like they wanted to be more than text. Like they remembered what it felt like to *burn*.

According to the text, Larkend was one of the few places in the world—outside the Three Woods—where raw magic had ever been documented. Not clean magic. Not filtered through bloodlines or rituals. This was magic still bleeding from the world's veins.

Unrefined. Untamed. Unforgiving.

"'Most believe the raw magic came from the Death Echo,'" I read aloud, voice hushed. "'A scar in the weave where too much death happened too fast. The Echo fractured time, bent magic, and left the boundaries between worlds so thin they trembled.'"

The book had detailed how remnants of raw magic were occasionally found in Larkend—stray, unrefined magic that lingered like mist in the air. Most researchers believed this phenomenon was linked to the town's Death Echo. The echoing of death on such a massive scale could have fractured the magical weave of the town itself, leaving raw magic exposed like nerves under torn skin. If Orlla had discovered a way to harness that, or if Matron Black wanted to bind the Death Echo itself, it could explain why Orlla had been so obsessed with Larkend. But why would they need an anchor of raw magic to bind a Death Echo? And what kind of spell needed something so dangerously potent?

I exhaled, hands shaking slightly. It made sense—Orlla's obsession, Matron Black's silence, the way everyone pretended like her disappearance wasn't worth mourning.

If Orlla had found a way to harness raw magic, to bind the echo and *use* it...

"I don't like this," Phontine whispered, her wings pressing tighter to my shoulder. "This kind of power...it never comes without a cost."

"No," I agreed, the weight of it sitting heavy in my chest.

A line from the book sparked inside my mind, etched behind my eyes like a brand:

Only the Woods hold raw magic willingly. All other places bleed for it.

And Blakewell was starting to bleed.

The next chapter unfolded like a wound—raw, red, pulsing with the kind of truth that didn't feel meant for mortal hands.

"'How Death Echoes Are Created.'"

My pulse kicked harder, the word burning across the page in jagged ink as I read aloud.

"'A part from an exceptional amount of lives taken at the hands of magic, a Death Echo could occur when a being of immense magical potential perishes in a place saturated with enchantment, their essence may remain—not as a ghost, but as a Death Echo. Caught in an endless loop of their final moments, these echoes are tethered to the very ground they died upon. Unlike spirits, they cannot move on. They do not evolve. They do not forget. Binding one can grant the caster temporary dominion over the dead...but the ritual demands precision. And an anchor of raw magic to stabilize the weave or risk being consumed.'"

The words blurred for a moment as I stared at them, the weight of their meaning pressing into my chest like a fist. My fingers clenched around the book's edges, the parchment crinkling under my grip.

Is this what Orlla had been chasing?

The raw magic that was documented in Larkend... Had someone tried to stabilize the Death Echo and failed?

Phontine shifted on my shoulder, her voice a breath of unease. "That's not ghost story stuff. That's...that's war magic."

I nodded, the taste of dread bitter on my tongue. "It would explain everything. Why Orlla disappeared. Why Matron Black's been clawing for her notes. Why the Black House feels like it's unraveling at the seams."

"If there's a Death Echo in Larkend..." Phontine's wings fluttered uneasily. "Why bind it? Why not try to stabilize it or end it?"

"Control," I whispered. "Control over death. Over what lingers. Maybe over who stays behind and who gets pulled back."

My voice cracked on the edge of the thought. Because that's what I wanted, wasn't it? Some way—*any* way—to speak to my father again. To hear his voice one more time.

But this...this wasn't love. This was power. Dark, unyielding power.

And I wasn't sure which was worse.

I shut the book softly, reverently. Like if I moved too quickly, the words might claw their way off the page and drag me under.

"Why would Matron Black want this kind of magic?" I murmured, almost to myself. "What's she trying to do? Raise the dead? Command them? Trap a soul?"

Phontine didn't answer. The silence between us vibrated with unease.

Then—movement. Just a flicker. A sliver of darkness at the edge of my vision.

My spine went rigid, a chill sliding through me like a phantom hand. I turned slowly, my breath held hostage in my lungs. Nothing. Just rows of shadowed shelves, the dim gold of enchanted lanterns, and the smell of old ink and secrets.

But I *felt* it. That watching. That *presence*.

Phontine's fingers curled tight into the collar of my shirt. "We need to go," she whispered. "Now."

I didn't argue.

I slid the book back into its slot, the leather spine cold against my fingers. My steps were quiet but quick as we moved through the stacks, each echo ringing a little too loud, a little too hollow. Whoever—or *whatever*—had been watching was gone.

But that didn't make me feel any safer.

The university ballroom loomed like a sanctum carved from glass and silence. Gleaming floors reflected the ashen light filtering through the towering windows, and students filtered out through the double doors in a soft tide of conversation and shuffling footsteps.

The scent of chalk dust clung to the air—sharp, dry, grounding—but it did little to settle the storm twisting in my gut.

At the far end of the room, a figure gathered papers with a kind of elegant absentmindedness. Dr. Niall Wren.

There was something *still* about him. Not stagnant—but deliberate. Like every movement was weighed, considered. His hair, streaked silver at the temples, gave him the kind of timelessness that made age hard to place. The sleeves of his ink-stained shirt were rolled to his elbows, revealing lean, weathered arms, and a satchel hung at his side, cracked leather worn thin from decades of use.

I stepped into the room just as he looked up. His eyes, a keen, unsettling blue, locked on mine.

"Miss Byrd?" His voice cut through the silence like a soft ripple across still water—low, refined, edged in weariness. "Administration said a young woman was stopping by my lecture hall."

Dr. Niall Wren stood by his desk, papers in hand, his presence more spectral than solid in the cavernous gloom of the ballroom. Light filtered through tall windows in fractured beams, catching on the silver streaks in his hair.

I nodded, forcing a small smile. "I was with Detectives McDara and Ashford the other day. I came to ask about Orlla."

His expression changed at her name—subtle but telling. A flicker of grief; a twitch at the corner of his mouth. He set the final paper into his satchel with reverent care, the soft clink of the buckle snapping shut like punctuation.

"Orlla was...a dear friend," he said, voice thickening. "If this is about her death...I'll tell you what I can."

I glanced around the now empty room. Shadows clung to the edges like they were waiting for something. Or listening. "I'm trying to understand what she was working on before she died. Why she was drawn to Larkend. I found something about Death Echoes in the library."

His reaction was sharp. Not dramatic—but sudden. A breath held. A tension pulled tight behind his eyes.

"Death Echo," he repeated, tasting the words like ash. "She never confirmed it outright. But she alluded to it. She said Matron Black had requested a spell...something dangerous. Something not meant to be bound."

My chest tightened. "A spell that required an anchor of raw magic?"

That got his full attention.

He leaned against the desk, steepling his fingers as if the gesture might stabilize him. "Yes. That, she admitted. Raw magic—pure, untouched. She said it was the only way to keep the spell from unraveling the caster. She believed there was still a pocket of it somewhere near Larkend. That it could either cleanse the town's curse...or, if twisted, amplify dark magic."

A shiver slid down my spine. "And the map?"

His eyes dropped. For the first time, his voice grew even quieter. "She said the map was the key. That it would lead to the anchor. I asked her what the Matron wanted it for. She wouldn't answer." He paused, his brow furrowed. "Only said...it frightened her."

Those words clung to the air like smoke—thick, suffocating. I could feel the weight of it pressing against my skin, cold and heavy.

"Do you think she left it behind?" I asked. "The map. Orlla knew they'd come for it if she didn't."

"She suspected as much," he said, his voice brittle with regret. "And if Matron Black hasn't found it yet...then yes. Orlla hid it. From them."

Before I could speak, a shift in the air stopped me cold.

A whisper. A flicker of shadow that moved without wind, curling around the base of one of the marble columns.

My body locked. My eyes scanned the room, but the space was still. Empty. At least to the eye.

Dr. Wren saw it too. He straightened, jaw tense. "You should be careful, Miss Byrd," he murmured. "Orlla wasn't the only one being watched."

My heart stuttered. Cold sweat beaded against my spine.

"Thank you," I whispered. "I need to—"

"Go," he said, already turning away. "And...should you find yourself in that House keep your eyes open."

I fled.

The ballroom swallowed my footsteps, the sound of my boots muted by polished floors and dread. Behind me, the whisper of magic coiled in the shadows, watching, waiting.

I didn't stop until I hit the sunlight. I didn't stop until my phone was in my hand.

I need to get to McDara. Now.

32

The cab ride back to McDara's apartment felt like crossing a war zone. The city blurred past the window, a smear of rain-streaked buildings and fog, but my thoughts were a storm louder than traffic. Dr. Wren's voice haunted me—his warnings, Orlla's secrets, the whisper of a Death Echo. I'd gone to the university searching for clarity. What I found had only sharpened the edges of the danger we were in.

And Matron Black? She wasn't circling this. She was at the center.

When the cab rolled to a stop, I sat there for a breath too long, staring at the apartment door like it might bite.

"Let's get this over with us." Phontine said.

My phone felt like a brick in my hand. Five missed calls. One text.

Where the hell are you?

My chest tightened. I shoved the phone into my pocket.

The door swung open before I could knock.

McDara filled the frame, broad shouldered and burning with tension. The air between us snapped tight as his eyes locked on me—wild, dark, storm-swallowed. He didn't wait for explanations.

He *moved.*

His steps were deliberate, each one radiating something electric and barely restrained. "Where have you been?" he demanded, voice low and rough like gravel under boots. "Why weren't you answering your phone? Are you hurt?"

"I'm fine—"

"You went off alone?" He was already reaching for me, his hands gripping my shoulders like he needed the touch to believe I was real. "Keyleth said you never made it to The Obsidian Quill. What were you thinking, Sonia? After what happened at the motel? You didn't even—"

"Cillian."

His name left my mouth in a hush, but it landed like a lightning strike.

He froze. His breath stilled. The tension in his hands melted into something else—something desperate. He closed his eyes like the sound of his name from my lips had cut through the static in his head. When he opened them again, he looked...shaken. Human.

"I thought it was happening again," he said, voice fraying. "The silence. The not knowing. I thought I'd find your body in some alley and—"

His words cracked in half. And so did something in me.

I reached up, covering his hands with mine, grounding him the way he always grounded me. "I'm okay. I found something. About Orlla. About the grimoire and a map."

"Oh boy." Phontine mumbled, "I'm going to see Keyleth. Bye." And she popped out of existence.

I guided him inside, our hands still tangled. He didn't let go.

Inside the apartment, I told him everything. Every word Dr. Wren had said. Every sickening revelation about Larkend, raw magic, and the Death Echo Orlla may have been trying to bind. He listened in silence, his expression shifting with each detail—from fury, to worry, to something darker. The detective in him was calculating, parsing it all out, but the man...the man looked like he wanted to punch through walls.

When I finished, I was breathless. My voice trembled, but I didn't try to hide it.

"There's more," I said quietly. "I want you to teach me how to use my magic."

His brows furrowed. "Sonia—"

"I'm not asking to become a Mage. Like a *real* Mage...I'm asking to survive." I stepped closer, my words soft but laced with steel. "I need to learn. You've seen the kind of things coming for me. And I trust you."

He looked at me like the word *trust* had hurt to hear. Like it didn't belong in the same breath as his name. "You shouldn't."

"But I do." My voice broke, but I didn't back down. "Please, Cillian."

He inhaled sharply, and that fragile moment between us stretched, taut and shimmering. Then he nodded, slow and solemn, like a man accepting a burden he couldn't refuse. The relief that flooded me was so sharp, it nearly buckled my knees.

But I wasn't finished.

"Before we start…" I stepped back just enough to look him in the eyes. "I need to know what's going on between us. You pulled back. You *patted* me this morning, like I was some stranger crashing on your couch. You barely looked at me at the station."

The air turned thick again. His jaw locked, a vein ticking near his temple. Then, as if retreating into armor, he let his hands fall from me entirely. The absence left a hollow ache in my chest.

"I'm not good at this," he said finally, voice low and hoarse. "You want an answer, Sonia? Fine. I want you to be safe. I never want to see you taken over by a ghost or nearly killed by a dark Mage but"—His eyes found mine, unflinching—"But starting something with you and keeping you safe aren't the same thing."

His words hovered between us, fragile as glass—too delicate to touch, too dangerous to ignore. I stood frozen in the silence, every heartbeat louder than the last, like my body was trying to scream through the stillness. What he'd said…it wasn't rejection, but it wasn't surrender either. It was somewhere in between. A precipice. And I was already leaning too far over the edge.

My voice cracked when I found it. "Do you…regret it?"

His breath hitched. The change in him was instant—his spine straightened, his lips parting in a soundless inhale. Like I'd just struck him where it hurt the most.

"Kissing me," I clarified, the words brittle, breaking apart at the edges. "Do you regret it?"

"Is that what you think?" His voice was low, hoarse. "That I don't want you?"

I blinked hard. "What else am I supposed to think, Cillian? One minute, you're all in, and the next, you're a million miles away. You treat me like I'm…like I'm a complication. Like I'm *in the way*."

He closed the distance between us like he was stepping through fire.

The air snapped tight. The space between us vanished, and suddenly he was right there—heat and storm and control wound tight enough to snap. I flinched back a step, turned my face away, but his hand came up, slow and sure, fingers tilting my chin until my eyes met his.

"I think about you constantly, Sonia." His voice was a raw rasp, like every syllable scraped his throat on the way out. "You're not a complication. You're *all I want*. And that's the problem."

My pulse hammered in my throat. "Why is that a problem?"

His other hand slid into my hair, threading through the strands like he needed to anchor himself. The moment his fingers curled against my scalp, the breath left my lungs. He tipped my head back, forcing my gaze up to him, and the look in his eyes—

Stars could burn and never match the heat I saw there.

His grip tightened—not enough to hurt, but enough to say *mine*. The air around us pulsed, thick with everything he wasn't saying, everything I *felt*.

"You have nowhere to go. Barely any money," he said, his forehead lowering until it brushed against mine, the heat of him seeping into my skin. "You're standing in the ruins of your life, Sonia. No one to rely on but me and I don't want you to feel like you have to...that you need to accept my advances because I'm the only option you have. I can't put you in that kind of position. I *won't*."

His words struck harder than any spell. They weren't rejection. They were fear—his, not mine. Fear of doing the wrong thing, of being something *I'd* one day resent.

"I didn't come here because I had nowhere else to go," I said softly, my breath mingling with his. "You think I couldn't call my mom and be on a plane back to Chicago tonight? Or that Keyleth wouldn't take me in if I called her?"

He stilled. Every muscle locked. The flicker of surprise in his eyes gave way to something deeper—something *breaking*.

"I'm not trapped, Cillian." I lifted a hand, placed it over his heart. His pulse leapt beneath my palm. "I'm *choosing* to be here. With you."

He didn't move. Didn't speak.

So, I stepped closer, into the space he tried so hard to protect. I pressed my chest to his, felt his breath stutter as I whispered, "I want you. Not because I need saving. Not because I don't have other options. But because it's *you*."

His control shattered.

He made a sound—low, guttural, torn from someplace buried—and then he was kissing me like it was the only language he had left. Like he could rewrite every word he couldn't say with his mouth on mine.

It was rougher than before, more desperate. His hands tangled in my hair, drawing me in like he couldn't stand the space between us. His lips moved against mine with a hunger that made my knees weak, his touch branding heat into my skin.

This wasn't a kiss of confusion or uncertainty.

This was *claiming*.

And when we finally broke apart, his breath ragged against my cheek, his arms still locked around me, I saw it—all of it. The war he was fighting. The guilt. The want. The aching tenderness he was trying so damn hard to hide.

"Tell me again," he said, voice like gravel and thunder.

"That I want you?" I asked, my voice thick with everything I felt.

He nodded.

I curled my fingers into the fabric of his shirt, felt the strength of him trembling beneath my touch. "I want you, Cillian. Every broken, beautiful, infuriating part of you."

And the way he looked at me then—like I was both the beginning and end of his story—was the kind of look that changed everything.

Forever.

McDara's lips met mine like a storm breaking—sudden, consuming, inevitable.

This wasn't the soft brush of someone unsure. This was heat. Possession. A kiss that stole the air from my lungs and gave it back as fire. His mouth moved over mine with purpose, every press and sweep a declaration. *Mine*, it whispered in every heartbeat. *Mine*, in every shiver that raced down my spine.

His fingers fisted in my hair, anchoring—grounding me as the world spun off its axis. I melted into him, clutching the front of his shirt like it might keep me from falling straight through the floor. His chest rose and fell beneath my palms, solid and strong and maddeningly steady compared to the chaos he'd lit inside me.

And then—just when the kiss deepened, just when I swore I'd lose myself in the taste of him—he broke away.

Our foreheads rested together, breath mingling in the charged space between us. His hands didn't leave me, fingers still threaded through my hair, his thumb stroking a slow path against my scalp like he couldn't quite stop touching me.

"You wanted to learn the basics of magic wielding," he murmured, his voice a rough velvet scrape over my senses.

I let out a breathless laugh, lips still tingling from the way he'd kissed me like he meant it. Like he might *never stop*.

"I wouldn't complain if we postponed the lesson," I said, the words low, teasing, meant to be light—but laced with the truth I couldn't bury anymore.

His smile was slow and wicked, his eyes dark with something that looked too much like want. "Oh, I have *plenty* of lessons I'd love to teach you." His hand slipped from my hair to brush the nape of my neck, and the contact lit up every nerve ending. "But first..." His voice dropped even lower. "Magic."

He stood, the spell between us not broken, just simmering beneath the surface now. I was already drunk on the heat of his skin, the rasp of his voice—and then he guided me toward the living room with a hand on my lower back, every step silent but electric.

With one clean sweep of his arm, he shoved the coffee table aside, clearing space in the center of the room. It wasn't just a living room anymore. It was a sanctum. A place carved from silence and fire and the need to understand something deeper—both in me, and in *us*.

"Sit," he said, voice firm but threaded with that same quiet reverence that had wrapped around every kiss.

I knelt on the rug, crossing my legs as the slit in my skirt slid open, baring more skin than I intended. His gaze caught—snared—and for a moment, he just *looked*, like he couldn't help himself.

My lips curled into a smirk. "Eyes up, Detective."

McDara cleared his throat, but a flicker of heat stayed in his eyes. "Close them," he said, quieter now. "We're starting with your source. Your center."

I obeyed, my lids slipping shut as I let the world fall away. I felt the room settle around me, the hum of magic like a breath held tight.

"Breathe," he instructed, voice a low anchor. "In through your nose. Out through your mouth. Slow. Steady."

I matched his rhythm, drawing air into my lungs, releasing it slowly. The silence between us wasn't empty—it pulsed with his presence. I could feel him next to me, kneeling close. Not touching, but near enough that my skin prickled with awareness.

"Your magic lives inside you," he said, voice softer now, intimate. "It's not a weapon you hold—it's a part of you. A heartbeat you haven't learned how to listen to yet."

The image painted itself behind my eyes. A flicker. A spark. Hidden deep in my chest, waiting.

"Find it," he whispered. "Let it rise."

And gods help me—I *did*.

A warmth unfurled low in my belly, spreading like ink in water. Faint at first, but pulsing now, with every breath. Not fire. Not light. Something older. Wilder. A quiet hum that sang in time with my bones.

"That's it," McDara breathed, and the pride in his voice made my heart stutter.

I reached for the thrum of it, not with my hands, but with something deeper. Something tethered to the storm inside me. And as the sensation swelled, something foreign brushed my skin—*his* magic. Subtle. Protective. A silent shield wrapping around me without ever touching.

My eyes fluttered open, and I found him watching me. Close. Too close. His expression was unreadable—part awe, part hunger, part something gentler that he didn't dare name.

Breathe in. Breathe out.

Eyes closed.

Breathe in.

Breath out. Find the spark.

And I did.

At first, it was a faint thrum at the center of my chest. Soft. Golden. Like the heartbeat of a star stitched beneath my skin. I reached for it—not with hands, but with the part of me that had always been silent. My will. My soul. My *self*. Magic answered.

It moved like silver light, threading through my body in webs of power I hadn't known existed. It wasn't loud—it was ancient. Familiar. *Mine.*

And I let it hold me.

I mapped the threads as they wove through me—some humming with life, others whispering like distant echoes. One, a thread thinner than a hair and colder than ice, shimmered at the edge of that warmth.

Dark. Wrong. *Calling.*

The moment I brushed it, everything shattered.

Magic bucked beneath my skin, the warmth gone in an instant. I fell—no direction, no gravity, only the lurching sensation of being ripped through dimensions by a force I couldn't fight.

And then—impact.

Cold, hard earth met me like a punishment. The air was thin and sharp, biting at my skin with every inhale. Mist clung to the twisted landscape, curling through dead trees like fingers trying to grasp what they couldn't hold.

The Deathscape.

It whispered through every breath I took. A realm stitched between life and decay. Dreamlike. Dreadful.

I knew it. Not because I'd seen it before, but because some part of me *belonged to it.*

A shadow fell across me.

And when I looked up—

He was there.

Not translucent. Not imagined. Not softened by the veil of the Living Lands.

Solid. Real. Terrifyingly beautiful.

Death.

His silver hair gleamed like moonlight on fresh snow, stark against the obsidian fall of his clothes. His eyes—silver, bottomless, alive with power—pinned me in place.

He didn't need to speak. His presence alone was enough to steal the air from my lungs. But when he did—

"Well, well…" His voice was a velvet knife, sliding between my ribs with lethal grace. "Miss me already?"

My mouth parted, but no sound came. He stepped closer.

"I—I didn't mean to come here," I whispered.

He crouched before me, movements fluid and wrong in that way only something otherworldly could be. "And yet…here you are." His eyes gleamed. "Tell me, Little Bird, what were you reaching for when you stumbled into *my* realm?"

I swallowed, the name heavy on my tongue. "I was training. With Cillian—McDara."

A shift. Subtle, but unmistakable. His expression didn't change, but the Deathscape pulsed with it—his irritation. The ground seemed to pulse beneath me, a heartbeat that didn't belong to anything living.

"Ah," he murmured. "*The detective.* He does seem…attached."

A chill bled into my bones. "I was just trying to connect with my magic."

Death tilted his head, his gaze sharpening like a blade. "You found more than that, Sonia. You touched the cord between us. The one you *should have* left buried."

I forced myself to sit straighter, though my limbs trembled. "I didn't know."

"No," he said, almost gently. "But you *do* now."

He reached out, not quite touching me. His hand hovered beside my cheek, and I swore I could feel him there—a ghost of a caress, made of cold fire and static. Every hair on my body lifted.

"Your magic is tangled with mine," he said. "Woven at the root. No matter how far you go, how deep you dig, you'll always find me waiting at the end of the thread."

A beat passed. His lips curled into something that looked like a smile, but it wasn't kind.

"Is that what you want, Little Bird?" he whispered. "To find me in every spell? In every shadow?"

I should have backed away. But I didn't. Because the terrifying truth was—

Some part of me did.

33

I stood, though my legs trembled like a newborn fawn's, each breath ragged in the ice-laced air. The Deathscape shifted around me like a living thing—coiled mist, twisted trees, and a sky the color of bone. The ground beneath my boots pulsed with a kind of dead heartbeat, as if this world breathed *in reverse*.

I took a step back.

A mistake.

Death moved—slow, deliberate, unhurried—like the reaper he was, a tide that had waited centuries to rise. His silver eyes locked onto mine, luminous and unblinking. I couldn't run. Couldn't *hide*. I was already seen.

"I warned you," he said, voice low and layered, like thunder echoing through stone. "What would happen if you came here unprotected."

My throat bobbed as I swallowed, but my voice barely found its way out. "Protection?" I whispered. "How can I have protection here?"

That smile. Sharp as a blade's kiss.

"The only protection in the Deathscape..." He took another step forward, shadows unfurling behind him like wings made of smoke. "Is mine."

His words coiled around my spine, cold and electric. The weight of his presence pressed against me, like gravity had bent itself around his body. My heart pounded—a violent, *living* sound in a realm where nothing should move, nothing should beat.

"I wasn't trying to come here," I said. "Every time I reach for my magic, it drags me under. I don't know how to stop it."

He tilted his head, slow and predatory. "Because you *can't*. You are a tether. A gate. You pull at threads meant to stay knotted, and now you've unraveled something you don't understand. Learning which threads not to mess with will save your life."

I inhaled, trying to steady my breath, trying to hold on to something *real*. "So, how do I stop this?"

His gaze darkened with something unreadable. "I could teach you."

The words slid between us, soft and lethal. Not an offer. A temptation.

My body tensed, every instinct screaming, *Don't trust him*—but fear was only one of the things I felt. Beneath it, tangled in the thorns, was longing. Because his power didn't just frighten me.

It *called* to me.

"You've never offered to help me before," I managed. "If you understand my magic so well, why not help me when you were in the Living Lands?"

"Have you begun to think me a friend, Little Bird?" he asked, and there was something dangerous in his voice—like a storm building behind the calm.

I opened my mouth. Closed it.

He took another step.

"You think me *harmless*," he murmured, voice suddenly laced with something sharp. "Because I cannot touch you in your world."

His eyes flared silver. The shadows responded, curling toward him like they *worshipped* him.

"All you do is mourn what I'm eating. You practically pout," I shot back, defiant despite the shake in my voice. "Not exactly terrifying."

He smiled—and it was beautiful, terrible, *inhuman*. "In your world, perhaps. But here?" His hand rose, skin shifting from pale to pitch, claws blooming from his fingers. "Here, I can touch you."

I froze as his hand hovered, just above my cheek. The air warped. The cold *kissed* my skin.

And then—he moved.

Death's hand slid around my throat, palm pressing against the mark he'd left on me—the one no one else could see. It flared to life beneath his touch; a brand made of flame and shadow. My breath hitched, every nerve ending caught fire.

Shadows curled tighter around us. The Deathscape responded to *him*, pulsing with each beat of his shadowed magic. The air itself thickened, breathing in time with my panic—or my desire. I couldn't tell.

Because where he touched me, I *burned*.

The connection between us roared to life. A bond. A tether. A thread spun of death and something *older*.

His lips parted as he leaned in, the soft brush of his breath like winter sliding across skin. His mouth ghosted over the shell of my ear, and my body betrayed me—shivering, breathless, caught in the snare of him.

"Do you want my protection, Little Bird?" he whispered.

His voice wrapped around my ribs like a vice. A dark promise.

"Because if you do...you'll have to give me more than fear."

My lungs forgot how to breathe.

Every inhale scraped like glass down my throat, every heartbeat a war drum trapped between his palm and my skin. Death's hand tightened just enough to feel the thunder of my pulse against his claws—just enough to remind me that I was his, in this moment, in this realm, on the knife's edge between surrender and survival.

His magic coiled through me like smoke and shadow, an anchor sinking into the marrow of my bones. It felt like possession. Like temptation. Like drowning in velvet darkness and not wanting to be saved.

I knew—bless the Wood, I knew—whatever protection he offered would come with a cost.

But the words wouldn't come. My mouth parted, but my voice was caught beneath the weight of him—his power, his promise, his *pull*. My thoughts frayed like old ribbon, unraveling beneath the sharp, brutal gravity of his attention.

Then—

A jolt.

Like lightning ripping through cloud cover, something *else* seized me.

An invisible tether yanked tight inside my chest. A force not born of shadow, but of stubborn, burning light. I gasped as the Deathscape wavered—its edges flickering like torn film. Death's grip snapped tighter, claws kissing skin, a warning written in ice and rage.

His snarl cracked through the void.

"He thinks he can take you from *my* realm?" His voice was a fury unleashed, deep and ancient, thunder shaped into sound.

McDara. *It had to be McDara.*

The pull grew stronger. A rope cinching around my ribs, winding tighter, tighter—threatening to split me in two. My spine bowed from the strain, my limbs stiff and weightless, the air too thin. A strangled sound escaped my lips, swallowed by the frostbitten wind of this place.

Death's fingers trembled. For a moment, I thought he'd hold me there. Claim me. Rip me from the living world and keep me shackled in silence and shadows.

But then—his face shifted.

The fury didn't fade. It fractured. Beneath the snarl, I saw something else. Grief. Ache. Longing.

He let go.

And it was like being dropped from a great height into cold water. I fell.

The world fractured—light and shadow breaking apart—and then I crashed back into myself.

My body hit the floor with a jarring thud, my cheek pressed to cool wood. I gasped, dragging air into my lungs like I'd never tasted it before. It burned, alive and real. I was back. The scent of garlic and rosemary still lingered in the room, but all I could feel was *him*—his shadow, his voice, his *mark*—haunting me like a second heartbeat.

"Sonia."

His voice wasn't an echo this time.

It was *real*. Sharp. Shaken.

McDara was beside me in an instant, his hands gripping my shoulders, steadying me. His face hovered just inches from mine, eyes wide and wild. A storm in human form. Fear and fury tangled in his features; his jaw locked against something that might've been panic.

"I've got you," he breathed, pulling me into his arms.

The warmth of him seared against my frozen skin. I clutched at his shirt, fingers curling into the fabric like I might fall away again if I let go. My whole body shook—teeth chattering, knees drawn to my chest, nerves shot through with lightning and frost. His arms wrapped around me, fierce and unyielding, his palm cradling the back of my head like I might shatter.

"You're safe," he murmured, voice breaking around the words. "You're here. You're safe. I've got you."

But I wasn't safe.

Not really.

Not from the cold that still crawled under my skin. Not from the burn of Death's claws. Not from the thread inside me that tugged toward the dark even now, even as McDara held me like I was his whole world.

I buried my face into his chest, breathing him in—cedar and salt and something that steadied the chaos—but the ghost of Death's hand still curled around my throat.

And I knew, with bone-deep certainty, that this wasn't over.

Not even close.

McDara wrapped the blanket around me like he could shield me from the realm I'd just escaped—like his touch alone could keep Death from reaching through the veil again. He tucked the edges in with careful, deliberate hands, as if fortifying a fortress around me. Like I was something fragile. Like I mattered.

The tea he pressed into my hands was scalding, but I welcomed the heat, curled my fingers around the ceramic like it was a lifeline. His hand lingered on mine—solid, callused, warm—and then he crouched in front of me. His eyes locked on mine, dark and steady, and for a moment, I couldn't look away. Couldn't breathe.

"What happened, Sonia?"

His voice was quiet—soft in sound but forged of steel beneath. Not a whisper of a question. A demand wrapped in velvet. And I knew—I *knew*—he would accept nothing but the truth.

I lifted the cup, just to buy myself time. The floral sweetness settled on my tongue, but it couldn't touch the chill coiled beneath my skin.

"I was trying to focus on my magic," I whispered. "Like you said. I thought I was getting close...but then I felt it again. That tether. It felt like a rope made of shadow and bone. And when I touched it, I—I fell. Into the Deathscape."

His jaw clenched. Sharp. Silent. His hand slid to my knee, grounding me with the strength in his touch, but the storm gathering in his expression made my heart hammer harder.

"He was there," I added. "Death."

McDara's lips parted, just slightly, and something flickered across his face—fear, edged with disbelief. "You've been there before?" he asked, voice barely above a breath.

I nodded, guilt burning down my spine. "Yes. A few times. I didn't mean to. It just...happens. When I reach for my magic, sometimes it pulls me through. I don't know why."

He exhaled hard through his nose, the hand on my knee tightening. The threads of his control were fraying. "I've only ever read about the Deathscape as a place of final judgment. No one should be able to access it—not while they're alive. Unless they're using Maleficaria."

"A regular Mage wouldn't be able to," I agreed. "But I'm a Ghost Whisperer. It's different. The veil's...thinner. I can see through it. Sometimes, I slip through."

His hand moved, trailing up to cup the side of my face. A callused thumb swept a strand of hair back behind my ear like I was breakable. His touch was careful, reverent—but his voice was still all grit and fire.

"And Death?" His gaze pinned me. "He rules it?"

"No," I breathed. "He *is* it. He *is* the Deathscape."

His expression fractured—horror, protectiveness, something darker flickering in the depths of his eyes.

"And you've been facing him alone this whole time?"

I nodded, the truth heavy on my tongue. "I didn't think anyone would believe me."

He went still. Not just quiet—still, like the moment before lightning splits the sky. "What did he say to you?"

The words felt like splinters in my throat. "He said we're bound. That I'm tethered to him through my magic. And if I come back unprotected...he'll keep me there."

McDara's thumb stilled against my cheek. His entire body radiated heat, fury banked beneath the surface like magma under stone.

"You're not going back there." His voice was a growl now. A vow carved in obsidian. "Not again. Not ever."

Tears blurred my vision. "I don't know how to stop it," I admitted. "It's like he's in my blood. In my *magic*. I reach for light and find him waiting in the dark."

His hand shifted, cupping my cheek fully now. His other moved to my waist, pulling me forward, into him. Into his warmth. His protection. "Then we'll stop it together. I don't care what it takes."

My breath hitched. "How? How do you protect someone from Death himself?"

His gaze held mine, and I saw it—everything. The war waging inside him. The need. The ache. The promise.

"I will learn every spell," he said, his voice quiet but laced with fire, "tear through every barrier, and break every law if I have to. I will walk into the Deathscape myself and drag you back if it comes to that. You are not his to take, Sonia."

My breath hitched—a sharp, traitorous inhale. The kind that came when desire tangled with fear. "Why?" The word slipped past my lips, barely a whisper, but it landed heavily between us. A question I wasn't sure I was ready to unravel.

McDara didn't hesitate. His hand slid into my hair, fingers threading through the strands like he'd been waiting to touch me again this way. His lips hovered a breath above mine, the heat of him seeping into me, pulling me under.

"Because you're mine, Sonia," he murmured, voice low and thunder dark. "And I don't share."

The air between us ignited—charged, humming with unspoken things. His magic curled around me, steady and warm, chasing away the lingering chill of the Deathscape like he was rewriting my temperature by sheer will alone.

His thumb brushed over my bottom lip, and I forgot how to breathe. The touch was tender, reverent, but underneath it lived a storm—one I was already drowning in.

I'd take McDara's fierce, aching possessiveness over Death's cold claim any day—if I chose to be with someone, let it be the man who held me like I was alive, not the shadow who wanted to own my soul.

"Promise me," he whispered, the words brushing my skin like silk. "Promise me you won't go back there."

I swallowed hard. The promise tasted like ash before it ever reached my tongue. "I promise." And I meant it—I *wanted* to mean it. But the tether still pulsed in the depths of my magic like a curse etched into my bones.

He kept his hand in mine, his thumb tracing slow circles over my knuckles. The room faded until there was only the echo of our breath, the hum between our bodies, the truth clawing at the edge of my lips.

If I leaned forward, just a little, our mouths would meet.

If I let go, just once, I wouldn't come back whole.

I cleared my throat, breaking the spell, barely. "We should look at the grimoire. Orlla's."

His gaze sharpened. The softness vanished, replaced by that focused, protective edge I was starting to crave.

"Dom and I flipped through it, but we didn't see a map. Maybe we missed something."

I nodded, fingers tightening around the mug still warm in my hands. "The spells she was working on—what Dr. Wren told me, what I read in the library—there has to be more. Something about the Death Echo. The anchor. I need to know what she was trying to do...and if Matron Black plans to finish it."

McDara's magic surged beneath his skin, visible in the tension of his jaw, the way his fingers gripped mine like he couldn't quite let go. "I'll get it." He moved, but I stopped him with a single touch, a silent plea.

"There's more," I said softly.

He turned back. The way he looked at me in that moment—like I was something rare and already halfway lost—nearly broke me.

"I need to learn control," I whispered. "I need to stop falling into the Deathscape every time I reach for my power. I need training—real training. Before it pulls me under for good. It's the only way I can keep myself safe and my promise to you."

McDara's entire frame stilled. Not with shock. With a stillness that felt like waiting for a war to start.

"I'll teach you," he said, every word thick with resolve. "But it might not be enough."

"I know," I said, my voice shaking. "And if it doesn't work...I may need to consider other options."

His brows lowered. The air shifted. "What kind of options?"

I hesitated. The name tasted like betrayal, but the truth had claws now, and it wouldn't stay buried. "Someone who understands what I am. Someone who's trained others like me."

His eyes narrowed. "Sonia..."

"Matron Black," I said.

The name landed like a dropped blade.

McDara stepped back, his hand slipping from mine. His expression iced over, all warmth replaced by a wall I couldn't climb. "Absolutely not."

"I'm not saying I *want* to," I said quickly, the sting of his distance hitting harder than I expected. "But if she can help—"

"She won't help. She'll own you."

His voice was colder than the Deathscape. Sharper than Death's claws.

"I *know* she's dangerous," I said. "But if I don't figure this out—if I lose control and Death drags me under—I won't come back. And I don't want to die, Cillian."

His eyes softened, just slightly—but it was enough to gut me. Beneath all that fury and fear, there it was again.

The ache.

"You're not going to," he said, the vow like steel catching fire. "Not on my watch."

He turned, jaw tight, and pulled out his phone. A few clipped words into the receiver, and then he faced me again. "Dom's bringing the grimoire."

I nodded, clutching the blanket tighter. "Good."

McDara hesitated, then added, "He's bringing Keyleth, too."

Surprise flickered through me. But the tension cracked—just a little—and I let a real smile tug at my lips. "Even better."

It wasn't long before a knock came like a crack in the tension-laced silence.

McDara moved first, his strides long and deliberate as he crossed to the door. When it opened, the cool air from the hall swept in, followed by the soft scent of wildflowers and something crisp, like spring rain. Keyleth stepped through, radiant as ever, her eyes sweeping the room until they landed on me.

"Sonia!" she breathed, already pulling me into her arms before I could form a greeting. Her embrace was grounding, the kind that didn't ask questions—it just gave. Her floral soap clung to her skin like memory, familiar and safe. I hadn't realized how much I needed safe until I was wrapped in it.

She stepped back, her gaze soft and searching. "Good to see you in one piece. I heard your day was...intense."

"You could say that," I murmured, glancing toward McDara.

He stood off to the side, arms crossed, watching everything with that silent protectiveness I'd come to rely on. Always there. Always steady.

Phontine flitted through the door next and hovered just beside my shoulder. Her wings made a soft shhh-shhh in the quiet. She didn't say anything, but her presence grew lighter—more playful—in Keyleth's aura. She never had that kind of ease around Dom.

And then he strolled in.

Dominic Ashford filled the space the way wildfire filled a field—loud, golden, and impossible to ignore. He tossed the grimoire onto the coffee table like it had insulted him.

"You owe me, Detective," he said with a grin, flopping onto the couch and stretching his arms wide. "That thing's cursed. I'm sure of it. At the very least, it's heavy as hell."

McDara didn't dignify that with a response. He moved to the book like it was sacred, not even bothering to sit before flipping it open. His brow furrowed, and the air around him shifted—charged and focused.

Keyleth folded herself gracefully onto the couch beside me, her voice curious. "What exactly are we looking for?"

"A map or a spell," I said quietly, my fingers brushing the aged leather cover. "Orlla's research pointed to something in Larkend. A source of raw magic—pure, unstable, unclaimed. We think it's what Matron Black wants."

Dom's easy grin slipped. "Raw magic?" He leaned forward. "That's not a power you play with. That's the kind of stuff that changes you—twists you."

"Exactly," McDara muttered, still flipping through the pages. "Which is why we have to get to it first."

The four of us bent over the grimoire, the room thick with candlelight and quiet urgency. The pages were worn, the margins full of scribbled notes and sketches, spell diagrams drawn with a precision that hummed faintly with residual magic. It felt like reaching back through time, like touching a ghost's blueprint for disaster.

I stopped at a passage, my pulse quickening. "Here. Orlla wrote that the spell she was designing needed a powerful magical source to function." I tapped the ink, old and faded. "That's what led her to Larkend."

Keyleth leaned in, her fingers brushing mine as she pointed to the margin. "She also noted a Death Echo. Look."

McDara's gaze met mine across the book, his eyes hardening. The way he looked at me then—it was as if he was already preparing to fight whatever this spell would awaken.

I spoke softly, the truth heavy in my chest. "Dr. Wren said she was afraid. That she thought Matron Black's plan went too far."

"A Death Echo," Dom muttered, raking a hand through his hair. "They're pure agony. Magical scars stuck on repeat. You bind one, you bind pain. You bind power that was never meant to be touched."

"And she was going to anchor it with raw magic," I said. "To control it."

McDara's fingers curled around the edge of the book, tension rolling off him in waves. "If we find it first..."

"We stop her," I finished, the final word falling like a stone.

A beat of silence passed. Keyleth folded her arms, her expression grim. "Larkend's a cursed place. No one comes out of there the same."

"No one's asking you to come with us," McDara said, his tone soft but firm.

Keyleth arched a brow. "I didn't say I wouldn't."

Dom gave a low whistle, the edge of a smile playing on his lips. "Well, if we're going to walk into a cursed town with ghosts and raw magic, might as well make it a party."

I turned another page—and there it was.

Drawn in ink so dark it looked fresh. A map.

The map lay open before us, sketched in Orlla's looping, deliberate handwriting—every line carved with purpose. A path wound through the heart of Larkend's scorched remains, cutting through ruins like a scar before ending at a single, marked point.

An abandoned chapel.

A place where the walls had likely listened to prayers...and now only echoed silence.

I stared at it, the weight of what it meant sinking into my bones. That had to be where the anchor was hidden. The source of raw magic. The thing Matron Black was willing to unravel a life to find.

Dom let out a breath through his teeth, shaking his head. "Well. That's ominous."

McDara's gaze lifted to mine—steady, unwavering. The kind of look that made promises without needing words. *I'll keep you safe. No matter what.* "We need to get there before she does," he said, his voice low and resolute.

I nodded, heart pounding, the hum of magic still lingering between our joined hands.

But then Keyleth raised her hand, her eyes narrowed as she scanned the map. "Wait," she said, cutting through our momentum like a blade. "We're all but convinced Matron Black set this in motion, right? But if Orlla had the map, if she was this close to finishing the spell...why would Matron Black kill her before getting what she needed?"

The question dropped into the room like a match in a dry forest. Silence sparked, tense and flammable.

I pressed my lips together, my thumb tracing the edge of the page. I wanted to say yes. I wanted to pin the blame on Matron Black. But...

"She doesn't have the map or the spell," I said quietly. "At least, not according to Calypso. Which means if she did kill Orlla, she did it before securing the only leverage she had. That doesn't make sense. Not even for her."

Dom blew out a slow breath, scrubbing a hand down his face. "Then we're back to square one."

McDara's fingers left the page, curling into a fist. "So why would someone want her dead?"

Keyleth shifted beside me. "If they didn't want Matron Black experimenting with Death Echoes, they might've killed Orlla to stop the spell from ever being completed."

The silence that followed was different this time. It wasn't confusion—it was clarity. The kind that tasted like blood.

Dom leaned back slowly, arms folding across his chest. "Which means whoever killed her...was likely in the Black House."

My stomach flipped.

Dom's gaze found mine, and something sharp gleamed behind his lazy smile. "We'd need someone on the inside."

Before I could speak, McDara's body tensed beside me—like someone had drawn a bowstring in his spine. His jaw locked, eyes flashing.

"No."

Dom raised a brow, calm and calculating. "I'm just saying—"

"I said no." McDara stood, towering, every inch of him radiating *don't you dare*. His voice wasn't loud, but it struck like thunder. Not rejection. Down right refusal. A line drawn in iron.

My fingers closed around his before I could think. I squeezed, gentle. Reassuring. His hand twitched like he wasn't expecting it—but he didn't let go. Instead, his shoulders eased, just a little. He stayed anchored. To me.

But he wasn't wrong to worry.

Because I *was* already inside. I was already being drawn deeper into Matron Black's world—because of my magic, because of everything I didn't understand and everything I needed to learn. I just hadn't figured out how to tell him that.

Dom leaned back with a shit-eating grin. "Well, I guess you two kissed and made up."

McDara's growl was more felt than heard. Dom looked absolutely delighted.

But I didn't rise to the bait. Instead, I leaned in without hesitation and pressed a soft kiss to McDara's cheek.

He froze.

For half a breath, the entire room seemed to still with him. And then his gaze shifted, meeting mine with heat. Real heat. The kind that curled behind the ribs and made it hard to breathe. He didn't say anything, but he didn't have to.

His grip on my hand tightened, like he didn't want to let go.

It might've turned into something more. Might've spiraled into something dangerous and tender. But then—

I felt it.

A flicker in the corner of the room. Like someone breathing against my spine.

I turned my head, heart stumbling.

And there—in the shadows—eyes. Silver. Watching.

Death.

But in the next blink, they were gone. Nothing but a dim corner, lit by the soft glow of the lamp.

Still, my pulse skidded sideways. I turned back, grounding myself in McDara's presence, in the solid feel of his hand in mine.

I was still here.

Still his.

For now.

34

The scent of fresh coffee hit me the moment I stepped into the kitchen—dark, rich, and inviting, curling around me like a lover's hand at the small of my back. It drew me forward before I was fully awake, before I remembered the ache in my chest and the weight of everything waiting outside this quiet sliver of morning.

McDara stood at the counter like he'd been sculpted there, already dressed and somehow infuriatingly composed. His broad shoulders moved with unhurried ease as he poured steaming, black coffee into a mug, his other hand braced against the edge of the counter near a glowing laptop. He looked like he hadn't slept. But he didn't look tired.

I padded in, barefoot and still in his oversized shirt, the hem brushing my thighs. I leaned against the opposite counter, arms crossed. "You're a morning person *after* staying up all night? That's...unnatural."

Without missing a beat, he handed me a mug, the ceramic warm against my fingers. "I run on spite and caffeine," he said, voice rough and deep from disuse. "It's a core skill in homicide."

I took a sip—smooth, bold, perfectly bitter—and narrowed my eyes at him over the rim. "Your coffee is always good. You're disgustingly competent."

He leaned back against the counter with a half smirk that did dangerous things to my insides.

"Dom and Keyleth leave?" I asked.

"About an hour ago. Crashed on the couch. I think Phontine was judging them." McDara's smirk twitched wider. "Speaking of the Pixie I think she's sleeping on the bookshelf."

I smiled at that, then hesitantly I asked, "Are they, uh...a thing?"

He snorted, setting down his own mug. "Dom might've tried once, but Keyleth would sooner hex him than date him. Why?" His voice dipped as he crossed the space between us, slow and sure, like a predator stalking something already his. "Jealous?"

"Of her? No." I tried to scoff, but the sound caught in my throat as he reached me.

His hands found my waist, fingers curling through the fabric of his shirt like he'd done it a hundred times. His hold was gentle, but there was a gravity to it—like I was the only thing in the room that mattered.

My breath caught. My free hand lifted, pressing lightly against his chest. I could feel the steady thrum of his heart, the heat of him bleeding through the cotton like a promise.

"This your new interrogation technique?" I murmured.

He smiled, slow and wicked. "Only when I like the suspect."

And then he kissed me.

Gods, he kissed me like he owned the moment. Like he was starving, and I was the only thing that could sate him. His mouth slanted over mine, confident and consuming, and I forgot about the coffee, the grimoire, the world. All I could feel was him—his hands, his lips, the low, guttural sound he made when I melted into him.

His fingers slid into my hair, angling my head back as his mouth deepened the kiss, tasting, claiming. There was nothing hurried about it. He kissed me like time had slowed, like he was memorizing every breath, every heartbeat.

And I let him.

I *wanted* to let him.

But then—his phone rang.

He didn't stop.

The device vibrated furiously on the counter, a mechanical buzz that felt like it belonged to another life. Still, McDara's lips stayed on mine, slower now, almost stubborn in his refusal to let go.

The phone rang again.

He broke the kiss with a frustrated growl, resting his forehead against mine. His voice was a rasp. "Ignore it."

The ringing persisted.

I exhaled, still tangled in the heat of him. "You should answer."

His grip on my waist tightened, like he was trying to decide if letting me go was worth the call. But then he muttered a curse under his breath and finally reached for the phone.

And just like that—the moment fractured.

His features hardened as he read the screen. The lazy warmth vanished, replaced by something cold and coiled.

"What is it?" I asked softly, coffee forgotten in my hand.

He didn't answer immediately.

But the tension rolling off him, sharp and sudden, told me everything I needed to know.

Something was very wrong.

His entire body snapped taut—shoulders squared, jaw clenched, every line of him transformed from warmth to steel in a heartbeat. The ease he'd worn like a second skin moments ago was gone, shattered by the voice crackling through the phone's speaker. Garbled. Frantic. I couldn't make out the words, only the fear coiling through the static like smoke.

McDara's eyes sharpened, scanning the apartment not like a man looking for comfort—but like a soldier already calculating exits and worst-case scenarios. Something was happening. Something bad.

"Where are you?" His voice sliced through the air, clipped and commanding, his hand darting out to grab his keys from the counter. His fingers clenched around them like they were a weapon—no, a lifeline.

"McDara?" I stepped forward, my voice low, hesitant.

He didn't answer. Didn't even glance at me. He just listened, then barked, "Give me the location."

And then it came—the sound that cleaved through whatever fragile peace remained. A boom.

Loud and low, vibrating through the phone speaker like thunder from the underworld. It wasn't just sound—it was impact. I felt it in my chest. In my gut.

More noises. Frantic now. Screaming? Crying? I couldn't tell. My skin prickled, my pulse racing.

McDara was already moving.

He shoved the front door open, one hand jamming his wallet into his jacket, the other clenching the phone like he could strangle answers out of it. Every motion radiated urgency. Purpose.

"McDara, wait—what's happening?" I reached for him.

He turned. Just for a second.

And gods, that second split me open.

His gaze hit mine like a blow—softened at the edges with something dangerously close to regret. But the steel was still there, braced behind it, unyielding. He was already gone, even before the words left his lips.

"I'll call you later."

And then he was out the door. Gone. The sound of it closing behind him was sharp and final, the echo slicing through the apartment like a blade. The warmth we'd built just hours ago was swept out in his wake, leaving only silence.

I stood there, pulse pounding, a ghost in the shell of a moment that had almost been something more.

Behind me, Phontine fluttered into the kitchen, eyes puffy with sleep, hair sticking out like she'd been caught in a windstorm. "What lit McDara's hide on fire?" she yawned.

I let out a breath I didn't remember holding, shoulders slumping. "I have no idea."

But my gaze was already drifting—to the counter. To the laptop McDara had left open.

Still glowing. Still active.

Still unlocked.

He *never* left things unsecure. Not his notes, not his case files. Not this. Whatever he'd been looking at when he made the coffee—when he teased me like the world wasn't coming undone—was still there, waiting. A flickering blue light pulsed from the screen. Steady. Silent. Beckoning.

My heart hammered.

It might be a clue. A warning. A trap.

And I didn't care.

I stepped forward.

My fingers twitched at my sides, the need to know clawing under my skin like something alive. I bit down on my bottom lip, hard.

I shouldn't.

I really shouldn't.

Phontine fluttered down to the back of a kitchen chair, wings barely disturbing the air, her expression caught between scandalized and intrigued. "You're not actually thinking about it," she said, tone heavy with reprimand. "Are you?"

I didn't answer. Just side-eyed her. "There's so much I don't know about him."

So many shadows clung to McDara's edges. Secrets wrapped in steel and silence. Things he never said—but always carried.

Phontine crossed her tiny arms, her expression sharpening like she was preparing to scold me into virtue. But then she tilted her head, her iridescent curls slipping over one shoulder. "I mean...we *are* living with him. It's not snooping. It's...environmental awareness."

I gave her a look. "That's not a thing."

She grinned, all teeth and mischief. "You were gonna do it anyway."

I sighed. "You're the worst."

"And you're stalling."

I was. Because part of me *did* care about his privacy. About not crossing the line that would fracture the fragile trust building between us. But curiosity had always been a hungry thing. And this was *McDara*—a man who kissed like he meant it, protected like he had something to lose, and pulled away like he didn't deserve to want.

He was tied to the Black House. To Orlla. To everything unraveling around me.

And if I didn't start pulling answers from somewhere, I was going to drown in all the unknowns.

So, I stepped forward.

His laptop glowed with passive defiance—open, unlocked, unguarded. That alone made my pulse spike.

My gaze flicked to the screen. An email window. Still active.

And there it was.

Matron Black.

A thread. Dozens of replies. Timestamps spanning weeks. Months.

My heart slammed against my ribs.

The subject line was vague. The content less so.

The most recent email from the Matron was coldly professional but laced with a thread of desperation.

The mist is destabilizing faster than projected. If it depletes before reinforcement, the exposure gap will be catastrophic. You know what's at stake. We need your help reestablishing the spread, or there will be consequences.

Consequences.

I scrolled farther, needing context. Needing anything that would make this feel *less* like the floor beneath me had vanished.

Without a steady mist barrier, she'd written in a thread below, *human-Magical tensions will spike. Memory dissonance in high-traffic zones will trigger instability. We've already had incidents—panic responses, unfiltered reactions to spellcasting, an entire block in New Town evacuated due to fear-fueled chaos. The longer the gap, the greater the risk of societal breakdown.*

My eyes stung, reading and rereading.

The mist wasn't just magical window dressing.

It was *sedation*.

It dulled fear. Eased hatred. Softened the edges of magic until humans could live beside Magicals without questioning it too hard.

How did I know that?

Hadn't I asked once?

Hadn't someone *told* me, and I just... forgot?

The sensation crawled over my spine.

My memory of the Mist felt *thinned*. Like someone had wiped away the edges.

McDara's reply had no punctuation. Just four words.

I don't work for you

But the next thing I did?

That was the real mistake.

I scrolled up.

An older message. Then another.

And suddenly the weight of my own body felt too heavy to hold.

McDara hadn't just *known* about the mist.

He'd *helped* implement it.

The details were cloaked in coded phrases—probability thresholds, perimeter management, veil disbursement—but the truth carved itself between the lines. McDara had been involved in laying the magical infrastructure that allowed the mist to spread.

We must repair the Veil Towers. Without the mist, we cannot guarantee the humans won't react with hysteria—it's the only thing dulling their senses enough to keep them from

seeing what we are. If it fails, McDara, we won't be managing discomfort—we'll be containing mass panic.

Veil Towers.

The phrase echoed in every message.

I blinked. My thoughts felt sluggish. Cold. But what was the mist? A vague memory came to me, Elias's face, lips moving but I couldn't hear the words.

My gaze dragged toward the window. Those strange, silent towers that dotted Blakewell like forgotten bones. Smooth. Unmarked. Looming in alleyways and rooftops. I'd passed dozens and never once thought twice about them.

But now...

Now I knew.

They weren't relics. They weren't mundane.

They were *active.*

They were *spreading the mist.*

And McDara—he'd helped *build* them.

McDara had ensured its reach.

The mist. The Veil Towers. The silence.

And all I could think was, *What the hell is it doing to the humans of Blakewell?*

What did they breathe in every day without knowing? What seeped into their lungs, their bones, while the Mage Council stood by and watched?

While McDara helped make it happen.

My stomach turned; a low, twisting sickness coiling tighter with every breath. If he knew—if he'd known all along—then why hadn't he stopped it?

Why hadn't he told *me?*

I clicked out of the Matron Black email thread, already feeling like I needed to scream or throw something or *run*—but something else caught my eye. Another message.

It sat in his inbox like a loaded gun. Ticking.

I didn't want to open it.

I *shouldn't* open it.

But my hand moved anyway.

They can't keep the magic from me.

A chill unfurled down my spine before I even read the first line. I already knew who it was.

Deidre.

The sickness I'd felt reading about the Veil Towers was nothing compared to this. This was something deeper. More personal. It felt like being stabbed with a dull blade and then told to smile through it.

The first email was a raw, bleeding thing. Anger and fear tangled in every word, desperation crawling through the screen.

CeeCee,

I know you don't want to hear this, but I can't sit back and do nothing. The doctors—humans—they're useless. It's spreading. I can feel it every day. They're already talking about options that are worse than the sickness itself.

And Matron Black? She won't help me. I begged her, Cillian. I begged her to do something. To use her magic, the magic she hoards and teaches to her favorites. But she said there are "lines" she won't cross.

Like she gets to decide what's too far when it's my damn life *on the line.*

I won't just sit here and die. They can't keep magic from me.

I sat frozen, my eyes locked on the screen, pulse a dull, thunderous beat in my ears.

Deidre. Sick. Dying. And no one helped her.

Not the humans.

Not the Mage Council.

Not Matron Black.

Especially not Matron Black.

McDara's response followed—measured, gentle. So careful. But his grief bled through every line, like he already knew how it would end.

Dee,

You're not alone in this. I need you to promise me that whatever you're thinking of doing—you won't.

Magic isn't the answer. You know that. You don't need to dig into things you don't understand, things that could make it worse. I will find another way, but I need you to trust me.

Please, Deidre. Promise me.

There were more after that. Weeks of updates. Test results. Hospital visits. Her hope draining away one line at a time.

And McDara, always responding. Always trying to save her.

Until he couldn't.

The next email was different. Deidre's tone had shifted—sharpened. Grief twisted into resentment.

I did what you asked. I waited. I let you search for answers. But the truth is, Cillian, there is no answer. Not one that you can stomach.

Matron Black has the power to help me, but she won't. She's a hypocrite. A liar. She talks about magic like it's something sacred, but she picks and chooses when it's worth using. If it were you, if it were someone she actually valued, would she still refuse?

And then came the line that felt like ice water down my back.

She doesn't guard those books as well as she thinks. I found something. Orlla caught me before I could take it, but...she didn't turn me in.

My breath hitched.

Orlla *knew.*

She'd found Deidre snooping through forbidden knowledge—dark magic, hidden texts—and instead of stopping her, she listened.

She'd *let it happen.*

Was that the moment it all started? Not when Matron Black refused to help, but when Orlla *did?*

When desperation met curiosity and they bloomed into something black and powerful.

Deidre's sickness hadn't just changed her—it had started a chain reaction. One that pulled Orlla into shadows, into risks, into secrets powerful enough to burn.

And McDara...he'd been caught between them. Between saving the sister he loved and holding the line of what was too far.

I gripped the edge of the counter to keep from sliding to the floor, the weight of it all pressing hard against my chest.

He had fought so hard to protect Deidre from dark magic.

But in doing so...he might've lit the match that pulled Orlla straight into the fire.

The door clicked shut behind me, the cool metal of McDara's spare key still warm in my palm. A breath of morning wind brushed my neck, but it carried something colder than air—something *other*.

Phontine flew over to a window box filled with peonies. I turned toward the stairs.

And nearly collided with a nightmare in silk and shadow.

Death stood too close, his presence swallowing the space between us like a black hole. One blink and he could've been inches away. Or everywhere at once.

My heart slammed into my ribs as I stumbled back a step, hand flying to my chest. "Seriously?" I wheezed. Phontine jerked around, saw me talking to something she couldn't see and stayed away. "You need to wear a damn bell. Or a glow stick. Or *something*."

No answer. No smirk. Not even a quirk of those too-perfect lips.

Death just *stared*.

The silence wasn't theatrical. It wasn't teasing.

It was...*wrong*.

The usual, razor sharp amusement was gone, replaced by something that crawled under my skin and stayed there.

I cleared my throat and started down the steps, trying—and failing—to pretend I wasn't hyperaware of him falling into step beside me, all grace and stillness and silent fury.

When I glanced sideways, I caught it.

The tension in his jaw. The faintest flare of silver beneath his lashes.

Death was annoyed.

Not curious. Not toying with me. *Irritated*.

I blinked. "Are you in a *bad mood*?"

His look could have flayed a lesser soul.

I stopped walking, planting my boots and crossing my arms. "Okay. Out with it. What's got the god of the in-between glowering like someone cursed your favorite cloak?"

"So relaxed." His voice curled low, cold smoke slipping between his words. "You used to tremble when I appeared. Eyes wide, heart racing. You feared me."

He took a slow step forward, the air thickening with his presence. "Now you just *stare*. And speak to me with far too much comfort. You've grown careless, Little Bird."

My pulse was steady despite the way the shadows coiled at his feet. "I'm not careless. I just know the rules now." I met his eyes without flinching. "In the Living Lands, you can't touch me. And that makes you a little less scary, doesn't it?"

His jaw tensed. A muscle ticked. "Keep telling yourself that."

"Oh, I intend to." A small, defiant smile tugged at my lips. "So, what's wrong? Tell me."

The expression that twisted across his face was feral. "Your detective," he said, each word precise and poisonous, "put up more *wards*."

I stared. "Wait. What?"

"He strengthened them," Death hissed, as if saying it burned. "After the motel. After *you* started staying."

It took a second for that to sink in.

Then—"Wards can keep you *out*?"

His silence was answer enough.

A sound unfurled from him—low, guttural, furious. The air around us rippled like heat on asphalt, and my skin prickled.

I hadn't known he *could* look this unsettled.

Gone was the cool detachment. In its place was something primal, raw. It twisted beneath his skin like smoke, like he was one step away from unraveling.

Then, just as quickly, the storm inside him stilled. He tilted his head, gaze cutting like a blade.

"It takes energy," he said coolly, "to project myself into the Living Lands. More than you comprehend. I am *anchored* to the Deathscape. I only allow fragments of my essence to slip through. But your detective"—he sneered the word like a curse—"is determined to keep me out."

Oh gods.

Death was *pouting*. Death. Was. Pouting.

The ancient, terrifying embodiment of the afterlife…was genuinely sulking because McDara had slapped a magical *Keep Out* sign on his turf.

It should've terrified me.

Instead, I bit the inside of my cheek, hard.

I met his glare head-on, unable to help the flicker of challenge in my voice. "So…McDara's magic actually keeps you out?"

His eyes flashed silver lightning. Dangerous. Daring me to say more.

But underneath the fury, I saw it—*uncertainty*. The flicker of something not quite possessive. Not quite power.

Jealousy.

And suddenly, I wasn't afraid.

I was *curious.*

"You don't like that, do you?" I murmured. "Being locked out. Shut out."

His nostrils flared. Shadows writhed at his feet.

But still, he didn't deny it.

Didn't have to.

Because the truth was right there in his silence.

McDara had done the one thing Death couldn't stomach.

He'd kept me from him.

His answer wasn't words—it was movement. A single step forward, slow and precise, and the world tilted. Shadows peeled from his form like they were alive, tendrils slipping across the sidewalk as if tasting the air. The smirk vanished from my face. My breath hitched. *Oh, hell.*

The space between us warped, thick with an unspoken threat, tension coiling like a storm cloud ready to split the sky. His silver eyes caught the light and devoured it, unreadable and ancient, twin eclipses fixed on me like I was something he meant to claim—or consume.

Then his gaze dropped. Slowly. Deliberately.

His eyes dragged down the length of me, and the heat that had burned across my skin just moments ago was replaced with something colder. Sharper. He took in the velvet dress hugging my frame, the slit that whispered secrets with every step, the leather jacket I'd thrown on like armor, and the choker at my throat—just above his mark.

That silver gleam in his eyes darkened.

"All dressed up, Little Bird," he murmured, voice low and honeyed, but there was steel beneath it. Possessive and coiled tight. "Tell me..." He stepped closer. I didn't move. "...is that for your detective?"

The way he said it—it wasn't a question. It was a challenge. The kind that dared me to lie.

And if the faint twitch in his jaw meant anything, he already knew the truth. He hated it. He hated the idea that McDara would see me like this.

I lifted my chin. "I dress for me, not for a man."

His hum was a mockery. "Mm. Of course. Nothing to do with the way he looks at you like he wants to drag that dress off you with his teeth?" My cheeks flushed, heat prickling at the edges of my control—but I refused to bite.

I turned from him. Stepped past. I didn't run. I didn't snap. But I walked like I meant it, combat boots thudding against the pavement, my back straight and unyielding.

Behind me, his laugh curled through the air—not warm, not amused. No. It was the sound of bone against metal. The sound of something not quite *human*.

"You're running off to find him?" His voice slithered behind me, smooth and cruel. "What exactly do you think you'll do, Sonia? Sniff him out like a stray? Beg him to let you in?"

I stopped. Cold.

"Because if your detective wanted you," he whispered, stepping close again—*too* close—"he wouldn't make you guess where he's gone."

His words landed like claws. Tearing into places I didn't want touched.

But I didn't turn around. Didn't give him the satisfaction of seeing the way they burrowed under my ribs.

Instead, I pivoted. Toward New Town. Toward the Black House.

"Phontine let's go."

My Pixie warily followed, grumbling about ghost and death. For once I was grateful she couldn't hear what Death was saying because if she did she'd know how deep his words cut me.

If McDara didn't want to tell me what he was doing, then fine. I wasn't going to chase him like some girl hoping to be chosen. I had magic to master. I had ghosts to find. I had a father to reach.

And no matter how close Death got, no matter how sharp his words became—I would *not* let him be the one to break me.

35

The taxi hadn't even peeled away from the curb before I snapped. I shoved the door shut with more force than necessary, the slam echoing off the concrete like the crack of thunder before a storm. Death drifted behind me, a living shadow made of silk and menace, pressing too close, as always.

Phontine hurried to follow me. "Sonia!"

"Do you ever *get tired* of badgering me?" I growled, tossing the words over my shoulder as I stalked toward the steps.

"Death's still here?" But it didn't sound like Phontine was waiting for my reply which was good all my senses were snared by the infuriating shadow plaguing my every step.

"Do you ever get tired of making it so easy?" His voice was *too* smooth—velvet wrapped around barbed wire. It scraped against every raw edge I was trying to keep hidden.

I spun to face him, my fury simmering just beneath the surface. "You're like a stray dog, following me around. Can't you haunt someone else for a change?"

His silver eyes flared like twin moons eclipsing all light. The corners of his mouth curved—not into a smile, but something colder. Sharper. "Careful, Little Bird." The softness of his voice was a blade at my throat. "Angering me is never wise."

A flicker of something primal stirred in my chest, but I buried it. Deep. I lifted my chin, defiant. "You can't touch me in the Living Lands. Remember?" The bravado in my voice was thinner than I wanted it to be. "And I'm not falling into the Deathscape again."

I turned, refusing to let him see the shiver that rolled down my spine at the weight of his stare. The heat of his presence faded into a cold hush, like standing too close to a frozen lake.

But I didn't stop walking.

The Black House rose before me, all gleaming glass and polished nothingness—like a lie built into the skyline. It loomed, hollow and pristine under the midday sun. A monolith of power pretending to be transparent. Every inch of it gleamed with cold perfection, its clear walls revealing only what it wanted the world to see.

No people. No movement. No sign that a single soul lived inside.

Phontine rang the bell. No answer. I reached past her and punched the button again. Nothing.

My frown deepened. A Mage House full of some of the most powerful casters in the city...and not *one* person was home? Yeah, right.

Beside me, Death made a low sound in his throat—something between a laugh and a warning. "Interesting," he murmured, voice brushing against my ear like a secret.

I ignored him. Stepped forward. And opened the door.

It wasn't locked.

"Breaking and entering?" he purred. "How delightfully reckless of you."

"It's not breaking if the door's open," I snapped. "Maybe they should learn to lock it."

The moment I crossed the threshold, the silence swallowed me whole.

I'd been here before. But now? It felt...wrong.

Too still. Too quiet. Like something had been drained from the walls.

The glass stretched high above me, reflecting fractured light in angles that felt unnatural. The air was sterile, scrubbed of life. No warmth. No magic humming through the glass.

No life. Just echoes.

There were no coats hung by the door, no half-empty coffee mugs, no signs of wear or personality. No proof that this was anything more than a stage.

I climbed the main stairway and passed the office hallway, the only place with photos—portraits so stiff and posed they looked more like headstones than memories. Every frame was cold. Every face frozen in polished, lifeless pride.

My boots made no sound on the obsidian marble, and that silence unnerved me more than Death's whisper ever could. By the time I reached Matron Black's office, a knot had twisted tight in my gut.

This wasn't just a home. It was a fortress. And today, it felt like a tomb.

The double doors loomed before me, cold and still. I hesitated.

Too easy. Too quiet. Like a snare waiting for the rabbit to step forward.

This was exactly what Matron Black wanted.

Before I could raise a hand, the doors creaked open of their own accord—slow, deliberate, the air crackling with the faint hiss of lingering spellwork.

And there she was. Matron Black. Sitting like a queen behind her fortress of a desk, one manicured hand raised just enough to show it had been *her* magic. As if to say: *You're expected. You're already playing the game.*

I barely had time to breathe before Death spoke beside me like smoke catching fire. "How predictable," he murmured, voice brushing my skin like the whisper of a blade. "Careful, Little Bird." And just like that—gone. Vanished into the folds of shadow, leaving behind only chill and warning.

Typical. The one time I wanted him to stay, to be something other than a riddle wrapped in silk and menace—he disappeared.

I rolled my shoulders back, grounding myself, and stepped into the room. I didn't sit. Not yet. I stood beside one of the massive leather chairs, a silent challenge.

Matron Black studied me like she already knew what cards I held and exactly how I'd play them. Her smirk was all teeth and wine-smooth poison. "Back so soon, Miss Byrd?" Her voice was velvet draped over iron. "I do hope you haven't come for an apology."

I said nothing, watching as she leaned back slightly, her gaze cutting.

"Though, you can't blame me for my suspicions," she continued, her tone lilting with faux amusement. "A stranger arrives, and that same night, one of my Mages is murdered? Curious timing, wouldn't you agree?"

The words hit hard, but I didn't flinch. I balled my fist, anchoring myself. "Actually Orlla died the night before I arrived." I said, tone even. "But I understand there's plenty of suspicion to go around."

Her eyes narrowed, just a flicker, like a blade sliding into place. "That, there is."

A beat passed. The silence was a held breath, stretched taut between us.

Then, "So tell me, Sonia. Why *are* you here?" The way she said my name—too casual, too familiar—made my skin prickle.

I sank into the chair, the leather cold beneath me, and folded my hands in my lap. "I want to know why Orlla left the Black House."

Matron Black's stillness was masterful. Only someone looking for the crack would have noticed the shift.

The air sharpened. "McDara knows why," she said flatly.

My spine stiffened. "He doesn't." Because if he did—if he *knew*—he wouldn't have kept us chasing ghosts.

Matron Black's lips curled, slow and serpentine. "That's odd," she said. "Because his partner"—She paused, the next word laced with contempt—"His *mutt* of a partner called me this morning. Asked me that very same question."

My stomach turned to ice. Dom.

"He wanted to know why Orlla left. Wanted to know the last thing we spoke about." Her eyes pinned me. "Isn't it sweet how hard they're trying to protect you?"

I kept my expression neutral even as my blood pounded. "And what did you tell them?" I asked, careful, steady.

Her fingers drummed once against the polished desk, deliberate. "House matters. Assignments. Routine leadership duties." She exhaled, long and slow. "The usual."

It was too clean. Too practiced. Each word laid out like a blade beneath silk.

She was hiding something. And I wasn't leaving until I knew what.

A hundred questions clawed at my throat, hungry and hollow. Each one more pointless than the last.

I could ask about the spell Orlla had been working on. About the map to the anchor of raw magic. About the Death Echo Matron Black might be trying to bind.

But I already knew what I'd get in return. A sharp smile. A veiled threat. A polished lie dressed in silk and power.

She wouldn't tell me a damn thing—not about the case. But there was one question I couldn't leave unasked. One truth that had burned in my chest for too long.

I inhaled slowly, letting the silence between us thicken. Letting her feel it wrap around us like tension before a storm.

Then I lifted my chin. Met her gaze. And asked, quiet but unyielding, "How do I find my birth parents?"

Matron Black's expression didn't shift immediately. But something flickered—just enough to crack the mask.

Not smugness. Not amusement. Not power.

Remorse. Subtle and fleeting, like a shadow slipping beneath a door.

I leaned forward, voice steady. "You're the Matron of this House. You know who comes and goes. You had to know where they went when they left."

The moment stretched, taut as a wire. And then, with the grace of someone preparing for a confession, Matron Black rose.

She circled her desk slowly, robes whispering over marble, and lowered herself into the chair beside mine. Too close. Too intimate. Too human.

I went still. My breath caught halfway in my lungs.

This wasn't the poised, untouchable woman I'd come to fear. This was someone about to bury the last of my hope.

Her eyes met mine. Her voice was careful. Precise. "Your parents are dead."

The world tilted.

It wasn't grief at first. It was noise—a roaring that swallowed everything. It filled my head, my chest, shook my ribs until I couldn't breathe.

"No." The word cracked from me, raw and immediate. I shook my head, once, twice, again, as if denial could undo what she'd said. "No. That's not—"

But she didn't correct herself. Didn't soften. She just watched. Immovable. Unblinking.

I searched her face for a lie, for a tell. There was nothing but finality.

The hope I'd carried all this way—every sleepless night, every aching step toward Blakewell—began to crumble.

Someone should have told me. Someone *would* have told me. There should've been a sign, a thread, anything.

But there had been nothing. Until now.

I opened my mouth. But the next protest withered in my throat.

Silence spread like frost.

Matron Black exhaled slowly, her voice cool and quiet. "I didn't want to blindside you when you arrived. If all you wanted was training, I saw no need to dredge up the past."

"How?" My voice broke. Rough. Bare. Like something torn loose inside me. "How did they die?"

Matron Black stilled. She composed herself with deliberate poise, but I saw the tension. The shadows.

"They died nearly twenty-two years ago," she said, "in the incident at Larkend."

And just like that, the roaring was back.

But this time, it wasn't grief.

It was shock. Rage. Revelation. It poured through my veins, hollowing me out from the inside. The place I'd been researching, the cursed town that held the key to everything—

Had also been the graveyard of my past.

"I don't know how much longer I have." The words were nothing but a whispers form my lips.

Matron Black's eyes sharpened, that endless dark narrowing with surgical interest.

"Much longer for what?"

"My dad, the man who raised me, my real dad, died six months ago." The words slipped out, brittle and broken, barely a breath. "What if he's already moved on? I *have* to learn how to use my magic to contact him before I loose my chance."

Matron Black tilted her head, and her lips curved—not kindly. More like a wolf scenting an open wound. "Fascinating."

The word coiled around me like a spell. My spine straightened. "What?"

Her gaze roamed over me like I was a book she hadn't finished reading. "The Deathscape," she said slowly, savoring each syllable. "Your ability to enter it. Your connection to the dead…It's rare. Raw. Dangerous."

There was hunger beneath her polished veneer now, slick and glittering like oil on water. I didn't like the way she said *dangerous*. I didn't like the way she said *rare*.

But before I could push back, she shifted forward. Not threatening. Not soft. Just deliberate. Power poised and waiting.

"You don't need your birth parents to master your magic."

That pulled me out of the grief haze. Sharpened every nerve.

"What are you talking about?"

Her fingers laced together in her lap, eyes gleaming. "The Mage who trained your birth mother—who taught her to wield her Ghost Whisperer magic—still resides in this House."

My stomach dropped. The air turned colder.

Matron Black smiled. That slow, elegant, devastating kind of smile. The kind that felt like a noose disguised as silk.

"She can train you, Sonia." Her voice was a lullaby now. "But only if you choose to join the Black House."

36

The air outside The Obsidian Quill sliced across my skin like a blade made of frost. Not the kind of cold that prickled—this one sank deep, bone deep, curling into my chest where Matron Black's voice still echoed.

It had been over an hour since I left the Black House, and I could still feel it—the tight coil of her offer, slick and poisonous, wrapping around my ribs like it had a claim.

Phontine shimmered into visibility the moment I'd stepped into daylight, her wings casting fractured light against the sidewalk like glass catching flame. She hadn't even let me shut the cab door before I spilled every broken thought in my head.

Now, coffee clutched in my hand like a lifeline, I did what I always did—pretended I could outrun what haunted me.

"Are you sure you made the right choice?" Phontine asked, her voice soft for once, brushing the edge of hesitant. "I hate that I had to wait outside."

"Matron Black doesn't seem to like Pixies." I said, "plus its safer for you to stay away from her."

We walked past old brick storefronts, glass panes dusted with golden, afternoon light. The street should've felt safe. Warm. Alive.

Instead, it felt like waiting.

I took a long sip, the heat of the coffee scalding my tongue, and welcomed it. Better the burn than the weight that hadn't stopped pressing against me since I walked out of the House of Masks.

"I hate when you get all broody and quiet. It's either silence or a floodgate of every sharp thing in your head." Phontine muttered, fluttering ahead of me. "Just say what you're thinking for once—"

The world dropped ten degrees in a breath.

A wave of unnatural cold hit us like a wall, slicing down the street with a force that stole the air from my lungs.

People around me cried out, clutching coats tighter, scarves dragged up over mouths. Breath misted like fog, curling in the sudden silence.

And I felt her.

Even before I saw her—I felt her.

Orlla.

She shimmered at the far end of the sidewalk, her translucent form flickering in and out like a bad signal, as if the world could barely contain what was left of her. Her eyes—hollow, wide, desperate—locked onto mine. She raised one ghost-pale hand.

Frost bloomed.

It wasn't random. It wasn't chaotic.

It was deliberate.

A message.

The glass windows around us bloomed with ice, every storefront erupting with the same jagged, mirrored pattern. Etched in frost: The outline of the caves.

My pulse slammed against my throat.

A couple behind me gasped. Someone dropped a coffee. A child cried out.

But all I could see was her. All I could feel was that silent, searing need pulsing from her ghostlight.

Follow.

My fingers fumbled as I yanked out my phone. McDara's name glowed back at me.

I called. It rang. And rang. No answer.

"Come on, come on," I whispered, trying again.

Voicemail.

"Damn it." My breath fogged the air, panic scraping up my throat like smoke.

Whatever this was—whatever Orlla was trying to show me—it wasn't something that could wait.

And I was alone.

Phontine hovered in close, her face pale as moonlight. "Tell me we're not about to follow the murder ghost into a death trap."

I downed the rest of the coffee in one scalding gulp and tossed the cup into the nearest bin.

"We're following the murder ghost."

Phontine let out a strangled groan. "Why are we like this?"

I turned without answering, boots crunching across frost-glazed pavement.

The forest writhed around us, black branches clawing at the sky like broken fingers.

Phontine and I tore through the trees, the air thick with a presence that didn't belong to the living. Orlla's magic coated everything, death-ice clinging to trunks and curling over leaves like veins of ice threading through the bones of the earth.

It had started as a shimmer, a whisper on the wind. Now it was a trail of white fire.

A command. A cry. A curse.

Each breath I dragged in felt sharp enough to cut, the cold crawling under my skin, fusing with my spine, coiling around my lungs. This wasn't just winter chill—it was unnatural, something that hollowed out the world as we ran through it.

"She's getting worse," Phontine gasped beside me, her wings twitching from the bite of the cold. Her glow was dimmer now, the frost clinging even to her magic. "Way worse. Maybe because we're too slow?"

"I'm *running*," I hissed, boots slipping over damp moss and frozen roots. The slit in my dress snapped against my legs, velvet dragging through icy brush, already soaked and shredded. The glamour of it was long gone—I wasn't a girl on her way to answers anymore. I was a girl chasing a ghost straight into the jaws of something very, very wrong.

But I didn't say what I was really thinking.

That we weren't alone.

There was a weight behind me. Not a shadow. Not a sound. A presence. It breathed down my neck without breath, pressed fingers into the back of my mind without touch. Not Orlla. Something else. Watching. Waiting.

The ice deepened—slick and glassy now, trailing up the trees in jagged lines. Orlla's ghost shimmered ahead, her shape flickering with violent urgency.

Hurry.

The word didn't enter my ears. It lanced straight into my bones.

We broke through the last line of trees.

The cave mouth loomed ahead—jagged, black, and hungry, rimmed in frost and shadows. The air turned to knives.

Then—footsteps.

I spun, chest heaving.

Two figures surged out of the tree line.

Calypso. Pandora.

Their faces flashed pale in the cold light, eyes wide with surprise. Calypso's hand was raised, a leather pouch clenched tight. Pandora's expression was already sharpening like a blade.

"What the hell are you doing here?" My voice cracked, half breath, half fury. I didn't have time for this.

Calypso faltered. "Sonia, we—"

"We could ask the same thing," Pandora snapped, her stance already shifting to defense.

But I didn't answer.

Because the cave screamed.

A thunderous blast detonated from deep inside the earth, shaking the forest floor, sending gravel skittering and ice shards splintering from the walls.

And then—the screaming.

Raw. Human. Tearing.

My blood went still. My body didn't.

I was already moving.

Straight into the dark.

37

I didn't feel the jagged cave walls clawing at my arms. Didn't register the slick, treacherous stone scraping beneath my boots. My body ran on instinct, heart a war drum pounding against my ribs, lungs burning from the effort—but none of it mattered.

Only one thing mattered: The magic.

It reverberated through the cave like a cry of grief given shape—alive, screaming, violent.

Phontine zipped ahead, her glow flickering like a dying star in the swallowing dark, barely cutting through the pitch around us. Calypso and Pandora's footsteps echoed behind me, but their voices blurred into static. They weren't what I was running toward.

I felt the source before I saw it—a pulsing force of corrupted magic that slithered through the air like it had teeth.

We hit the final bend.

The chamber yawned before us, vast and echoing, shadows clawing at every edge.

And in the center of it, hunched near the far wall—

A figure. Trembling. Consumed.

Magic poured from their hands in slick, serpentine ribbons of black and sickly green, the tendrils cracking along the floor like lightning turned to liquid. It hissed as it moved, alive and starving, the sound almost...mournful.

I stepped forward, unthinking, my soul hollowed out by the weight of what I already knew but couldn't believe.

The figure jerked, spine arching unnaturally, and a sound escaped them—a cry. A scream. A *wound* given voice.

Then the hood fell.

And the world shattered.

Deidre.

My legs locked. My lungs stopped. The magic inside me stilled, as if even it recoiled.

Her face was twisted in pain, mouth parted in a voiceless scream, hands clawing at her own chest where the dark magic boiled from her skin, eating away at her. Like it had fused with her bones. Like it was already part of her.

This wasn't the girl who had smiled shyly over coffee. This wasn't the sister McDara protected like his own soul.

This was a girl losing herself to something that should never have touched her in the first place.

And I knew—*I knew*—McDara didn't know. He couldn't.

Because if he did, he would've burned the world down to stop it.

His sister. His responsibility. His line in the sand.

This was his nightmare made flesh.

My stomach churned, bile clawing up the back of my throat as Deidre doubled over, fingers dragging bloody streaks through her shirt, her body convulsing against the force of the magic she couldn't contain.

This wasn't just sickness anymore.

This was corruption. This was possession. This was destruction from the inside out.

And all I could think—all I could scream inside the silence of my own bones—was one, sharp question that wouldn't let me breathe:

Who taught her?

Deidre had promised him.

But she had learned dark magic.

And now, she was drowning in it.

The truth stood before me in flesh and ruin—black magic pouring from her like blood, thick and writhing, seeping from every pore. If it hadn't been Matron Black...

Had it been Orlla?

The thought made my stomach revolt. The timeline. The secrecy. The map. The Death Echo spell. It fit. Too well.

And that meant Deidre wasn't just using Maleficaria—

She *was* the Malifax Mage.

The Malifax Mage who'd tried to kill me...

It was her.

"Deidre..." Her name broke in my throat, barely more than a breath, too soft for the roar of magic shrieking through the cavern.

She didn't hear me. Couldn't.

Her body swayed beneath the weight of it, magic oozing from her like some malignant second skin. It lashed at the rocks, sizzled against the floor, as if trying to anchor her in place. As if the Deathscape itself was dragging her closer.

She was unraveling.

A gasp cut through the silence—Calypso.

Pandora didn't speak. Didn't blink. Her body went taut, her aura shifting. *Predatory.*

And then—

McDara.

He exploded from the nearest tunnel like a storm made flesh, a blur of movement and fury. Dust and rock spiraled in his wake as he planted himself between us and the wreckage of his sister.

His body was rigid; every muscle braced like a wall against the inevitable.

He was ready to defend her. Not just from them. From me.

His gaze found mine first. And what I saw in his eyes wasn't confusion or fear.

It was desperation. Wild and raw.

Then his gaze slid—to Calypso. To Pandora.

And everything in him *coiled*.

That same protectiveness I'd felt when he pulled me from the Deathscape—that fire-forged promise that he'd never let harm touch me—It was aimed at her now.

Not me. Her.

The realization struck like a punch to the chest, splintering through my ribs, stealing my breath. Not because I didn't understand it—but because I did.

Then it hit me.

The weight I'd felt crawling across my skin, that *awareness* I'd tried to dismiss in the panic—

Calypso and Pandora weren't here by accident.

They were Black House Mages.

And in the world of Mage Courts, there was no redemption for what Deidre had become.

There was only one kind of justice for a Malifax Mage. Final. Unforgiving. Cold.

I felt the shift in the air—static and promise.

Calypso's hand twitched.

Pandora's eyes locked on Deidre.

And McDara…McDara moved to stand in front of his sister. And readied himself to burn the world down.

The cave pulsed like a living thing. The air wasn't just thick—it pressed, wrapped around my neck like invisible fingers. Every breath scraped down my throat, every heartbeat a thunderclap of dread.

Pandora's voice sliced through the stillness, clean and brutal. "How long have you been experimenting with dark magic, Deidre?"

Deidre recoiled, as if the words had slapped her. Her body hunched, trembling, and the shadows around her surged—black and green tendrils of magic lashing out like a wounded animal, striking at stone, at air, at *us*.

And McDara moved.

Fast. Instinctively. Like he'd always been ready.

His body a barricade of muscle and magic. His shoulders squared. His magic flared. "That's enough."

Steel. Final. Unmovable.

But Pandora didn't flinch. Her eyes cut to him, sharp as a blade drawn between ribs. "So, you *did* know."

And that—that broke something inside me.

Because he didn't answer.

He didn't deny it. Didn't blink. Didn't even *look at me.*

He just stood there. Solid. Silent. A wall built between us.

The silence *split* through me—cracking something deep, something raw and already bruised from too many secrets.

My mouth went dry. My thoughts screamed.

How long had he known? How long had he let her rot in shadows, hoping no one would notice the stench?

Deidre—the girl who had sat beside me. Who had smiled like she carried only warmth. She had tried to kill me.

And McDara—the man who'd kissed me like I was something holy, who held me like I was his last chance at light—had kept this from me.

Had he known when we kissed? Had he known when he'd told me I was safe in his arms?

Had I been living in the same house with a man who was protecting the very thing hunting me?

The betrayal hit like a blade under my ribs, twisting, carving its name into my lungs with every breath. And still—*gods help me*—I didn't want to believe it.

Even now, even here, with the truth seeping into the cracks between us like poison—I wanted to trust him.

I wanted him to turn to me. To *say something*. To reach for me, pull me back from the edge, and swear that none of it meant what it looked like.

But he didn't.

He stood guard. Not for me. For her.

And the space between us yawned open like a chasm—wide and cruel and cold.

Because the truth was no longer a whisper.

It was a question with no answer: What would McDara do to protect his sister?

And what would he sacrifice to keep her safe?

Even if it was me?

The air in the cave thinned, heavy and trembling—like a breath the world was too afraid to exhale.

Magic prickled along the stone walls, buzzing low and angry and *alive*. Pandora's hands flexed at her sides, a warning in every twitch of her fingers. Magic shimmered beneath her skin, sharp and electric, pulsing like the charge before a storm.

"You do realize what this means, don't you?" Her voice came razor sharp, too calm to be safe. Her eyes didn't leave Deidre. Then McDara. "Matron Black will—"

Calypso moved like a blade slipping between ribs—fast, quiet, deliberate. "Let's take a second." Her voice cracked, taut and splintering. She stepped between her twin and the unraveling magic at McDara's back, hands raised in fragile peace. Her gaze found

Pandora's, steady and pleading. "Think for yourself for once, yeah? We don't have to do this by the book."

Pandora's expression twisted, lips curling like the words left a bad taste. "Of course we do. You know how she operates. You want to go against protocol?"

The word *protocol* rang out like a sentence.

A pulse of dread carved into my chest.

"What's protocol?" My voice cut through the tension like a whip.

Pandora didn't even blink. "That's not your business."

My fingers curled into the zipper of my jacket, desperate to feel something real—something solid. But the cold in my gut was spreading, seeping into my bones, turning the air around me to ice.

Calypso's shoulders lifted on a sharp breath. "It should be." Her tone was brittle glass. "It should be her business. I hate that we can't tell her anything. That she's just a pawn in Matron Black's game. It's not right."

And that—*that* was it.

The thing I'd felt every time Calypso held back. Every time she lied with her words and not her eyes. It wasn't malice. It was fear.

Gratitude swelled in my throat like a sob, but it barely had time to bloom before the tension snapped tighter—like a bowstring pulled to breaking.

Pandora's stance turned lethal. Magic curled at her feet like smoke, hungry for release. And McDara—he didn't move. Didn't speak. Just stood there. Solid. A wall of fury and devotion between his sister and the people who might hurt her.

His choice had already been made.

And it wasn't me.

My pulse thundered. If Pandora attacked—if Calypso folded beneath duty, if Deidre lashed out again—McDara would throw himself into it. Would bleed for her. Would burn for her.

And I—*the Wood damn me*—I would burn too.

Would I fight Calypso? Pandora? Would I fight the very people I thought were my allies?

A tremor danced up my spine, every emotion inside me a tangled storm of betrayal and fear, and the worst one of all: *Love.*

I couldn't let McDara be collateral in this war. Even if I didn't know which side he was really on.

"Sonia, you need to calm down." Phontine hovered near, her wings a frantic blur.

I turned to her, fury flashing through the tears that hadn't yet fallen.

"Don't tell me to calm down." Because this wasn't a moment for calm.

This was a moment for choosing. And whether anyone liked it or not...I was about to make mine.

"We're in a cave with a Malifax Mage bleeding dark magic like it's oxygen, two House-trained enforcers who would burn her down without blinking, and McDara"—My eyes snapped to him, to the man I didn't know how to trust anymore—"who looks like he'd take on the world for her."

Phontine's glow flickered, dimming like a guttering candle. "That's *exactly* my point," she hissed. "You don't have active magic, and mine's not even close to strong enough to stop what's coming. You need to leave. Before you're caught in the middle of this."

But I couldn't move.

Because McDara hadn't. He stood there—*a wall of muscle, magic, and mourning*—between us and his sister, body braced like he expected the whole damn cave to collapse around him.

I couldn't leave him.

I stepped forward, voice shaking but loud enough to cut through the still churning air. "McDara," I said, and his eyes snapped to mine—wild, wrecked, *ready.* "Deidre needs help."

He didn't speak. His jaw locked so tight I could see the twitch in the muscle. I pressed on.

"She's being consumed from the inside out," I said, my voice cracking. "This isn't sustainable. This—this magic is eating her alive. If we don't do something—"

"You want to hand her over to Matron Black?" he cut in, the words low and furious, like fire being forced through clenched teeth. "That would be a death sentence."

From behind me, Pandora's voice lashed out like a whip. "And what's your plan, then? Hide her until she *explodes* again?" Her magic flared, the static in the air sharp enough to taste.

But McDara didn't flinch. Didn't even look at her. His gaze stayed locked on *me.*

"She's not a monster," he said. No, *pleaded.* "She's *sick.* She never wanted this. She only turned to the darkness because no one else would help her—"

The words stabbed. Because I knew that desperation. Because it sounded *too much like me.*

But I couldn't ignore what had already happened. I couldn't erase it.

"She tried to kill me."

The cave went *silent*.

The confession hit the air like a dropped blade—final, undeniable. It carved through the magic, through the tension, through the fragile thread between me and the man who had held me like I was worth saving.

McDara flinched. His face twisted, shattered—but it wasn't surprise in his eyes. *It was guilt.* Devastation. Grief.

But not denial.

And that was the moment everything inside me cracked.

"You knew," I breathed. A whisper. A curse. A truth.

McDara's body tensed, his expression cracking at the edges. He took a step toward me, frantic, reaching, his mouth parting—

"YOU KILLED ORLLA!" Pandora's scream detonated through the chamber like thunder, her magic igniting the air with searing heat. "You're coming with us Deidre!" Fire surged down her arms, crawling like a serpent made of vengeance and flame.

McDara spun, throwing up a shield of raw force, his own magic flaring bright and furious.

And then—

Chaos.

The cave exploded into light and motion. Magic collided. Rock split. And all I could do was hold my breath—as the war finally began.

38

The scream tore from Deidre like a soul unspooling.

Black-green magic exploded out of her in a wave—violent, feral, *wrong*—like something ancient and hungry had finally been set loose. The air convulsed with it, vibrating like a struck chord. McDara lunged through the chaos, magic crackling up his arms, his entire being tuned to one thing: His sister.

Protect. Shield. Save.

Calypso swore, hands slamming together as she summoned a shield of iridescent light. The first pulse of Deidre's power slammed into it like a battering ram, sending a spray of sparks arcing into the cavern's gloom.

The air thickened, humming with raw, uncontained force. *You killed Orlla* still rang in the space like a curse—like the moment time had fractured.

Deidre staggered, her body shaking from the inside out. "No," she breathed, the word so brittle it might've shattered under its own weight. "No, no—I didn't—"

The temperature plummeted.

Frost crawled across the cave floor, snaking like veins of ice through the stone. It climbed Deidre's boots, laced up her legs, whispering promises of judgment. Of reckoning.

And then she appeared.

Orlla.

No longer the faint shimmer of memory. No longer the ghost pleading for help.

Now, she was *wrath made manifest.*

Her presence surged through the cave like a cold front from hell. Her features were distorted, twisted by grief and rage, her form splintered with light that fractured like shattered glass. Ice bloomed in her wake—sharp, spectral, endless.

My breath hitched.

She wasn't just here to be seen. She was here to *punish.*

Deidre's knees buckled, the frost clamping around her like manacles. "I didn't mean to," she sobbed, panic splintering her voice. "I didn't mean to—"

But the words rang hollow.

Orlla's spectral eyes burned. No softness. No mercy. Just the cold clarity of vengeance.

McDara's voice snapped through the tension like a whip. "Sonia—she's here, isn't she?"

I nodded, throat tight. "Yes."

And then I moved.

The cold bit into my skin like needles, but I pushed forward, past the ice that crept like a living thing, toward the wraith I'd once promised to help.

"Orlla," I called, voice trembling but unyielding. "This isn't justice—this is rage. You *don't have to do this.*"

But she didn't turn. Didn't flinch.

She *chose* not to hear me.

The ice surged higher, locking Deidre in place from the waist down. The cave floor groaned beneath the pressure, fissures spidering out like shattered bone.

Deidre screamed.

And the darkness inside her *responded.*

Magic detonated from her chest, uncontrolled and feral, bursting outward like a nova of rot and shadow. The air cracked apart as if reality itself had fractured.

Then—

An arm around my waist. Steel-strong. Sure.

McDara.

He yanked me against him, his body the shield I didn't have, his magic slamming into place in a dome of blistering heat and golden light. The dark wave slammed into it and *broke,* scattering across his shield like acid rain on glass.

The shockwave still hit—my ears rang, the stone beneath my feet buckled—but McDara's arms didn't loosen.

His breath was ragged against my hair. "I've got you."

Above us, stone shifted. Cracked. Groaned. The cave itself protested, ancient rock trembling as the magic tore deeper.

But none of it could drown out the presence still pulsing through the air.

Orlla's fury.

A storm with no eye. No calm.

The cave had become a battlefield carved from ice and grief.

Orlla was no longer the woman I had seen in fleeting glimpses—no longer a whisper in the dark.

She was *vengeance incarnate.*

Frost surged up Deidre's body like a punishment written in ice, cracking through the floor, spider-webbing across the stone. With every second Orlla lingered, the air turned colder—sharper. The oxygen thinned. Each breath felt like a razor dragged down my throat.

A deep rupture split the cave in two, a jagged scar of dark energy cleaving Pandora and Calypso from the rest of us. It pulsed like a heartbeat—wild, unsteady, waiting to erupt again.

Deidre shook, trembling like a thread about to snap. Her hood was gone, her face hollowed by pain and desperation, her eyes glowing with frenzied defiance.

"They knew!" she cried, the words cracking on the cavern walls. "Matron Black knew about the Larkend magic—what it could do! And she *left me to* rot!"

McDara froze. His entire body locked up, tension rippling through him like a cord drawn too tight. His magic still lingered, humming protectively around me like a shield—but I could feel him slipping. His control thinning. His heart bleeding out.

I turned just in time to see him step forward, hands raised—not casting, not threatening. Just open.

A brother trying to reach the last pieces of his sister.

"Deidre," he said, voice raw. "You don't have to fight anymore. Just let me help you—"

"Help?" Her voice splintered, a brittle, breaking thing. "Help like before? When you begged them to save me and they laughed in your face? When they let me *drown*?"

Her hands lifted, black magic pouring from her palms like venom.

"I won't go back, Cillian!" she screamed. "You'll have to *drag me*!"

The next pulse of magic was merciless.

It slammed forward like a tidal wave—and would've hit McDara square in the chest if I hadn't moved.

I lunged, grabbing his arm and yanking him back just as the blast hit the stone where he stood. The impact left a crater in the cave floor, magic still hissing, sizzling like acid as it ate through the rock.

He stared at me, breathless. Shaken.

But it was already too late.

The frost surged again.

Deidre screamed as the ice cinched higher, locking her in place from the knees up, jagged edges biting into her skin.

"*Stop!*" McDara roared, rounding on me. "Orlla—she's still here?"

"Yes," I choked out, heart pounding. "And she's not stopping."

Orlla's fury bloomed like a hurricane, her magic pressing down on my skull, a pressure so intense it blurred my vision, warped the air. I staggered under it. She wasn't just haunting me anymore. She was *claiming judgment*.

And she was going to kill Deidre.

This wasn't justice. It was a slow, merciless execution.

No.

I closed my eyes, reached inward, past the rising panic—past the memories of Orlla whispering in the dark, past the sick twist in my stomach telling me I'd trusted her.

I tunneled into the storm of my magic.

It rose around me, wild and golden, untamed and *alive*. Like diving into open sea during a lightning storm—terrifying and beautiful and real. I followed McDara's voice in my memory, that steady anchor pulling me back every time I drifted too far.

Don't fall into the Deathscape. Don't fall into the Deathscape.

The Deathscape loomed—always just beneath me, a shadow waiting to swallow—but I pushed through, gritting my teeth, holding the thread tighter.

There.

Orlla.

Not a ghost now. Not even a spirit.

She was fury. Ice. A specter made of raw grief and betrayal.

A *wraith*.

I wrapped my magic around her, pulling, gripping tight, fighting her rage with everything I had left.

"*Orlla,*" I shouted, my voice breaking across the ice. "*Stop!*"

My magic snapped into her like a tether.

The words I spoke cracked the air like thunder, laced in something older than language—etched in grief, carved in raw power.

And for a heartbeat, it *worked*.

Orlla froze.

The frost stopped.

Deidre gasped, her body heaving, barely able to stay upright as her magic writhed around her like a creature in agony, desperate and directionless. Shadows spilled from her fingers in violent coils, striking the air, searching for anything to anchor to.

The cave held its breath.

Then—she *screamed*.

Pain ripped from her throat, wild and animal. Her magic surged like a dam breaking, and I felt it—my hold on Orlla slipping, unraveling, disintegrating beneath the weight of everything she was and everything she couldn't control.

I fought to hold it.

Fought to *hold her*.

But Orlla was fury given form. She wasn't just a ghost—she was retribution, frozen and unforgiving, and I had dared to try and stop her.

The frost began again, crawling up Deidre's legs in jagged, bone-white ridges. It split the stone beneath her, threading through the cave like a curse etched into the earth.

"*Orlla, please!*" My voice cracked, raw with fear and fury. "*Stop!*"

But she was past hearing.

She was already *gone*.

I closed my eyes and plunged deeper—into the heart of my magic, into the place where light met shadow, where my fear had always lived. I pushed harder, demanding more from the thing inside me, begging it to obey.

And then I felt it.

A cold that wasn't ice.

A presence that wasn't Orlla's.

A chill slid down my spine, not sharp like frost—but heavy, slow, *inevitable*.

I opened my eyes.

He was there.

Death.

A silhouette in black and silver, silver eyes catching every shard of light, his gaze already on mine.

Watching.

Always watching.

"Help me," I whispered, the words torn straight from the center of my soul.

But he didn't move.

Didn't blink.

Didn't *breathe*.

He just looked at me like he was *waiting*. Like my pain, my desperation—like *Deidre's agony*—was part of some test I didn't understand.

I wanted to scream at him.

But a crack of dark magic snapped me back to the present.

Deidre's magic convulsed, snarling in the air. Her body bucked beneath it.

And then McDara was there.

Moving faster than anyone should've been able to move.

"*Deidre!*" His voice was ragged, desperate, each syllable torn from a heart already breaking. "*Look at me—please.*"

She did.

Her eyes—wild, fevered—met his.

And for the first time, something *changed*.

The magic faltered.

Not much. Not enough. But enough to make hope spark in the silence.

"I can fix this," McDara said, his voice lower now, trembling at the edges. "Just trust me, Dee. I swear to you. I *swear it.*"

She hesitated.

Just for a breath.

Her hands dropped a fraction. Her shoulders dipped. A flicker of light broke through the shadows coiled around her.

She was listening.

She was *trying.*

I held my breath.

And then—

I lost my grip.

The thread of magic I had wrapped around Orlla slipped through my fingers like silk, and she *lunged.*

A blur of spectral light and biting frost, her scream silent but deafening.

She collided with Deidre in a storm of ice and grief, and the cavern erupted in light.

Deidre screamed again—this time not from fear, but from the sheer force of it.

Her magic *detonated.*

It didn't lash.

It *exploded.*

A bolt of dark energy tore through the air like lightning—and I didn't even see where it struck until McDara's body jerked backward.

His head snapped, his limbs went slack, magic bled from him in ribbons of fractured light.

He hit the ground.

And didn't move.

39

The sound of his body hitting stone shattered something in me.

It wasn't a noise. It was a *cataclysm*.

I heard myself scream—heard the raw, feral edge in it—but it was distant, swallowed by the roaring panic thundering through my skull. Everything narrowed, tunneled in on him.

McDara.

His body convulsed where it had fallen, arching off the ground in a violent, unnatural spasm. Dark veins—tainted with corrupted magic—raced beneath his skin like poison come to life, pulsing, writhing, *spreading*.

"*McDara!*" His name tore from my throat like a battle cry. I moved, didn't think—just *moved*, powered by a fear so sharp it bordered on agony—

A blast of dark magic hit the wall beside me and rock began to fall. Nailing me in the leg.

The impact sent me flying. My back slammed into the rock; the air punched from my lungs. Pain sparked across every nerve ending, but none of it mattered.

I couldn't breathe. Couldn't think.

I can't lose him—gods, I can't lose him—

I forced the fear down and locked onto my magic like a lifeline, yanking it up from the depths of me, demanding control.

"*STOP!*" I screamed, the command infused with power, fury, *grief.*

Orlla *froze.*

Her spectral form halted mid-lunge, ice crystals scattering around her like shattered stars.

I clenched my jaw, muscles trembling as I *redirected* her—not as a weapon. Not as vengeance. As a *shield.*

"Protect him," I whispered.

And she did.

The ice surged, not toward Deidre, but between us—between McDara and the dark tide of magic still pouring off her in frenzied waves. A wall of jagged, living ice erupted from the ground, catching the brunt of the next strike and *held.*

Orlla stepped in front of me, her translucent body solidifying, luminous and haunting, her magic flaring like a beacon. She became a barrier between us and the black-green chaos still tearing through the cave.

I collapsed to my knees, breath sawing in and out of my lungs, heart pounding like a war drum.

McDara was still down.

Still shaking.

That cursed magic was eating him alive.

But I couldn't move to help him—not yet. Because Deidre was still standing.

And Death—*Death was still watching.*

A silent sentinel at the edge of the world.

This wasn't over.

Deidre screamed—not with sound, but with movement. She *ripped* at the ice climbing her arms, her fingers clawing at it like an animal caught in a trap. Her legs cracked free of their frozen bonds, her limbs shaking with every breathless surge of resistance. Her magic flared and twisted around her like a storm without direction, feral and wild.

Then she broke loose.

And her eyes—those dark, frenzied eyes—*found me.*

Through Orlla's form, she stared straight at me. The madness, the magic, the fury—

And then her gaze shifted.

To *him*.

McDara.

On the ground.

Convulsing.

Because of *her*.

The noise that left Deidre's lips wasn't human. It wasn't a scream.

It was a sound torn from a soul as it shattered.

Hollow. Shaking. *Ruined*.

Her body swayed as the truth struck her like a blade to the heart. Her hands trembled, still crackling with magic she could no longer control.

She staggered back.

Her lips parted like she wanted to say it wasn't her. Like she wanted to scream, *This wasn't supposed to happen—*

But she *knew*.

She had done this.

She had hurt him.

And the pieces of her were coming apart, right before our eyes.

Dark magic coiled through the air, thick as smoke, seething and wild. It pulsed off Deidre like a second heartbeat—sick and ravenous—and I knew, in that breathless, suspended moment, that I couldn't hold Orlla much longer.

She was trembling with fury in my grasp, her form flickering, breaking apart at the edges like ice under strain. I couldn't move her. Couldn't shield McDara more. Couldn't *stop* what was coming.

And Deidre—

Her breath rasped through the cave, each exhale shallower than the last, and the magic wrapped around her reeled back once—

Then *snapped* tighter.

I braced.

But before the next wave could strike, the sickly green wall sealing off the tunnel behind us shattered like glass. Chunks of corrupted magic rained down, sizzling where they struck the rock, disintegrating on impact.

The pressure in the air shifted. A crack of wind blasted through the space—and with it, a flicker of *hope*.

Calypso and Pandora burst through the ruin of the barrier like twin storms unleashed.

Phontine let out a breathless gasp on my shoulder. "Oh, *thank the Wood*—"

For a heartbeat, I believed it too.

Then Deidre *screamed*.

Her hands flung forward and a blast of magic ripped through the chamber. Calypso's fingers snapped up, lips moving fast, spellwork forming on instinct as she caught the assault midair and twisted it away. Her shield glittered like starlight over water, catching the wild chaos and *weaving* it into harmless collapse.

Pandora didn't speak.

She stepped into the storm like she *was* the storm—controlled, inevitable. Her magic coiled around her in pulses of deep violet, ancient syllables falling from her tongue like hammers striking iron.

I felt the spell building before I understood it.

It was old. Heavy. Final.

No.

"Wait—what is she doing?" I gasped.

But I knew.

She was sealing Deidre in. Locking her down. Not striking to kill—binding. *Silencing.*

The cave trembled with every word Pandora spoke. Magic rippled like a living current, rolling through the stone, the walls, the air itself. She wasn't casting a curse. She was *constructing a cage.*

And Deidre—

She fought it.

Screamed against it. Magic burst from her again, wild, feral, fueled by panic—but Pandora held.

And it stunned me.

Because she *wasn't* ending it. She wasn't trying to rip Deidre apart. She was *trying to put her down gently.*

Why?

Why spare her?

Why now?

But I didn't have time to ask.

Because I was slipping.

My hold on Orlla unraveled like water through a sieve. My magic frayed, my vision swam. The cold gripped my ribs like iron fingers.

"Hold—hold—*hold*—"

I clamped my eyes shut, trying to force Orlla back into place—but then—

"*Deidre!*"

The scream cracked through the cave like lightning.

I turned.

McDara.

He was still on the ground, broken, veins laced with black, breath ragged—but *alive*.

And reaching for her.

His hands clawed through the dirt, dragging himself toward her, his entire body trembling with pain. "*Don't let this take you!*" he cried, voice raw, wrecked. "*You can't have my sister!*"

Deidre's head whipped around.

Her eyes locked on him.

And for one, impossible moment, she stilled.

I *thought* she would stop.

I *thought*—

A bolt of dark magic sliced past my face.

So close it burned.

I twisted, spinning on instinct—

And that's when I saw *him*.

Death.

He stood at the mouth of the chamber, still and silent, as if carved from shadow and moonlight. Silver eyes gleamed in the dark, twin stars burning cold.

But he wasn't looking at me.

Not at Deidre.

Not even at McDara.

He was watching *Calypso*.

And for the first time since this chaos began—

I looked too.

And what I saw—

Terrified me.

Because Calypso wasn't just defending.

She was *commanding.*

Dark magic ripped through the air toward her—and she *took* it. Snatched it mid-flight like it was hers by right. She didn't redirect it. She *absorbed* it. Molded it. Bent it like metal softened in flame.

Her magic flared, and the corruption didn't fight her.

It *obeyed.*

She twisted it around her fingers like silk thread, folding it into her spellwork like it belonged there.

No Mage should be able to do that.

No *human* should be able to do that.

And yet Calypso moved like a conductor of storms, like the dark magic was just another element in her arsenal.

Not an enemy.

A *tool.*

And Death—

Death was smiling.

Not his usual mocking grin. Not the flirtatious tilt of a mouth full of riddles and secrets.

No.

This smile was *dark.*

It was old.

Something like recognition.

And that terrified me more than anything.

The spell snapped into place like a noose.

Pandora's magic locked with finality, the air thrumming as if the very bones of the cave recognized the weight of it. The storm had broken—but its aftermath was still unraveling. Threads of power curled through the cavern like smoke after a fire, shimmering and crackling with the echo of fury and fear.

And at the center of it all—Deidre collapsed.

Her knees hit the stone with a wet crack. Her hands followed, trembling, claws of spent magic twitching around her fingers. Breath sawed from her lungs in jagged, broken gasps, and for the first time, she looked small. Hollowed.

McDara moved.

He shouldn't have been able to—not with the poison still devouring him from the inside, not with blood smearing his mouth and darkness spidering under his skin—but pain didn't matter to him. Not when it came to family.

He crawled through the wreckage; every inch of progress carved from sheer will.

Desperate.

Desperate.

I staggered, nearly going down myself. My magic frayed like silk caught in thorns, and my knees threatened to buckle beneath me.

And then—

He was there.

Death.

Silent as shadow, solid as nightmare. One breath, and he was beside me, his presence sliding over my skin like velvet laced with frost.

He didn't touch me—he couldn't. But gods, he *looked* like he wanted to. The silver in his eyes dimmed for half a heartbeat, something unreadable tightening his features. Concern? Or just fascination with watching me bleed out my magic like lifeblood?

"I'm losing control," I rasped, the truth scraping raw from my throat.

Death's lips curved. Not kindly.

"Oh, Little Bird." His voice coiled through the air like smoke. "You can endure a little more. I know you can."

A chill shivered down my spine, but I met his gaze, fire sparking behind my exhaustion. "You enjoy this," I hissed. "Watching me break."

He smiled, slow and cruel, like I'd given him a gift.

"I enjoy watching you *fight* not to."

My hand itched to slap that grin off his face. But I didn't have the strength. So, I stood—barely. Trembling. Fraying. But *standing*.

And Death watched me like I was the most beautiful thing he'd ever seen.

Across the chamber, McDara reached Deidre.

He collapsed beside her and pulled her into his arms like the world was ending. And maybe, for him, it was. He cradled her like she was everything he'd ever sworn to protect. Like if he just held her tight enough, he could will her heart to keep beating.

"I've got you," he whispered. Voice ruined. Soul broken. "You're okay, Dee. You're okay."

She wasn't.

We all knew it.

Her limbs jerked, twitching like something was unraveling her from the inside out. The sleep spell shimmered over her skin, trying to lock her down, press her into unconsciousness like a gentle, lethal lullaby.

And then the air changed.

Magic cracked.

I felt it—like static over my skin, like pressure in my chest that shouldn't have been there.

Deidre's back arched. A sound tore from her throat—half gasp, half growl—and suddenly a bolt of dark magic shot from her chest.

It wasn't just a flare.

It was a scream made of shadows and rage.

It hit Pandora's sleep spell like a beast unchained, wild and venomous and all wrong. The entire chamber vibrated. My teeth clacked together from the shock of it.

She was fighting it.

The spell. The dark magic. Everything.

And her body...couldn't take it.

Blood—black and thick as tar—began to trickle from her ears.

Then her mouth.

I staggered forward, hand instinctively out, like I could do something. Like I could stop it.

McDara held her tighter, panic scrawled across every inch of his face. "No, no, no—stay with me, Dee. You're fine. Just breathe, you're okay, I've got you—"

She wasn't breathing right.

She wasn't breathing at all.

But then—her lips moved.

"I was...so close..." Her voice was barely more than a wet whisper. "CeeCee...she said...just needed...more time..."

McDara froze.

His arms shook around her. "Who?" he breathed, eyes wild, flicking over her bloodied face. "Deidre, who told you that?"

She didn't answer.

Couldn't.

Her eyes had already lost focus.

And then—gods—she went still.

Her head lolled against his shoulder.

Black blood coated her lips.

Gone.

McDara didn't move.

Not at first.

He just stared.

Then he let out a sound—low, cracked, and utterly inhuman.

It shattered something inside me.

He gripped her tighter, rocking her like a child clinging to a storm-drenched doll. "No. No, no, no—don't do this to me—come on, Dee, wake up, please—"

His magic flared out of him in vicious, lashing waves. I felt the pulse of it slam into the stone. The air bent around him, and for a second, I swore the whole cave trembled.

Pandora stepped forward.

McDara didn't even look at her. "Don't," he snarled, voice hollow and vicious. "Don't you come near her."

Tears slipped from his eyes—hot and silent.

He pressed his forehead to hers. "You were supposed to make it. I was supposed to save you."

And I just stood there.

Frozen.

The echoes of her last words still clawed at the edges of my mind.

Deidre said *she* just needed more time.

Whoever *she* was...she was still out there.

And McDara?

I saw it in the way his magic twisted the air.

He would burn Blakewell to the ground to find her.

And gods help whoever got in his way.

40

The cave burned with silence.

Not the peaceful kind. Not the kind that offered rest or reverence.

This silence was heavy—suffocating. It clung to the walls like smoke after a fire, thick with everything unsaid and everything too broken to fix.

Tension laced the air like razor wire—one wrong word and someone would bleed.

"I'm taking her to Matron Black."

Calypso's voice shattered the stillness, low but unyielding. Controlled. But beneath it, I heard the tremor. The fear. She took a step forward.

McDara didn't look up.

He was still on his knees, Deidre limp in his arms, black blood staining both of them. He held her like she was something sacred. Like if he just stayed still enough, long enough, the world might reverse course and give her back.

Then he lifted his head.

"No." That single word came out a snarl, guttural and wrecked. "Go to hell."

It landed like a curse, sharp enough to cut the air in two.

I flinched.

Pandora stepped forward, her magic crackling around her like static before lightning. "There still dark magic in her body, McDara—"

"She's my sister." His voice. It wasn't just grief. It was war. Thunder and blade and the end of something sacred. "No one touches her."

"You think that changes what she is?" Pandora shot back, her eyes fierce, her hands already tingling with spell-light.

"Yes." His voice cracked like stone under pressure, but there was no hesitation in it.

Calypso raised her hands, palms up, like she was approaching a feral beast. "The dark magic that is still infused in her needs to be contained. You saw what it did to her. Matron Black is the only one who can—"

"I don't care."

Those words.

That voice.

It was a death sentence. A vow. A man carving a line into the earth and daring anyone to cross it.

And I just stood there.

Helpless.

I wanted to go to him—to touch his shoulder, to offer something, anything. But what could I give him? Deidre was dead. There was no spell to undo it, no comfort that could make this right. I didn't know how to help him, didn't know how to fix the way his soul was caving in on itself right in front of me.

He rocked slightly, holding Deidre's body tighter, blood smeared across his hands and cheek. His breath came in short bursts now—shallow, too fast. His injuries were catching up to him, I realized. The dark magic. The impact. The heartbreak.

And I—I couldn't take it anymore.

A scream clawed in my throat, but it wasn't mine.

Orlla.

Her fury bled into me like spilled ink—icy, consuming. I staggered back, the cold crawling under my skin, wrapping around my spine like a noose.

"No," I whispered, barely audible. "Not again. You don't get to decide what's enough."

But Orlla wasn't listening.

She wasn't *feeling*.

She was a blade now, forged in betrayal and lit by rage, and she was straining against my hold, her spectral form flickering, twisting, reaching for Deidre like she meant to take the vengeance she was robbed of.

I grit my teeth, fingers trembling. "Stop."

But I was losing her.

Losing control.

And then—

He moved.

Death didn't speak.

He didn't smirk.

He *looked.*

And the moment his silver eyes found mine, the world constricted.

There was no wind, no warning—just the snap of finality as he lifted a single finger.

And Orlla vanished.

Like she had never existed.

Gone.

The space she had occupied howled with the emptiness of it.

I choked on the silence, stumbling back, every nerve screaming with the loss. My knees nearly gave out. The void she left behind felt like it had carved *through* me.

And then—I felt him.

Death.

Closer than breath. Closer than fear.

He didn't have a body. But gods, that didn't stop him.

His presence *devoured* the space between us, wrapping around me like shadow-wrought chains, pressing against my skin like phantom fingertips—cold, precise, *claiming.*

I couldn't breathe.

Didn't dare move.

If he'd been solid, we'd be chest to chest.

He didn't need to touch me.

He was already inside me—threaded through my pulse, my breath, my *magic.*

His mouth—if that was what it was—hovered by my ear. I felt the shape of him more than saw it, his voice threading into my blood like ice water laced with something sweet and ruinous.

"I like it when you look at me like that," he murmured, the words smoke and silk and sin. "Desperate. Needing."

A violent tremor tore through me. A barely masked whimper.

I hated that it felt like a confession.

Because my magic *did* want him.

His magic traced my throat, a phantom breath that wasn't real but stole my breath all the same. I was burning cold, breaking open, held together by nothing but sheer will and the fading edge of fear.

And in that moment, I knew.

I had *accepted* the bond.

I hadn't said yes, hadn't made the deal.

But some part of me had let him in.

Some part of me had already *belonged* to him.

And Death—Death never let go of what he claimed.

Then—he vanished.

Like a nightmare sliding back beneath the bed.

No sound.

No trace.

But I could still feel him.

In my veins.

On my skin.

I stood there, shivering, the cave forgotten, voices distant.

My pulse thundered. My magic ached.

And I knew—bone deep and soul heavy—

He wasn't done with me.

Not even close.

Phontine's voice broke through the fog, small but urgent. "Sonia. We need to leave."

But I wasn't looking at her.

I was looking at *them*.

At Pandora, dragging Deidre's body across the fractured cave floor like she wasn't McDara's world gone sideways.

At Calypso, her hands raised and glowing, holding McDara back with barely restrained magic.

He fought against it anyway, his body trembling, blood still smeared across his jaw, his magic flickering like a candle caught in a storm. His teeth were clenched in a snarl, his eyes wild. He wasn't done fighting. Not for his family.

But he was losing.

Too much damage.

Too much grief.

Too late.

I took a step toward him before I could stop myself, my pulse cracking like lightning in my veins. "McDara—"

He swayed.

Then collapsed.

The sound of his body hitting the stone floor tore through me like glass.

And he didn't get back up.

The Black House had a dungeon.

Not the kind with rusted chains and rats and stone floors—no. This was cold, sleek, clinical. Magic shimmered faintly along the walls, woven into every tile, humming beneath every surface. It was built to contain power. To strip a Mage of their advantage. To remind them that even the strong could be caged.

I stood outside his cell, arms crossed tight over my chest, pulse pounding like a war drum in my ears. The glass between us was enchanted—one way. He couldn't see us.

But I could see *him*.

McDara sat on the bench inside, the black blood scrubbed from his skin but not from the hollows of him. His hands gripped the edge of the seat, white-knuckled, like if he let go, he'd shatter. He looked composed—too composed. Shoulders squared like a soldier in parade rest, spine ramrod straight. But the grief was there, bleeding out in the tremble of his fingers, the tight lock of his jaw, the way his eyes didn't seem to see anything at all. I knew better. He wasn't still. He was breaking—quietly, completely.

And he was doing it alone.

I turned away before I could crumble, too.

Matron Black stood beside me, spine straight, expression unreadable. But I saw it—just for a flicker—in the line of her mouth. The smallest fracture in her armor.

Guilt.

Or maybe grief.

McDara had been a part of the Black House. Had Matron Black watched him and Deidre grow up? Learn their magic? And now she watched as he was locked in a glass cage like a threat.

I met her gaze, my voice low and sharp. "Why?"

Matron Black arched a brow. "Why what?"

"Why put *him* in a cell instead of calling the police?"

There was amusement in her eyes, like my outrage was quaint. Predictable. Beneath her. She gestured to the two House guards flanking her, but my gaze snapped to one of them—

Elias.

Standing there like a phantom. Still as a blade waiting to be drawn. His dark, golden eyes flicked to mine, unreadable. A shadow in the background of every power game, and yet always exactly where he needed to be.

He wasn't here by accident.

Matron Black turned her attention back to the cell, and I followed her gaze—just in time to see McDara shift, pain tightening the muscles in his jaw.

"I would rather our House deal with this," she said, voice smooth as glass. "And when it's over, I would rather McDara walk free and return to his life."

His life.

Like there was anything left of it.

Deidre was gone. His purpose had fractured with her.

And him?

He was breaking.

With a snap of Matron Black's fingers, the spell on the glass shimmered.

McDara looked up.

His gaze slammed into mine—and *burned.*

Rage.

Betrayal.

Desperation so raw it made my breath hitch.

But then his eyes slid past me—and locked on *her.*

And something inside him *ignited.*

He was on his feet in a second, slamming toward the glass like it might shatter beneath the weight of what he felt.

"Where is she?" His voice cracked like thunder. Not loud, but dangerous. *Final.*

"Her body is on House grounds," Matron Black said, her voice as sterile and emotionless as the cell we stood in. Each word clipped, sharp edged, clinical—like she was reading off a medical chart. Not talking about the girl McDara had bled for. The sister he'd held as she died choking on black blood.

"And the dark magic within her is contained."

Contained.

The word slammed into me like a fist. Like a curse.

Like a cage.

McDara stiffened, his fists curling, knuckles white. I could feel the heat building in his skin—magic coiling under it like a live wire ready to snap.

Contained. Like she was a biohazard. A mistake.

"She will be sent to the Mage Council," Matron Black continued, as if she hadn't just dropped a blade into the center of McDara's chest.

He snapped.

One second, he was frozen. The next—he detonated.

Magic erupted from him, lighting the dungeon like a white-blue inferno. The walls, the glass, the very air trembled with the force of it.

"THE HELL SHE WILL!"

His voice wasn't just fury—it was grief, betrayal, a howling wound torn wide open.

The sound cracked through me like thunder. The reinforced glass between us vibrated under the pressure of it, light fracturing across its surface like veins of barely contained rage.

If that barrier hadn't been spelled a dozen times over, he would've burned it down.

I barely remembered to breathe.

Matron Black didn't flinch. Not even a blink.

"She is still saturated with dark magic," she said, like she hadn't just been nearly incinerated. "The Council has protocols. Facilities. Specialists. They are the only ones equipped to cleanse her body before the corruption spreads or—reactivates."

McDara's chest heaved. "I'm going with her."

"No."

The word was flat.

His eyes burned like open wounds. "She was my sister."

"And now she is a vessel of unstable, cursed magic," Matron Black replied. "Your grief does not change the facts."

"I *need* to see what they're doing to her!" His voice cracked, raw. "I need to see it with my own eyes—I *have* to bring her home. I *will* bury her myself."

Matron Black's gaze didn't waver. "That will not be possible."

McDara swayed like she'd physically struck him. I reached for him instinctively, but he didn't notice. He was already unraveling.

"She died in my arms," he rasped. "I held her. And now you're telling me I don't even get to bury her?"

"She will be taken care of with dignity," Matron Black said.

My breath caught.

McDara let out a broken, guttural sound—half scream, half sob. His body trembled. Magic still sparked under his skin, but it was disjointed now. Fractured.

I stepped in front of him, desperate, useless. "Please. Just let him go with her. Just to see—"

"No." Matron Black's eyes locked on mine like steel. "You know what Deidre became. This is not a funeral. This is containment."

McDara crumpled.

It didn't happen all at once.

His knees buckled like the fight had finally been carved out of him. Like the last tether snapped. He stumbled forward, catching himself on the glass wall.

Elias took a sharp step forward, the shadows clinging to him tightening like a second skin, magic flaring just under the surface—coiled and ready.

But Matron Black didn't move.

She didn't flinch.

She *watched*.

Like she'd expected the explosion. Like she'd accounted for it. Like this moment had already played out in her mind a dozen times.

McDara's chest heaved. His magic danced over his skin in dangerous arcs, crackling against the cell's protective wards. But he didn't move forward. Didn't speak again. His rage poured out of him in silence now, simmering, suffocating.

I saw it happen.

The tension in McDara's frame faltered. His magic dimmed, reluctantly pulled back into him. His hands unclenched, though his jaw was locked so tight I thought his teeth might crack.

Not because he believed her.

Because he didn't have another option.

Because she knew he didn't.

And that—

That was what gutted me.

I'd seen him furious. I'd seen him protective. I'd seen him restrained and reckless and impossible.

But I'd never seen him like this.

Defeated.

Like someone had carved out the fight from inside his ribs and left him hollow.

My heart twisted, even as anger still burned inside me—for what he'd hidden, for what he'd let happen.

But this? This was the moment I realized something else.

McDara hadn't just lost a battle.

He'd lost *her.*

Matron Black studied him with something colder than indifference—*understanding.* Like she was watching a blade finally snap from too much strain. Her voice softened by degrees, cautious now, like she was approaching wreckage she'd helped cause.

"I know," she said, gently—too gently—"that Deidre has been your only family for a long time. Since your father—"

"*Don't.*"

The word was ice and razors and shattered glass.

Matron Black froze mid-sentence.

McDara's head lifted. Slowly.

His eyes met hers.

And for the first time since she'd locked him in that cell, I saw *true warning* flare in them.

He was a man with nothing left to lose.

And if she touched that wound again—

She wouldn't survive what came next.

"You promised," he said. Each syllable was precise, deliberate. A warning. "You swore to me that you would never speak of him."

Matron Black stilled, her spine straight, her eyes narrowing by a fraction. "I did."

"Then keep that promise."

The command in his voice cracked the air between them. Not a plea. Not a threat. A line drawn in stone.

Matron Black studied him—longer than necessary. The kind of look that sifted through memories better left buried, that unearthed truths no one else was meant to survive. Then, finally, she gave a single nod.

No retort. No defense.

Just a nod.

Like they'd stood on this battlefield before. And whatever existed behind that name, that *promise*, was a war neither of them wanted to revisit.

My pulse surged. The realization hit fast and brutal.

There's a history here.

And suddenly, I wasn't sure if the man I had kissed just hours ago—the man whose silence I thought I understood—was someone I even *knew*.

Maybe I never had.

Maybe McDara's ghosts were darker than anything I'd ever conjured.

Matron Black turned to me, and before she even spoke, I already knew the script.

"You may have as much time as you need," she said, her voice a blade in velvet. "The guards stay."

She didn't look at McDara. Not even once.

Just turned and walked away, heels echoing softly off polished stone, silk trailing in her wake like shadows stitched into fabric.

No glance over her shoulder.

No parting words.

And McDara—he didn't flinch. Didn't move.

But the second her presence vanished, his eyes found mine.

And suddenly the air thickened.

My pulse spiked. My chest tightened. And every breath scraped like it had to claw its way past the tension choking the space between us.

I could barely feel my fingers as I turned to Elias. "Open the cell."

His brows twitched. "Are you sure?"

His hand landed on my shoulder—steady, grounding.

That small, simple touch nearly undid me.

"Yes," I whispered, the word brittle as shattered glass. "I'm sure."

Elias didn't argue. He just looked at me a moment longer, then withdrew.

But not before McDara's eyes locked on his hand.

Watching. Tracking.

The moment Elias stepped back, a muscle in McDara's jaw jumped. His shoulders went rigid, his stare thunderous.

He said nothing.

Didn't need to.

With a flick of Elias's fingers, the door unsealed with a soft hiss, magic dissipating like smoke from a snuffed flame.

I stepped through.

Slow. Measured.

Like approaching a wounded predator.

McDara didn't move. But I saw it—all of it.

The lines of exhaustion etched beneath his eyes. The way his hands trembled from effort, from restraint. The silent fury barely caged in his posture.

I hovered just inside the threshold, words knotting in my throat.

Because I was angry.

I was furious.

I still didn't know if he'd known—*really* known—that the Malifax Mage was his sister. That she was the one who nearly ended me in that motel.

But none of that mattered in this moment. Something needed to be said first.

Because I could still see the bloodstains on his shirt. Not when his sister's body had been ripped away from him like she was nothing more than a cursed artifact to dissect.

"I'm sorry," I said softly. The words scraped my throat raw. "For Deidre. I'm so—so sorry you lost her."

McDara didn't look at me. His jaw flexed once, sharp. But he didn't speak.

I swallowed past the lump in my throat, took one hesitant step closer.

I was selfish for what I was about to do.

His world was just shattered but I...There were answers I needed. From him.

Because this morning, I'd tasted his kiss like it was a promise.

And tonight?

Tonight, I didn't know if I'd survive the truth.

41

I stopped just short of him, the silence stretching taut between us, vibrating with every breath I couldn't quite take.

"When did you know?" I asked, the words cutting sharper than I meant them to.

McDara stiffened.

"Sonia—"

"When," I snapped, my voice slicing through the stale dungeon air, "did you know the Malifax Mage was Deidre?"

His entire body recoiled—like I'd slapped him.

And then—gods help me—he whispered my name. Just that. Like it was everything. Like it was the only word left in a world that was crumbling around him.

It broke something in me.

And I hated it.

I hated the ache behind my eyes, the pressure behind my ribs, the way my hands wanted to tremble. So, I clenched them into fists instead. Grounded myself.

"Tell me."

His composure cracked. Splintered.

Then he was in front of me—his hands on my arms, gripping like I was his last lifeline. His head dipped low, eyes catching mine, holding me there like his gaze alone could stop the storm between us.

"Is that what you think?" he asked, voice raw, barely holding together. "That I *knew*? That I watched you walk into danger, knowing it was *my sister*?"

I yanked free, the heat of betrayal rising like wildfire through my veins. "What else was I supposed to think, McDara? You didn't say anything. You let me believe—"

His hands caught me again, firmer this time, more desperate.

Not controlling.

Clinging.

His face was close now, so close I could feel the unsteadiness of his breath, see the wild edge in his dark, devastated eyes.

"Sonia." My name again. But this time, it was a vow. "I didn't know."

I shook my head, denial digging in deep.

"I got a call from Deidre this morning," he rushed out, voice harsh, broken. "She sounded—*gods*, Sonia, she sounded like she was dying. I could barely understand her, but I knew something was wrong. I knew she was losing control of her magic."

His hands tightened on my arms like I might vanish, like he was fighting time itself to make me hear him.

"I didn't tell you because I didn't know what the hell I was walking into. I just—" He exhaled raggedly. "I just needed to get to her before it was too late."

His voice fractured. Splintered. "I didn't know it was her. Not until I saw her in the cave."

The rest didn't need to be said.

By then, he'd been too busy trying to save her. By then, there hadn't been time to tell me anything.

I sucked in a breath that didn't help, didn't *reach* the hollowed out place inside me.

Because even if it wasn't betrayal, even if it wasn't a lie—

He had still chosen her first.

His sister.

The person who had tried to kill me.

But as I stood there, trembling beneath the weight of everything that had happened, everything I had felt, I asked myself: *Would I have done any different?*

If it had been Phontine?

If it had been my mom?

Would I have stopped to explain, to warn, to trust someone else with the people I loved?

No.

I wouldn't have.

And *gods*, I hated that I understood.

I hated the part of me that softened, that cracked all over again, because *understanding* didn't erase the pain of the last twenty-four hours. It didn't rewrite the moments I thought I'd left behind.

And still—

"I would never let anyone hurt you, Sonia." His voice was quiet now. Steady. A blade sheathed in truth. "Not even my sister."

The words struck low. Deep.

They wound around my chest, curled into the fractured places, and *held*.

My breath stuttered. My bones remembered how to ache.

And he stepped closer.

Not forcing.

Not demanding.

Just *there*—offering himself without walls, without armor, for the first time since I'd met him.

And I couldn't move.

Because even with the silence still screaming between us...

I didn't want him to let go.

"I didn't know," he said again, quieter now, voice raw with something unshakable. Something I wanted to believe in. "If I had—if I even suspected—" His throat worked, a muscle jumping in his jaw. "You think I would have let you stay in that motel? Alone? You think I would have let you walk around Blakewell without telling you? Without protecting you?"

My stomach twisted.

Because no. I didn't think that. McDara, for all his walls and sharp edges, had always been the first to protect me. The first to put himself between me and whatever wanted to tear me apart.

A tremor ran through my limbs. I hated that I wanted to believe him. Hated that I was already believing him.

"I care about you." His voice was hushed, like he was afraid to say it too loud. Like it was the most fragile truth he had.

My pulse stuttered.

The hurt inside me still coiled tight, but...I knew he meant it.

McDara wasn't a man who handed out reassurances easily. Wasn't someone who softened for just anyone. But he had softened for me.

I exhaled shakily. Let my eyes flutter shut for just a second.

And then, I let him pull me in.

His arms wrapped around me carefully. As if I might break.

I sank into his warmth, my cheek pressing against the rough fabric of his shirt, my hands fisting into the material.

McDara exhaled against my hair, his hands settling firm against my back, his whole body solid. Unwavering.

"I won't lose you," he murmured, barely more than a breath. "Not to this."

I let my eyes close, let myself sink into this one moment.

Because, for the first time in far too long, I felt like I wasn't standing alone in the dark.

I pulled back just enough to look at him.

McDara's little smile was warm, real—a flicker of who we were before everything shattered. It hit me so deeply, so unexpectedly, that my chest clenched, my breath tangling in my ribs.

But then—movement.

I turned my head just in time to see a guard approaching with a tray of food.

McDara's dinner.

I took a small step back, exhaling, trying to ground myself, trying to breathe through the storm still raging inside me.

The guard hesitated, shifting the tray in his hands, and I moved to the cell door, reaching for it. As I did, a prickle of awareness crawled down my spine.

Elias.

He was watching me.

Not like before—with the weight of quiet attentiveness he carried so well.

Something else.

Something sharp and unreadable.

A strange unease flickered through me, but I ignored it, turning back to McDara.

The tray hit the floor with a metallic *crash*, but I barely heard it.

Because all I could see was *him*.

McDara—my storm-eyed protector, the man who held me like I was the only thing tethering him to the world—was slipping.

Literally slipping.

His body was *flickering*. Not shaking, not fading from consciousness—*flickering*. Like light through fog. Like shadow through smoke. Like a ghost.

"No," I whispered, my voice already breaking. "No, no, no—"

His shoulders sagged, the strength in them bleeding out too fast. His knees gave and I barely managed to catch him, my arms wrapping tight around his weight as we hit the ground. I sank with him, his body heavier than it should've been, yet insubstantial in a way that made me want to scream.

"Cillian!" My voice cracked open the room. Shattered it. "Stay with me—*look at me!*"

His lashes fluttered. His eyes met mine.

And I froze.

Because they weren't his.

They weren't the warm, storm-dark eyes that had looked at me like I was worth saving. Worth wanting.

They were *silver*.

Pale, blinding, *impossible* silver.

Death's silver.

And it was *taking him*.

"No—*no!*" My fingers curled into the fabric of his shirt as I shook him, as if sheer desperation could pull him back. "Don't you fucking dare. Don't you *dare* leave me."

He exhaled—a breath that barely felt real, like it passed through another world before it reached me.

And I felt it.

The flicker.

The shift.

That *moment* when someone passes too close to the Deathscape.

I *knew* it.

And this time, it wasn't me being dragged toward it.

It was him.

"*Help!*" I screamed, voice ragged, shaking the walls. "Get help—*NOW!*"

Footsteps thundered behind me. Voices overlapping. A scramble of panic. But it was all background noise.

Because I couldn't look away from him.

Couldn't stop *touching* him, holding him, anchoring him to this world with every shred of magic I had.

His hands twitched—like he wanted to reach for me but didn't know how.

Like his body didn't remember *how* to stay.

I cradled his face, my thumb brushing over his cheekbone, trying to ground him.

Trying to remind him where he belonged.

"With me," I whispered. "*With me.* Do you hear me?"

His lips parted like he wanted to say something.

But no sound came out.

Only light.

Only silver.

I wasn't letting him go.

Not now.

Not *ever*.

His body flickered again—too much like the ghosts that haunted me.

I squeezed my eyes shut, pressing my forehead to his, shaking. This couldn't be happening.

I would not watch him die.

Not like this.

Not like this.

42

The beep…beep…beep of the heart monitor sliced through the silence like a lifeline.

Steady. Solid. Proof he was still here.

The hospital—the only Magical hospital in the country, as far as I knew—was tucked away in Blakewell, hidden from human eyes. A place that shouldn't exist but thank the gods it did.

I stood at McDara's bedside, barely breathing, watching the faint rise and fall of his chest like it was the only thing tethering me to the ground. His skin was too pale, his lips too still, the shadows beneath his eyes deep enough to swallow light. But he was *breathing*.

That was all that mattered.

Magic hummed softly across his arms, pale blue runes pulsing just beneath the skin—healing sigils glowing with a rhythm meant to mimic life. The healer said the worst of the dark magic had been burned out, that the death-pull had been severed.

But he hadn't woken up.

Not yet.

Not *fast* enough.

Across the room, Dom sat slouched in a plastic chair, legs sprawled, arms crossed. He looked relaxed. Like a man half asleep.

He wasn't.

He hadn't slept since we had gotten here.

A soft knock sounded at the door.

I turned, half hoping for a nurse.

Instead, silk swept into the room.

Matron Black.

My spine went stiff.

She glided forward like she *owned* the floor beneath her. Every movement precise, robes whispering secrets with every step. Her gaze swept over McDara's unmoving form, unreadable—until it wasn't.

Something flickered behind her eyes.

Regret. Or maybe just the echo of it.

Dom stirred.

Not slow. Not groggy.

Predator alert.

His head lifted, jaw tightening, tail stilling by the chair's leg, and his stare locked on Matron Black with the kind of disdain that could kill a man in the wild.

Matron Black turned her head, cool and aloof.

"Shifter," she said, like the word offended her mouth.

Dom smiled. Sharp. Lazy. Dangerous.

"Mage."

The word was a blade dressed like a shrug.

A single twitch of her jaw gave her away.

Dom unfolded from the chair, rising to his full height—tall, broad, built like a battering ram in boots. No magic in the world could match the force of *presence* he exuded.

And right now?

He was pure, wild, primal instinct in a man's skin.

"So." He tilted his head. "You send a body bag instead of a cure, huh?"

Matron Black's eyes narrowed.

Dom didn't blink. Didn't budge.

She arched a brow, that cold smirk blooming like rot. "My *niece*," she said, crisp and pointed, "is not your concern."

My breath hitched.

Wait.

Her *what?*

Dom's expression didn't shift, but I saw it—just the faintest flicker of realization behind his eyes.

"No grief for the one who stayed loyally by your side?" he said slowly.

"My niece caused her own downfall." Matron Black's chin lifted. "And, unfortunately, she was also your friend. Where is your grief for one of your own?"

"Grief? You have no fucking clue what I feel." He nearly spat. "And *my friend* wouldn't have gotten into that shit if not for you."

"You do not know of what you speak, Shifter."

"She's dead. My friend is *dead*." Dom shot back, his tone hardening. "And now your *other* protégé is lying in a hospital bed because you refused to help her."

The air snapped with tension.

Matron Black stepped closer to McDara's bed, her voice a low murmur. "He chose to protect her."

"No," Dom said, stepping between them. "Deidre chose *you*. And you let Cillian bleed for it. Again."

The silence that followed was brutal.

Matron Black's expression remained composed. But her eyes?

Her eyes *burned*.

Before I could fully process the quiet violence in Matron Black's gaze, her next words detonated like a curse bomb in my chest.

"I want to visit with my nephew in private."

My eyes snapped to McDara.

Nephew.

I turned back to her, heart slamming against my ribs. "You're lying." The words came out sharp, brittle, but even as I said them, they rang hollow.

She tilted her head with that precise, venom-laced grace. "Am I?"

The room spun, every thread of logic unraveling at once. McDara. Her nephew. *Her family.*

How had he never told me?

Matron Black studied me like a glass about to crack. "McDara disowned anything to do with his mother's side of the family a long time ago," she said, tone smooth as silk and twice as cold. "I suggest you ask him about it...if he'll tell you."

Disowned.

The word struck like a slap, lodging in my ribs and bleeding slow.

Dom shifted beside me, and I could feel the growl coil in his throat before he swallowed it. He looked like he wanted to launch himself between us—say something reckless and satisfying—but instead, he exhaled sharply and turned to me.

"I'm getting coffee. You want one?"

"Yeah," I breathed, my voice raw and too small for the moment.

He didn't even glance at Matron Black as he left. Just walked out like the whole room wasn't burning behind him.

The air thinned the second he was gone.

Matron Black turned back to me, gaze sharp enough to carve bone. "How is he?" she asked, nodding faintly toward McDara's still form.

I forced the knot in my throat down. "The healer removed the dark magic residue. He's stable."

A beat passed.

And then—*something* shifted. Barely. The kind of change that only meant anything because it came from *her.*

Relief. Barely visible. But real.

And for the first time, I saw her.

Not the iron mask. Not the Black House Matron.

She still cared.

Even after McDara had severed everything. Even after Deidre had shattered it all.

She just didn't show it the way *normal* people did.

And McDara?

He'd been running. Not just from a legacy—but from *her.*

From everything she stood for.

And suddenly, I wasn't sure I knew him at all.

Her attention returned to me like a blade sliding into its sheath. Controlled. Elegant. Deadly.

"I assume nothing has changed for you," she said, voice calm, like she wasn't holding a loaded truth in her palm. Like she wasn't testing me.

Like she didn't just reveal that *everything* was far more tangled than I thought.

The silence stretched. My throat tightened.

But when I answered, my voice was steel.

"Nothing has changed."

A pause.

Then—she smiled.

Not cruel. Not sharp.

Just...knowing.

"Then I'll see you Monday," she said, and turned on her heel, disappearing like a queen exiting a battlefield she knew she'd already won.

And I stood there, staring at the empty doorway, still reeling from the aftershocks.

Because now I wasn't just walking into the Black House.

I was walking into *his past.*

And the ghosts waiting inside? They wore his last name.

I was joining the Black House.

Matron Black's gaze shifted—just barely—but in her world, that was a storm. Then she reached out and pressed her hand gently to my shoulder.

I stiffened.

The touch was careful. Intentional.

Oddly maternal.

"You may not have found your birth parents," she murmured, voice low and razor-thin, meant only for me. "But it will be good to have a Guen in the House again."

Guen.

The name hit harder than it should have. A name I hadn't spoken aloud. A name I hadn't even known until Blakewell.

She didn't call me Sonia. Didn't use the name I'd grown up with.

She called me by blood.

Matron Black's fingers tightened—once—then released. And just like that, she swept from the room. Silent. Serpentine. Absolute.

She had claimed me.

And I had let her.

My hand curled around the edge of McDara's bed frame, grounding myself against the chaos spinning behind my ribs.

I turned—and froze.

McDara was awake.

Watching me.

His dark eyes, raw and unblinking, locked onto mine like he'd been tracking me through a dream.

He'd heard *everything*.

The confession cracked through me before I could stop it. "I know what you're going to say." My voice rushed, tripping over itself, frantic. "That I shouldn't join the Black House. That it's dangerous. That I'm walking into something I can't come back from—"

"Sonia—"

"But I *have* to." I barreled on, breath short, hands fisting at my sides. "I can't keep slipping into the Deathscape every time I tap into my magic. I can't keep *losing control*—not after Orlla. Not again. I need training. Real training."

I swallowed hard, my voice breaking.

"My dad has been gone six months. What if he's already moved on before I learn how to find him in the Deathscape?"

McDara's breath hitched. I saw the way his eyes flickered, the way his chest tightened.

"If I can't control my magic..." My voice collapsed into a whisper. "I'll lose my only chance to see my dad again."

The ache in my chest fractured open. I tried to blink the sting from my eyes, tried to stay steady—but this truth always undid me.

McDara's jaw clenched, his throat working like he was holding something back.

But then, quiet. Sharp.

"What did she mean?"

I blinked.

"What?"

"Matron Black," he rasped. "When she called you a *Guen*."

I stared at him. Of all the things I'd said—all the pain I'd laid bare—*this* was where he landed?

"It's..." I hesitated, still breathless. "It's my birth mother's last name."

The color drained from McDara's face.

His entire body locked. Breath hitched. His fingers clenched into the sheets like he'd just been punched in the chest.

"McDara?" I stepped forward, panic surging sharp and fast. "What—?"

He shook his head. Violently. Like he could shake off whatever horror had just swallowed him whole.

But his eyes—gods, his *eyes*—they never left mine.

And something in them looked like goodbye.

"McDara, *what is it?*" I gripped his hand, desperate to anchor him. Desperate to anchor *myself.*

"I'll be safe," I whispered. "Matron Black can train me. My birth parents aren't even here anymore—"

He gripped my hand *hard*.

And then he said it.

Not softly. Not gently.

A broken thing.

"They didn't leave, Sonia." His voice barely scraped out. "Your birth parents didn't leave Blakewell."

I stilled.

"They died," I said quietly, nodding. "I know. Matron Black told me. She said they died in Larkend—"

"No," he interrupted, voice hollow. "Not like that."

He wasn't looking at me anymore. He was looking *through* me.

Like he couldn't bear to be in the moment he was about to destroy.

I stepped closer, blood roaring in my ears. "Then *what is it?* Why are you looking at me like that?"

McDara's throat bobbed. His hand flexed beneath mine like he was holding a blade.

"I don't know how to say it," he whispered. "But you need to know."

My world narrowed.

And then he looked at me.

Really *looked.*

Not like the man who had kissed me under moonlight. Not like the man who had caught me in the ruins of everything I thought I knew.

This was different.

This was grief.

"There's a curse," he said, voice stripped to its bones. "A blood curse on the Guen family."

My heart clenched.

He didn't stop.

"Every member of the Guen line dies at twenty-five."

Silence.

Stillness.

My world fractured.

A roar started in my chest. Deep. Hollow. Screaming.

And I couldn't breathe.

Because my name wasn't just a name.

It was a countdown.

And the clock had already started.

The world tilted—sharply, violently—and I would've crumpled right there if Mc-Dara's hand hadn't caught mine.

His grip was the only thing keeping me from vanishing into the abyss.

"No." The word tore from my throat, ragged and raw. "That's—that's not—"

But truth didn't wait for permission.

It slammed into me like a freight train.

My birth parents hadn't died in some tragic accident. They hadn't left me for a better life.

They were *cursed*.

And now that curse was mine.

Twenty-five.

The number clanged through my skull like a funeral bell.

I was twenty-four.

It was almost November. My birthday was February 8th. Four months. That's how long I had before this curse...

A sharp, broken sound clawed its way out of me. A laugh—but not really. It was the kind of sound people made when the ground caved in beneath them. When there was nothing left to hold on to but fear and fury.

I couldn't breathe.

I couldn't *think*.

My lungs locked. My pulse roared. The room felt like it was closing in, walls pressing tighter with every second, every beat of that cursed heart monitor.

McDara's hand squeezed mine, grounding—desperate.

"Sonia—"

I ripped away.

The motion yanked his IV. The monitor spiked into a frantic scream. But he didn't care.

He didn't even flinch.

His eyes stayed on me. Wild. Hollow. Shattered.

His hands hovered like he wanted to gather me up, piece me back together.

But nothing could hold me now.

I was a splintered thing, unraveling in real time.

My fate—my *expiration date*—was clawing its way through my skin, wrapping around my ribs like a noose I couldn't tear loose.

Four months.

That's all I had.

Four months until I became a name whispered in the past tense.

A Guen.

Another body cursed and buried.

McDara's voice was low, desperate, but it felt like it came from the other side of a storm. "I will stop this. Sonia—*look at me*. I'll find a way. I *swear* it."

I blinked against the burn in my eyes, but tears slipped through anyway. My heart slammed against my ribs like it wanted out.

This was too much.

Too much.

Too *much*.

I staggered back a step.

Then another.

His face twisted—broken lines, wrecked hope—but he didn't chase me.

Right now, he couldn't.

"Sonia—"

I turned.

And walked out.

I didn't look back.

Because if I stayed a second longer, I was going to shatter into a thousand pieces.

And I didn't know if I'd survive putting them back together again.

43

The night air was thick. Saturated with magic that didn't belong to this world.

It clung to the hospital's back lot like a living thing—buzzing, restless, feral. The kind of residue left behind after something unnatural had been torn from the ground, bleeding power in its wake.

Matron Black stood motionless at the edge of the lot, a silhouette of cold authority beneath the harsh white floodlights. Her gaze was fixed on the armored van parked twenty feet ahead. Its reinforced doors bore sigils that pulsed faintly with containment runes—etched in blood and silver. Strong enough to hold a Mage far more powerful than the girl inside.

Deidre McDara.

Her body dead but not the magic that thrashed inside of her.

Beside Matron Black stood a cloaked figure, faceless beneath the heavy hood.

Silent.

Unmoving.

They didn't need to speak. Not here. Not for this.

Matron Black's head tilted slightly, her sharp gaze catching the flicker of gold at the figure's wrist. A single bangle. Smooth. Unadorned.

A reminder.

A leash.

A debt she'd called in more than once.

She inhaled slowly. The air tasted like frost and smoke and something rotting beneath the surface.

"No one has survived this long with that much Maleficaria rotting through their veins." Her voice was soft. Controlled. But underneath it—certainty.

The figure said nothing.

"The Council will dissect her." Matron Black's gaze didn't waver. "Not just physically. They'll unravel her magic. They'll want to understand how the curse embedded itself so deeply—why it didn't kill her outright."

She let the words hang. Let them weigh the air down.

Still, the figure didn't move.

Didn't flinch.

Didn't dare.

The armored van gave a low mechanical groan as the final locking mechanism clicked into place.

Sealed.

The girl was no longer a person.

She was a warning.

Matron Black folded her hands neatly in front of her, her expression unreadable as the metal door slammed shut.

"Ensure Cillian never finds where her body is." The words were final as if the order had already come to past. "This level of dark magic might never be completely eradicated. To have it out of containment would be disastrous."

The figure gave a single, slow nod. A shadow acknowledging command.

No protest.

No resistance.

Just inevitability.

The air thickened—hummed with finality.

And then the figure turned, their cloak whispering against the pavement like a death knell and walked into the dark.

Matron Black didn't watch them go.

Her gaze remained fixed on the van as it rolled away, its tires whispering across asphalt like a hearse.

Deidre McDara was gone. An unfortunate sacrifice.

And the Council?

They thought they were salvaging a case study. A rarity.

They had no idea what was curled inside that girl's bones. What darkness had made a home there. What curse was waiting to wake.

Matron Black's lips curved.

Not cold.

Not cruel.

Knowing.

She turned in a swish of silk, her steps silent as she disappeared into the night.

And the shadows swallowed her whole.

To find out if Sonia survives her curse and the men that want her, continue reading with **Ghost Curse**.

Acknowledgements

I wrote *Ghost Whispers* in the thick of new motherhood, often between naps, tears, and very strong cups of coffee. So first, to my Sweetheart—thank you for being my constant, my encourager, and the one who always makes space for my dreams. You never once doubted that I could do this, even when I did. We did it!

To my two little ones—you may not understand just yet, but you've already shaped this story in more ways than you'll ever know. Thank you for being the heartbeat behind everything I do.

To my incredible beta readers—Brooke, Emily, Sydney, Kari, Winter, Aimee, Dani, Kelsey and Ashley (my favorite cousins lol), Angel, Freebs, Katrina, Alyssia, Fyra, Stevie, Laurie, Sammy—your insight, enthusiasm, and support made this book stronger in every way. You helped me find the soul in this story, and I'm forever grateful.

To my editor, Katherine at Oak Moss Editorial LLC, thank you for your sharp eye, your kind guidance, and your belief in this book's potential. It was a blast working with you!

To my family—thank you for cheering me on, asking about the book even when you had no idea what I was talking about, and for letting me ramble endlessly about ghosts, bloodlines, and fictional crushes.

To my ladies—Sarah, Courtney, and Linnea—thank you for being the ones who always listened to the wild behind-the-scenes chaos, the business brainstorms, and the story spirals. You made space for my words long before they hit the page, and your encouragement meant more than I can say. I'm so lucky to have you in my corner.

And to my grandmother, who unknowingly sparked this obsession by letting me watch an outrageous amount of *Murder, She Wrote* as a kid—this mystery-loving heart started with you.

Finally, to *you*, dear reader—thank you for picking up this book, for stepping into Blakewell, and for taking this journey with Sonia. Your time, your heart, your curiosity—it means everything. I hope you find something here that lingers with you, the way good ghost stories always do.

Brittany lives with her husband, two tiny adventurers-in-training, and a caffeine addiction that's probably sentient by now. With a background in literature, history, and a lifelong obsession with fairy tales (the darker the better), she was destined to write magic—and mayhem.

She writes romantasy for readers 18+ who want their magic dangerous, their love interests morally gray, and their romance served with the *right* amount of spice. Expect shadow-laced worlds, fantastical chaos, and at least one murder mystery she swears she *didn't* plan. (The stories have minds of their own, okay?)

When she's not wrangling plot twists or toddlers, you'll find her wandering in nature on her lunch break, daydreaming about curses, closed doors, and enemies who *really* should've kissed sooner.

She hopes her books make you laugh, gasp, ache—and maybe stay up too late whispering *"just one more chapter."*

Books by Brittany Arden: where ghosts whisper, tension smolders, and someone's definitely lying.